In the spirit of the g P9-DFX-178
by Douglas Preston and Lincoln Child,
Clive Cussler, Raymond Khoury, and Steve Berry,
THE ALEXANDER CIPHER keeps the pages
turning with a rip-roaring ride through history,
archaeology, and the great deserts of Egypt.

ACCLAIM FOR
THE ALEXANDER CIPHER

Please turn this page for more reviews and turn to the back of this
book for a preview of Will Adams's new novel, *The Exodus Quest*.

THE
ALEXANDER
CIPHER

Books by Will Adams

The Alexander Cipher
The Exodus Quest

THE
ALEXANDER
CIPHER

✝

WILL ADAMS

GC

GRAND CENTRAL
PUBLISHING

NEW YORK   BOSTON

The events and characters in this book are fictitious. Certain real locations and public figures are mentioned, but all other characters and events described in the book are totally imaginary.

Grand Central Publishing
Hachette Book Group
237 Park Avenue
New York, NY 10017
Visit our website at www.HachetteBookGroup.com

Grand Central Publishing is a division of Hachette Book Group, Inc.
The Grand Central Publishing name and logo is a trademark of Hachette Book Group, Inc.

Printed in the United States of America

Originally published in hardcover by Hachette Book Group
First mass market edition, March 2010

10 9 8 7 6 5 4 3 2 1

For my parents

ACKNOWLEDGMENTS

This book has been over a decade in the contemplation and writing, and during that time I've received help, encouragement, and advice from a great many people—too many to acknowledge individually. But I would particularly like to thank my UK and U.S. agents, Luigi Bonomi and George Lucas, and my editors, Wayne Brookes and Jaime Levine, both for seeing something they liked in the original manuscript and for helping me make it better. I'd also like to thank Colin Clement for correcting my worst excesses about life and archaeology in Alexandria and Egypt. It goes without saying that where any mistakes remain, they are mine alone.

After Alexander the Great's death in Babylon in 323 BC, his body was taken in a magnificent procession to Egypt for eventual burial in Alexandria, where it remained on display for some six hundred years.

Alexander's mausoleum was considered a wonder of the world. Roman emperors including Julius Caesar, Augustus, and Caracalla made pilgrimages there. Yet, after a series of earthquakes, fires, and wars, Alexandria fell into decline and the tomb was lost.

Despite numerous excavations, it has never been found.

THE
ALEXANDER
CIPHER

Prologue

THERE WAS A FRESHWATER SPRING at the lowest point of the cave, like a single black nail at the tip of a twisted, charred, and mutilated leg. A thick layer of lichen and other scum clotted its surface, barely disturbed in centuries except to ripple and shiver at the touch of one of the insects that lived upon it, or to dimple with bubbles of gas belched from deep beneath the floor of the surrounding desert.

Suddenly, the skin burst and the head and shoulders of a man erupted from the water. His face was turned upward, and instantly he gasped huge heaves of air through his flared nostrils and gaping mouth, as though he'd been underwater beyond the limit of his endurance.

There was no light at all in the cave, not even a phosphorescence of water, and the man's relief at surviving his underwater flight quickly turned to distress. Had he merely exchanged one mode of death for another? He felt around the edge of the pool until he found a low ledge. He heaved himself up, twisted around to sit on it. Almost as an afterthought, he reached beneath his soaking tunic for his dagger, but in truth, there was little danger of pursuit. He'd had to fight and kick his way through every inch of that watery escape. He'd like to see that fat, sword-wielding Libyan try to follow; for sure, he'd cork in the passage, and it wouldn't spit him out till he'd lost some flesh.

Something whirred past his cheek. He cried out in terror and threw up his hands. The echo was curiously slow and deep for what he'd imagined to be a small cave. Something else flapped past him. It sounded like a bird, but no bird could navigate in such darkness. Perhaps a bat. He'd certainly seen colonies of them at dusk, swarming the distant orchards like midges. His hopes rose; if these were the same bats, there had to be a way out of here. After surveying the rock walls with his hands, he began to climb the gentlest one.

He wasn't an athletic man, and the ascent was nightmarish in the dark, but at least the rough walls offered good holds. Each time he reached a dead end, he simply retreated and found another route. Hours passed, and more hours. He grew hungry and tired, but he didn't allow himself to give up, and finally he reached a precarious ledge high above the cavern floor, just wide enough for him to kneel. He crawled forward and upward, the rock face to his left, nothing at all to his right, only too aware that a single mistake would plunge him to certain death. The knowledge didn't impede him but rather sharpened his concentration.

The ledge closed around him so that it felt as if he were crawling inside the belly of a stone serpent. Soon the darkness wasn't so complete as it had been, and then he emerged shockingly into the setting sun, so dazzling after his long blindness that he had to throw up a forearm to protect his eyes. The setting sun! A day at least had passed since Ptolemy's ambush. He inched closer to the lip, looked down at nothing but a sheer cliff face and certain death. He looked up instead—still steep, but manageable. The sun would soon be gone, so he began to climb at once, looking neither down nor up, contenting himself with progress rather than haste. The last glow of daylight faded as he reached an overhanging brow. He steeled himself and committed to it, hauling himself up with his fingernails and palms and elbows, scrabbling frantically with his knees and feet, scraping his skin raw on the rough sandstone, until finally he made it over and rolled onto his back, staring thankfully up at the night sky.

Kelonymus had never claimed to be brave. He was a man of healing and learning, not war. Yet he still felt the silent reproach of his comrades. "Together in life, together in death" had always been their vow. When Ptolemy had finally trapped them, the others had all taken without qualm the distillation of cherry laurel leaves that Kelonymus had concocted for them, lest torture loosen their tongues. Yet he himself had balked, swept by the terrible fear of losing the wonderful gift of life—the sight, the smell, the touch, the taste, the glorious ability of thought. Never again to see the high hills of home, the lush banks of its rivers, the forests of pine

and silver fir! Never again to listen at the feet of the
wise men in the marketplace. Never to have his mother's
arms around him, or tease his sister, or play with his two
nephews! So he had only pretended to take his poison.
And then, as the others died around him, he'd fled into
the caves.

The hilltop he'd reached was sheer only on one side,
and the descent was simple enough with the moon to
light his way. But as he made his way down, he began
to realize just how alone he was. His former comrades
had been shield bearers in Alexander's army, daunt-
less lords of the earth. No place had felt safer than in
their company. But he was no soldier himself; he was
here only because his beloved brother Akylos, the man
Kelonymus looked up to above all others in the world,
had summoned him from Macedonia to help with this
single task. And now that he had lost his brother and
his comrades, he felt weak and fragile, adrift in a land
of strange gods and incomprehensible tongues. He
walked down the slope, faster and faster, the fear of
Pan welling in him until he broke into a headlong run,
only to stumble in a rut and fall hard onto the compacted sand.

He had a growing sense of dread as he pushed himself
up, though at first he wasn't sure why. But then shapes
began to take form in the darkness around him. When
he realized what they were, he began to wail. He came
to the first pair of crucifixes, where he found his comrade Bilip on one, the same Bilip who had carried him
when his own strength failed him outside Areg; and opposite him, Iatrocles, a kindly man with a never-ending

supply of wondrous tales of distant lands. Cleomenes and Herakles were next, their shins and wrists nailed to the crudely cut wood with fat iron spikes, splinters of bone showing through the bloodied skin. No matter that they had already been dead—crucifixion was the Macedonian punishment for criminals and traitors, and Ptolemy had evidently wanted it known that that was what he considered these men. Yet it wasn't these men who had betrayed Alexander's dying request regarding his burial. It wasn't these men who had put personal ambition above the wishes of their king. No. These men had merely sought to do what Ptolemy himself should have done: build Alexander a tomb in sight of the place of his father.

He looked down the avenue of crosses ahead. Something about their symmetry caught his eye. They were in pairs. All the way along, they were in pairs. Yet their party had been himself and thirty-three others. An odd number. How could they all be in pairs unless someone else had gotten away? Hope fluttered weakly. He began to hurry down the horrific corridor of death. Old comrades on either side, yes—but not his brother. Twenty-four crosses, and none his brother's. Twenty-six. He prayed silently to the gods, his hopes rising all the time. Twenty-eight. Thirty. Thirty-two, and none his brother, and no more crosses! He felt an exquisite euphoria, but it lasted only a moment. Like a knife plunged between his ribs, he realized the diabolical plan that Ptolemy had hatched, why he had taken Akylos's body away with him. He cried out in anguish and rage, and he fell to his knees on the sand.

When his anger finally cooled, Kelonymus was a different man, a man of purpose. Fixed and certain. He had betrayed his oath to these men once already, but he wouldn't betray it again. *Together in life, together in death.* Yes. He owed them that much, whatever it took.

Chapter One

DANIEL KNOX was dozing happily on the bow of the dive boat when the girl came to stand with deliberate provocation, blocking the afternoon sun. He opened his eyes and looked up a little warily, because Max had made it clear that she was Hassan al-Assyuti's for the day, and Hassan had a proud and thoroughly warranted reputation for violence, especially against anyone who dared tread on his turf. "Yes?" Knox asked.

"So are you really a Bedouin?" she gushed. "I mean that guy Max said like you were a Bedouin, but I mean you don't look it. I mean, don't get me wrong, you kind of look it, I mean your complexion and your hair and eyebrows, but—"

It was no surprise she'd caught Hassan's eye, thought Knox, as she rambled on. He was a sucker for young blondes, and this one had a charming smile and startling turquoise eyes, as well as an attractive complexion, with its smattering of pale freckles and pinkish hints of acne, and a slender figure perfectly showcased by her lime-green and lemon-yellow bikini. "My father's mother was Bedouin," he said to help her out of her labyrinth. "That's all."

"Wow! A Bedouin gran!" She took this as an invitation to sit. "What was *she* like?"

Knox pushed himself up onto an elbow, squinting from the sunlight. "She died before I was born."

"Oh, I'm sorry." A damp blond lock fell onto her cheek. She swept her hair back with both hands, holding it there in a makeshift ponytail so that her chest jutted out at him. "Were you brought up here, then? In the desert?"

He looked around. They were on the deck of Max Strati's dive boat, tethered to a fixed mooring way out in the Red Sea. "Desert?" he asked.

"Tch!" She slapped him playfully on the chest. "You know what I mean!"

"I'm American," he said.

"I like your tattoo." She traced a fingertip over the blue-and-gold sixteen-pointed star on his right biceps. "What is it?"

"The Star of Vergina," answered Knox. "A symbol of the Argeads."

"The who?"

"The old royal family of Macedonia."

"What? You mean like Alexander the Great?"

"Very good."

She wrinkled her nose. "You a fan, then? I always heard he was just a drunken brute."

"Then you heard wrong."

She smiled, pleased to be put down. "Go on, then. Tell me."

Knox frowned. Where did you even start with a man like Alexander? "He was besieging this town called Multan," he told her. "This was towards the end of his campaigns. His men were fed up with fighting; they just wanted to go home. But Alexander wasn't having that. He was first up the battlements. The defenders pushed away all the assault ladders except his, stranding him up there alone. Any normal man would have leaped for safety, right? You know what Alexander did?"

"What?"

"He jumped down *inside* the walls. All on his own. It was the one sure way to make his men come after him. And they did, too. They tore the citadel apart to save him, and they only just got to him in time. The wounds he took that day probably contributed to his eventual death, but they added to his legend, too. He used to boast that he carried scars on every part of his body—except his back."

She laughed. "He sounds like a psycho."

"Different times," said Knox. "You know, when he captured the mother of the Persian emperor, he put her under his personal protection. After he died, she was so upset, she starved herself to death—not when her own son died, mind, but when Alexander died. You don't do that for a psychopath."

"Huh," she said. It was clear that she'd had enough talk of Alexander. She rose onto her knees, placed her left palm flat on the deck on the far side of Knox, then reached across him for the red-and-white icebox. She threw off its lid and tested each of the bottles and cans inside for coldness, taking her time, her breasts swinging free within her dangling bikinitop as she did so, the nipples pink as rose petals. Knox's mouth felt a little dry suddenly—knowing you were being worked didn't make it ineffective. But it reminded him forcibly of Hassan, too, so he scowled and looked away. She sat back down with a thump, an open bottle in her hand, a mischievous smile on her lips. "Want some?" she asked.

"No, thanks."

She shrugged and took a swallow. "So have you known Hassan long?"

"No."

"But you're a friend of his, right?"

"I'm on the payroll, love. That's all."

"But he's kosher, right?"

"That's hardly the smartest way to describe a Muslim."

"You know what I mean."

Knox shrugged. It was too late for her to be getting cold feet. Hassan had picked her up in a nightclub, not a Sunday school. If she didn't fancy him, she should have said no, simple as that. There was naive and there was stupid. It wasn't as though she didn't know what she was doing with her body.

At that moment, Max Strati appeared around the line of cabins. He walked briskly over. "What happens here, then?" he asked frostily. He had come to Sharm el-Sheikh on vacation twenty years ago and had never gone home. Egypt had been good to Max, and he wouldn't risk that by pissing off Hassan.

"Just talking," said Knox.

"On your own time, please, not mine," said Max. "Mr. al-Assyuti wishes his guests to have a final dive."

Knox pushed himself up. "I'll get things ready."

The girl jumped up, too, clapping with false enthusiasm. "Great! I didn't think we'd be going down again."

"You will not join us, I think, Fiona," Max told her flatly. "We have not enough tanks. You'll stay here with Mr. al-Assyuti."

"Oh." She looked suddenly scared, childlike. She put her hand tentatively on Knox's forearm. He shook her off and walked angrily toward the stern, where the wet suits, fins, masks, and snorkels were stored in plastic crates next to the steel rack of air tanks. A swift glance confirmed what Knox already knew: there were plenty of full tanks. He felt a sudden tightness in the nape of his neck. He could feel Max's eyes burning into his back, so he forced himself not to look around. The girl wasn't his problem, and she was old enough to look after herself. He had no connection to her, no obligation. He had worked his balls off to establish himself in this town, and he wasn't going to throw that away just because some brat had misjudged the price of her lunch. Of course, his self-justifications did little good. He felt sick in the pit of his stomach as he squatted down by the crates and started checking equipment.

The MAF Nile Delta excavation, Northern Egypt

"HELLO!" CALLED OUT GAILLE BONNARD. "Is there anyone here?"

She listened patiently for an answer, but none came.

How odd. Kristos had been clear that Elena, who needed her help translating an ostracon, would be waiting for her in the magazine, where they stored and documented all their finds. But there was no sign of her or her truck, and the magazine was closed. Gaille felt a rare flicker of irritation. She didn't mind making the fifteen-minute walk from the cemetery site, but she did mind having her time wasted. Then she noticed that the door of the hut was hanging ajar—something she had never seen before. She knocked, pulled it open and looked within, allowing in a little sunlight. The interior walls were lined with shelves stacked with battery lamps, hammers, mattocks, baskets, rope, and other archaeological equipment. There was a dark square hole in the floor, too, from which protruded the top of a wooden ladder.

She crouched, cupped her hands around her mouth, and called down, but there was no answer. She waited a few seconds, then called down again. Still hearing nothing, she stood with her hands on her hips, brooded. Elena Koloktronis, head of this Macedonian Archaeological Foundation excavation, was one of those leaders who believed all her team incompetent and who therefore tried to do everything herself. She was constantly running off in the middle of one task to see to another. Maybe that was what had happened here. Or maybe there had just been a mix-up with the message. The trouble was, with Elena it was impossible to do the right thing. If you went looking for her, you should have stayed where you were. If you stayed, she was furious that you hadn't come looking.

Gaille crouched again, her hams and calves aching from her long day's work, and called down a third time, feeling just a tremor of alarm. What if Elena had fallen? She turned on a battery lamp, but the shaft was deep and the beam was lost in its darkness. She had a sudden vision of Elena lying unconscious at the foot, her neck twisted, in urgent need of medical attention.

Gaille had little head for heights, so she took a deep breath as she put her hand on the ladder, reached one foot tentatively onto the top rung, then the other. When she felt secure, she began a cautious descent. The ladder creaked, as did the ropes that bound it to the wall. The shaft was deeper than she had imagined, perhaps six meters. You couldn't normally go down so far in the delta without reaching the water table, but the site was on the crown of a hill, safe from the annual inundation of the Nile— one reason it had been occupied in ancient times. She called out again. Still silence, except for her own breathing, magnified by her narrow confines. Displaced earth trickled past. Curiosity began to get a hold of her. She had heard whispers about this place, of course, though none of her colleagues dared speak openly about it.

She reached the bottom at last, her feet crunching on shards of basalt, granite, and quartzite, as though old monuments and statues had been smashed into smithereens and dumped. There was no sign of Elena, but a narrow passage led away to the left. She called out again, more quietly this time, half hoping there would be no answer, so that she would have the opportunity to explore a little. Her lamp started flickering and stuttering, then went out altogether, so she tapped it against the wall and it sprang back on. The stone chips under her feet crackled as she advanced. There was a painting on the left wall, its colors remarkably bright. It had evidently been cleaned, perhaps even retouched. A profiled humanoid figure dressed as a soldier but with the head and mane of a gray wolf was holding a mace in his left hand and, in his right, a military standard, its base planted between his feet, a scarlet flag unfurling beside his right shoulder in front of a turquoise sky.

Ancient Egyptian gods weren't Gaille's specialty, but she knew enough to recognize Wepwawet, a wolf god who had eventually merged with others into Anubis, the jackal. He had been seen primarily as an army scout and had often been depicted on *shedsheds*—Egyptian military standards such as the one he was holding here. His name had meant "Opener of the Ways," which was why the miniaturized robot designed to explore the mysterious air shafts of the Great Pyramids had been christened with a version of his name, Upuaut. He had gone out of fashion during the Middle Kingdom, around 1600 BC, so this painting should be over three and a half thousand years old. Yet the shedshed that Wepwawet was holding told a different story. For a handsome young man was depicted on it, his face tilted up like that of some renaissance Madonna. It was hard to know for sure when you were looking at a portrait of Alexander the Great, since his impact on iconography had been so profound that for centuries afterward people had aspired to look like him. But if this wasn't Alexander himself, it was unquestionably influenced by him, which meant it couldn't possibly date to earlier than 332 BC. And that begged an obvious question: What on earth was he doing on a standard held by Wepwawet, over a millennium after Wepwawet had faded from view?

She set this conundrum aside and continued on her way, still murmuring Elena's name, though only as an excuse should she suddenly encounter anyone. Her battery lamp went out again, plunging the place into complete blackness, and again she tapped it on the wall until it sprang on once more. She passed another painting—identical to the first, as far as she could tell, though it was not yet fully cleaned. The walls began to show signs of charring, as though a great fire had once raged here. She glimpsed a flash of white marble ahead, and two stone wolves lying prone yet alert. More wolves. She frowned. When the Macedonians had taken Egypt, they gave many of the towns Greek names for administrative purposes, often basing the names on local cult gods. If Wepwawet was the cult god of this place, then surely this must be—

"Gaille! Gaille!" From far behind her, Elena was shouting. "Are you down there? Gaille!"

Gaille hurried back along the passage. "Elena?" she called up. "Is that you?"

"What the hell do you think you're doing down there?"

"I thought you'd fallen. I thought you might be in trouble."

"Get out!" ordered Elena furiously. "Get out now."

Gaille started to climb. She saved her breath until she reached the top, then she said hurriedly, "Kristos told me you wanted to—"

Elena thrust her face in Gaille's. "How many times have I told you this is a restricted area?" she yelled. "How many times?"

"I'm sorry, Ms. Koloktronis, but—"

"Who the hell do you think you are?" Her face was red; tendons stood out on her neck, reminding Gaille of a straining racehorse. "How *dare* you go down there? How *dare* you?"

"I thought you'd fallen," Gaille repeated helplessly. "I thought you might need help."

"Don't you dare interrupt me when I'm talking."

"I wasn't—"

"Don't you dare!"

Gaille stiffened. For a moment she considered snapping back. It had barely been three weeks ago, after all, that Elena had called her out of the blue and begged her—*begged* her—to take a month out from the Sorbonne's Demotic Dictionary project to fill in for a languages assistant who had fallen ill. But Gaille knew instinctively how well she matched up against other people, and she didn't stand a chance against Elena, not when she lost her temper like this. The first time Elena exploded, it had left Gaille shell-shocked. Her new colleagues always shrugged it off, telling her that Elena had been that way ever since her husband died. Full of internal rage, she boiled like a young planet, erupting unpredictably in gushes of indiscriminate, molten, and sometimes spectacular violence. It had become almost routine now, something to be feared and placated, like the wrath of ancient gods. So Gaille stood there and took on the chin all Elena's scathing remarks about the poverty of her abilities, her ingratitude, and the damage this incident would doubtless do her career when it got out, though she herself of course would do her best to protect Gaille.

"I'm sorry, Ms. Koloktronis," she said when the tirade finally began to slacken. "Kristos said you wanted to see me."

"I told him to tell you I was coming over."

"That's not what he told me. I just wanted to make sure you hadn't fallen."

"Where did you go?"

"Nowhere. I just checked at the bottom."

"Very well," said Elena grudgingly. "Then we'll say no more about it. But don't mention it to Qasim, or I won't be able to protect you."

"No, Ms. Koloktronis," said Gaille. Qasim, the on-site representative of the Supreme Council, was every bit as secretive about this place as Elena herself. No doubt it would be embarrassing for Elena to have to admit to him that she'd left the door unlocked and unguarded.

"Come with me," said Elena, locking the steel door then leading her across to the magazine. "There's an ostracon I'd like your opinion on. I'm ninety-nine point nine nine percent sure of its translation. You can perhaps help me with the other naught point naught one percent."

"Yes, Ms. Koloktronis," said Gaille meekly. "Thank you."

"ARE YOU AN IDIOT?" GROWLED MAX, having followed Knox to the stern of the dive boat. "Do you have a death wish or something? Didn't I tell you to leave Hassan's woman alone?"

"She came to talk to me," answered Knox. "Did you want me to be rude?"

"You were flirting with her."

"*She* was flirting with *me*."

"That's even worse. Christ!" He looked around, his face suffused with fear. Working for Hassan would do that to people.

"I'm sorry," said Knox. "I'll stay away from her."

"You'd better. Trust me, you get on Hassan's wrong side, you and your mate Rick can forget about your little project, whatever the fuck it is."

"Keep your voice down."

"I'm just warning you." He wagged a finger as if he had more to say, but then he turned and walked away.

Knox watched him go. He didn't like Max; Max didn't like him. But they had a valuable relationship. Max ran a dive school, and Knox was a good, reliable dive instructor who knew how to charm tourists into recommending him to others they met on their travels—and he worked for peanuts, too. In return, Max let him use his boat and side-scan sonar for what he disparagingly referred to as their "little project." Knox smiled wryly. If Max ever found out what he and Rick were after, he wouldn't be so dismissive.

Knox had arrived in Sharm nearly three years ago, needing a place to lie low for a while. While he was sitting by the seafront one evening enjoying a beer, a powerfully built Australian man had come up to him. "Mind if I join you?" he had asked.

"Help yourself."

"I'm Rick."

"Daniel, but everyone calls me Knox."

"Yeah, so I've been told."

Knox squinted at him. "You've been asking?"

"They say you're an archaeologist."

"Used to be."

"You gave it up to become a dive instructor?" Rick sounded skeptical.

"*It* gave *me* up," explained Knox. "A bust-up with the establishment."

"Ah." He nodded at Knox's arm. "Interesting tattoo you've got there."

"You think?"

Rick nodded. "If I show you something, you'll keep it to yourself, right?"

"Sure," said Knox.

Reaching into his pocket, he pulled out a matchbox. Inside, embedded in cotton wool, was a fat golden teardrop about an inch long, with an eyelet at the narrow end for a clasp or a chain. Specks of pink were accreted from where it had apparently been chiseled out of coral, and on its base a sixteen-pointed star had been faintly inscribed. "I found it a couple of years back," said Rick. "I thought you might be able to tell me more about it. I mean, it's Alexander's symbol, right?"

"Yes. Where'd you find it?"

"Sure!" snorted Rick. "Like I'm going to tell you that." He took it back and replaced it jealously in its matchbox, which he returned to his pocket. "Well? Any idea?"

"It could be anything," said Knox. "A tassel for a robe, a drinking cup, something like that. An earring."

"What?" frowned Rick. "Alexander wore earrings?"

"The star doesn't mean it belonged to him personally. Just to his household."

"Oh." He looked disappointed.

Knox frowned. "And you found it in these reefs, yes?"

"Yeah. Why?"

"It's odd, that's all. Alexander never came near here. Nor did his men."

Rick snorted. "And I thought you said you were an archaeologist! Even *I* know he came to Egypt. He went to visit that place out in the desert."

"The Oracle of Ammon in Siwa Oasis. Yes. But he didn't travel via Sharm, believe me. He cut across the north coast of Sinai."

"Oh. And that was his only visit, was it?"

"Yes, except for . . ." And Knox's heart suddenly skipped as a wild idea occurred to him. "Jesus Christ!" he muttered.

"What?" asked Rick, excitedly.

"No, no, it couldn't be."

"What? Tell me."

Knox shook his head decisively. "No. I'm sure it's nothing."

"Come on, mate. You've got to tell me now."

"Only if you tell me where you found it."

Rick squinted shrewdly at him. "You reckon there's more? That's what you're thinking, yeah?"

"Not exactly, but it's possible."

Rick hesitated. "And you're a diver, yeah?"

"Yes."

"I could do with a buddy. The place isn't easy on my own. If I tell you, we'll go look together, yeah?"

"Sure."

"Okay. Then spill."

"Fine. But you've got to remember, this is pure specu-lation. The chances of this being what I think it is—"

"I get the point. Now, spill."

"Long version or short?"

Rick shrugged. "I've got nowhere I need to be."

"I'll need to give you some background first. Alexander only came to Egypt once during his life, like I said, and then only for a few months. Across north Sinai to the Nile Delta, then south to Memphis, the old capital, just south of Cairo, where he was crowned. After that it was north again to found Alexandria, westwards along the coast to Paraeto-nium, modern Marsa Matruh, then due south through the desert to Siwa. He and his party got lost, apparently. Ac-cording to one account, they'd have died of thirst except that two talking snakes guided them to the oasis."

"Those talking snakes—always there when you need them."

"Aristobulus tells a more plausible story, that they fol-lowed a pair of crows. Spend any time in the desert, you're pretty much certain to see some brown-necked ravens. They're about the only birds you will see in many places. They often travel in pairs. And they're cheeky buggers, too; if they can't find any snakes or locusts to eat, they'll happily scout around your campsite looking for scraps, before heading off back to the nearest oasis. So if you were to follow them . . ."

Rick nodded. "Like dolphins in the Sea of Sand."

"If you want to put it that way," agreed Knox. "Any-way, they got Alexander to Siwa, where he consulted the oracle, and then it was back into the desert again; but this time he headed east along the caravan trails to Bahariyya Oasis, where there's a famous temple dedicated to him, and then back to Memphis. That was pretty much that. It was off beating up Persians again. But then, after he died, he was brought back to Egypt for burial."

"Ah! And you think this was from then?"

"I think it's possible. You've got to bear something in mind. This was Alexander the Great we're talking about. He led thirty thousand Macedonians across the Hellespont to avenge Xerxes' invasion of Greece, knowing that he'd face armies ten times larger. He hammered the Persians not once, not twice, but three times, and then he just kept on going. He fought countless battles, and he won them all, making himself the most powerful man the world has ever seen. When his best friend, Hephaiston, died, he sent him on his way on top of a beautifully carved wooden pyre eighty meters high—like building Sydney Opera House, then putting a match to it, just to enjoy the blaze. So you can imagine, his men would have insisted on something pretty special when Alexander himself died."

"I get you."

"A pyre was out of the question. Alexander's body was far too precious to be burned. Apart from anything else, one of the duties of a new Macedonian king was to bury his predecessor. So whoever possessed Alexander's body had a serious claim to kingship, especially as Alexander hadn't left an obvious successor, and everyone was jostling for position."

Rick nodded at Knox's empty glass. "You fancy another?"

"Sure. Thanks."

"Two beers!" shouted Rick at the barman. "Sorry. You were saying, people jostling for position . . ."

"Yes. The throne was pretty much open. Alexander had a brother, but he was a half-wit. And his wife, Roxanne, was pregnant, but no one could be sure she'd have a son; and anyway, Roxanne was a barbarian, and the Macedonians hadn't conquered the known world to be ruled by a half-breed. So there was an assembly of the army in Babylon, and they came to a compromise. The half-wit brother and the unborn child, if he turned out to be a boy—which he did, Alexander the Fourth—would rule together; but the various regions of the empire would be administered for them by a number of satraps all reporting to a triumvirate. You with me?"

"Yes."

"One of Alexander's generals was a man named Ptolemy. He was the one who made the claim about the talking snakes leading Alexander to Siwa, as it happens. But don't let that fool you—he was a very shrewd, very capable man. He realized that without Alexander to hold it together, the empire was bound to fragment, and he wanted Egypt for himself. It was rich, out of the way, unlikely to get caught up in other people's wars. So he got himself awarded the satrapy, bedded himself in, and eventually became pharaoh, founding the Ptolemaic dynasty that ended with Cleopatra. Okay?"

Their beers arrived and they clinked them in a toast. "Go on," said Rick.

"It wasn't easy for Ptolemy, making himself pharaoh," said Knox. "Egyptians wouldn't recognize just anyone.

Legitimacy was very important to them. Alexander was different, a living god of unquestioned royal blood, who'd driven out the hated Persians—there was no shame in being ruled by such a man. But Ptolemy was a nobody as far as the Egyptians were concerned. So one of the things he needed was a symbol of kingship."

"Ah," said Rick, wiping froth from his upper lip. "Alexander's body."

"Ten out of ten," grinned Knox. "Ptolemy wanted Alexander's body. But he wasn't the only one. The head of the Macedonian triumvirate was called Perdiccas, and he had ambitions of his own. He wanted to bring Alexander's body back to Macedonia for burial alongside his father, Philip, in the royal tombs of Aigai in Northern Greece. But getting him from Babylon to Macedonia wasn't easy; you couldn't just load him on the first boat. He had to travel in a certain style."

Rick nodded. "I'm the same way, myself."

"A historian called Diodorus of Sicily gave a very detailed description of all this. Alexander's body was embalmed and laid in a coffin of beaten gold, covered by expensive, sweet-smelling spices. And a catafalque—that's a funeral carriage to you and me—was commissioned. It was essentially a giant golden temple on wheels, so spectacular that it took over a year to get ready. It was six meters long, four meters wide, and it had a high vaulted roof of gold scales set with jewels that was supported by gold ionic columns twined with acanthus. A golden mast rose from the top, flashing like lightning in the sun, and at each of its corners there was a golden statue of Nike, the ancient goddess of victory, holding out a trophy. The gold cornice was embossed with ibex heads, from which hung gold rings supporting a bright, multicolored garland. The spaces between the columns were filled with a golden net, protecting the coffin from the scorching sun and the occasional rain. Its front entrance was guarded by golden lions."

"That's a whole lot of gold," said Rick skeptically.

"Alexander was seriously rich," replied Knox. "He had over seven thousand *tons* of gold and silver in his Persian treasuries alone. It took twenty thousand mules and five thousand camels just to shift it all around. You know how they used to store it?"

"How?"

"They used to melt it and pour it into jars and then simply smash off the earthenware."

"Holy shit," laughed Rick. "I could do with finding one of those."

"Exactly. Anyway, the generals didn't dare stint on the funerary carriage. Alexander was a god to the Macedonian troops, and skimping would have been the quickest way to lose their loyalty. But it was eventually completed, though it was so heavy that the builders had to *invent* shock-absorbing wheels and axles for it, and even then the route had to be specially prepared by a crew of road builders, and it took sixty-four mules to draw it along." He paused to take another sip of his beer. "Sixty-four mules," he nodded. "And each of them wore a gilded crown and a gem-encrusted collar. And each of them had a golden bell hanging on either cheek. And each of these bells would have had inside it a golden pendant tongue just exactly like the one you've got in your matchbox."

"You're fucking with me," said Rick, the shock legible on his face.

"And, more to the point," grinned Knox, "this entire catafalque—all this gold—simply vanished from history without a trace."

Chapter Two

MOHAMMED EL-DAHAB kept a framed photograph of his daughter Layla on his desk. It was taken two years ago, just before she fell sick. He had developed the habit, while he worked, of glancing at it every few moments. Sometimes it gladdened him to see her face, but mostly these days it made his heart sink. He pinched the bridge of his nose between his thumb and index finger and muttered a short but heartfelt prayer. He prayed for her like this perhaps thirty times each day, as well as during his formal *rek'ahs*. His prayers had done little good so far, but faith was like that—without testing it was nothing.

There were incongruous noises outside: shouting, jubilant laughing. He glanced irritably through his office window. Work on the building site had come to a halt while his crew congregated in a corner, and Ahmed was dancing like a dervish at a *moulid*. Mohammed hurried out angrily. Allah had cursed him with the laziest crew in all

Egypt. Any excuse! He scowled to put himself in the right
frame of mind for delivering a proper tongue-lashing, but
when he saw what had caused the commotion, he forgot
about it. The mechanical digger had ripped a great, gaping
hole in the ground, exposing a spiral staircase that wound
around a deep, black shaft, still thick with settling dust. It
looked yellow, dark, and old—old as the city itself.

Mohammed and his men all gazed at each other with
the same thought. Who knew how long this had lain hidden? Who could guess what riches might lie at its base?
Alexandria was not only one of the great cities of antiquity, it boasted a lost treasure of world renown. Was there
a man among them who hadn't dreamed of discovering
the golden sarcophagus of the city's founder, Iskandar
al-Akbar, Alexander the Great? Young boys dug holes
in public gardens; women confided in their friends the
strange echoes they heard when they tapped the walls of
their cellars; robbers broke into ancient cisterns and the
forbidden cellars of temples and mosques. But if it was
anywhere, it was here, right in the heart of the city's ancient Royal Quarter. Mohammed was not given to idle
dreams, but gazing down into this deep shaft, his gut
clenched tight as a fist.

Could this be his miracle at last?

He beckoned for Fahd's flashlight, then lowered his
left foot slowly onto the top step. He was a big man, Mohammed, and his heart was in his mouth as he rested his
considerable weight upon the rutted stone, but it bore him
without protest. He tested more steps, his back turned to
the rough limestone of the outer wall. The inner wall that
separated the spiral staircase from the great central shaft

was built of crumbled bricks, many of which had fallen away, leaving jagged black gaps. Mohammed tossed a pebble through a gap and waited, breathless, until it clattered four heartbeats later at the foot. The spiral closed above him, and he saw that the entire staircase was carved from the rock—a sculpture rather than a construction! It gave him confidence. He continued his descent, around and around. The spiral at last straightened out, doubled back through an arched portal into a large, circular room, calf deep with sand, rock, and fallen bricks. At the center, four sturdy pillars surrounded the open base of the central shaft. The thin reflected daylight was thick with chalky motes, swirling slow as planets, clotting like salve on his lips, tickling his throat.

It was cool down here, gloriously quiet after the incessant din of the building site. Including the stairwell from which he had just emerged, four arched doorways led off this rotunda, one for each point of the compass. Curved benches with oyster-shell hoods were recessed into limestone walls sumptuously carved with prancing gods, hissing medusas, rampant bulls, soaring birds, bursting flowers, and drapes of ivy. A dark, downward-sloping corridor showed through the first doorway, humped with rubble and dust. Mohammed swallowed with distaste and premonition as he tore aside its cobweb veil. A low side passage led off the winding corridor into a vast, tall chamber, its walls pocked by columns of square-mouthed openings. A catacomb. He went to the left wall, lit up a dusty yellow skull with the flashlight, and tipped the dome aside with a finger. A small, blackened coin fell from its jaw. He picked it up, examined it, set it back down. He

shone his flashlight deep into the niche, lighting up a heap
of skulls and bones pushed to the far end to make room
for later occupants. He grimaced at the sight and retreated
to the main corridor to continue his survey. He passed
four more burial chambers before descending a flight of
twelve steps, then another five before he reached the top
of another flight of steps and the water table. He returned
to the rotunda. Ahmed, Husni, and Fahd had come down,
too, and were now on their hands and knees, scrabbling
through the rubble. He was puzzled that they hadn't ex-
plored farther until he realized it was the only spot with
natural light—he had taken their one flashlight.

"What is this place?" asked Ahmed. "What have I
found?"

"A necropolis," answered Mohammed flatly. "A city of
the dead." Vaguely angered by their presence, he moved
off, walking through a second portal into a high-ceilinged
chamber lined with limestone blocks. A banqueting hall,
perhaps, where mourners would have come each year to
commemorate their loved ones. A short flight of steps led
down through the final portal into a small forecourt. On a
raised step, a pair of tall, blackened studded metal doors
with hexagonal handles were set into a white marble wall.
Mohammed pulled the left door. It opened with a grinding
screech. He squeezed through into a broad, high, empty
antechamber. Plaster had fallen away in places from the
walls to reveal rough limestone beneath. Two lines of ancient writing were carved into the lintel above the arched
doorway in the facing wall, but Mohammed could make
nothing of them. He crossed a high step into a second, main
chamber, of similar width and height but twice as deep. A

knee-high plinth stood in its center, giving the strong impression that something important like a sarcophagus had once lain upon it. If so, it had long since vanished.

A dull bronze button shield was pinned to the wall beside the doorway, and Ahmed tried to wrest it free. "Stop!" cried Mohammed. "Are you mad? Will you truly risk ten years in Damanhur for an old shield and a handful of broken pots?"

"No one knows of this but us," retorted Ahmed. "Who can tell what treasures are here? Enough for us all."

"This place was looted centuries ago."

"But not of everything," pointed out Fahd. "Tourists will pay mad prices for all kinds of ancient rubbish. My cousin has a stall near al-Gomhurriya. He knows the value of such things. If we bring him down—"

"Listen to me," said Mohammed. "All of you, listen. You'll take nothing and you'll tell no one."

"Who gave you the right to make decisions?" demanded Fahd. "Ahmed found this, not you."

"But this project is mine, not yours. This site is mine. If one word of this gets out, you'll answer to me. Understand?" He faced them down, one by one, until they broke and stalked away. He watched them uneasily. Entrusting secrets to such men was like entrusting water to a sieve. Alexandria's slums writhed with villains who would cut twenty throats on the mere rumor of such a prize. But he wasn't going to back down because of that. Though he had striven to be good all his life, since Layla had fallen ill, he cared only for making her better. The question was how to turn this find to that end. Looting it was impractical. For all Ahmed's optimism, there wasn't enough to go around; and if he tried to cut out the others, they would sneak on him to his bosses, maybe even to the police, and that would go hard for him. As site manager, he was legally bound to report this find to the Supreme Council for Antiquities. If they learned he had kept it quiet, he'd lose his job, his license to operate, and almost certainly his liberty, too. He couldn't risk that. His salary was pitiful, but it was all that stood between Layla and the abyss.

The solution, when it finally came to him, was so simple that he couldn't believe he hadn't thought of it at once.

"EXCUSE ME. You please will help me with this?"

Knox looked up to see Roland Hinz holding up his huge black wet suit. "Of course," he smiled. "Forgive me. I was miles away."

He stood behind the big German to make sure he didn't tumble as he tried to pull on the neoprene leggings—that wouldn't go down well. Roland was a Stuttgart banker considering investing in Hassan's latest Sinai venture. Today's outing was largely in his honor, and he was making the most of it, too, giggly with champagne, more than a little coked, getting on everyone's nerves. In truth, he shouldn't be allowed anywhere near the water, but Hassan paid well to have the rules stretched. And not just rules. Getting Roland into his wet suit was like trying to stuff a duvet into its cover: he kept plopping out in unexpected places. Roland found this intensely funny, but then, he found everything funny and seemed to think people found him charming. He tripped over his own feet and laughed hysterically as he and Knox spilled inelegantly onto the deck, then looked around at the other guests as though expecting rapturous applause.

With a strained smile, Knox helped him back up, then knelt down to pull on his booties for him. He had bloated, pinkish-yellow feet with dirt caked between his toes, which looked as though he hadn't washed between them for years. Knox distracted himself with thoughts of the quest he and Rick had embarked on. The afternoon when he'd shared his ideas about Alexander's catafalque had been just the beginning, though the big Australian's initial euphoria hadn't lasted long. "So this procession came through Sinai, did it?" he had asked.

"No," said Knox. "Not according to any of our sources."

"Oh, ballocks, mate," protested Rick, sitting back in his chair. "You had me all excited for a minute."

"You want me to tell you what we know?"

"Sure," he said, still annoyed. "Why not?"

"Okay," said Knox. "The first thing you need to understand is that our sources are unreliable. We don't have any eyewitness accounts of Alexander's life or campaigns. Everything we have, we have from later historians citing earlier ones—second-, third-, even fourthhand accounts."

"Chinese whispers," suggested Rick.

"Exactly, but it's even worse than that. When Alexander's empire split up, each of the various factions wanted to paint themselves in the best light, and all the others in the worst, so there was a lot of propaganda written. Then the Romans came along, and while the Caesars worshipped Alexander, the Republicans loathed him. Historians were selective in their stories, depending on which camp they belonged to. One way or another, most of what we have is very badly slanted. Working out the truth is a nightmare."

"Duly noted."

"But we're pretty sure that the catafalque traveled along the Euphrates from Babylon to Opis, then northwest along the Tigris. A magnificent procession, as you can imagine. People trekked hundreds of miles just to see it. And, sometime in 322 or 321 BC, it reached Syria. After that, it's hard to know. Bear in mind that we're talking about two things here. The first is Alexander's embalmed body, lying in its coffin. The second is the funeral carriage and all the rest of the gold. Okay?"

"Yes."

"Now, we know pretty much what happened to Alexander's body and coffin. Ptolemy hijacked it and took it to Memphis, probably with the collaboration of the escort commander. But we don't know what happened to the rest of the catafalque. Diodorus says that Alexander's body was eventually taken to Alexandria in it, but his story is confused, and it seems clear he's actually talking about the coffin, not the catafalque. And the most vivid description comes from a guy called Aelian. He says that Ptolemy was so fearful that Perdiccas would try to seize Alexander back that he dressed a likeness of his body in royal robes and a shroud, then laid it on a carriage of silver, gold, and ivory, so that Perdiccas would charge off in pursuit of this decoy while Ptolemy took Alexander's body on into Egypt by another route."

Rick squinted. "You mean Ptolemy left the catafalque behind?"

"That's what Aelian suggests," said Knox. "You've got to remember, the main prize was Alexander. Ptolemy needed to get him back to Egypt quick, and you couldn't travel quickly with the catafalque. Estimates suggest that it moved a maximum of six miles a day, and that was with a large team of sappers preparing the road. It would have taken months to reach Memphis. And it couldn't exactly have traveled discreetly, either. Yet I've never come across any account of it being seen traveling the obvious route south from Syria through Lebanon and Israel to Sinai and the Nile; and surely someone would have seen it."

"So he left it behind, like I said?"

"Possibly. But the catafalque represented an enormous amount of raw wealth. I mean, put yourself in Ptolemy's shoes. What would you have done?"

Rick considered a few moments. "I'd have split up," he said. "One lot scoots ahead with the body. The other takes a different route with the catafalque."

Knox grinned. "That's what I'd have done, too. There's no proof, of course. But it makes sense. The next question is how. Syria's on the Mediterranean, so he might have sailed down. But the Med was notoriously infested with pirates, and he'd have needed ships on hand; and if he felt it was possible, he'd surely have taken Alexander's body that way—and we're pretty certain he didn't."

"What were his alternatives?"

"Well, assuming that he couldn't move the catafalque as it was, he could have had it chopped up into manageable pieces and taken southwest along the coast through

Israel to Sinai; but that was the route he almost certainly took himself with Alexander's body, and there's not much point splitting up if you're going to go the same way. So there's a third possibility: that he sent it due south to the Gulf of Aqaba, then by boat around the Sinai Peninsula to the Red Sea coast."

"The Sinai Peninsula," grinned Rick. "You mean past these reefs here?"

"These very dangerous reefs," agreed Knox.

Rick laughed and raised his glass in a toast toward the sea. "So all that gold might just be sitting out there waiting for us?" he said. "What say we go find it, eh?"

And that was exactly what they had been trying to do ever since, though without success. On the other hand, the more they searched, the more Rick had learned, and the more he had caught the archaeological bug. He had originally been a Clearance Diver in the Australian Navy—the closest they had to Special Forces—and working in Sharm had allowed him to keep diving, though he missed that sense of mission. Their quest had restored it to him, so much so that he determined to make a new career in underwater archaeology. So he was studying hard, borrowing Knox's books and other materials, pestering him with questions.

Roland's booties were now on. Knox stood and helped strap him into his buoyancy control device, then ran through his safety checks. He heard footsteps on the bridge above him and glanced up as Hassan sauntered into view, leaning on the railing and looking down. "You guys have fun, now," he said.

"Oh, yes," enthused Roland, giving the thumbs-up. "We have great fun."

"And don't hurry back." He beckoned behind him, and Fiona came reluctantly into view. She had put on long cotton trousers and a thin white T-shirt, as though more modest clothing could somehow protect her, yet still she was shivering visibly. When Hassan caught Knox staring at her, he grinned wolfishly and put his arm around her shoulders, almost daring Knox to do something about it.

It was said on the streets of Sharm that Hassan had slit the throat of a second cousin for sleeping with a woman he had put his mark on. Another story held that he had beaten an American tourist into a coma for protesting when Hassan propositioned his wife.

Knox lowered his eyes and looked around, hoping to share the burden of responsibility. Max and Nessim, Hassan's ex-paratrooper head of security, were checking out each other's dive gear. He'd get no joy there. Ingrid and Birgit, two Scandinavians Max had brought along to keep Roland company, were already suited and waiting by the stern ladder. Knox tried to catch Ingrid's eye, but she knew what he was up to, and kept her eyes firmly averted. He glanced back up at the bridge. Hassan was still grinning down at him, aware of exactly what was going through Knox's mind. An alpha male in his prime, savoring the challenge. He ran his hand slowly down Fiona's flank to her backside, cupping and squeezing her buttock. The man had risen from nothing to make himself the most powerful shipping agent on the Suez Canal by the age of thirty, and you didn't achieve that by being soft. Now they said he was bored, looking to extend his empire every way he could, including through tourism, buying

up waterfront properties in the slump that had followed
recent terrorist outrages.

Roland was ready at last. Knox helped him down the
ladder into the Red Sea, then knelt to pass him his fins.
The big German kept losing his balance as he tried to pull
them on, splashing around wildly, guffawing maniacally,
slapping the water.

"Hold on," said Knox tightly. "I'll be with you in a
second." He geared up, shrugged on his BCD and tank,
goggles loose around his neck, fins in his hand, and
started down the ladder. He was about to let go when
he glanced up at the bridge one last time. Hassan was
still staring down at him, while beside him, Fiona had
her arms crossed anxiously over her chest. Her hair was
tousled, her shoulders hunched and forlorn. She looked
her age suddenly, or lack of it—a child who had met
a friendly Egyptian man in a bar and thought she'd
worked herself a freebie for the day, confident she could
wriggle and flirt her way out of any expectations he
might have. Her eyes were wide, lost, and frightened,
yet somehow still hopeful, as though she believed that
everything would work out fine, because people were
basically nice.

Just for a moment, he imagined it was his sister, Bee,
standing there.

Knox shook his head angrily. This girl was nothing
like Bee. She was an adult. She made her own choices.
Next time she would know better. He glanced over his
shoulder to make sure the sea was clear behind him, put
his regulator into his mouth, bit down hard, and threw
himself backward to explode like fireworks into the Red

Sea. He resolutely didn't look back as he led Roland toward the reef, staying a modest four meters deep, in easy reach of the surface should anything go wrong. A pageant of tropical fish watched their progress intently but without alarm. Sometimes it was difficult to know which was the show and which the audience. A Napoleon fish, surrounded by a shoal of angels and wrasse, turned regally, effortlessly away. He pointed it out to Roland with exaggerated diving gestures—beginners always enjoyed feeling like initiates.

They reached the coral shelf, a wall of ochre and purple that fell dizzily away into blackness. The waters were still and unclouded; visibility was extraordinary. He glanced around unthinkingly and saw the dark hull of the boat and the menacing blurs of distant big fish in the deeper, cooler waters, and he felt a sharp twinge as he suddenly remembered the worst day of his life, visiting his sister in an intensive care unit in Thessalonike after the car crash. The place had been oppressive with the sounds of life support: the steady wheeze of ventilators, the low yet precarious pulse of monitors, the respectful, funeral home whispering of staff and visitors. The doctor had tried her best to prepare him, but he had still been too numb from his trip to the morgue, where he had to identify his parents, and so it had come as a shock to see Bee on the business end of a respirator and all the other attachments. He had felt dislocated, as though watching a play rather than real events. Her head had been unnaturally swollen, her skin pale and blue. He could still remember its waxy pallor, its uncharacteristic flabbiness. And he had never before realized how freckled she was around her eyes and in the crook of her elbow.

He hadn't known what to do. He had looked around at her doctor, who gestured for him to sit down beside her. He had felt awkward putting his hand on hers; they'd never been a physically demonstrative family. He pressed her cool hand beneath his own, felt intense and startling anguish, something like parenthood. He squeezed her fingers between his own, held them to his lips, and remembered how he had joked to friends about what a curse it was to have a younger sister to look after. But having a younger sister wasn't something he had to worry about any longer.

He tapped Roland on the arm and pointed upward. They surfaced together to find the boat perhaps sixty meters away, with no sign of anyone on deck. He felt a flutter of nerves in his chest as he spat the regulator from his mouth. "Stay here," he warned Roland. Then he set out in strong strokes across the crystal water.

MOHAMMED EL-DAHAB clasped his case protectively in front of his chest as the woman led him up to the private office of Ibrahim Beyumi, head of the Supreme Council for Antiquities in Alexandria. She knocked once on the door, then pushed it open, beckoning Mohammed through. A dapper and rather effeminate-looking man looked up from where he sat behind a pine desk. "Yes, Maha?" he asked.

"This is Mohammed el-Dahab, sir. A builder. He says he's found something on his site."

"What kind of something?"

"Perhaps he should tell you himself," she suggested.

"Very well," sighed Ibrahim. He gestured for Mohammed to sit at his corner table. Mohammed looked around, dispiritedly assessing with a builder's eye the bulging wood-paneled walls, the fractured high ceiling with its missing clumps of plaster, the mildewed drawings of Alexandria's monuments. If this was the office of the top archaeologist in Alexandria, there wasn't as much money in antiquities as he had hoped.

Ibrahim read his expression. "I know," he complained. "But what can I do? Which is more important, excavation or my comfort?" Mohammed shrugged as Ibrahim came to sit beside him. *He*, at least, looked expensive with his sharp suit and gold watch. Settling his hands primly in his lap, he asked: "So you've found something, then?"

"Yes."

"You care to tell me about it?"

Mohammed swallowed. He was a big man, not easily cowed by physical dangers, but educated people intimidated him. Yet there was something kindly about Ibrahim; he seemed like a man who could be trusted. Mohammed set his case on the table, opened it, withdrew his framed photograph of Layla, and laid it facing Ibrahim. Touching and seeing her image restored his courage. "This is my daughter," he said. "Her name is Layla."

Ibrahim squinted curiously at Mohammed. "Allah has indeed blessed you."

"Thank you, yes. Unfortunately, Layla is sick."

"Ah," said Ibrahim, leaning back. "I'm sorry to hear that."

"They call it Burkitt's lymphoma. It appeared in her stomach like a grape, and then a mango, beneath her skin. Her surgeons removed it; she had chemotherapy. We thought she'd conquered it."

Ibrahim rubbed his throat. "Maha said you'd found something—"

"Her doctors are good people," said Mohammed. "But they're overworked, underequipped, and they have no money. They wait for—"

"Excuse me, but Maha said you'd found—"

"They wait for her disease to progress so far that there's nothing more they can do." Mohammed leaned forward and said softly but fiercely: "That time is not yet here. My daughter still has one chance."

Ibrahim hesitated, then asked reluctantly, "And that is?"

"A bone marrow transplant."

A look of polite horror crossed Ibrahim's face. "But aren't those incredibly expensive?"

Mohammed waved that aside. "Our Medical Research Institute has a program of publicly funded transplants, but they won't consider a patient unless they've already identified a donor match. But they'll not run tests for a match unless the patient is already in the program."

"But that makes it impossible—"

"It's their way of choosing without having to choose. So unless I can finance these tests, my daughter will die."

Ibrahim said weakly: "You can't expect the SCA to—"

"These tests aren't expensive," said Mohammed urgently. "It's just that the chances of a match are low. My wife and I, our closest family, our friends—we've all taken the tests, but without success. I can persuade others, more distant cousins, friends of friends, but only if I organize and pay. I've tried everywhere to borrow money for this, but already this disease has put me so far in debt that . . ." He felt tears coming; he broke off, bowing his head to prevent Ibrahim from seeing.

There was silence for a while. Then Ibrahim murmured, "Maha said you'd found something on your site."

"Yes."

"Am I to understand that you want money for these tests in exchange for telling me about it."

"Yes."

"You realize you're legally obliged to inform me anyway."

"Yes."

"That you could go to jail if you don't."

Mohammed lifted his face and met Ibrahim's gaze with perfect calmness. "Yes."

Ibrahim nodded, gestured around his shabby offices. "And you understand I cannot promise anything?"

"Yes."

"Very well. Why don't you tell me what you've found."

Chapter Three

KNOX REACHED THE DIVE BOAT QUICKLY. He took off his fins, tossed them aboard, and climbed up. He could see no sign of Fiona or Hassan. Now that he was here, he wasn't certain what to do. He felt conspicuous and rather foolish. He unbuckled and slipped off his BCD and tank, carrying them with him as he walked quietly across the deck to the port-side cabins. He tested the doors one by one, looking inside. He finally came to one that was locked. He rattled it. There was a muffled cry inside, then silence.

Some people enjoyed and sought out violence. Not Knox. He had a sudden vision of himself standing there, and it unnerved him badly. He turned and walked away, but then the door opened behind him. "Yes?" demanded Hassan.

"I'm sorry," said Knox, without looking around. "I made a mistake."

"Come back!" said Hassan irritably. "Yes, you. Max's boy. I'm talking to you. Come here now."

Knox turned reluctantly, walked back toward Hassan,

eyes submissively lowered. Hassan didn't even bother to block his view, so that Knox could see Fiona lying on the bed, forearms crossed over her exposed breasts, cotton trousers half pulled down around her clenched and lifted knees. There was a cut above her right eye; her upper lip was bleeding. A torn white T-shirt lay discarded on the floor.

"Well?" demanded Hassan. "What did you want?"

Knox glanced again at Fiona. She shook her head at him, to say it was all right, she could cope with this, he shouldn't get involved. The selfless gesture triggered a protective urge in Knox that in turn suffused him with rage. He swung his scuba tank like a wrecking ball into Hassan's solar plexus, doubling him over. Then he clubbed him on the side of his jaw, which sent him reeling backward. Now that he'd started, he couldn't help himself. He hit Hassan again and again until the man collapsed on the floor. It was only when Fiona pulled him away that his mind cleared.

Hassan was unconscious, his face and chest painted with blood. He looked so badly beaten that Knox knelt and was relieved to find a pulse in his throat.

"Quick," said Fiona, tugging his hand. "The others will be coming back."

They ran together out of the cabin. Max and Nessim were indeed swimming back toward the boat, while Roland and the two women watched from farther off. Knox ran to the bridge, where he ripped wiring from beneath the two-way radio and ignition. All the keys were kept in a plastic tub on the floor, and he grabbed the lot. The speedboat was tied by a single rope to their stern. He hurried down the ladder, hauled the speedboat toward them, helped Fiona into its bow, and followed her. Untying the

towrope, he then jumped into the driver's seat and slipped
the key into the ignition just as Max and Nessim reached
them and started to climb aboard. When Knox spun the
boat in a tight circle and roared away, the wash of water
ripped Max free, but the burly security man, Nessim, held
on, pulled himself aboard, and stood up. He was a tough
bastard and angry as hell, but he was hampered by his wet
suit and tank. Knox threw the boat into another tight spin,
this time sending him flailing over the side.

Knox straightened out and roared off toward Sharm.
He shook his head at himself. He'd done it now. He'd
fucking done it. He needed to reach his Jeep before Hassan or Nessim could put the word out. If they caught
him . . . *Christ!* He felt sick at the prospect of what they
would do. He needed out of Sharm, out of Sinai, out of
Egypt altogether—and he needed out tonight. He glanced
around and saw Fiona sitting on the bench seat at the
back, head bowed, teeth chattering, a blue towel wrapped
tight around her trembling shoulders. For the life of him,
he couldn't think how she had reminded him of Bee. He
slammed the heel of his hand against the control panel in
anger at himself. If there was one thing he hated, it was
memory. You worked your balls off to build a life in a
place like this that had no links whatever with your past—
no friends, no family, nothing to weigh you down. But it
wasn't enough. You took your memory with you wherever
you went, and it would fuck you up in a heartbeat.

IBRAHIM BEYUMI walked Mohammed down to the street to wish him farewell, then thanked him for reporting his find at the building site and watched him disappear around the corner of the street.

Maha, his assistant, started to rise when he returned upstairs, but he settled her with a palm, then went to consult the vast street map of Alexandria pinned to the wall behind her. As ever, it filled him with wistful pride, marked as it was with every antiquity in his beloved city, including Pompey's Pillar, Ras el-Tin, the Latin Cemeteries, the Roman theater, Fort Qait Bey. There were some fine sites among them, and he boasted vigorously about them to anyone who would listen, but he knew in his heart that none of them were in the first rank of Egyptian antiquities. Alexandria boasted no pyramids, no Karnak or Abu Simbel, no Valley of the Kings, despite the fact that two thousand years ago its buildings had been something to marvel at. The Pharos lighthouse had been one of the Seven Wonders. The Mouseion had led the world in learning and culture. The Temple of Serapis had awed worshippers with its splendor and the trickery of its flying statues. The Royal Palaces of Cleopatra were imbued with extraordinary romance. And most of all, the city had boasted the mausoleum of the city's patriarch, Alexander the Great himself. If just one of these great marvels had survived, Alexandria would surely now rival Luxor or Giza on the tourist trail. But none had.

"That man," said Ibrahim.

"Yes?"

"He's found a necropolis."

Maha looked around. "Did he say where?"

"In the old Royal Quarter." Ibrahim traced out the approximate area with his finger, then tapped its heart. Remarkably, it was impossible to be sure of the outlines of the ancient city, let alone the position of a particular street or building. Alexandria was virtually surrounded by water, with the Mediterranean to the north, Lake Mariut to the south and west, and the marshy Nile Delta to the east, limiting its room for growth. When new buildings had been needed, therefore, old ones had simply been torn down to make way for them. Fort Qait Bey was built on the ruined foundations of the Pharos lighthouse. And the limestone blocks of Ptolemaic palaces had been reused for Roman temples, Christian churches, and then Islamic mosques, mirroring the various ages of the city.

He turned to Maha with a storyteller's smile. "Did you know that Alexander marked out our city's walls himself?"

"Yes, sir," she replied dutifully but without looking up.

"He leaked a trail of flour from a sack, only to have birds of all colors and sizes come feast upon it. Some people might have been put off by such an omen. Not Alexander."

"No, sir."

"He knew that it meant our city would provide shelter and sustenance for people from all nations. And he was right. Yes, he was right."

"Yes, sir."

"I'm boring you."

"You said you wanted these letters out today, sir."

"I do, Maha. Indeed I do."

Alexander hadn't lived to see his city built. It had been Ptolemy and his progeny who benefited, ruling Egypt with gradually diminishing authority until the Romans took over, themselves displaced by the Arab conquest of AD 641. The administrative capital had been transferred south, first to Fustat, then to Cairo. Trade with Europe had fallen off; there was no longer such need for a Mediterranean port. The Nile Delta had silted up; the freshwater canals had fallen into disuse. Alexandria's decline had continued inexorably after the Turks took control, and by the time Napoleon invaded at the turn of the nineteenth century, barely six thousand people lived here. But the city had since proved its resilience, and its harbors had come back to life, thanks to a boom in Mediterranean trade, so that today some four million souls were packed together into high-density housing that rendered systematic excavation impossible. Archaeologists like Ibrahim, therefore, were at the mercy of developers, who were still tearing down old buildings to erect new ones in their place—and every time they did so, there was a glimmer of a chance that they would uncover something extraordinary.

"He did describe one area in great detail," he said. "A forecourt with bronze doors leading to an antechamber and main chamber. What do you make of that?"

"A tomb?" hazarded Maha. "Ptolemaic?"

Ibrahim nodded. "Early Ptolemaic—very early." He took a deep breath. "Indeed, it sounded to me like the tomb of a Macedonian king."

Maha stood and turned, her fingers splayed on her desk. "You can't mean . . . ," she began. "But I thought Alexander was buried in a great mausoleum, not an underground necropolis."

Ibrahim remained silent for several seconds, vicariously enjoying her excitement, wondering whether to deflate her gently now or risk sharing his wilder hopes. He decided to let her down. "He was, yes. It was called the Sema; the Greek word for 'tomb,' you know. Or perhaps Soma, their word for 'body.' "

"Oh," said Maha. "So this won't be Alexander's tomb, then?"

"No."

"What is it?"

Ibrahim shrugged. "We'll need to excavate to find that out."

"How? I thought we'd spent all our money."

And that was the nub. Ibrahim's entire budget for the year was already allocated, and he'd begged as much from the French and the Americans as they could give. It happened like that here, precisely because excavation was such an opportunistic affair. If too many interesting sites were found in the same financial period, he simply couldn't handle them all. It became a matter of triage. At this precise moment, all his field archaeologists were involved, directly or indirectly, in projects across the old city. Excavating this new site would demand new money, specialists, and crew. And it wasn't as if he could put it on hold until the next financial year. The stairwell was slap in the middle of the new hotel's prospective parking lot; Mohammed could accommodate a couple of weeks of excavation, but any more would ruin his schedule. That was a real concern to Ibrahim. In uncovering ancient Alexandria, he depended almost entirely on property developers and construction companies to report significant finds. If ever he got a reputation for causing excessive delays or being difficult to work with, they'd simply stop notifying him, regardless of their legal obligations. In many ways, this latest site was a headache he didn't need. But it was also an early Macedonian tomb, quite possibly a very significant find indeed, so he couldn't let it slide by.

There was one possible source of funds, he knew. His mouth felt tacky and dry just thinking of it, not least because it would mean contravening all kinds of SCA protocols. Yet he could see no alternative. He forced a smile. "There's that Greek businessman who keeps offering to sponsor us," he said.

Maha raised her eyebrows. "You can't mean Nicolas Dragoumis!"

"Yes," he said. "That's the one."

"But I thought you said he was . . ." She caught his eye and trailed off.

"I did," he acknowledged. "But do you have a better suggestion?"

"No, sir."

Ibrahim had been delighted when Nicolas Dragoumis first contacted him, for sponsors were always welcome. Yet something about his manner had made Ibrahim apprehensive. After finishing that first phone call, he had immediately checked the Dragoumis Group's corporate Web site, with all its links to subsidiaries in shipping, insurance, construction, media, import-export, electronics, aerospace, property, tourism, security, and more. He had found a sponsorship section explaining that the Dragoumis Group supported only those projects that helped demonstrate the historical greatness of Macedonia or worked to restore the independence of Aegean Macedonia from the rest of Greece. Ibrahim didn't know much about Greek politics, but he knew enough not to want to get involved with Macedonian separatists.

Elsewhere on the site, he'd found a page with a group photograph of the company's directors. Nicolas Drag-oumis was tall, lanky, handsome, and well dressed. But it had been the man standing front and center who un-nerved Ibrahim. Philip Dragoumis, the Group's founder and chief executive, fearsome-looking, swarthy, lightly bearded, with a large plum-colored birthmark above his left cheekbone, and a disturbingly potent gaze, even in a photograph. He seemed like a man to steer clear of. But at this point Ibrahim had no choice. His heart beat a little faster, a little louder, as though he were standing on the very edge of a high cliff. "Good. Then, could you find me his telephone number, please?"

KNOX BEACHED THE SPEEDBOAT near his Jeep and waded ashore. Fiona had pulled herself together and was now insisting on returning to her hotel. From the way she wouldn't meet his gaze, it seemed she'd figured out that Hassan's wrath would be at Knox, not her, and that therefore the safest place was anywhere away from him. Not so dumb after all. Knox revved the Jeep furiously as she hurried off along the seafront. He was glad not to have her to worry about, but it pissed him off anyway. His passport, cash, and plastic were in his money belt. His laptop, clothes, books, and all his research were in his hotel room, but he dare not go back for them.

At the main road, he faced his first major decision: northeast to the Israeli border or up the west coast highway toward the main landmass of Egypt. Israel was safety, but the road was in bad repair, slow, and choked with army checkpoints. West, then. He'd arrived here nine years ago on a boat into Port Said; it seemed a fitting way to leave. But Port Said was on the Suez, and the Suez belonged to Hassan. No. He needed out of Sinai altogether. He needed an international airport—Cairo, Alexandria, or Luxor.

He jammed his cell phone against his ear as he drove, warning Rick and his other friends to watch out for Hassan. Then he turned it off altogether, lest they use the signal to trace him. He pushed the old Jeep as fast as it would go, engine roaring. Blue oil fires flickered ahead on the Gulf of Suez, like some distant hell. They matched his mood. He'd been driving for less than an hour when he saw an army checkpoint up ahead, a chicane of concrete blocks between two wooden cabins. He stifled the sudden urge to swing around and flee. Such checkpoints were routine in Sinai; there was nothing sinister about this. Waved to the side of the road, he felt the bump as he left the road, then cloying soft sand beneath his wheels. An officer swaggered across, a short, broad-shouldered man with hooded, arrogant eyes. He held out his hand for Knox's passport, then took it away with him. There was little traffic; the other soldiers were chatting around a radio, automatic rifles slung nonchalantly over their shoulders. Knox kept his head down. There was always one who wanted to show off his English.

A long, green insect was walking slowly along the rim of his lowered window. A caterpillar—no, a centipede. He put his finger in its way. It climbed unhesitatingly onto it, its feet tickling his skin. He brought it up to eye-level to inspect it as it continued on its way, unaware of just having been hijacked, of the precariousness of its situation. He watched it move up and around his wrist with a sense of fellow feeling. Centipedes had held great significance for the ancient Egyptians. They'd been closely connected with death, but in a welcome way, because they fed on the numerous insects that themselves feasted on corpses, and so had been seen as protectors of the human body, guarding against decomposition, and thus an aspect of Osiris himself. He gently tapped his hand against the outside of the Jeep's door until it fell off and tumbled to the ground. Then he leaned out the window and watched it creep away until he lost it in the darkness.

Inside the cabin, the officer was reading details from his passport into the telephone. He replaced the handset and sat perched on the edge of his desk, waiting to be called back. Minutes passed. Knox looked around, noting that no one else was being kept—just cursory inspections and then a wave through. The phone in the cabin finally rang, and Knox watched apprehensively as the officer reached out to answer it.

Chapter Four

A church outside Thessalonike, northern Greece

*T*HE RAM WHICH THOU SAWEST *having two horns are the kings of Me'dia and Persia,"* intoned the old preacher, reading aloud from the open Bible on his pulpit. *"And the rough goat is the king of Gre'cia: and the great horn that is between his eyes is the first king."* He paused and looked around the packed church. "Every Bible scholar will tell you the same thing," he said, leaning forward a little, lowering his voice, confiding to his audience. "The ram Daniel speaks of represents the Persian king Darius. The king of Gre'cia represents Alexander the Great. These verses are talking about Alexander's defeat of the Persians. And do you know when Daniel wrote them? Six hundred years before the birth of Christ, *two hundred and fifty years before Alexander was even born*. Two hundred and fifty years! Can you even begin to imagine what will be happening in the world two hundred and fifty years from now? But Daniel did it."

Nicolas Dragoumis nodded as he listened. He knew the old preacher's text word for word, because he'd written much of it himself, and then they had worked together in rehearsals until every word was perfect. But you could never really tell with something like this until you took it to the people. This was their first night, and it was going well so far. Atmosphere—that was the key. That was why they had chosen this old church, though it wasn't an official service. The moon showed through the stained-glass windows. A bird hooted in the rafters. Thick doors excluded the outside world. Incense caught in nostrils, covering the smell of honest sweat. The only lighting came from lines of fat white candles, just bright enough for the congregation to be able to check in their own Bibles that these verses were truly from chapter 8 of the Book of Daniel, as the preacher had assured them, but dark enough to retain a sense of the numinous, the unknown. People in this part of the world knew that things were stranger and more complex than modern science tried to paint them. They understood, as Nicolas did, the concept of mysteries.

He looked around the pews. These haggard people. People with compacted lives, old before their time, taking on backbreaking work at fourteen, becoming parents at sixteen, grandparents at thirty-five, few of them making it past fifty. Unshaven faces gaunt from stress, sour from disappointment; skin leathery and dark from too much sun; hands callused from their endless struggle against hunger. And angry, too, simmering with resentment at their poverty and the punitive taxation they paid on what little they earned. Anger was good. It made them receptive to angry ideas.

The preacher stood up straighter, relaxed his shoulders, and continued his reading. *"Now that being broken, whereas four stood up for it, four kingdoms shall stand up out of the nation, but not in his power."* He gazed out into his congregation with the slightly manic blue eyes of a madman or a prophet; Nicolas had chosen him well. " 'Now that being broken,' " he repeated. "That phrase refers to the death of Alexander. 'Four kingdoms shall stand up out of the nation.' And that refers to the breakup of the Macedonian Empire. As you all know, it was broken into four parts by his four successors: Ptolemy, Antigonus, Kassandros, and Seleucus. And remember, this was written by Daniel *nearly three hundred years earlier.*"

Unrest and anger weren't enough, reflected Nicolas. Where there was poverty, there was always unrest and anger, but there wasn't always revolution. There had been unrest and anger in Macedonia for two millennia, as first the Romans, then the Byzantines and Ottomans had oppressed his people. And every time they struggled free from one yoke, another had been placed on them. A hundred years ago, prospects had at last looked bright. The 1903 Ilinden Uprising had been brutally crushed, but then, in 1912, a hundred thousand Macedonians had fought side by side with Greeks, Bulgarians, and Serbs, finally to expel the Turks. It should by rights have been the birth date of an independent Macedonia, but they were betrayed. Their former allies turned upon them, the so-called Great Powers collaborated in the infamy, and Macedonia was cut up into three parts under the wretched Treaty of Bucharest.

Aegean Macedonia had been awarded to Greece, Serbian
Macedonia to Serbia, and Pirin Macedonia to Bulgaria.

" '*And out of one of them came forth a little horn,
which waxed exceeding great, toward the south, and toward the east, and toward the pleasant land.*' The little
horn is Demetrios," asserted the preacher. "For those of
you who may not remember, Demetrios was the son of
Antigonus, and he had himself proclaimed king of Macedonia, even though he was not of Alexander's blood."

The Treaty of Bucharest! Just the name had the power
to twist and torture Nicolas's heart. For nearly a hundred years, the borders it had laid down had remained
largely unchanged. And the loathsome Greeks, Serbs,
and Bulgars had done everything they could to eradicate
Macedonian history, language, and culture. They had
shut down free speech, imprisoning anyone who showed
the slightest defiance. They had appropriated the properties of Macedonian farmers and resettled outsiders on
them. They razed villages, orchestrated mass murders
and rapes, turned Macedonians into slaves, and then
worked them to death. They committed ethnic cleansing on a grand scale, without a peep of protest from the
wider world.

But it hadn't worked. That was the thing that gave
Nicolas hope. The spirit of Macedonian nationhood still
burned strong. In pockets across the region, their language
survived, as did their culture and church. They lived on in
these simple yet proud people, in the glorious sacrifices
they had already made and would soon make once more
for the greater good. Someday soon his beloved country
would finally be free.

"*And it waxed great, even to the host of heaven; and it cast down some of the host and of the stars to the ground, and stamped upon them. Yea, he magnified himself even to the prince of the host, and by him the daily sacrifice was taken away, and the place of his sanctuary was cast down.*' 'And the place of his sanctuary was cast down,' " repeated the preacher. "That's this place. That's Macedonia. The land of your birth. It was Demetrios, you see, who began the chaos that has engulfed Macedonia ever since. Demetrios. In two hundred and ninety-one BC. Mark that date. Mark it well. Two hundred and ninety-one BC."

In Nicolas's pocket, his cell phone began to vibrate. He gave few people this number, and his assistant, Katerina, had strict instructions not to put any calls through tonight. He stood and walked to the back doors. "Yes?" he asked.

"Ibrahim Beyumi for you, sir," said Katerina.

"Ibrahim who?"

"The archaeologist from Alexandria. I wouldn't have bothered you, but he says it's urgent. They've found something. They need a decision at once."

"Very well. Put him through."

"Yes, sir."

The line switched. Another voice came on. "Mr. Dragoumis, this is Ibrahim Beyumi here. From the Supreme Council in—"

"I know who you are. What do you want?"

"You've been generous enough to offer sponsorship in certain—"

"You've found something?"

"A necropolis. A tomb. A *Macedonian* tomb." He took

a deep breath. "From the description I was given, it sounds just like the Royal Tombs at Aigai."

Nicolas clutched his phone tight and turned his back on the church. "You've found a Macedonian royal tomb?"

"According to this description, maybe. But I won't know for sure until I've inspected it myself."

"And when will you do that?"

"First thing tomorrow—providing I can arrange financing, at least."

In the background, the preacher was still talking. " *'Then I heard one saint speaking,'* " he intoned, squeezing every sonorous drop from the biblical prose, " *'and another saint said unto that certain saint which spake, How long shall be the vision concerning the daily sacrifice, and the transgression of desolation, to give both the sanctuary and the host to be trodden under foot?'* How long shall Macedonia and the Macedonians be trampled underfoot? How long shall we pay the price for Demetrios's sin? Remember, this was written three hundred years before the sin of Demetrios, which took place in two hundred and ninety-one BC!"

Nicolas clamped a hand over his ear, the better to concentrate. "You need financing *before* you inspect?" he asked sardonically.

"We have a peculiar situation," said Ibrahim. "The man who reported the find has a very sick daughter. He wants funds before he'll talk."

"Ah." The inevitable baksheesh. "How much? For everything."

"In money terms?"

Nicolas clenched his toes in frustration. *These people!*

"Yes," he said, with exaggerated patience. "In money terms."

"That depends on how big the site proves to be, how much time we have, what kind of artifacts—"

"In U.S. dollars. Thousands, tens of thousands, hundreds of thousands?"

"Oh. It typically costs six or seven thousand American dollars a week for an emergency excavation like this."

"How many weeks?"

"That would depend on—"

"One? Five? Ten?"

"Three. Two if we're lucky."

"Fine. Do you know Elena Koloktronis?"

"The archaeologist? I've met her once or twice. Why?"

"She's on a dig in the Delta; Katerina will give you her contact number. Invite her tomorrow. If she vouches for this tomb of yours, the Dragoumis Group will give you twenty thousand dollars. I trust that will meet all your excavation costs, plus any more sick children who turn up."

"Thank you," said Ibrahim. "That's most generous."

"And get Katerina to talk you through our terms."

"Terms?"

"You don't think we'd provide funds on this scale without terms, do you?"

"But—"

"As I said, talk to Katerina." And he snapped the phone shut.

" 'And he said unto me, Unto two thousand and three hundred days; then shall the sanctuary be cleansed.' Two thousand and three hundred days!" cried the preacher

exultantly. "Two thousand and three hundred days! But
that's not precisely what the original Bible text says.
The original text talks about the 'evenings and morn-
ings of sacrifices.' And those sacrifices took place once
each year. Two thousand three hundred days, therefore,
doesn't mean two thousand three hundred days at all. No.
It means two thousand three hundred *years*. And who can
tell me what date is two thousand three hundred years on
from the sin of Demetrios? No? Then let me tell you. It is
the year of our Lord two thousand and nine. It is now. It
is today. Today our sanctuary is finally to be cleansed. It
says so in the Bible, and the Bible never lies. And remember, this was all predicted exactly by Daniel, *six hundred
years before the birth of Christ.*" He wagged a finger in
both admonition and exhortation. "It is written, people. It
is written. This is our time. This is *your* time. You are the
chosen generation, chosen by God to fulfill his command.
Which of you dare refuse his call?"

Nicolas watched with gratification as people turned
to look at one another, murmuring in astonishment.
This was indeed their time, he reflected, and it wasn't
a fluke. He'd been working toward it for fifteen years
now, his father for forty. They had operatives in every
hamlet, town, and village. Vast caches of weapons and
food were waiting in the mountains. Veterans of the Yu-
goslavian wars had trained them in ordnance and guer-
rilla campaigns. They had sleepers in local and national
government, spies in the armed services, friends in the
international community and among the Macedonian
diaspora. And the propaganda war was in full swing,
too. The schedules of Dragoumis TV and radio were

crammed with programs designed to stir Macedonian fervor, their newspapers filled with stories of Macedonian heroism and sacrifice, alongside tales of the opulent lifestyles and unthinking cruelty of their Athenian overlords. And it was working. Anger and hatred were building across northern Greece, even among those who had little sympathy with the separatist cause. Civil disturbance, riots, increasing incidents of ethnic assaults. All the telltale trembling of an imminent earthquake. But they weren't there yet. Much as Nicolas craved it, they weren't quite there. A revolution needed people so worked up they *wanted* martyrdom. Break out the guns now, and it would look promising for a while, but then everything would fizzle. The backlash would come. The Greek army would deploy on the streets; families would be menaced, and businesses investigated. There would be arbitrary arrests, beatings, and counterpropaganda. Their cause would be set back years, might even be irreversibly crippled. No. They still needed something more before it could begin. Something particular. A symbol that the Macedonian people would be prepared to fight to the death for.

And it was just possible that his recent phone call from Egypt might provide it.

THE EGYPTIAN ARMY OFFICER was still speaking on the phone. He seemed to be talking for a very long time.

He came out with a pen and a pad of paper and crouched to jot down the license number of Knox's Jeep. Then he went back inside and read it out to whoever was at the other end of the phone.

The Jeep's keys were in the ignition. For a crazy moment, Knox contemplated driving for it—if Hassan caught him, he was finished anyway. But though the Egyptian soldiers looked cheerful and relaxed enough, that would change in a heartbeat if he fled. The threat of suicide bombers was simply too high around here for them to take risks; he'd be shot dead before he made it fifty yards. So he forced himself to relax, to accept that his fate was out of his hands.

The officer replaced the handset carefully, composed himself, then walked over. He wasn't swaggering anymore. He looked thoughtful, even apprehensive. He gestured to his men. Immediately, they became alert. He stooped a little to talk through the Jeep's open window, tapping the spine of Knox's passport against the knuckles of his left hand as he did so. He said, "I am hearing whispers of a most remarkable story."

Knox's stomach squeezed. "What whispers?"

"Of an incident involving Hassan al-Assyuti and some young American man."

"I know nothing about that," said Knox.

"I'm glad," said the officer, squinting down the road to Sharm as though expecting a vehicle to appear at any moment. "Because, if the rumors are true, the young foreigner in question has a very bleak future."

Knox swallowed. "He was raping a girl," he blurted out. "What was I supposed to do?"

"Contact the authorities."

"We were in the middle of the fucking sea."

"I'm sure you'll have your chance to tell your side."

"Ballocks," said Knox. "I'll be dead within an hour."

The officer flushed. "You should have thought of that before, shouldn't you?"

"I should have covered my arse, you mean? Like you're doing now?"

"This isn't my fight," growled the officer.

Knox nodded. "People in my country, they think that all Egyptian men are cowards and thieves. I tell them they're wrong. I tell them that Egyptian men are honorable and brave. But maybe I've been wrong."

There was an angry muttering. One of the soldiers reached in the open window. The officer clamped his hand around his wrist. "No," he said.

"But he—"

"No."

The soldier retreated, a little shamefaced, while the officer looked down thoughtfully at Knox, clearly uncertain what to do. A pair of headlights crested a hill behind. "Please," begged Knox. "Just give me a chance."

The officer had noticed the approaching headlights, too. His jaw tightened as he came to his decision. He tossed the passport onto the passenger seat, then signaled his men to stand aside. "Get out of Egypt," he advised. "It's no longer safe for you."

Knox let out a long breath. "I'm leaving tonight."

"Good. Now go before I change my mind."

Knox put the Jeep into gear, accelerated away. His hands began shaking wildly as his body flooded with the euphoria of escape. He held himself back until he was a distance down the road, then he whooped and punched the air. He'd done a stupid, reckless thing, but it looked as though he'd got away with it.

NESSIM, HASSAN AL-ASSYUTI'S HEAD OF SECURITY, arrived in Knox's Sharm backpacker hotel to find the middle-aged concierge snoring raucously behind his desk. He came awake with a strangled shriek when Nessim slammed down the wooden access hatch. "Knox," said Nessim. "I'm looking for Daniel Knox."

"He's not here," said the concierge, breathing heavily.

"I know he's not here," said Nessim coldly. "I want to see his room."

"But it's his room!" protested the concierge. "I can't just show it to you."

Nessim reached into his jacket pocket for his wallet, making sure that the concierge caught a glimpse of his shoulder holster while he was at it. He took out fifty Egyptian pounds and set them down on the counter. "This is me asking nicely," he said.

The concierge licked his lips. "Just this once, I suppose."

Nessim followed the fat man upstairs, still brooding on what had happened on the boat, the humiliation of being bested by some beach bum foreigner. At first, he had thought that Knox would be easy to track down, but it wasn't proving that simple. He had word back from a contact in the army that Knox had somehow bluffed his way through a checkpoint. When he heard about that, he had felt a spike of intense anger and frustration. How simple it might have been! But he knew better than to make waves. Only a fool took on the army in Egypt, and Nessim wasn't a fool.

The concierge unlocked and opened Knox's door, looking around nervously lest other guests see what was happening. Nessim went inside. He had one night to capture Knox, and he had that only because Hassan was on morphine to manage his pain. When he woke in the morning, he would demand to know what progress had been made.

He would want Knox.

Nessim fingered the shabby clothes hanging in the wardrobe, checked the side pockets of the red canvas bag in the bottom, crouched to inspect the books lined up on the floor against the walls—a few comic novels and thrillers, but mostly academic works on Egypt and archaeology. There were CDs, too—some music, others for his laptop. He picked up a comb-bound document. The front page, in both English and Arabic, read:

Mallawi Excavation
First Season Notes
Richard Mitchell and Daniel Knox

He flipped through it. Text and photographs of an excavation near an ancient Ptolemaic settlement a few kilometers from Mallawi in Middle Egypt. He put it back thoughtfully. Why would an Egyptologist be working as a dive instructor in Sharm? He checked a few more documents. Maps and photographs of reef systems, as best he could make out. He took the canvas bag from the wardrobe and packed all Knox's documents inside. Then he packed up Knox's laptop, too, and his work-related CDs and floppy disks. In the top drawer of Knox's desk, he found photocopies of his passport and driver's license, presumably in case he lost the originals, and a strip of color passport-size photographs, no doubt for one of the myriad documents foreigners needed to work in Sinai. He scooped these up and tucked them away in his jacket pocket. Then he picked up the canvas bag and laptop to take away with him. The concierge gave a little whimper. "Yes?" asked Nessim. "Is something the matter?"

"No," said the concierge.

"Good. A word of advice. I'd clear the rest of his stuff out if I were you. I very much doubt your friend will be coming back anytime soon."

"No?"

"No." He handed him one of his business cards. "But call me if he does."

Chapter Five

THE MOSQUITOES were in a malevolent mood that evening. Gaille had buttoned her white chemise tight around her throat and wrists, tucked her long trousers into her socks, then sprayed all her remaining exposed skin to a shine with repellent; yet they still somehow found a way to feed off her and then boast of it afterward with that infuriating trumpeting of theirs, retreating to the high hotel ceiling well out of range of reprisal even when she stood on a chair. Whatever had happened to the notion of sisterhood? There it was again, that gloating buzz behind her ear. She slapped at her neck, but only as a gesture to punish herself for being so easily caught. The damage was done. The side of her right hand began to pulse and redden. Her mouse hand was an easy target as she typed up these damned excavation notes every night. She paused momentarily and glanced at her window. Just one night off wouldn't hurt. A cold beer and a little conversation. But if Elena caught her in the bar . . .

Her door opened without warning, and Elena herself

strode in as though she owned the place. She had no regard for anyone else's privacy, but heaven help you if you dared so much as knock on her door without first giving two weeks' written notice! "Yes?" asked Gaille.

"I've just had a phone call," said Elena. She squinted belligerently at Gaille, as though she found herself at a disadvantage and expected Gaille to make the most of it. "Ibrahim Beyumi. You know him? He's head of the Supreme Council in Alexandria. Apparently he's found a necropolis. He thinks part of it may be Macedonian. He wants me to check it out with him. He also said he was putting together a team for possible excavation, and asked if I could provide specialist support. I had to remind him I had my own excavation to run. Still, I mentioned you were available."

Gaille frowned. "He needs support with languages?"

"It's an emergency excavation," snorted Elena. "The job is to record, remove, process, and store. Translation will come later."

"Then . . . ?"

"He needs a photographer, Gaille."

"Oh!" Gaille felt bewildered. "But I'm not a photographer."

"You've got a camera, haven't you? You've been taking pictures for us, haven't you? Are you telling me they're no good?"

"I only took them because you asked me to—"

"So it's my fault, now, is it?"

Gaille asked plaintively, "What about Maria?"

"And who will *we* be left with? Are you claiming to be as good a photographer as she is?"

"Of course not." The only reason she had brought her camera at all was to photograph badly faded ancient ostraca, so that she could use her laptop's image software to make the writing clearer. "I just said I'm not a—"

"And Maria doesn't speak Arabic or English," pointed out Elena. "She'd be useless to Ibrahim, and all on her own. Is that what you want?"

"No. All I'm saying is—"

"All you're saying is!" mocked Elena spitefully, imitating her voice.

"Is this about what happened earlier?" asked Gaille. "I told you, I didn't see anything down there."

Elena shook her head. "This has nothing to do with that. It's very simple. The head of the Supreme Council in Alexandria has asked for your help. Do you really want me to tell him you refused?"

"No," replied Gaille miserably. "Of course not."

Elena nodded. "We're doing an initial survey first thing tomorrow morning. Make sure you're packed and ready to leave at seven." She took a look round Gaille's messy hotel bedroom, shook her head in exaggerated disbelief, then slammed the door behind her as she left.

IT SADDENED KNOX to abandon his Jeep in long-term parking. It had been his one constant companion since he'd been in Egypt. Eight hundred thousand already on the clock, and more left beneath the hood. You grew to

love a car when it had done that well for you. He left
his keys and the parking lot receipt beneath the seat.
He'd give one of his Cairo friends a call, see if they
wanted it.

The airport was busy. There was so much refurbish-
ment going on that everything was squeezed into half the
space. Knox pulled his baseball cap down over his eyes,
though it seemed unlikely that Hassan's people would be
ahead of him. He had a choice of flights. Many planes arrived in Egypt late at night, turning around to reach their
home airports around dawn. He wandered along the bank
of check-in desks. New York? Screw that. When you'd
fucked up your life, the last thing you wanted was to be
reminded of it by the success of old friends. Athens was
out, too. When he'd lost his marbles in the wake of family tragedy, Greece had been put off limits to him. London? Stuttgart? Paris? Amsterdam? The thought of such
places depressed him horribly. A dark-haired woman in
the queue for Rome caught his eye and smiled coyly. It
seemed as good a reason as any. He went to the inqui-
ries counter to see if there were tickets. The man in line
ahead of him was moaning about freight surcharges for
his computer, but Knox tuned him out. "Go home," that
checkpoint officer had urged. But Egypt *was* his home.
He'd lived here ten years. He'd grown to love it, for all
its heat, discomfort, chaos, and clamor. He loved the desert most of all: its searing clean lines, its extraordinary
gift of solitude, the kaleidoscopic sunsets and the chill
mists in the dune valleys in the moments before dawn.
He loved the hard labor of excavation, the thrill of poten-
tial discovery, that glorious kick it gave you getting out

of bed each morning. Not that he ever got the chance to excavate anymore.

The man ahead of him finally paid up. Knox stepped forward, fluttery with nerves. If he was going to have problems, this was where he'd find out. The booking clerk smiled blandly. He asked about seats; she assured him there were plenty. Knox handed across his passport and a credit card. She tapped keys, glanced up. *"Mi scusi un momento."* She took his passport and card and vanished through a door at the back of her booth. He leaned forward to see what it said on her screen. He saw nothing to alarm him. He looked around the concourse. Everything appeared normal. The clerk returned. She wouldn't quite meet his eye. She kept his passport and credit card in her hand, fractionally out of his reach. He glanced around again. Teams of security guards appeared almost simultaneously through doors at either end of the concourse. Knox lunged forward to snatch his passport and card from the startled clerk, then turned, ducked his head, and walked briskly away, his heart pumping wildly. To his left, a security guard yelled. Knox abandoned all pretense and raced for the exit. The doors were automatic, but they slid open so slowly that he turned shoulder-first and still crashed into them, forcing his way through, spinning around. A guard on duty outside unslung his rifle from his shoulder so hastily that he fumbled it and it fell clattering to the floor. Knox fled left, away from the bright lights of the terminal building and into the darkness beyond. He vaulted a rail, ran down a steep embankment to a poorly lit airport bus stop, leaped between a group of young travelers sitting on their backpacks, then smashed into the wall of an underpass, grazing his palm. Two uniformed janitors sharing a cigarette looked at him in astonishment as he ran between them, the whiff of their black tobacco catching in his throat. He turned left, sprinting hard, ignoring the shouting and the sirens. There were trees to his left; he ducked into their cover, running for another ten minutes until he couldn't manage anymore, and came to a stop, bent double, hands on his knees, heaving for air. Car headlights were slowly patrolling the roads, flashlights sweeping through the trees. The sweat on his shirt cooled; he shivered as he caught the scent of himself. This was bad. This was truly fucking awful. If the police got to him, it wouldn't matter that he could prove his case— Hassan would already have him by the balls. He thought through his options. The air- and seaports were clearly on alert. Border crossings would have his photo. You could get any document in the world forged in Cairo, but Hassan's reach was long. He'd soon know Knox was in Cairo, and he'd put out the word. No. He needed to get away as quickly as possible. He could flag down a taxi or a bus, but the drivers would remember him. Trains were often packed with soldiers and police. Better to risk going back for his Jeep.

There was shouting from his left, a single gunshot. Knox flinched and ducked. It took him a moment to realize they were shooting at shadows. He had his breath back now, and his bearings. He crouched and kept moving until he reached the perimeter wire fence of long-term parking—high but not barbed. He climbed it by a concrete post and dropped down the other side, the joints of his fingers raw from the thin mesh. He ran low between the pools of light and the ranks of parked cars. The place was deserted. Departing passengers were already in the terminal; arrivals had long since driven off. Once back in his Jeep, he drove up to the booth and handed money to a sleepy attendant. The barrier lifted.

Blue police lights flashed away to his left as he pulled out onto the main road. He turned right instead, heading toward Cairo. The lights shrank and then disappeared from his mirror. Police cars with flashing lights hurtled past on the other side of the highway. He found that he was holding his breath, had to make himself start again. Where the fuck was he going to go now? He couldn't stay in Cairo, but he needed to avoid checkpoints, too. That cut out Sinai, the Western Desert, and the south. Alexandria, then. It was just three hours north, and of all Egypt's cities, he liked it most. He had friends there, too, so he could avoid hotels. But he was a fugitive; he couldn't inflict himself on just anyone. He needed someone who'd believe in him, someone with strong nerves who relished a little transgression from time to time, just to keep the blood pumping. Put like that, there was only one contender. Knox felt his spirits lifting for the first time in hours. He stamped down on the accelerator and roared north.

Chapter Six

MAIS ATTENDS!" yelled Augustin Pascal at whatever bastard was pounding at his door. *"J'arrive! J'arrive!"* He clambered across the naked girl lying with her face down between his pillows. With that long, wavy, tawny hair, it looked like Sophia. He lifted her mane to make sure. *Shit! Shit!* He'd been excited for a week at the prospect of nailing her, and now he'd gone and wasted it while too drunk to remember.

A terrible thing, growing old.

The pounding on the door began again, resonating with the demolition works inside his skull. He checked his alarm clock. Five thirty! Five fucking thirty! But this was unbelievable! *"Mais attends!"* he yelled again. He kept emergency bottles of water and pure oxygen on his bedside table. He alternated long swallows from one with deep breaths from the other, until he felt able to stand without keeling over. He wrapped a ragged towel around his waist, lit a cigarette, and went to open his front door. Knox was standing there. "The fuck do you want?" demanded Augustin. "You know what fucking time this is?"

"I'm in trouble," said Knox simply. "I need help."

IBRAHIM BEYUMI, Head of the SCA in Alexandria, felt in high spirits as he drove through his beloved city. The sun had only just risen, but he'd been too excited to stay in bed. He'd had a dream during the night. No, that wasn't quite right. He'd been lying there half awake, waiting for his alarm to sound, when he was suddenly overwhelmed by a sense of exquisite and intense well-being. He couldn't shake off the idea that he was on the verge of something momentous, and not even the occasional twinge of anxiety about taking Nicolas Dragoumis's money could touch his mood.

He pulled up outside the apartment block that Mohammed, the man who had reported this mysterious underground necropolis, had given as his home address. It was a wretched-looking place, tall and pockmarked with discolored gray walls, its front doors broken and hanging loose, intestinal wires spilling out of the intercom. Mohammed was already waiting in the lobby. His eyes lit up when he saw Ibrahim's Mercedes, and he walked proudly and slowly across, turning around as he did so, like an actor or a sportsman milking his time on the stage, wanting as many of his friends and neighbors as possible to see him climb in.

"Good morning," said Ibrahim.

"We travel in style, then," said Mohammed, pushing back the passenger seat as far as it would go to accommodate his legs, yet still struggling to fit.

"Yes."

"My wife's very excited," said the big man. "She's convinced we have found Alexander." He glanced slyly at Ibrahim, as though to gauge his reaction.

"I doubt it, I'm afraid," said Ibrahim. "Alexander was buried in a huge mausoleum."

"And this isn't part of it?"

Ibrahim shrugged. "It's very unlikely. It wasn't just Alexander, you see. The Ptolemies were buried there, too." He smiled across at Mohammed. "They wanted Alexander's glory to rub off on them. It didn't work all that well, though. When the Roman emperor Augustus made his pilgrimage to Alexander's tomb, the priests asked him if he'd like to see the bodies of the Ptolemies, too. You know what he replied?"

"What?"

"That he'd come to see a king, not corpses."

Mohammed laughed loudly. Alexandrians had always enjoyed watching the powerful get taken down a peg or two. Ibrahim was so pleased that he ventured another anecdote. "You know Pompey's Pillar?"

"Of course. I can see it from my site."

"Did you know it had nothing to do with Pompey? It was actually erected in honor of the emperor Diocletian after he led an expeditionary force here to quash an uprising that had made him so angry he vowed to revenge himself on the Alexandrians until his horse was knee-deep in blood. Guess what happened?"

"I can't think."

"His horse stumbled and grazed its knees, so that they became covered in blood. Diocletian took this as a sign and spared the city. His officials put up his pillar and statue in remembrance. But do you know what the Alexandrians did?"

"No."

"They built a statue, too. But not to Diocletian—to his horse."

Mohammed guffawed and slapped his knee. "To his horse! I like that!"

They were drawing closer to the city center. "Which way?" asked Ibrahim.

"Left," said Mohammed. "Then left again." They paused for a tram. "So where *was* Alexander's tomb?" he asked.

"No one knows for sure. Ancient Alexandria suffered terribly from fires, riots, wars, and earthquakes. And then there was a catastrophic tsunami during the fourth century. First it sucked away the water from the harbors, luring citizens out to pick up the fish and valuables just lying there. Then the wave struck. They never stood a chance."

Mohammed shook his head in wonder. "I never heard."

"No? Anyway, the city fell into ruin and all the great sites became lost, even Alexander's mausoleum. And we've never found it since, though we've tried, believe me." Countless excavators had tried, including Heinrich Schliemann, fresh from his triumphs at Troy and Mycenae. All had come up empty.

"You must have some idea."

"All the sources agree that it was on the northeast of the ancient crossroads," said Ibrahim. "The trouble is, we're not sure where that was. All these new buildings, you see. Two hundred years ago, yes. A thousand years ago, easy. But now . . ."

"People say Alexander is buried beneath the Mosque of the Prophet Daniel. They say he's in a golden casket."

"They're wrong, I'm afraid."

"Then why do they say this?"

Ibrahim was quiet for a moment, collecting his thoughts. "You know that Alexander appears in the Qur'an?" he asked. "Yes, as the prophet Zulkarnein, the two-horned one. Leo the African, a sixteenth-century Arab writer, talked of pious Muslims making pilgrimages to Alexander's tomb, and he said it was near the church of Saint Mark, as the Mosque of the Prophet Daniel also is. And Arab legends talk of a prophet Daniel who conquered all Asia, founded Alexandria, and was buried here in a golden coffin. Who else could that be but Alexander? You can certainly see why people might confuse the mosque with Alexander's tomb. And then, oh, about a hundred and sixty years ago now, a Greek man claimed he'd glimpsed a body wearing a diadem on a throne in the mosque's vaults. It's a very seductive idea. There's only one problem with it."

"Yes?"

"It's completely wrong."

Mohammed laughed. "You're sure?"

"I've searched the vaults myself," said Ibrahim. "Believe me, they're Roman, not Ptolemaic. Five or six hundred years too late. But the idea has stuck, not least because our best map of the ancient city marks Alexander's mausoleum very near the mosque."

"There you are, then!"

"The map was made for Napoleon the Third," said Ibrahim. "A nephew of Napoleon Bonaparte who became emperor of France. Anyway, he was writing a biography of Julius Caesar, and he needed information on ancient Alexandria, so he asked his friend Khedive Ismail for a map of it. But there wasn't one at the time, not a reliable one at least, so Khedive Ismail commissioned a man called Mahmoud el-Falaki to make it."

"Research is certainly easier if you're an emperor."

"Quite," agreed Ibrahim. "And it's a really fine piece of cartography, too. But not perfect, I'm afraid. He fell for the old legends, too. He marked Alexander's tomb near the mosque, and all the modern guidebooks and histories now reprint it, keeping the myth alive. The poor imam of the Nabi Daniel Mosque is constantly being pestered by tourists hoping to find Alexander, but they won't find him there, believe me."

"Where should they be looking?"

"On the northeast side of the old crossroads, as I said. Near the Terra Santa cemetery, probably. A little northwest of the Shallalat Gardens."

Mohammed was looking downcast. Ibrahim patted his forearm. "Don't give up hope just yet," he said. "There's something I haven't told you."

"What?"

"I haven't told anyone. I don't want rumors to start, you know."

"Tell me."

"The thing is, Alexander didn't have just one tomb in Alexandria. He had two."

"Two?"

"Yes. The Soma, the great mausoleum I told you about, was built around 215 BC by Ptolemy Philopater, the fourth of the Ptolemaic kings. But, before that, he had a different tomb, almost certainly more in the traditional Macedonian style. More, as it happens, like the one you and your men found yesterday."

Mohammed looked wonderingly at him. "You think this is what we have found?"

"We won't know until we see it," said Ibrahim. "But don't get too excited. This was Alexander, remember; the Ptolemies would surely have built something spectacular for him." Not that they knew what. They didn't even know when Alexander's body had been brought up here from Memphis, where it had been held while his mausoleum was being built. The modern consensus was 285 BC, nearly forty years after his death, though no one had satisfactorily explained why the transfer should have taken so long. "Apart from anything else, we believe that they would have wanted to keep his body on display, so it's unlikely he'd have been kept deep underground. But that's the wonderful thing about archaeology," grinned Ibrahim. "You never know for sure."

There was something else, too, though nothing he felt like sharing with Mohammed. It was that ever since he'd been a small boy, listening to his father murmur him to sleep with tales of the founder of this great city, he'd had a sense of destiny. One day, he would play his part in the rediscovery of the tomb of Alexander. And this morning, as he lay awake in bed, he had a reprise of that feeling, a conviction that the time was upon him. And for all his intellectual misgivings, he was sure in his heart that it had something to do with the tomb they were on their way to inspect.

NESSIM HAD BEEN ON THE GO ALL NIGHT, working furiously to catch Knox before Hassan woke. But he had failed. Fifteen minutes ago he received his summons, and now here he was, steeling himself with a clenched fist before knocking on his boss's bedroom door at Sharm's medical center.

Nessim had joined the Egyptian Army at the age of seventeen and had become a paratrooper, one of the elite. But a twisted knee put an end to his hopes of active service, so he resigned his commission out of boredom to become a mercenary in the endless African wars. When a mortar round had landed fizzing practically in his lap yet hadn't exploded, it convinced him that it was time for another change of pace. Back in Egypt, he had made a name for himself as a bodyguard before being recruited by Hassan as his head of security. Nessim didn't scare easily; if he did, he would never have survived such a life. But Hassan scared him. Having to report bad news scared him.

"Come in," muttered Hassan. His voice was softer than usual, and a little wheezy. He'd lost a tooth and suffered severe bruising of his ribs, too, which evidently made breathing painful. "Well?" he asked.

"Would you please excuse us?" Nessim asked the doctor sitting beside his bed.

"With pleasure," said the doctor, a shade too emphatically for his own good.

Nessim closed the door behind him. "We've got the girl," he told Hassan. "She was going for a bus."

"And Knox?"

"We almost had him. At Cairo Airport. He got away."

"Almost?" said Hassan. "What good is almost?"

"I'm sorry, sir."

Hassan closed his eyes. Evidently, yelling hurt too much. "You call yourself my head of security?" he said. "Look at me! And you let the man who did this wander around Egypt like some kind of *tourist*?"

"You'll have my resignation as soon as—"

"I don't want your resignation," said Hassan. "I want Knox. I want him here. Do you understand? I want you to bring him to me. I want to see his face. I want him to know what he's done and what's going to happen to him because of it."

"Yes, sir."

"I don't care what it takes. I don't care how much you spend. I don't care what favors you have to call in. Use the army. Use the police. Whatever is necessary. Am I clear?"

"Yes, sir."

"Well?" asked Hassan. "Why are you still here?"

"With respect, sir, there are different ways to catch him. One, as you rightly suggest, is by using our contacts in the police and the army."

Hassan squinted. He was a shrewd man, for all his wrath. "But?"

"It was easy enough to secure their help last night. We simply told them that Knox had caused a serious incident on a boat though the details were still unclear. But tomorrow and the day after, if we still want their active help, they'll want evidence of this serious incident."

Hassan looked at Nessim in disbelief. "Are you saying what he did to me isn't sufficient evidence?"

"Of course not, sir."

"Then what *are* you saying?"

"So far, very few people know anything more than rumors. I picked your medical team myself, and they know better than to talk. I've had my own people guarding your door; no one has been allowed in without my explicit permission. But if we involve the police, they'll want to investigate for themselves. They'll send officers to interview you and take photographs and talk to the other guests on the boat, including your Stuttgart friend and the girl. And I wonder if that would be helpful at this particular moment—or, indeed, whether it would be good for your reputation to have photographs of your injuries reaching the newspapers or the Internet alongside exaggerated reports of how they were incurred, which could easily happen, because we both know you have enemies as well as friends in the police. And you should ask yourself what it would do for your personal authority if people got to see what a mere dive instructor had done to you—and that he'd managed to escape, too, even if only for a little while."

Hassan frowned. He knew the value of being feared. "What's our alternative?"

"We drop the charges. We say it was all a misunderstanding, and we put the fear of god into the girl and then get her out of the country. You lie low until you've recovered. Meanwhile, we go after Knox ourselves."

There was a long silence. "Very well," said Hassan finally. "But you're to take personal charge. And I expect results. Understand?"

"Yes, sir. I understand entirely."

Chapter Seven

It was Gaille's first visit to Alexandria, and it didn't make much of a first impression, with traffic barely moving along the Corniche, the city's famous seafront. The masts of fishing boats and yachts in the Eastern Harbor jangled in a light breeze that brought with it a faint acidic tang. She rested her head back, shielding her eyes from the early morning sun as it flickered between tall, rectangular, sun-bleached hotels, apartment blocks, and offices, all pocked with satellite dishes. The place was coming to life like a gigantic yawn. Alexandria had always been the late riser of Egyptian cities. Shops were raising steel shutters, lowering canopies. Groups of portly men sipped coffees at pastry cafés and watched benignly as ragged boys and girls wended through the traffic selling packs of napkins and cigarettes. The alleys leading away from the harbor front were tight, dark, and faintly menacing. A tram already crammed with passengers paused to take on more. A policeman in a dazzling white uniform and flat cap held up his hand to divert them right. An ancient commuter train clanked and rattled with taunting slowness through a crossing. Young boys played chase in its open cattle cars.

Elena glanced pointedly at her watch. "You're sure this is the right way?"

Gaille shrugged helplessly. Her only map was a crude photocopy from an outdated backpacker guidebook. She had a nagging suspicion that she had already gone badly wrong, though she had learned enough about her new boss not to admit it. "I think so," she equivocated.

Elena sighed loudly. "At least you could make an effort."

"I'm doing my best." Gaille couldn't shake off the suspicion that she was being punished for her intrusion into the site yesterday or was at least being opportunistically expelled from the Delta dig because of it. They were approaching a large intersection. Elena looked at her expectantly for directions. "Turn right," said Gaille.

"Are you sure?"

"It should be somewhere along here on the left or right."

"Somewhere along here on the left or right?" snorted Elena. "That's really helpful."

Gaille leaned forward, staring through the windshield, her brain aching from lack of sleep and too much coffee. There was a construction site ahead, a huge concrete high-rise with steel rebar waggling like spider legs from the top. She said in desperation, "I think this must be it."

"You *think* this must be it; or this is *actually* it?"

"I've never been to Alexandria before," protested Gaille. "How should I know?"

Elena huffed noisily and shook her head, but she signaled and swung through double gates, then bumped along a rutted track. Three Egyptian men were conferring animatedly at the far end. "That's Ibrahim," muttered Elena, with such obvious chagrin that Gaille had to fight back a smile. If Elena thought she was gloating . . . They parked. Gaille quickly opened her door and jumped down, suffering a momentary, debilitating flutter of shyness. Normally she was confident in professional situations, but she had no faith in her skills as a photographer and consequently felt like a fraud. She went around to the back of the flatbed, ostensibly to check her belongings and equipment, but in truth to hide.

Elena yelled out for her. She took a deep breath to compose herself, fixed a smile to her lips, then walked around to meet them. "Ibrahim," said Elena, indicating the elegant man in the center of the group, "I'd like you to meet Gaille."

"Our esteemed photographer! We are truly grateful."

"I'm not really a—"

"Gaille's an excellent photographer," said Elena, with a sharp glance. "What's more, she's an ancient-languages expert, too."

"Splendid! Splendid!" He gestured to his two companions, who were spreading out a site map on the ground. "Mansoor and Mohammed," he said. "Mansoor is my right hand. He runs all our excavations in Alexandria. I couldn't survive without him. And Mohammed is the construction manager for this hotel."

"Pleased to meet you both," said Gaille.

They glanced up from their map and nodded politely. Ibrahim smiled distractedly, glanced at his watch. "Just one more to come. You know Augustin Pascal?"

Elena snorted. "Only by reputation."

"Yes," nodded Ibrahim seriously. "He's a fine underwater archaeologist."

"That wasn't what I meant," said Elena.

"Oh."

An awkward silence followed, broken only when an engine roared at the mouth of the site. "Ah!" said Ibrahim. "Here he is."

A thirty-something man cruised up the approach on a gleaming black-and-chrome chopper, wending around potholes, bare-headed, allowing his long dark hair to flow free. He was wearing mirror shades, two days' worth of stubble, a leather jacket, jeans, calf-high black biker boots. He rode the chopper up onto its kickstand, stepped off, and fished a cigarette and a brass Zippo from his shirt pocket.

"You're late," said Ibrahim.

"*Desolé,*" he grunted, shielding the flame. "Something came up."

Mansoor asked wryly, "Sophia, I suppose?"

Augustin grinned wolfishly. "You know I'd never take advantage of my students like that." Elena clucked her tongue and muttered a Greek obscenity beneath her breath. Augustin grinned and turned to her, spreading his hands. "Yes?" he asked. "You see something you like, perhaps?"

"How could I?" retorted Elena. "You're standing in the way."

Mansoor laughed and slapped Augustin on the shoulder, but Augustin looked unruffled. He looked Elena up and down, then gave her a grin of frank approval, perhaps even of intent, for she was a striking woman, and anger added a certain something to her coloring. Gaille winced and took half a step back, waiting for the inevitable eruption, but Ibrahim stepped between them just in time.

"Well," he said, with nervous jauntiness. "Let's start, shall we?"

The ancient spiral steps looked precarious, and Gaille descended warily, but they reached the bottom without alarm and gathered in the rotunda. The corner of a black-and-white pebble mosaic showed beneath the rubble. Gaille pointed it out in a murmur to Elena. "Ptolemaic," declared Elena loudly, going down on her haunches to brush away the dust. "Two-fifty BC, give or take."

Augustin pointed to the sculpted walls. "Those are Roman," he said.

"Are you suggesting I can't tell a Macedonian mosaic when I see one?"

"I'm suggesting that the carvings are Roman."

Ibrahim held up his palms. "How about this?" he suggested. "Perhaps this site started out as a private tomb for some wealthy Macedonian, which would explain the mosaic. Then, when the Romans came three hundred years later, they decided to turn it into a necropolis."

"That would explain the staircase," admitted Elena grudgingly. "Macedonians didn't usually build in spirals. Only straight lines or squares."

"And they'd have needed to widen the shaft when they expanded it into a necropolis," agreed Augustin. "For light and ventilation, and to lower corpses, and to take out quarried stone. They used to sell it to builders, you know."

"Yes," said Elena scathingly. "I did know, thank you."

Gaille was barely listening. She was staring dizzily up at the circle of sky high above her head. Christ, but she was out of her depth. An emergency excavation offered no second chances, so within the next two weeks, the mosaic and all these exquisite carvings and everything else in this place would need to be photographed. After that, the place would probably be sealed forever. Artifacts like these deserved a professional photographer, someone with an eye for the work, experience, sophisticated equipment, lighting. She plucked anxiously at Elena's sleeve, but Elena brushed her off, following Mohammed down the steps into the forecourt of the Macedonian tomb. They paused to admire the shining white marble blocks of the facade and entablature, then pressed on through the half-open bronze door into the tomb's antechamber.

"Look!" said Mansoor, pointing his flashlight at the side walls. They went closer to inspect them. There was paint on the plaster, though terribly faded. It had been common practice in antiquity for important scenes from the dead person's life to be painted in or around the tomb. "You can photograph these?" asked Mansoor.

"I'm not sure how well they'll come out," said Gaille wretchedly.

"You must wash them first," said Augustin. "Lots and lots of water. The pigment may look dead now, but give them some water and they will spring back to life like beautiful flowers. Trust me."

"Not *too* much water," warned Mansoor. "And don't set up your lights too close. The heat will crack the plaster."

Gaille looked around desperately at Elena, who studiously refused to meet her eye. Instead, she shone her flashlight at the inscription above the portal into the main chamber. "Akylos of the thirty-three," said Augustin, translating from the Ancient Greek. Elena fumbled and dropped her flashlight at that moment, cursing violently, so Ibrahim turned his light on the inscription instead, allowing Augustin to complete his translation. "Akylos of the thirty-three. To be the best and to be honored above the rest."

"It's Homer," murmured Gaille. Everyone turned to look at her in surprise. She felt her cheeks burn. "It's from the *Iliad*," she said.

"That's right," nodded Augustin. "About a man called Glaucus, I believe."

"Actually, it comes up twice," said Gaille timidly. "Once about Glaucus and once about Achilles."

"Achilles, Aklyos," nodded Ibrahim. "He evidently thought a great deal of himself." He was still staring up at the inscription when he followed Mohammed into the main chamber, so that he tripped over the low step and went sprawling onto his hands and knees. Everybody laughed as he picked himself up and brushed himself down with the self-deprecating smile and shrug of the accident prone.

Augustin went to the shield pinned to the wall. "The shield of a hypastist," he said. "A shield bearer," he explained when Ibrahim frowned. "Alexander's special forces. The greatest unit of fighting men in the most successful army in the history of the world. Maybe he wasn't being so boastful after all."

MORNING SUNLIGHT fell on Knox's cheek as he lay on Augustin's couch and tried to catch up on sleep. He groaned and turned his back, but it was no good. The day was already too sticky. He rose reluctantly, took a shower, ransacked Augustin's room for clothes, then ground some beans and set the coffeemaker brewing. He slathered a croissant with butter and *confiture de framboises,* then wolfed it down as he wandered the apartment looking for ways to divert himself. Egyptian TV was gruesome at the best of times, but Augustin's flickering black-and-white portable made it completely unwatchable. And there was nothing to read except tattered newspapers and some comic books. This was not an apartment for killing time in. It was an apartment for sleeping in, and preferably not alone.

He walked out onto the balcony. Identical high-rises on every side, all in the same disheartened beige, washing hung out to dry on the balconies, ubiquitous gray dishes all turning to their satellites like the faithful to Mecca. Yet still he felt glad to be here. Few Egyptologists would say it openly, but they looked down their noses at Alexandria. They barely considered the Greco-Roman era to be Egyptian at all. But Knox didn't think that way. To him, this was Egypt's golden age, and Alexandria its golden city. Two thousand years ago, it had been the greatest metropolis on earth, nurturing the finest minds of antiquity. Archimedes had studied here; so had Galen and

Origen. The Septuagint had been translated here. Euclid had published his famous works here. Chemistry took its very name from here; al-Khemia was the black land of Egypt, and alchemy the Egyptian art. Aristarchus had proposed the heliocentric theory here, well over a millennium before it was rediscovered by Copernicus. Eratosthenes had calculated almost exactly the circumference of the earth by extrapolating from discrepancies in the lengths of shadows cast at the sun's zenith both here and in Aswan, some 850 kilometers to the south, on the summer solstice. What imagination! What intellectual curiosity and endeavor! An unprecedented collision of cultures, an effervescence of thought the equal of Athens and unmatched again until the Renaissance. It was beyond him how anyone could dismiss such achievements as second best or think that—

His meditations were interrupted suddenly by a noise from inside, as though someone was trying surreptitiously to clear his throat. Had his sanctuary been discovered already? He stepped to the edge of the balcony, so that he couldn't be seen through the glass doors, and pressed himself flat against the wall.

IBRAHIM FOLLOWED CLOSE BEHIND MOHAMMED as he led them down the corridor into the main body of the necropolis. For all that he'd been dampening his hopes before visiting this place, he still felt a sense of anticlimax that the tomb had proved to be for a common soldier, not a king. But he was a professional, and he concentrated hard, the better to understand what he was dealing with.

They came to a chamber, its walls cut with columns of loculi, like the drawers of a massive morgue. It seemed to confirm his theory that this whole complex had started off as a private Macedonian tomb for Akylos before being expanded into a public necropolis. He took a closer look. The niches were crowded with bones, half buried in dark sandy dirt, others scooped out onto the floor by grave robbers looking for treasure. Amid the debris they found a broken faience figure, some green and blackened coins dating from the first to fourth centuries AD, numerous fragments of terra-cotta from funerary lamps, jars, and statuettes. There were chunks of stone and plaster, too. Loculi had typically been sealed after burials, but the looters had smashed these seals to get at the contents.

"Will you find mummies, do you think?" asked Mohammed. "I took my daughter to your museum once; she became fascinated by the mummies."

"It's very unlikely," answered Ibrahim. "The climate here isn't kind; it eats away everything but bone. And even if they had survived the humidity, they'd never have survived the tomb robbers."

"Robbers stole mummies?" frowned Mohammed. "What for?"

"People often hid jewelry and other valuables in their body cavities, so the robbers would take them up into the sunlight to tear them apart and search them. But the mummies themselves had real value, too. Particularly in Europe."

"You mean museums?"

"Not at first, no," said Ibrahim. "You see, about six hundred years ago, Europeans came to believe that bitumen was very good for the health. It was the wonder cure of its time. Every apothecary had to stock it. Demand was so great that supplies ran short and traders started looking for new sources. You know how black mummified remains can get? People became convinced they'd been soaked in bitumen. That was where the word 'mummy' came from, you know; '*mumia*' was Persian for 'bitumen,' and most of the original supplies of bitumen came from Persia, because it forms naturally there, in great congealed pools."

Mohammed grimaced. "People used mummies as medicine?"

"Europeans did, yes," said Ibrahim, giving the big builder a grin. "But, anyway, Alexandria was right at the center of this trade, which is one reason we've never found even fragments of mummy here, though we know for sure that mummification was practiced."

They moved on to another chamber. Mansoor lit up a plaster seal with his flashlight. It had faint traces of paint on it, a scene of a seated woman and a standing man clasping right hands.

"The wife has died," Ibrahim explained to Mohammed. "This painting is known as a *dexiosis,* a kind of farewell, with them saying good-bye for the last time."

"Maybe he's in there with her, too," muttered Mohammed. "They seem pretty crowded, these tombs."

"That's because there were so many people in Alexandria, and not enough space. Some estimates say that a million people lived here in ancient times. Have you seen the necropolis at Gabbari?"

"No."

"It's huge. A true city of the dead. And there's Shatby and Sidi Gabr, too. But still they weren't enough. Particularly after Christianity became popular."

Mohammed frowned. "Why so?"

"Before the Christians, many Alexandrians opted for cremation," he explained. "See these niches in the walls? They're designed for urns and caskets. But Christians believed in resurrection, you know. They needed their bodies."

"This is a Christian necropolis, then?"

"It's an Alexandrian necropolis," answered Ibrahim. "You'll find believers in the Egyptian gods, the Greek gods, the Roman gods, Jews, Christians, Buddhists— every religion on earth."

"And what happens to them now?"

Ibrahim nodded. "We'll study them. We can learn a great deal about diet, health, mortality rates, ethnic mix, cultural practices. Many other things."

"You'll treat them with respect?"

"Of course, my friend. Of course."

They went back out, into another chamber. "What's this?" asked Augustin, pointing his flashlight through a hole in the wall to a short flight of steps disappearing down into the dark.

"I don't know," shrugged Mohammed. "I didn't see it before."

Ibrahim had to duck low to get beneath, and Mohammed had to go on his hands and knees. Inside was what appeared to be the tomb of a wealthy family, separated by a line of carved pillars and pilasters into two adjoining spaces. Five stone sarcophagi of different sizes stood against the walls, all decorated with a rich confusion of styles and faiths. A portrait of Dionysus was carved into the limestone above depictions of Apis, Anubis, and a solar disk. Stone recesses above each of the sarcophagi held Canopic jars, perhaps still containing their original contents: the stomach, liver, intestines, and lungs of the deceased. Other objects glittered on the floor: fragments of funerary lamps and amphorae, scarabs, small items of silver and bronze jewelry studded with dulled stones. "Marvelous," murmured Augustin. "How can the robbers have missed these?"

"Perhaps the door was concealed," suggested Ibrahim, kicking at the rubble. "An earthquake, or just the passage of time."

"How old?" asked Mohammed.

Ibrahim glanced at Augustin. "First century AD?" he suggested. "Maybe second."

They came at last to the level of the water table. Steps disappeared tantalizingly down into it, hinting at more chambers beneath. The water had risen and fallen dramatically over the centuries; if they were lucky, it might have prevented the robbers from looting whatever lay beneath. Augustin stooped and made ripples with his hand. "Do we have the budget for a pump?" he asked.

Ibrahim shrugged. Pumping was expensive, noisy, dirty, and all too often completely ineffective. It would also mean running a fat pipe along the passage and up the stairwell, which would get in the way of the main excavation. "If we must."

"If you want me to explore first, I'll need a buddy. These places are death traps."

Ibrahim nodded. "Whatever you wish. I leave it up to you."

NESSIM WAS DRIVING through Suez when his cell phone rang. "Yes?" he asked.

A man's voice. "It's me."

Nessim didn't recognize his caller, but he knew better than to ask. He'd contacted a great many people last night, and few of them were keen on having their connection with Hassan known. Cell phones were notoriously vulnerable; you had to assume you were being monitored at all times. "What have you got?"

"Your man has a file."

Ah! So the Egyptian Security Service had a file on Knox. Intriguing. "And?"

"Not over the phone."

"I'm on my way to Cairo now. Same arrangement as last time?"

"Six o'clock," the man agreed. And the phone went dead.

KNOX WAS STILL STANDING out on Augustin's balcony, expecting at any moment that the glass doors would be pushed open and the intruder would step out. Only now did he realize what a death trap this apartment was. The fire escape, elevator, and main stairs were all outside the front door. Other than that . . . There weren't any other balconies to leap onto, or any ledge to inch along. He gripped the rail tight and leaned out to look six stories down to the unyielding concrete of the parking lot. He could conceivably drop down to the balcony directly beneath his own, but if he mistimed his release . . . His toes went numb just thinking about it.

Inside Augustin's apartment, the coughing was growing worse. A strange intruder to break into an apartment only to stand there hacking away. He risked a quick glance through the glass doors but saw nothing to alarm him. Another cough, then some hissing, and finally he understood. He went back in, shaking his head at his paranoia, to find Augustin's percolator spluttering out the last few drops of coffee. He poured himself a cup and toasted himself mockingly in the mirror. He wasn't good at this kind of thing, not least because he found confinement hard to bear. Already he could feel a kind of cabin fever building, a slight cramping in his upper arms and the backs of his calves. He longed to take a brisk walk, burn off some nervous energy, but he dare not show his face outside. Hassan's men would surely already be showing his photograph at train stations, hotels, and taxi companies, scouring parking lots for his Jeep. Knox knew he needed to lie low. But still . . .

Augustin had rushed off first thing to inspect some

newly discovered antiquity. By Christ, he wished he were down there with him.

IBRAHIM FELT DEEPLY APPREHENSIVE as he, Mohammed, and Elena ascended the spiral stairs back into daylight. He had to make a report to Nicolas Dragoumis, and he was all too aware that more than his excavation funds rested on the outcome; Mohammed's hopes for his poor daughter did, too. He squeezed the big man's forearm to reassure him as best he could, then walked a little way off and dialed the Dragoumis Group switchboard, gave his name and business, and was put on hold.

"Well?" demanded Nicolas, picking up.

"It's a fine site," said Ibrahim. "There are some wonderful—"

"You promised me a royal Macedonian tomb. Is it a royal Macedonian tomb or not?"

"I promised you something that looked like a royal tomb," said Ibrahim. "And it does. Unfortunately, it seems to be the tomb of a shield bearer, not a king or noble."

"A shield bearer?" sneered Nicolas. "You expect the Dragoumis Group to spend twenty thousand dollars on the tomb of a shield bearer?"

"The shield bearers were Alexander's elite," protested Ibrahim. "This man Akylos would have been—"

"*What?*" interrupted Nicolas. "What did you say his name was?"

"Akylos."

"Akylos? You're absolutely sure?"

"Yes. Why?"

"Is Elena there?"

"Yes."

"Put her on. Now! I want to speak to her."

Ibrahim shrugged and passed her his phone. She walked a little distance away and turned her back so he couldn't overhear. She spoke for a good minute before returning his phone. "You have your money," she said.

"I don't understand," said Ibrahim. "What's so special about this man Akylos?"

"I don't know what you mean."

"Yes, you do."

"Mr. Dragoumis wants to be kept fully informed."

"Of course. I'll call him myself whenever we—"

"Not by you. By me. He asks that I be given unrestricted access."

"No. I couldn't possibly agree to—"

"Mr. Dragoumis insists, I'm afraid."

"But those weren't our terms."

"They are now," said Elena. "If you want his continued support . . ."

Ibrahim glanced at Mohammed, twisting his hands as he waited. "Very well," he sighed. "I'm sure we can arrange something." He nodded at Mohammed to let him know he'd got his money. The big man closed his eyes and sagged in relief, then walked unsteadily to his office, no doubt to make phone calls of his own.

Mansoor emerged from the stairwell and walked over to join Ibrahim. "Well?" he asked. "Do we go for it?"

"Yes."

"Destructive or nondestructive?"

Ibrahim nodded thoughtfully. A good question. In a fortnight, if the hotel group got their way, tons of rubble would be bulldozed down the stairwell as a makeshift landfill site; its mouth would be sealed and a parking lot laid over the top, so that no one could ever get down there again. If that were to happen, then they first needed to remove everything of value, including the wall paintings and sculptures and the mosaic from the rotunda floor. It was perfectly possible, but it took time, expertise, and heavy equipment, and they'd need to start planning now. On the other hand, Alexandria was wretchedly short of historic sites, particularly early Ptolemaic ones. If they could negotiate permanent access with the hotel group, this site would make a valuable addition to the city tour, but only if these original features remained in place and were properly protected during the excavation. "Non-destructive," said Ibrahim finally. "I'll talk to the hotel people. Perhaps they'll realize the value of having an antiquity on their property."

Mansoor snorted. "And perhaps they'll give us complimentary penthouse suites whenever we ask, out of the kindness of their hearts."

"Yes, well, let me deal with them. But you can handle the excavation, yes?"

"It won't be easy," said Mansoor. "I can put Shatby on hold. There's no great urgency with that. We can transfer the crew and the generator and the lighting. But we'll still need more people."

"Put the word out. You have a budget."

"Yes, but with a large crew we'll need ventilation; and I don't want people removing rubble up those steps. That's a recipe for accidents. We'll need to put a lift above the stairwell. And Augustin will want a pump; I know he will. And it's not just what we'll need on site. There are fifteen hundred loculi to be emptied, which means six or seven thousand sets of human remains turning up at the museum or the university over the next fortnight. We'll need to have trained specialists ready to receive them." He snapped his fingers. "Our two weeks will be gone like that, you realize."

Ibrahim smiled. Mansoor always liked to build up a problem in his mind so that his satisfaction at solving it would be all the greater. "You'd better get started, then," he advised.

AKYLOS! Nicolas could scarcely believe it. But what was written was written. And the restoration of Macedonian greatness *was* written, and not just in the book of Daniel.

"What was all that about, then?" shouted Julia Melas over the roar of his Lamborghini Murciélago roadster's engine. She was an aspiring journalist from a Canadian newspaper, interviewing him and his father for a feature on Macedonia. There was a large expatriate community in Canada—a source of both moral and financial support. And she wasn't at all bad to look at, either. Maybe if things panned out well . . .

"We in the Dragoumis Group sponsor historical research all over the world!" he shouted back. "Truth isn't restricted to one location, you know." He braked to turn up into the hills, but a white truck appeared around the corner ahead, hurtling downhill faster than its age and size would suggest prudent. Nicolas was in no mood to wait, not with such a pretty girl beside him. He gave the Murciélago a squirt of acceleration and cut in front of it, and the driver braked and veered and sounded his horn impotently. Julia gave a little shriek and glanced admiringly at him. Nicolas laughed exultantly. He felt good. Things were moving at last. Life was like that: nothing for a year, two years, and then everything all at once.

"You were telling me about Aristander," she yelled, the wind swirling her skirt up around her thighs, so that she had to press it coyly back down.

Nicolas slowed a little so they could talk in more reasonable voices. "He was Alexander's favorite seer," he told her. "After Alexander died, Aristander had a vision that the land which held his body would be unconquered through the ages."

"And?"

"A man called Perdiccas, Alexander's heir apparent, wanted to bury Alexander in the royal tombs at Aigai, alongside his father, Philip." They crested a hill; the fertile plains of northern Greece spread out beneath them. He pulled to the side, parked, got out, and pointed Aigai out to her. "The tombs were discovered thirty years ago. They're magnificent. You should go visit."

"I will," she nodded. "But this man Perdiccas—he obviously didn't bring Alexander's body back here."

"No," acknowledged Nicolas. "Another Macedonian general, Ptolemy, took it to Egypt instead." He shook his head regretfully. "Think of it! But for that, Macedonia would have been unconquered through the ages!"

Julia frowned. "You can't seriously mean that."

"Why not?"

"But . . . it's just a prophecy."

Nicolas shook his head. "No. It's a historical fact. Consider: Perdiccas was the one man with the authority to hold the entire empire together. And he tried to recover Alexander's body from Ptolemy, but Ptolemy hid on the other side of the Nile, and Perdiccas lost hundreds of men to drowning and to the crocodiles when he tried to cross it. His own officers were so angry that they murdered him in his tent. After that, the empire was doomed. Alexander's legitimate heirs were assassinated, and it became every man for himself. But, now, just imagine if Perdiccas had succeeded . . ."

"Yes?"

He put his left arm around her shoulder, pulling her to stand beside him, then sweeping his other arm around the magnificent vista, all the way down to the dazzling blue Aegean. "Look at that," he said proudly. "Macedonia. Isn't that a fantastic sight?"

"Yes," she agreed.

"Perdiccas was an honorable man. He'd have protected Alexander's son from assassination and kept his empire still together. And if Alexander the Fourth had been one tenth the man his father had been, Aristander's prophecy would indeed have come true."

"I thought you said Alexander's body was taken to Egypt," observed Julia. "And Egypt hasn't exactly been unconquered through the ages, has it?"

Nicolas laughed. He liked a pretty girl with spirit. "No," he acknowledged. "But look at what did happen. The Ptolemies kept the throne for as long as they respected Alexander's remains. But then Ptolemy the Ninth melted down his golden coffin to pay his troops, and that was the end of them. And who took over from the Ptolemies?"

"Who?"

"The Caesars. They revered Alexander, you know. Julius Caesar wept because he fell so far short of Alexander. Augustus, Septimus Severus, Caracalla, and Hadrian all made pilgrimages to sacrifice at his mausoleum. He was their hero. But then there were riots, Alexander's tomb was desecrated, and the Romans lost Egypt to the Arabs. The message is clear, isn't it?"

"Is it?" Julia frowned.

"Honor Alexander and prosper. Ignore him and perish. And in Macedonia, of all places on the earth, Alexander would most certainly have been honored. So it follows that we'd never have been conquered."

Julia backed away from him, clearly a little disconcerted. She checked her watch and forced a smile. "Perhaps we should get moving," she said. "Your father's expecting me."

"Of course," said Nicolas. "We mustn't keep Father waiting." He climbed back in his roadster, started it up, savoring its throaty roar. The way he drove, it was just fifteen more minutes to his father's house.

"Wow!" muttered Julia as it came into view.

"A recreation of the royal palace at Aigai," said Nicolas. "Only bigger." His father now rarely left this estate. He'd grown increasingly reclusive with the years, had largely handed over his business empire to professional managers so that he could concentrate on his true ambition.

Costis, his father's head of security, came out to greet them. "This is Julia," said Nicolas. "She's here to interview my father. But I need a few minutes with him first."

"He's in the vaults," replied Costis.

Nicolas nodded at Julia. "Perhaps I can take you back to town later."

"Thanks," she said warily. "But I'm sure I can get a taxi."

He laughed again, enjoying her discomfort. She'd looked troubled ever since he told her about the Aristander prophecy. Westerners today! They took fright at the merest hint of the sacred. It was just as well that she hadn't been in church last night, that he hadn't told her about the book of Daniel—the full prophecy, that is, including the description of the man predicted to bring about Macedonian liberation.

The only way to reach the vaults was via a secure elevator. Nicolas stepped into it now; the steel doors closed smoothly. He presented his eyes to the retinal scanner; then it began its slow descent, shuddering a little under its own weight when it came to a halt. An armed guard was stationed by the vault, where his father kept all his greatest treasures. Nicolas punched in his code, and the steel door opened. He went through, still thinking about the book of

Daniel, and particularly those verses that, twenty-five hundred years before, had promised his people a savior.

> *And in the latter time of their kingdom, when the transgressors are come to the full, a king of fierce countenance, and understanding dark sentences, shall stand up.*
>
> *And his power shall be mighty, but not by his own power: and he shall destroy wonderfully, and shall prosper, and practice.*
>
> *And through his policy also he shall cause craft to prosper in his hand; and he shall magnify himself in his heart, and by peace he shall destroy.*

His father, as if by some kind of telepathy, was already standing in front of the glass-topped cabinet in which were displayed a few samples of the Mallawi papyri, his hands resting like a priest's on the walnut frame as he gazed down at the yellowed reeds and the faded black writing. A feeling of intense love, awe, and pride burned in Nicolas's chest when he beheld him. A king of fierce countenance indeed!

Dragoumis looked up and drilled his son with his emotionless black eyes. "Yes?" he asked.

"They've found Akylos," Nicolas blurted, his excitement almost too much. "It's started."

Chapter Eight

A BLUE TRUCK CUT IN FRONT OF ELENA as she drove back south to the Delta, forcing her to slam on her brakes. She blasted her horn until the truck moved aside; then she wound down her window, shook her fist, and yelled some choice Arabic phrases at the bewildered driver. She was in a troubled mood. It was speaking to Nicolas that had done it. That, and that damned Frenchman. So smug. Between them, they'd stirred memories of her late husband, Pavlos, and Elena hated that, because it just reminded her of her loss.

She'd known of Pavlos long before she'd ever met him, had been infuriated and entertained in equal measure by the tone, anger, and wit of his articles ridiculing Macedonian nationalism. She'd been intrigued, too, by the gossip of besotted women throwing themselves at him. She was a proud and independent woman herself, and like so many of her kind, she had yearned to fall helplessly in love. They had finally met on either side of a radio debate in Thessalonike, and he had surprised her from the start. She had expected someone sharp, assertive, dressy, plausible, but Pavlos hadn't been like that at all. Though he wasn't exactly arrogant, she had never met a man so confident of himself. She knew from their first handshake that she was in trouble. He had an unsettling way of looking at her, then and later, as though she were completely exposed to him, as though he understood not just everything she said but all its subtext, too. He had watched her as though she were a movie, one he had seen before.

He had trodden all over her in their debate, defusing her best arguments with humor, hammering relentlessly at her weakest points. Disconcerted, she tried to press him back by citing Keramopoullos on the idiosyncratic style of Macedonian ceramics, before remembering that the words had come from Kallipolitis. She glanced up fearfully to see him grin, and for a terrible moment her scholarly reputation had been at his mercy. That moment—the moment of being at his mercy—had changed her life.

For two days after the debate, Elena had wandered her museum from room to room, hugging herself like an addict. Each time she tried to work, a craving like hunger would disturb her. She had never needed to call men, but she called Pavlos. Scared he would mock her, she introduced herself brusquely, remarked that he had raised interesting points in the debate. He thanked her. Then her nerve had failed. She held the phone against her cheek, wanting to say something clever or hurtful but not knowing what. When he asked her to have dinner with him, she could have cried.

How had it been? It had been everything. She remembered little of the detail, as though the intensity of her love had simply been too much for her memory. But she could remember the joy of it. Even now sometimes, she could experience an exquisite moment of bliss, catching sight of his double on the street, smelling his brand of cigarette in some passerby's hand, or having some man look at her in the way Pavlos had—as that arrogant Frenchman had, certain he could take her to bed whenever he damned well chose.

Pavlos's death had devastated Elena. Of course it had. She still hadn't recovered from it. How could she? Grief hadn't been as she imagined, any more than love had been. She had imagined grief as a great sea swell that lifted you into wretchedness for a while before setting you back down again much where you'd been before. But it hadn't been like that. Grief had changed the fabric of who she was as completely as blown carbon changes molten pig iron.

Yes, she thought, the metaphor worked: grief had turned her into steel.

THE WOMAN DROPPED THE MANILA ENVELOPE through the open rear window of Nessim's Saab as he paused to buy a packet of cigarettes from a vendor. He drove off in a flurry of dust back to his hotel's underground parking lot, then took it up to his room to read. It was disappointingly thin, as files went, but then, he hadn't expected Knox to have a file at all. He flipped through the pages, the print barely legible from being photocopied too often, the photographs almost completely black.

It quickly became clear that the Security Service hadn't really been interested in Knox at all. They had been interested in another man, a Richard Mitchell, with whom Knox had worked for several years. Mitchell, it seemed, had a big mouth; he had accused the extremely well connected head of the SCA of selling papyri on the black market. A piece of recklessness that had achieved precisely what one would expect: his isolation from the Egyptological community and the refusal of any further permissions to excavate.

That at least explained what Knox had been doing in Sharm: killing time until the dust settled, dreaming of treasure on the seafloor. But it wasn't much help when it came to tracking him down. The last sheet in the file, however, was a different matter. It was a list of all Knox's known friends and associates, and it gave their home addresses, too.

NUR GREETED MOHAMMED AT THE DOOR. She looked haggard, which meant Layla had had a bad day. "You look beautiful," he said, kissing her cheek and handing her a small bouquet of tired blooms.

"How can you afford these?" she protested tearfully.

"They're a gift," he said gently. "Sharif wanted you

to have them." He looked past her, down the hallway, to Layla's room. "Is she awake?"

Nur nodded. "But tired."

"I won't be long." He knocked gently on Layla's door, opened it, and walked in. His daughter smiled to see him. He knelt beside her bed, reached into his pocket, and produced a black queen he'd carved and varnished. He liked to whittle. In the rare lulls on-site, he would scour the bins for ends of wood that he could attack with his linoleum knife. It was good therapy. When you could do nothing for your child's health, you could at least do something for her happiness.

Her eyes went wide with wonder and delight. She took the varnished mahogany, licked it with the very tip of her tongue, clutched it tight against her chest, like a doll. For some reason, Layla had turned against real dolls since learning of her disease, making do with these carved figures instead. He couldn't even tempt her with sweets any more. It was as though her life had become too serious for childish distractions. "You'll read for me tonight?" she asked.

"Of course."

She snuggled down, seemingly content. Now that Ibrahim had promised funding, he had called everyone he could think of and begged them to take the tests. That had felt good, as though he was contributing. But now he was dependent on others again. Now he was *waiting*. It was the hardest thing in the world for a parent, waiting.

He felt wretched when he left Layla's room. Nur bit her lip, but she couldn't hold back her tears. She spent her life weeping, drying herself out from the inside. Mohammed took her in his arms, held her tight to comfort her. Sometimes he felt so close to despair, he almost craved for the worst to happen, just so it would be over. His fine career, his beautiful wife and daughter. Everything that had once seemed so perfect. He murmured tentatively, "Is she well enough to go out?"

"Out?" There was an edge of hysteria in Nur's tone. "Where?"

"The site."

Nur pushed him away. "Are you *crazy*?" she cried.

Mohammed embraced her again. "Listen to me," he said. "This archaeologist Ibrahim I told you about, the one with the Mercedes who's paying for our tests. He has money; he has influence. He moves in a different world from ours. Layla needs all the friends she can get in that world."

"He can help?"

Mohammed hesitated. Nur had a habit of punishing him for promises he made to soothe her through the harder times. "Who can say?" he murmured. "But he's a kind man, a gentle man. Once he knows Layla for himself, who knows what Allah would have him do?"

"Look what I have!" said Augustin cheerfully, hoisting up two plastic bags. "Falafel baguettes and beer, yes? Just like the old days."

"Great."

Augustin frowned. "You don't sound too happy."

"A little stir-crazy," admitted Knox.

"One day? You can't even survive one day?"

"It's all these bloody *Tintin* books of yours," said Knox, helping him unpack. "Can't you get me something decent to read?"

"Such as?"

"Something archaeological. How about your excavation reports from the harbor? I'd love to know what you've been finding."

"Sure," nodded Augustin. "No problem. I'll bring them back tomorrow night. But if you're suffering . . ."

"Yes?"

"This site I visit today. A necropolis. It goes all the way down to the water table and then some, but Ibrahim doesn't want to pump. He wants me to explore. I was going to take Sophia, but if you're really going crazy . . ."

A little tremor of fear and anticipation ran through Knox. "Are you serious?"

"Why not? She's prettier than you, yes, but not so good a diver. You know how dangerous enclosed spaces can be."

"How would I even get to the site?"

"On the back of my bike," said Augustin, passing Knox a cold bottle of Stella. "You can wear my helmet; someone should. No one will stop us, I promise. The police in the city are a disgrace. Ten years I am here, I am never once stopped. And if we are, *tant pis*! I still have my papers from my last visit to Cyrene. Those Libyan bastards refused me entry under my real name! Me! Just because of some letter I wrote about that mad fop Gadhafi. So I had to go in as Omar Malik. A truck driver from Marsa

Matruh, would you believe? If I can pass for a truck driver from Marsa Matruh, so can you."

Knox shook his head. He couldn't believe he was even considering this. But Augustin had an admirable lack of respect for the ordinary rules of behavior, and his attitude was infectious. "And inside the site?"

"No problem. Leave any talking to me. Not that there'll be much. Up top there's a working building site, remember. Down below there are God knows how many chambers, a hundred loculi in each, every one stuffed with bones and artifacts, all of which Mansoor wants in the museum inside two weeks. It's chaos. Excavators from the museum, from the university, from along the coast. Just one security guard at the mouth of the stairwell, but all you need to get past him is a standard SCA pass, and I can issue you one of those myself. Some forgettable name. John Smith. Charles Russell. Mark Edwards. Yes! Perfect. Mark Edwards. You look exactly how a Mark Edwards should look."

Knox shook his head uncertainly. "You know what Cairo thinks of me. If I'm found out, it could mean trouble for you."

"Fuck Cairo," scowled Augustin. "I still feel sick at what that bastard Yusuf did to you and Richard. Believe me, helping you will be a pleasure. Besides, how will anyone find out? I'm not going to talk. Are you?"

"Someone might recognize me."

"I don't think so. Ibrahim, maybe, but he's a good man; he wouldn't take it any further. Anyway, he never visits sites anymore; he might get his suit dirty. Other than that, there's no one you know. And they're all friends, except for this gorgeous angry Greek woman called Elena and her—"

"Elena?" Knox put a hand to his brow. "Elena Koloktronis?"

Augustin pulled a face. "You know her?"

"No," snorted Knox. "Just a lucky guess."

"How do you know her?"

"You remember what happened to my parents and my sister?"

"Of course. Why? She had something to do with that?"

"It was her husband who was driving."

"Oh. And he . . . ? He also . . . ?"

"Yes."

"I'm sorry," said Augustin. "I'm sorry both for you and for her. But it won't matter; she's not there tomorrow."

"You're certain?"

"She runs an excavation in the Delta. She only came today to bring in her French photographer girl. Gaille Dumas, something like that. You know her?"

"A photographer?" Knox shook his head. "No."

"Then we're fine," said Augustin. He grinned and held out his beer bottle to clink in a toast. "What could possibly go wrong?"

Chapter Nine

AUGUSTIN WAS RIGHT about getting into the site the next morning. It proved a breeze. He was right, too, about the excitement Knox felt at being part of a proper excavation again. It had been too long. Far too long. Just being there made him happy: the noise, the smells, the banter. Up top, a generator was roaring away, powering a winch lift hauling an almost nonstop stream of excavation baskets cut from old truck tires, filled with rubble to be sifted in sunlight, then sent either to the museum or to landfill; lamps and ventilator fans were spread throughout the necropolis on miles of white power cables; and excavators in breathing masks and white gloves knelt in the confined tombs, carefully removing artifacts and human remains.

Augustin had brought down all the diving equipment before collecting Knox. They didn't waste any time sightseeing but hurried straight down to the water table and suited up, inspecting each other's gear with great care. People who had dived as often as they had were sometimes cursory with their safety checks. But in an enclosed labyrinth like this, you couldn't simply dump your weight belt and kick for the surface if things went wrong. There *was* no surface.

Augustin held up a reel of red nylon cord, borrowing a trick from Theseus. But there was nothing to anchor it to. "Stay here," he said, and vanished briefly, returning with an excavation basket weighted with rubble. He tied the cord to it and gave it a couple of tugs. They hooked themselves together with a lifeline, turned on their dive lamps, and made their way down into the water, Augustin feeding out the cord behind him. Neither man wore fins. They had weighted themselves to walk. They kicked up more sediment that way, but it made it easier to keep one's bearings. Almost at once, they found the entrance to a chamber, most of its loculi still sealed. On one of them, Augustin's underwater flashlight picked out a haunting portrait of a large-eyed man staring directly back at them. The mouth of the neighboring loculus had rotted away, and their flashlights glinted on something metallic inside. Augustin carefully pulled out a funerary lamp, which he tucked into his pouch.

They visited three more chambers, the connecting corridor kinking this way and that. The cord snagged on something, and Augustin had to tug it loose. The water grew murkier and murkier, sometimes swirling so badly they could barely see each other. Knox checked his air: down to just a 130 bar. They had agreed to dive in thirds: one-third out, one-third back, one-third for safety. He showed Augustin, who nodded and pointed back the way they had come. There was evidently some slack in the cord, for he began to reel it in and kept on reeling. He turned to Knox with a look of alarm perceptible even inside his mask. Knox frowned and spread his hands, and Augustin held up the loose end of the red cord, which should have been tied around the handles of the excavation basket, but which had somehow come free.

CHILDREN MADE IBRAHIM UNCOMFORTABLE. An only child himself, he had neither nieces nor nephews, nor any prospects of fatherhood. But Mohammed had bent over backward to accommodate him and his team on this excavation, so Ibrahim could scarcely refuse his daughter a tour, though he thought it crazy to bring a sick child into such a dusty, death-filled place.

One of Mohammed's construction crew tracked them down in a tomb chamber. "A call for you," he grunted. "Head office."

Mohammed pulled a face. "Forgive me," he told Ibrahim. "I must deal with this. But I'll be straight back. Could you hold Layla a minute?"

"Of course." Ibrahim braced himself as Mohammed passed him the bundle of blankets and swaddling, but the poor girl, ravaged by her disease, was light as air. He smiled nervously down. She smiled back. She looked terrified of him, painfully aware that he must consider her a nuisance. She pointed to the skull in the loculus: "This man was not

Egyptian, then?" Mouth ulcers made her slurp and wince with every word.

Ibrahim winced with her. "That's right," he replied. "He was Greek, from north across the sea. Your father is a very clever man; he knew this man was Greek, because he found a coin called an obol in his mouth. The Greeks believed that spirits needed this to pay a ferryman called Charon to row them across the River Styx into the next world."

"The next world?" asked Layla. Her eyes were large with wonder, as though her skin had been pulled back around them. Ibrahim swallowed and looked away. For a moment, he felt the threat of tears. So young a girl; so harsh a fate.

His arms were aching badly by the time Mohammed finally returned. He beamed at Layla with such affection as he took her back that Ibrahim felt lost, shamed, as though he had no right to his place in the world, to the air and space he consumed, to his easy life. He felt overcome by the need to do something to help Layla. "Those tests we were able to help you with," he murmured to Mohammed. "Where might I get one done myself?"

KNOX AND AUGUSTIN looked at each other with concern, but they were experienced divers; they didn't panic. They checked their air; they each had twenty minutes, twenty-five if they didn't waste it. Augustin pointed ahead, and Knox nodded. They needed to find their way out, or at least a pocket of air where they could wait until the sediment resettled and they could see again.

They reached a dead end. Knox brought his gauge up to his goggles to check air pressure, which was dropping relentlessly. They kept their hands to the walls to steer through the blinding haze. On night dives in Sharm, his colleagues had talked glibly of zero visibility, but with all the muck he and Augustin had stirred, this was indescribably worse. Knox could barely see his gauges even when he held them in front of his mask. They hit another dead end, maybe the same one. They could all too easily be going around in circles. Fifteen bar. They began swimming, completely turned around now, their sense of direction gone, the fear building, breathing faster, burning up their precious air, so little of it left—just five bar, deep into the red hazard zone—and then Augustin seizing his shoulder and thrusting his face into his, tearing out his regulator, pointing desperately at his mouth. Knox passed him his spare, but he was down to the last few gasps himself. They reached another fork; Augustin pointed right, but Knox was sure they had gone right last time, so he tugged left, fighting over it. Augustin insisted on going right, however, and Knox decided to trust him, both men now swimming flat out, hitting and kicking each other, scraping rough wall and ceiling, Knox gagging as his tank ran dry, pressure on his lungs, hitting another wall, Augustin wrenching him upward against steps and then bursting up into open air.

Knox spat out his regulator and breathed in gratefully, lying alongside Augustin, their chests pumping like frantic bellows. Augustin laid his head sideways to look at Knox, a glint already in his eye, as though he'd thought of something funny but couldn't yet get it out. "There are old divers," he panted finally. "There are bold divers."

Laughter hurt Knox's lungs. "I reckon you should get a pump, mate."

"I think you're right," agreed Augustin. "And we tell no one about this, okay? Not for a year or two, anyway. I'm supposed to be professional."

"Mum's the word," nodded Knox. He pushed himself tiredly up, unbuckled his BCD, and dropped it and the empty tank onto the stone floor.

"Look!" said Augustin. "The basket's disappeared."

Knox frowned. Augustin was right. In his relief at getting out alive, he had forgotten what triggered the trouble in the first place. "What the hell?" He crouched down where the excavation basket had been. He had assumed that Augustin's knot had just come loose. "You don't think this was Hassan's doing, do you?"

A rueful expression spread over Augustin's face. "No," he said. "I fear it was simpler than that."

"What?"

"It was an excavation basket full of rubble," observed Augustin. "And what is Mansoor's number one priority?"

Knox winced and closed his eyes. "Clearing the site of rubble."

"This is our lucky day, my friend."

Soft footsteps approached down the corridor. Knox looked up as a slender, dark-haired, attractive young woman appeared out of the shadows, a digital camera on a strap around her neck. "Your lucky day?" she asked. "Have you found something?"

Augustin jumped up and walked over, interposing himself between her and Knox. "Look!" he said, taking out his funerary lamp, waving a hand at the water. "Chamber after chamber of sealed loculi!"

"Fantastic." She glanced past Augustin at Knox. "I'm Gaille," she said.

He had no option but to stand. "Mark," he replied.

"Nice to meet you, Mark."

"Likewise."

"How's the photography going?" Augustin asked her, touching her shoulder.

"Fine," said Gaille. "Mansoor's brought down all his lighting from the museum so I can photograph the antechamber, but it gets too hot to keep on long. The plaster, you know—we don't want it cracking."

"Indeed no." He put an arm around her shoulder, tried to turn her away from Knox. "Listen," he said. "I understand you're alone in town, yes? Perhaps we could have dinner together? I can show you old Alexandria."

Her eyes lit up. "That would be great, yes." She sounded so enthusiastic, she blushed and felt compelled to explain herself. "It's just, there's nowhere to eat in my hotel, and they won't let guests take food back to their rooms, and I really hate eating alone in restaurants. I feel so *conspicuous,* you know. As though everyone's watching."

"And why wouldn't they watch?" asked Augustin gallantly. "A pretty girl like you. Which hotel are you staying at?"

"The Vicomte."

"That terrible place! But why?"

She shrugged sheepishly. "I asked my taxi driver for somewhere central and cheap."

"He took you at your word, then," laughed Augustin. "Tonight, then. Eight o'clock, yes? I'll pick you up."

"Great." She looked past him to Knox, standing in the shadows. "You'll come, too, yes?" she asked.

He shook his head. "I don't think I'll be able to make it, I'm afraid."

"Oh." She patted her hips and made a shrugging kind of face. "Well, then," she nodded. "Until later." And she retreated up the corridor away from them with a slightly stilted walk, as though she sensed—quite correctly—that she was being watched.

Chapter Ten

Bᴀᴄᴋ ᴀᴛ Aᴜɢᴜsᴛɪɴ's ᴀᴘᴀʀᴛᴍᴇɴᴛ, Knox sat on the couch and tried to kill time. It wasn't easy. *Tintin* was bad enough once. He paced around the sitting room, went out onto the balcony. It seemed forever before the sun set. And still no sign of Augustin. The phone rang at seven thirty, but Knox dared not answer, letting the answering machine chug out its message. "It's me," shouted Augustin, loud music thumping in the background along with raucous laughter and the clinking of glasses and bottles. "Pick up, will you."

Knox did so. "Where the hell are you? You said you'd be back hours ago."

"Listen, my friend," replied Augustin. "A difficult situation at work."

"Work?" asked Knox dryly.

"I need you to call that photographer girl for me. Gaille Dumas. The one from the Vicomte. Explain to her that I'm in the middle of a crisis; I'm putting out fires."

"She's in town all on her own," protested Knox. "You can't stand her up."

"Exactly," agreed Augustin. "That's why I need you to do it for me. After all, if she hears this noise, maybe she'll wonder if I'm telling her the complete truth."

"Why don't you ask her to join you?"

"I have plans. You know that Beatrice I mentioned?"

"For Christ's sake! Do your own dirty work."

"I'm asking as a friend, Daniel. How was it you put it? Yes. I'm in trouble. I need help."

"Okay," sighed Knox. "Leave it to me."

"Thanks."

"And good luck with your crisis," said Knox venomously. He picked up the phone directory and flipped through it for the Vicomte Hotel. He felt bad for the girl, and vicariously guilty. He was puritanical about such things, he supposed. When you asked a girl out, particularly one who so evidently hankered for company, you showed up. The shadow of a long evening stretched out ahead of him. No one to talk to, nothing to read, nothing to watch on TV. *Sod it,* he thought. *Sod Hassan and his thugs.* He needed to stay hidden, but Alexandria was a vast city, and its streets offered the cover of crowds. He went into Augustin's room for a clean shirt and a baseball cap. Then he went down to the street and hailed a cab.

IBRAHIM COULDN'T GET COMFORTABLE at home that evening. His upper arm itched from where the nurse had taken blood for his HLA test, and he kept thinking of that poor girl's wide brown eyes. He kept thinking of her predicament, her courage. In the end, he couldn't sit at home anymore. He went through to his study and plucked a book down from the shelves, one from which his father had read to him as a child. Then he went out to his car.

Mohammed's apartment was on the ninth floor, but the elevators were broken. When Ibrahim finally made it up the stairs, he had to put his hands on his knees a minute, and wheezed for breath. What an effort it must be with an invalid child! It made him think about his own privileged childhood and education, everything made easy by his father's wealth. He heard, inside, the suppressed rancor of a married couple on whom too much strain has been placed, trying not to let their beloved child overhear. He felt embarrassed suddenly, an intruder. He was about to walk away again when the door opened unexpectedly and a woman emerged, a scarf over her hair, dressed formally as if off on a visit. She looked as startled to see him as he was to see her. "Who are you?" she demanded. "What are you doing here?"

"Excuse me," he said, flustered. "I have something for Mohammed."

"What?"

"Just a book." He pulled it from the bag. "For his daughter. Your daughter."

The woman looked at Ibrahim in bewilderment. "This is for Layla?"

"Yes."

"But . . . who are you?"

"My name is Ibrahim."

"The archaeologist?"

"Yes."

She bit her lower lip thoughtfully. Then she went back inside her flat. "Mohammed," she said. "Come here. Your archaeologist friend is visiting."

Mohammed appeared from a side room, ducking his head beneath the low lintel. "Yes?" he asked anxiously. "Is there a problem at the site?"

"No," said Ibrahim, showing a bit more of the book. "It's just . . . my father used to read to me from this. I thought maybe you and your daughter . . ." He opened the book and flipped through the pages, showing off the gorgeous illustrations inside: pictures of Alexander from history and myth.

"It's beautiful," gaped Mohammed. He glanced at his wife, who hesitated then nodded. "Layla's been talking about you all evening," said Mohammed, coming to grasp Ibrahim by the elbow. "I know it would mean a great deal to her if you gave it to her yourself."

ALEXANDRIA WAS USUALLY one of the most welcoming of Egyptian cities, but the tensions between the West and the Arab world had reached here, too, and Knox took a cool nod from a young Egyptian man out with his woman as he paid his taxi driver on the street outside Gaille's hotel.

Normally, he would have shrugged it off, but with Hassan to worry about, it preyed on his mind. All these people. How could he tell which ones were dangerous? The ones who smiled, the ones who scowled?

Like many of the city's cheaper hotels, Gaille's was on the top two floors. The old lift rattled and shook as it ascended past floors of gloom and darkness. He pulled back the mesh door and stepped out. Behind the reception desk, the balding middle-aged concierge was talking with a young bearded man. They both looked at Knox without even trying to hide their disdain. "Yes?" asked the concierge.

"Gaille, please," said Knox.

"The Frenchwoman?"

"Yes."

"And you are?"

Knox had to think for a moment to remember the name Augustin had given him. "Mark," he said. "Mark Edwards."

"Sit, please." The concierge turned back to his friend, picking up their conversation again. Knox sat in a blue armchair, white fluff leaking from the tattered upholstery. A minute went by. Still the concierge made no effort to alert Gaille. Another minute passed. The two men were chatting away, not looking his way, their contempt clear. Knox had no wish to make himself conspicuous, but there came a point when doing nothing would be more memorable than doing something, so he stood up, brushed fluff from his trousers, went back over to reception. "Call her for me," he said.

"In a minute."

He put his hand on the counter. "Call her," he said. "Now."

The concierge scowled but picked up his phone and dialed her extension. A phone tinkled dully down the hall. "You have a visitor," he told her. He put the phone back down and resumed his conversation with his friend without a word to Knox.

Another minute passed. A door opened and closed. Footsteps hurried on the hard wooden floorboards. Gaille appeared around a corner, wearing sneakers, faded jeans, and a baggy black sweatshirt. "Mark," she frowned. "What are *you* doing here?"

"Augustin couldn't make it, I'm afraid. Crisis at work. I hope you don't mind a last-minute substitute."

"Not at all." She looked down at her dowdy clothes, pulled a face. "Are we going anywhere fancy?" she asked.

"You look fine," Knox assured her. "You look gorgeous."

"Thanks." She smiled shyly. "Then shall we just go? I'm starving."

He ushered her inside the elevator. The concierge and his bearded friend glared as he slammed closed the mesh door a little more vehemently than necessary. It was dim and tight inside; two people was all it could comfortably take. They stood shoulder to shoulder as it clanked slowly down six floors. "Charming man," he muttered once they were out of earshot.

"My guy in Tanta was even worse, would you believe?" said Gaille. "He gave me those looks—you know, as if he held women to blame for every evil in the history of the world. I felt like asking him, why run a hotel? Why not run a YMCA or something? Just nice young boys."

Knox laughed and hauled open the door again as they reached the ground floor. "You like seafood?"

"I *love* seafood."

"There's this restaurant I used to visit a lot. I haven't been there for a while, but I thought we might give it a try."

"That sounds great. You know Alexandria well, then?"

"I used to." Down the hotel's front steps, he steered Gaille away from the bustling and carnival-like Sharia Nabi Daniel, along a quieter road. With Hassan on his tail, he needed to stay in the shadows. He kept looking around, sensing eyes on him, people frowning, taking a second look. In the darkness behind, a man in pale blue robes was talking quietly but urgently on his cell phone, darting glances his way.

"Are you all right?" asked Gaille. "Is something the matter?"

"No," he said. "Forgive me. Just a little distracted." They came to a fork in the road, a minaret on its corner, giving him the opportunity to cover his jitters with conversation. "The Attarine Mosque," he said, pointing it out. "Did you know that that's where they found what might be the sarcophagus of Alexander the Great?"

"No."

"It was your man Napoleon," Knox explained. "He had his people scour Egypt for treasures. Anyway, they found this huge breccia sarcophagus covered in hieroglyphics, which no one could decipher back then but which the locals swore blind had been Alexander's. Alexander was Napoleon's hero, so he decided to be buried in it himself and ordered it back to France. But it got diverted to the British Museum instead, where it's now on show near the Rosetta Stone."

"I'll look out for it."

The man was still the same distance behind, talking earnestly on his cell phone. Knox felt his anxiety increase. He steered Gaille down a narrow side road to see if that would dislodge him. "Of course," he said, "when hieroglyphics were finally cracked, it turned out that it wasn't Alexander's sarcophagus at all, but Nectanebo the Second's."

"Ah."

He glanced around once more, but the road was clear. "Exactly," he said, allowing himself to relax a little. "Nothing annoys a Brit more than being sold a pup by the natives. And no one even considered that there might be a glimmer of truth to the story. After all, Ptolemy would surely never have put Alexander the Great in the cast-off sarcophagus of some fugitive pharaoh like Nectanebo, would he?"

"It does seem unlikely."

"Exactly. Do you know much about Nectanebo?"

Gaille shrugged. "A little."

"The last native Egyptian pharaoh. He defeated the Persians in battle and commissioned lots of new buildings, including a temple in Saqqara, city of the dead for Memphis, Egypt's capital at the time."

"I'm not completely ignorant, you know. I do know Saqqara."

"He also commissioned this sarcophagus," grinned Knox, "though he never got to use it. The Persians came back, and Nectanebo had to flee. So, when Ptolemy took Egypt twenty years later and needed somewhere to keep

Alexander's body while he built him a proper mausoleum in Alexandria, Nectanebo's temple and sarcophagus were both lying empty."

"You're suggesting he used them as a stopgap?"

The man who had been following them earlier suddenly appeared ahead of them, still talking quietly but earnestly on his phone. He glanced their way and immediately dropped his eyes. Knox steered Gaille down a side alley, prompting her to frown at him. He quickly regretted his choice. The alley was deserted and dark, and their footsteps rang and echoed on the pavement, emphasizing just how alone they were. And when he glanced around, he saw the man entering the alley behind them.

"What is it?" asked Gaille. "What's wrong?"

"Nothing," said Knox, taking her arm and hurrying her along. "Just hungry, that's all."

She frowned, unconvinced, but let it go. "You were telling me about the sarcophagus," she prompted.

"Yes." He glanced back and was relieved to see that they had put some distance between themselves and their tail. "Ptolemy certainly needed a stopgap. I mean, it was several decades before he transferred Alexander to Alexandria. And it would explain how the sarcophagus came to be here. I mean, you should see this thing. It's a beast. But perfect for protecting Alexander's body in transit."

"It makes sense from an Egyptian point of view, too," agreed Gaille. "You know they believed Alexander to be the son of Nectanebo the Second?"

Knox frowned. "You don't mean that old *Alexander Romance* story?" The *Alexander Romance* had been a runaway best-seller of ancient times, a book of half-truths, exaggerations, and lies about Alexander, including a story that Nectanebo II had visited the Macedonian court, where he seduced Philip's wife, Olympias, and fathered Alexander.

"It's more than that. When Alexander beat the Persians at Issus, he didn't just make himself de facto ruler of Egypt. To Egyptian eyes, it proved he was Nectanebo's legitimate successor. Did you know that one of his Egyptian throne names was 'he who drives out the foreigners,' just like Nectanebo?"

"Hey!" protested Knox. "I thought you said you didn't know anything about Nectanebo?"

"I said I knew a little," smiled Gaille.

"So you think the *Alexander Romance* story is credible, then?" he asked, steering her to the right, taking another look back as he did so. Their tail was still there—closer, if anything. And then two men walked around the corner ahead. Knox readied himself to run. But the two men kept on walking, paying no attention to Knox or their tail.

"Well, obviously it's not true," said Gaille. "Nectanebo never went anywhere near Greece. But I can certainly believe that such a story gained currency among the Egyptians. Maybe Alexander even encouraged it. He was incredibly skilled at winning hearts and minds. I've always thought that was one reason he visited Siwa. I mean, everyone assumes that he went because the Oracle of Ammon was so revered by the Greeks. But the Egyptians revered it, too, and had for centuries. Did you know that all the Twenty-Eighth Dynasty pharaohs traveled to Siwa to be acknowledged, and that they were all depicted with rams' horns, too, just like Alexander?"

They finally emerged onto the Corniche. A breaker crashed against the rocks, spraying spume over the high wall, leaving the road shining black. Knox glanced around again to see their tail put his phone away in his pocket then look anxiously all around him. "Is that right?" asked Knox.

Gaille nodded vigorously. "The Egyptians were sticklers for legitimacy in their pharaohs. Alexander succeeded Nectanebo, so in a sense, *of course* he was his son. The story about Nectanebo sleeping with his mother was just a convenient way of explaining it." She smiled apologetically. "Anyway, enough shop. Where's this restaurant of yours?"

"Just up here." He glanced around a final time. Their tail was advancing with a broad smile on a dark-haired woman and two young children, picking them up, laughing joyfully as he spun them around. Knox breathed a sigh of relief. Nothing but paranoia. Then he reminded himself sternly that just because it had proved benign this time didn't mean he could afford to relax.

They reached the restaurant, a plush place overlooking the waterfront. Gaille looked at Knox in horror, then down at her shabby clothes. "But you told me it wasn't fancy!" she protested.

"It isn't. And you look beautiful."

She pursed her lips, as if she thought he was lying, even though he wasn't. She had the kind of looks he had always found irresistible, shining with gentleness and intelligence. She said, "I only put on these horrid things because I didn't want to give your friend Augustin any encouragement. If I'd known it'd be you . . ."

A grin spread across Knox's face. "Are you saying you *do* want to give me encouragement?"

"That's not what I meant at all." Gaille blushed furiously. "I only meant that I think I can trust you."

"Oh," said Knox gloomily, opening the door for her, ushering her inside. "Trustworthy. That's almost as bad as being nice."

"Worse," smiled Gaille. "Much worse."

They climbed a flight of stairs to the dining area. "Avoid anything freshwater," he advised, helping her to a seat with a view out over the Eastern Harbor. "The lakes around here, it's a miracle anything survives in them. But the seafood will be good."

"Duly noted."

He flapped out a napkin as he sat. "So how's your photography going?"

"Not bad. Better than I expected, if I'm honest." She leaned forward over the table, eager to confide. "I'm not actually a photographer at all, you know."

"No?"

"I'm a papyrologist, really. The camera just helps me reassemble fragments. You can do amazing things with the software these days."

"So how did you get this job, then?"

"My boss volunteered me."

"Ah, Elena. Very kind of her. So you're working with her in the Delta, yes?"

"Yes."

"What on?"

"An old settlement," she enthused. "We've found traces of city walls and dwellings and cemeteries. Everything from Old Kingdom up to Early Ptolemaic."

"Wow. What's the place?"

"Oh." She looked hesitant suddenly, aware she'd said too much. "We haven't made a definitive identification yet."

"You must have some idea."

"I can't talk about it," said Gaille. "Elena made us all sign agreements."

"Come on. I won't tell a soul, I swear. And you just said I was trustworthy."

"I can't. Honestly."

"Give me a clue, then. Just one clue."

"Please. I really can't."

"Of course you can. You want to. You know you do."

She pulled a face. "Have you ever heard the expression, 'putting your head in the wolf's mouth'? That's like crossing Elena. You don't do it twice, trust me."

"Fine," grumbled Knox. "So how come you're working for her? I mean, it's a Greek excavation, isn't it? You don't strike me as particularly Greek."

"Elena's expert fell ill and she needed a replacement. Someone gave her my name. You know what it's like."

"Yes."

"She just called up one afternoon. I was really flattered, and I had nothing I couldn't get out of. Besides, it's all very well reading about Egypt in books, but it's not the same, is it?"

"No," agreed Knox. "So is this your first excavation?"

She shook her head. "No, but I hate talking about myself. It's your turn. You're an underwater archaeologist, yes?"

"An archaeologist who knows how to dive."

"And an intellectual snob, too?"

He laughed. "Raging."

"Where did you study?"

"Yale."

"Oh!" She pulled a face.

"You don't like Yale?" protested Knox. "How can you not like Yale?"

"It's not Yale exactly. Just someone who used to study there."

"An archaeologist?" he grinned. "Excellent! Who?"

"Oh, I'm sure you won't know him," she said. "His name's Daniel Knox."

Chapter Eleven

MARVELOUS!" LAUGHED AUGUSTIN, clapping his hands, when Knox reported back later that evening. "But that's just marvelous. What did you do?"

"What the fuck could I do?" grumbled Knox. "I told her I'd never heard of him, and changed the subject."

"And you've no idea why she dislikes you so much? You didn't perhaps fuck her one time, then never call?"

"No."

"You're sure? That's what it usually is with me."

Knox scowled. "I'm certain."

"Then what?"

"I don't know," he shrugged helplessly. "I can't think. Unless . . ."

"What?"

"Oh, no," said Knox, his cheeks suddenly ablaze. He put his hand on his forehead. "Oh, Christ!"

"What?"

"Her name's not Gaille Dumas, you idiot. It's Gaille Bonnard."

"Dumas, Bonnard." He shrugged indifferently. "I knew it was something to do with the arts. And who is she anyway, this Gaille Bonnard?"

"She's Richard's daughter," answered Knox. "That's who she is." Then he added bleakly, "No wonder she hates me."

IT WAS STICKY IN GAILLE'S ROOM, even with her balcony doors wide open. That flicker on Mark's face when she'd mentioned Daniel Knox, his hurried change of subject, the way he was so ill-at-ease afterward. She cursed herself for her big mouth; she had been having a really good time until then. Of course they would have known each other. Frankly, it would have been astonishing if two Yale-educated archaeologists of similar age hadn't been friends.

Some hatreds were based on principle; others were personal. Whenever Gaille thought of Knox, though she'd never even met him, she felt a fusion of the two, snakes writhing in her chest. Her mother, a nightclub singer, had had a brief fling with her father and gotten pregnant, coercing him into a marriage that never stood a chance, not least because he finally realized that he preferred men. Gaille had been just four when her father finally gave up and fled to Egypt. Her mother, struggling to come to terms with a homosexual husband and a career on the skids, had taken it out on Gaille. She had also found solace in abusing every substance she could lay her hands on until, finally, on the eve of her fiftieth birthday, she had misjudged one of her periodic cries for help and taken her own life.

As a child, Gaille had done what she could to cope with her mother's self-hatred, anger, and violence, but it had never been enough. She might have gone crazy from the strain of it, except that she had a safety-valve, a way to relieve the building pressure. It had been the one month every year when she joined her father on one of his excavations in North Africa or the Levant, and she'd loved every second.

When she was seventeen, Gaille had been due to join his second season near Mallawi in Middle Egypt. For eleven months, she'd been studying Coptic, hieroglyphics, and Hieratic in a desperate effort to prove her value so conclusively that her father would take her on full-time. But three days before she was due to fly out, he had arrived unexpectedly at their Paris apartment. Mama had thrown one of her tantrums and refused to let him see Gaille. She'd had to kneel outside the cramped sitting room door and listen through its plywood panels. A nearby television had been loud with sporadic canned laughter, so she hadn't heard everything—but enough. He was postponing Mallawi to deal with an urgent personal situation. Now it wouldn't take place until after Gaille was back at school.

That season had proved her father's crowning triumph. Just eight weeks later he had found a Ptolemaic archive so important that Yusuf Abbas, the future secretary general of the Supreme Council for Antiquities, had taken personal control. Gaille should have been there, but no. A precocious young Yale Egyptologist called Daniel Knox had been recruited in her place. That was her father's urgent personal situation! An itch in his pants. The betrayal had been so hurtful, Gaille had shunned him from that moment on. Though he had tried to contact her and apologize, she never gave him a chance. And though she was too committed to Egyptology to see merit in any other way of life, she had avoided Egypt until he was long dead and Elena's offer had taken her by surprise.

She had never met Knox, had never wanted to. But he had written her a letter of condolence that included a moving account of her father's last years. He claimed that her father had thought and spoken constantly of her, that when he fell to his death rock climbing in the Western Desert, there was nothing anyone could do to save him, and that his last thoughts had been of her, that his dying request had been of her, asking Knox to contact her himself and tell her so. She had found this, perversely, both deeply upsetting and immensely consoling. Then a parcel had arrived from Siwa Oasis, containing all her father's belongings and papers. It included the police report into the accident, and transcripts of statements made by the two guides who had been on that fateful climb. Both testified that Knox could have pulled her father to safety had he acted quickly enough, but that he had stood there watching instead. They both stated, too, that the fall had been instantly fatal, that his body was already cold by the time they or Knox or anyone reached him. That there was no way, therefore, that he could have communicated any last wishes. It had all been a lie.

Before she received and read that report, she had hated Knox only on principle. Since then, it had become personal as well.

NESSIM HAD LEARNED as a soldier to be aware of the physiology of fear. Knowing what was happening inside your body was a good way to control it. Your heart beat faster, making your breath hot in your mouth; that metallic tang in the back of your mouth was nothing but your glands flooding your system with adrenaline in preparation for fight or flight; the tingling in your fingers and toes and the looseness of your bladder and bowels was blood being reallocated to places that needed it more.

He stood by his hotel window to dial Hassan's number, looking down at the river ten stories below. "Have you found him?" asked Hassan when he was put through.

"Not yet, sir. But we're making progress."

"Progress?" enquired Hassan acidly. "Is this the same progress you told me about yesterday?"

"I've put together a strong team, sir."

"Oh, good. A team."

"Yes, sir." It was true, too, for all Hassan's scorn. Old comrades, keen for the work, who had proved themselves both reliable and discreet. He'd given them each Knox's name, his license plate, copies of his photograph, and the few other details he had, then he set some to watch the homes of Knox's known associates, others to tour hotels and stations. He had arranged a trace on Knox's cell phone, too, so that if he ever turned it on, they'd be able to triangulate his position to within a hundred meters. He had put a trace on Knox's various bank accounts and credit cards, too. Anything was possible in Egypt if you had money.

"Listen," said Hassan, who had no interest in such operational details. "I don't want progress. I want Knox."

"Yes, sir."

"Call tomorrow. Have good news for me."

"Yes, sir." Nessim replaced the handset with a slightly trembling hand and sat down on his hotel bed, shoulders sagging. He wiped his forehead. His wrist came back with the hairs slicked with sweat. Another of the symptoms. A full house. For a moment, he contemplated pillaging his bank account and simply vanishing. But Hassan knew too much about him. He knew about his sister. He knew about Fatima and their son. Besides, Nessim's sense of honor balked at running from a professional duty just because it was difficult or dangerous. So instead he got out Knox's Secret Service file and stared at the old, blackened text some more. It hadn't been updated for years. Several of the people on it had moved or had left Egypt altogether. Others they couldn't track at all. But it was Nessim's best hope of success all the same.

Chapter Twelve

AUGUSTIN AND KNOX headed into the site first thing, eager to get started, hopeful that the pump would have won them enough headroom to explore. They both knew all too well that pumping out an antiquity in Alexandria wasn't easy. The limestone bedrock was extremely porous, holding water like a giant sponge. As soon as they started pumping, this sponge would start releasing its reservoir, replacing what they were taking out until equilibrium was restored. They couldn't hope to beat it, not with the resources they had available. They could only buy a little time.

It was obvious from the moment they arrived on-site, however, that something was seriously wrong. The pump engine was wheezing like a chronic smoker chasing after a bus. They hurried down to find that a seal had evidently failed. Water spilled and sprayed down the camber of the rotunda floor into the Macedonian tomb, where lamps gleamed like pool lights beneath the murky water.

Augustin sprinted back up the stairwell to kill the pump engine. Knox unplugged the power cables, plunging the place into temporary darkness, then turned on his flashlight, removed his shoes and trousers, and collected all the lamps and coiled them up on the steps, safely out of the water. The electrical equipment was supposedly waterproof, because flooding and humidity were always a risk on Alexandrian sites, but better to be safe than sorry.

Augustin had evidently turned off the pump engine, for the contents of the pipes were gurgling and retreating. Knox waited for silence, then plugged the power cables back in and shed light on the mess. Augustin joined him on the top step, shaking his head in dismay. "*Merde!* Mansoor will have my testicles."

"Can we bring the pump in here?"

"I only *arranged* for the beast," grumbled Augustin. "I don't know how it works." But a look of inspiration then crossed his face. He vanished and returned with four excavation baskets, tossing two to Knox, then used the others to scoop up water.

"You can't be serious!" protested Knox.

"You have a better idea?" retorted Augustin, already hustling off down the corridor to the water table. Knox did likewise. The heavy baskets strained his shoulder and elbow joints and left red welts across his fingers. They grinned at each other as they dumped the loads and jogged back up. After a few trips, other excavators began trickling in. They saw what had happened, and grabbed baskets for themselves. Soon, a whole crew of them were at it.

After a dozen trips, Knox's legs were like rubber. He took a breather in the main chamber, out of the way of the ongoing effort. Despite his initial skepticism, Augustin's idea was working well. The water level had already fallen so far that the high steps between the forecourt and the antechamber, and between the antechamber and the main chamber, were now acting as dam walls, creating three separate reservoirs. Down on his haunches to bathe his throbbing palms and fingers in the cool water, he noticed something curious. The water level in the main chamber was lower than in the antechamber—and lower than the step that separated them, too.

He frowned, his weariness forgotten, then went out into the forecourt. "Has anyone got any matches?" he asked.

GAILLE ARRIVED TO FIND THE SITE IN BEDLAM. She hadn't finished photographing the main chamber, yet, so her first reaction was anxiety that she might have missed her chance. She kicked off her shoes, rolled up her trousers, and waded in to take a closer look. Her dinner companion from the night before was already in there, throwing broken matchsticks into the corners. "Avoiding the heavy lifting, huh?" she asked.

"Look!" he said, pointing at the antechamber. "See how the water level's higher in there?"

Gaille got the significance at once. "So where's it draining to?"

"Exactly," agreed Knox keenly. "This place is supposed to be quarried out of solid rock." He threw the last of his matchsticks into the corners; then they watched raptly together as they slowly converged.

"I had a really good time last night," murmured Gaille.

"I did, too."

"Maybe we could do it again some time."

"I'd like that," he said. But then he pulled a face. "Listen, Gaille, there's something I need to tell you first."

"It's about Knox, isn't it?" she said. "He's your friend, isn't he?"

"This really isn't the place to discuss it. Can I come by the Vicomte later?"

She smiled eagerly. "We'll go out afterwards. My treat this time."

There was splashing in the antechamber; then Mansoor appeared, bringing Elena with him. "What's going on?" demanded Mansoor angrily. Gaille turned to her companion, expecting him to explain, but he only ducked his head, grabbed his baskets, and fled, leaving Elena and Mansoor staring openmouthed after him. "Who the hell was that?" asked Mansoor.

"Augustin's dive buddy," explained Gaille. "I think the pump might have been partly his idea."

"Ah!" said Mansoor. "I hope he doesn't think I'm angry at him. It's that damned Augustin I want a word with." He shook his head with a mix of amusement and exasperation. "What are the matchsticks for?" he asked.

"No one's been emptying from here," explained Gaille, pointing out the discrepancy in water levels. "We just wanted to know where it was draining."

"And?"

"They seem to be converging on the plinth." They crouched around it, their flashlights illuminating the

dozens of silver trails of air bubbles escaping from beneath. "Akylos of the thirty-three," murmured Gaille,
struck by a sudden thought. "To be the best and honored
above the rest."

"The inscription from above the doorway?" frowned
Mansoor. "What about it?"

"The Greeks loved their puns, you know."

"Spit it out, girl," said Elena.

Gaille pulled a face, worried they might think her crazy.
"It's just, you don't think the inscription could mean that
the rest—the other thirty-two, that is—are honored *below*
Akylos."

Mansoor laughed and squinted oddly at her. "You're a
photographer?"

She blushed, aware of Elena's burning stare. "Languages, really."

"I'll get Ibrahim down here," said Mansoor. "He needs
to see this for himself."

KNOX FOUND AUGUSTIN by the water table, putting on
his wet suit. "Did Elena recognize you?" he asked Knox.

"I don't think so. Did Mansoor catch you?"

"Not quite." Augustin flapped his hand as though it had
been scalded. "A close thing, though. *Houf!* I think for
sure I am lobster bisque." He nodded at the water. "A wise
man would stay out of the way for a little while. You want
to explore?"

"Let's do it," agreed Knox.

Despite the pump's failure, it had made good progress during the night, so that the water came up only to their chins. They soon discovered what a maze it was, such an interconnected complex of passages and chambers that it made them even more aware of their luck at getting out alive the day before. In one chamber, the far wall had been painted with the outlines of loculi but hadn't been cut. It took Knox a moment to work out why. There was a ragged hole in the ceiling, as though the workmen had accidentally broken through into another space. "Hey, mate," he said, shining up his flashlight. "Look at this."

Augustin came to join him. "What the hell?" he frowned.

"Give me a leg up."

Augustin made a stirrup of his hands, hoisting Knox up into the new chamber. It was just high enough for him to stand without banging his head. He put his hand on the facing wall, built of limestone blocks, the mortar between them now crumbled to dust.

"Help me up, damn you," said Augustin. "I want to see for myself."

Knox reached down for his companion. When they were both up, they set about exploring. A narrow lane led right. There was a narrow gap at its end into a parallel lane flanked by a second block wall, then into a third with an outer wall of solid rock. So: a single chamber, some six meters square and two meters high, divided by internal walls into three lanes connected at one end, forming a capital "E." They went together to the end of

the central aisle. A flight of five steps led upward, then
turned at right angles into a second flight, which vanished into the ceiling. Dull thumps sounded from above,
shaking dust from the walls. "Jesus!" muttered Knox.
"What was that?"

Augustin banged his fist against the ceiling. A smile of
understanding broke on his face. "The rotunda," he said.
"This must be the original staircase. Yes. The Macedonians dug too far; they reached the water table. So? They
built these limestone walls for support, they laid a new
floor; they covered it with a mosaic. *Parfait!* The builders
of the necropolis simply broke in here by accident five
centuries later."

THE MAIN CHAMBER had drained completely by the
time Ibrahim arrived on site. Bringing heavy-lifting
equipment down here wasn't easy, so Mansoor had
recruited Mohammed instead. The two men worked
the tips of crowbars beneath one end of the plinth and
levered it up. It made cracking, popping sounds as
it gave, protesting after all those centuries of being
bonded to the floor. They raised it a few inches, their
chests and arms bulging, crowbars flexing beneath
the strain.

Ibrahim and Elena went down onto their knees to shine
their lights beneath. There was a round, black hole in the
floor, perhaps a meter in diameter. The plinth was too

heavy for even Mohammed and Mansoor to hold long. Mansoor went first, giving a warning cry, then Mohammed, too, letting it crash back down, throwing up dust, which caught in Ibrahim's nostrils and throat, sending him into a coughing fit.

"Well?" asked Mansoor, slapping his hands together.

"There's a shaft," said Ibrahim.

"You want us to move the plinth?" asked Mohammed. "Is that possible?"

"I'll need some help and some more equipment, but yes."

Ibrahim felt all eyes expectantly upon him, but still he hesitated. Nicolas had promised twenty thousand dollars, but they'd received only half so far, the rest due upon satisfactory completion. Katerina had laid great emphasis on the word "satisfactory," making it abundantly clear that failure to report a find like this would be considered highly *un*satisfactory. And it wasn't as if he could keep it secret, not now that Elena knew. He had a sudden mental image of Mohammed's daughter, her life hanging by a thread. "Give me a moment," he said. "I need to make a call." He beckoned Elena to follow him up the stairwell, then called the Dragoumis Group, clamping a hand over his ear to shut out the din of the building works. Tinny folk music played as he waited to be connected. He rubbed the bridge of his nose fretfully.

The music stopped abruptly. "Yes? This is Nicolas."

"It's Ibrahim. From Alexandria. You said to call if we found anything."

"And?"

"There's something beneath the Macedonian tomb. Perhaps a shaft."

"A shaft?" Ibrahim could hear the excitement in Nicolas's voice. "Where does it lead?"

"Almost certainly nowhere. These things rarely do. But we'll need to move the plinth to make sure. It's just, you made it clear that you wanted to be informed at once."

"Quite right."

"I'm going to have the plinth moved now. I'll call you back as soon as we—"

"No," said Nicolas emphatically. "I need to be there for this."

"This is an emergency excavation," protested Ibrahim. "We don't have time for—"

"Tomorrow afternoon," insisted Nicolas. "I'll be with you by one. Do nothing before then. Understand?"

"Yes, but really, it's almost certainly nothing. You'll come all this way and there'll be nothing and—"

"I'm going to be there," snapped Nicolas. "That's final. In the meantime, no one goes in there. I want guards. I want a steel gate."

"Yes, but—"

"Just do it. Send Katerina the bill. And I want to speak to Elena. Is she there?"

"Yes, but—"

"Put her on."

Ibrahim shrugged helplessly. "He wants to speak to you." She nodded and took his phone and walked off a little distance, making a wall of her back so that she couldn't be overheard.

NICOLAS PUT DOWN THE PHONE and sat back in his chair, breathing a little heavily. *Well, that was a phone call.* Elena had been certain she recognized Daniel Knox! And on his site, too! At this most sensitive of times. He stood and walked to his window, rubbing his lower back hard with his hands, which had suddenly become unaccountably stiff.

His office door opened. Katerina came in with a stack of papers. She smiled when she saw him working his spine. "What's the matter?" she joked. "Have you heard from Daniel Knox or something?" He gave her a look that would have peeled onions. "Oh!" she said, putting the papers down on his desk and quickly withdrawing.

Nicolas sat back down. Few people had ever managed to get under his skin like Knox had. For six weeks, ten years ago, the man had made a series of outrageous slanders against his father and his company, and they'd all stood around and done . . . precisely nothing. His father had granted the man immunity, and his father's word was law; but Nicolas still burned with the humiliation. He rocked forward and buzzed Katerina. "I'm sorry, sir," she blurted out before he could speak. "I didn't mean to—"

"Forget about it," he said curtly. "I need to be in Alexandria tomorrow afternoon. Is our plane free?"

"I believe so. I'll check."

"Thank you. And that Egyptian man we bought those

papyri through—he arranges other kinds of business, too, doesn't he?" He didn't need to spell out for Katerina what kinds of business he was referring to.

"Mr. Mounim? Yes."

"Good. Get me his number, please. I have a job for him."

Chapter Thirteen

IBRAHIM GATHERED HIS TOP TEAM in the rotunda to announce their sponsor's visit. He tried to sound enthusiastic about it. He tried to make out that it had been his idea. He asked people to be available to do show-and-tells, if needed, and promised tea and coffee and cakes and a buffet lunch afterward in the museum, then reminded them all subtly that this man was paying their wages. He suggested they make an event of it. In short, he did everything he could to spin it into a good thing. When he was done, he invited questions. No one said a word. They were archaeologists; they detested sponsors. The meeting broke up and everyone returned to work.

IT WAS LATE AFTERNOON, and Hosni was beginning to regret saying yes to Nessim's offer of a job looking for some fugitive Westerner. He'd forgotten how boring surveillance work could be.

He was half asleep in the driver's seat of his battered green Citroën when the black-and-chrome chopper pulled up outside the apartment block, two men riding on it. The driver was in jeans, a white T-shirt, and a leather jacket; the pillion passenger in pale cotton trousers, a blue sweatshirt, and a red crash helmet, which he removed to talk to the driver. Hosni grabbed his photograph of Knox, but he couldn't tell for sure at such a distance, not from such a small photograph. The two men shook hands. The passenger went inside while the driver turned in a tight circle and roared off. Hosni counted floors. Augustin Pascal lived on the sixth. About twenty seconds later, through his field glasses, he saw the balcony doors open and the pillion passenger step out, stretching his arms wide. Hosni fumbled for his cell phone, then speed-dialed Nessim's number.

"Yes?" asked Nessim.

"It's Hosni, boss. I think I've found him."

Nessim sucked in breath eagerly. "You're sure?"

"Not one hundred percent," said Hosni, who knew Nessim too well to give false hope. "I've only got this photograph. But yes, I'm pretty sure."

"Where are you?"

"Alexandria. Augustin Pascal's place. You know? The marine archaeologist."

"Good work," said Nessim. "Don't lose him. And don't let him know you're onto him. I'll be with you as soon as I can."

ELENA KOLOKTRONIS had no appetite to drive back to her Delta excavation for the night, just to come back to Alexandria first thing in the morning, so she'd booked herself a room in the famous Cecil Hotel. It was only a ten minutes' walk from Gaille's fleabag, but in every other way it was a different world. She could scarcely waste precious excavation funds pampering a mere languages expert, after all, but for herself it was different. She was here as the senior representative of the Macedonian Archaeological Foundation. She owed it to the dignity of that institution to travel in a certain style.

She spent the early evening catching up on her paperwork. It was extraordinary how bureaucratic running an excavation in Egypt could be. She was beginning to weary of it when she heard a knock on her door. "Come in," she said. It opened and closed behind her. She finished adding up a column of figures, then half turned in her chair to see, with a disturbing little thrill, the Frenchman from the necropolis standing there in his jeans and leather jacket. "What the hell are you doing here?" she demanded.

Augustin walked to her window as though he owned the place. He pulled back a curtain to gaze out over the harbor. "Very nice," he nodded. "All I have is other people's laundry."

"I asked you a question."

He turned his back on the window and leaned against her air-conditioner. "I've been thinking about you," he said.

"What!"

"Yes. Just like you've been thinking about me."

"I assure you," she said, "I haven't given you a moment's thought."

"Is that right?" he mocked.

"Yes," said Elena. "That's right." But something trembled in her voice, and Augustin's insolent smile grew even broader. Elena scowled. She was an attractive, successful, and wealthy woman, well accustomed to being hit on by womanizers like this. She normally dealt with them without even thinking, by deploying a scornful electric flytrap of a glare that incinerated their interest so efficiently that she didn't even notice anymore the sharp spark of death as these little flies tumbled to the floor. But when she now threw this glare at Augustin, there was no spark, and he didn't fall. He simply absorbed it with that offensive smirk of his and carried on staring at her. "Please leave," she said. "I have work."

But he didn't leave. He just stood there, his back to the window. "I've booked a table," he said. "I wouldn't want to hurry you, but—"

"If you don't leave," she said coldly, "I'll call security."

He nodded. "You must, of course, do whatever you think best."

She felt flutters in her stomach as she pulled the phone toward her. It was one of those old analogs. She dialed the first number, expecting that would be enough for him. But he made no move. He just stood there with that same damned conceited smile on his face. The dial made that low metallic purr as it returned to its starting position. She dialed the second number. The handset felt cool against her cheek. She put her finger in the hole to dial the third number, but then her arm just seemed to die on her, as though all her muscles had atrophied at once.

He walked across and plucked the handset from her, resting it back in its cradle. "You'll want to freshen up," he said. "I'll be downstairs."

"WE'VE FOUND HIM," said Nessim.

There was a moment's silence on the other end of the phone. After so many disappointments, Hassan seemed rather thrown. "Are you sure?"

"Hosni spotted him," said Nessim. "He's staying in a friend's apartment. I drove up here as soon as I got the call. He came out fifteen minutes ago, not a care in the world. He must think we've stopped looking. But it's him, all right."

"Where's he now?"

"In a taxi. Heading towards Ramla."

"You're following?"

"Of course. You want him picked up?"

That silence again. Then, "Listen to me: this is what I want."

Knox was surprised and gratified by the warmth
with which Gaille greeted him that evening. "Perfect timing," she enthused. "Ibrahim's asked me to do a show-
and-tell on the antechamber paintings tomorrow. I need a
victim to practice on." She led him back to her room, de-
fying the toxic glare of her concierge. Her balcony doors
were open to a cacophony on the street below: youngsters
talking and laughing excitedly in anticipation of their
evening, a distant tram clanking on its rails like an overworked kitchen. Her laptop was open on her desk, her
screen saver painting weird patterns on the monitor. She
nudged her mouse, and a colorful wall painting of two
men sprang up.

He leaned in, frowning. "What the hell? Is this from
the site?"

"The side walls in the antechamber."

"But . . . they're just plaster. How did you get them to
look like this?"

She grinned with pleasure. "Your friend Augustin. He
told me to use water. Lots of water. Not quite as much as
you pumped in this morning, maybe, but . . ."

He laughed and softly smacked her shoulder in reproach, triggering an unexpected spark of contact that
gave them both a little jolt. "You've done a great job," he
said, pulling himself together. "It looks fantastic."

"Thanks."

"You know who these guys are?"

"The one on the left is Akylos. The occupant of the tomb."

Knox frowned. The name Akylos was strangely familiar. But why wouldn't it be? It had been common enough among Greeks. "And the other?" he asked.

"Apolles or Apelles of Cos."

"Apelles of Cos?" asked Knox incredulously. "You don't mean the painter?"

"Is that who he is?"

Knox nodded. "Alexander the Great's favorite. Wouldn't have his portrait made by any other artist. He often dropped by his studio to bore everyone silly with his views on art, until finally Apelles told him to shut up, as even the boys grinding the colors were making fun of him."

Gaille laughed. "That took some courage."

"Alexander liked people with a bit of brass. Besides, Apelles knew how to flatter as well as mock. He painted Alexander with a bolt of lightning in his hand, just like Zeus. Where is this? Does it say?"

"Ephesus, as far as I can make out, but you can see the lacunae for yourself."

"It would make sense," said Knox. "Alexander went there after his first victory over the Persians." He reached past her, closed the file, and brought up another: soldiers wading through water. "Perga," he said. He glanced at her. "You know about this?"

"No."

"It's on the Turkish coast, opposite Rhodes. If you want to head south from there, you can hike over the hills, which is hard work, or you can go along the coast. Trouble is, you can only manage this route when a northerly is blowing, because it pushes the sea back far enough for you to get through. There was a southerly when Alexander set out, but you know Alexander—he just kept on going, and the wind switched just in time, lasting just long enough for him and his men to get through. Some people say that it was the seed for the story of Moses parting the Red Sea. Alexander passed through Palestine shortly afterwards, after all, while the Bible was still a work in progress."

Gaille pulled a face. "That's a little fanciful, isn't it?"

"You shouldn't underestimate the impact of Greek culture on the Jews," said Knox. "They wouldn't have been human if they hadn't been a little dazzled by Alexander." Many Jews had tried to assimilate, but it hadn't been easy, not least because a centerpiece of Greek social life had been the gymnasium, and "*gymnos*" was Greek for naked, so everything, by definition, had been on show. The Greeks had prized the foreskin as a fine piece of divine design and had considered circumcision barbaric. Many Jews had therefore tried to reverse the mohel's work by cutting free the skin around the base of their glans or by hanging metal weights from what little they had.

"I don't mean fanciful like that," said Gaille. "I'm only saying that bodies of water miraculously drying up to enable the hero to get through aren't exactly unknown in ancient myth. Nor are floods sent to destroy enemies. If I had to put my money on a historical precursor, I'd bet on King Sargon."

"The Akkadian?"

Gaille nodded. "A thousand years before Moses, two thousand before Alexander. There's a source describing how the Tigris and the Euphrates dried up for him. And he already has an established point of similarity with Moses."

Knox frowned. "How do you mean?"

"His mother put him in a basket of rushes and set him on the river," said Gaille. "Just like with Moses. He was found by a man called Akki and raised as his son. Mind you, changelings were a common enough motif. It gave the poets a way to show a kind of cosmic justice at work. Take Oedipus, left out by his father to die from exposure, only to return to kill him."

Knox nodded. "It's amazing how the same stories keep cropping up again and again across the entire Eastern Mediterranean."

"Not that amazing," replied Gaille. "It was a massive trading block, after all, and merchants have always loved trading tall tales."

"And the region was infested by minstrels, of course. And you know what minstrels have always been famous for."

"Wandering," grinned Gaille, glancing up and around. Their eyes met and held for a moment, and Knox felt unsettling flutters in his chest. It had been too long since he'd had a woman to share his life and passions with, not just his bed. Far too long. He turned in mild confusion back to the screen. "So this is a map of Alexander's campaigns?" he asked.

"Not exactly," said Gaille, a little flustered herself. "Of Akylos's life. The two just happen to be the same." Without looking his way, she brought up another picture: a walled city surrounded by water being menaced by an outsize satyr, an anthropomorphic Greek god, part man, part goat. "This one has me puzzled. I thought it might be Tyre, looking at the walls and water, but—"

"It's Tyre, all right," said Knox.

"How can you be so sure?"

"Tyre was famously impregnable," he told her. "Even Alexander had problems with it. One night during his siege he dreamed that a satyr was mocking him. He chased and chased it, but it kept eluding him, until finally he caught it and woke up. His seers interpreted it by pointing out that '*satyros*' was made up of two words, '*sa*' and '*Tyros*,' meaning 'yours' and 'Tyre.' Tyre will be yours. It'll just take time and effort. And so it proved."

"Unhappily for the inhabitants."

"He spared everyone who took sanctuary in temples."

"Yes," said Gaille tightly. "But he slaughtered two thousand of their fellow citizens by nailing them to crosses."

"Maybe."

"There's no maybe about it. Read your sources."

"The Macedonians often crucified criminals after they were dead," replied Knox calmly. "Like the British hanging them on gibbets. To discourage others."

"Oh," frowned Gaille. "But why would Alexander consider the Tyrians criminals? They'd only been defending their homes."

"Alexander sent in heralds to discuss terms before laying the siege. The Tyrians murdered them and hurled their bodies from the ramparts. That was an absolute no-no back then." He glanced at Gaille again, puzzled by something. "This is one hell of a tomb for a shield bearer, don't you think? I mean, a forecourt, an antechamber, and a main chamber. Not to mention Ionic columns, a sculpted facade, bronze doors, and all these paintings. It must have cost an incredible amount of money."

"Alexander paid well."

"Not that well. Besides, this is how Macedonian kings were buried. It feels, I don't know, *presumptuous,* doesn't it?"

Gaille nodded. "They're raising the plinth tomorrow afternoon. Maybe that'll give us some answers. You're going to be there, aren't you?"

"I doubt it, I'm afraid."

"But you must come," she said earnestly. "We wouldn't have discovered it without you."

"Even so."

"I don't understand," she complained. "What's going on?"

There was pain in her eyes, as well as confusion. Knox knew he couldn't prevaricate any longer. He pulled a face to let her know he had a difficult subject to broach, then stood up straight, putting distance between them. "You know how I said earlier there was something I needed to tell you?"

"It's that damned Knox, isn't it," scowled Gaille. "He's your best bloody friend or something."

"Not exactly."

"Let's not let him come between us," she begged. "I was just shooting my mouth off last night. Honestly. He means nothing to me. I've never even met the man."

Knox looked steadfastly into her eyes, until realization began to dawn. Then he nodded. "Yes, you have," he told her.

Chapter Fourteen

IT TOOK GAILLE a moment to assimilate fully what Knox was saying. Then her expression went cold. "Get out," she said.

"Please," he begged. "Just let me—"

"Get out. Get out now."

"Look. I know how you must feel, but—"

She went to her door and threw it open. "Out!" she said.

"Gaille," he pleaded. "Just let me explain."

"You had your chance. You sent me that letter, remember."

"It wasn't what you think. Please just let me—"

But the concierge had overheard the commotion. Now he arrived outside Gaille's room, grabbed Knox's arm, and dragged him out. "You leave," he said. "I call police." Knox tried to shake him off, but he had surprisingly strong fingers, which he dug vengefully into Knox's flesh, giving him no choice but to go with him or start a fight. They reached the lobby. The concierge bundled him into the elevator, punched the button for the ground floor, then slammed the mesh door closed. "No come back," he warned, wagging his finger.

The elevator juddered downward. Knox was still in a daze when he stepped out into the ground-floor lobby and down the front steps. The look of anger on Gaille's face had not only shocked him, it had made him realize just how hard he was falling for her. He turned right and right again, heading down the alley at the rear of her hotel, converted, like so many alleys in Alexandria, into an improvised parking lot, so that he had to wend his way between tightly packed cars.

He remembered, suddenly, the letter he'd sent her, all the deceits he'd filled it with. His face burned hot; he stopped dead in the alley so abruptly that a man walking behind him barged into his back. Knox held up his hand in apology, started to say sorry, but then he caught a whiff of something chemical, and suddenly a damp, burning cloth was clamped over his nose and mouth, and the darkness began closing in. Too late, he realized that he'd allowed himself to stop worrying about Sinai, about Hassan. He tried to fight, to pull away, but the chloroform was already in his system, and he collapsed tamely into the arms of his assailant.

IT WAS BARELY ELEVEN THIRTY when Augustin brought Elena back to the Cecil Hotel. He had invited her on to a nightclub; she pleaded weight of work. He insisted on escorting her into the lobby all the same. "There's no need to come up," she said drily when they reached the elevators. "I'm sure I'll be safe from here."

"I see you to your room," he announced gallantly. "I would never forgive myself if anything happened."

She sighed and shook her head but didn't make a point of it. There was a mirror in the elevator. They each checked themselves out in it and then each other, their eyes meeting in the glass, smiling at their own vanity. She had to admit that they made a striking pair. He walked her right to her door. "Thank you," she said, shaking his hand. "I had fun."

"I'm glad."

Elena took her key from her purse. "I'll see you tomorrow, then."

"No doubt." But he made no move to leave.

"You haven't forgotten where the elevators are already?" she asked pointedly.

He smiled wryly. "I think you're the kind of woman not to be afraid of what she wants. I'm right about this, yes?"

"Yes."

"Good. Then let me make this clear. If you ask me to leave once more, I truly will leave."

There was silence for a few moments. Elena nodded thoughtfully to herself as she unlocked her door and went inside. "Well?" she asked, leaving the door open behind her. "Are you coming in or not?"

KNOX SLOWLY RETURNED TO CONSCIOUSNESS, aware of his lips, nostrils, and throat burning, of nausea in his gut. He tried to open his eyes. They were glued shut. He tried to lift a hand to his face, but his wrists were bound behind his back. He tried to cry out, but his mouth was taped. When he recalled what had happened, his heart plunged into panicked tachycardia and his body shuddered in a great spasm, arching him off the floor. Something clumped him hard behind the ear, and he slumped back into darkness.

He was more circumspect when he came around again. He let his senses gather information. He was lying on his front. Some kind of soft carpet with a lump in the middle that pressed against his ribs. His ankles and wrists were so tightly bound that his fingers and toes tingled. His mouth was coppery and tacky from a cut on the inside of his cheek. The air smelled thickly of cigarette smoke and hair oil. He felt the soft vibration of an expensive engine. A vehicle passed at speed, its sound warped by Doppler. He was on the floor of a car, and he was probably being taken to Hassan. That lurch of panic. Vomit welled in his throat, stopping only at the back of his mouth. He inhaled deeply through his nose until the nausea subsided. He reached for a calm thought. It wasn't necessarily Hassan's men who had snatched him. Maybe it was freelancers after blood money. If he could just get them to talk, he could establish rapport, negotiate, outbid. He tried to sit up and was again thumped brutally on the back of his head.

They swung left and began to jolt over rough terrain. It was all Knox could do to buffer himself. His ribs were banged and bruised. They drove for what seemed an age, then stopped abruptly. Doors opened. Someone grabbed him beneath his arms and hauled him out, dumping him on sandy ground. He was kicked onto his back; fingernails picked at the tape on his cheek. It was ripped from his eyes, taking some lashes with it, leaving his skin tender. Three men stood above him, dressed in black sweaters and balaclavas, and the sight of them turned Knox's guts to water. He tried to tell himself they wouldn't be hiding their faces unless they thought he'd live. It didn't help. One of the men dragged Knox by the legs to a wooden post hammered into the ground. He gathered together several loose strands of barbed wire and wrapped them around Knox's ankles.

Though their car was parked obliquely, Knox could just make out its rear license plate. He burned it into his memory. A second man popped the trunk and pulled out a coil of rope, which he dumped on the sand. He tied a knot in one end, looped it around the tow bar, and tugged it hard to make sure it would hold. He made a hangman's noose in the other end, came over to Knox, slipped it around his neck, and tightened it until it bit into the soft skin of his throat.

Knox had lost sight of the third man. Now he saw him ten paces away, recording everything on the camera phone. It took Knox a moment to see the significance. He was filming a snuff movie to send to Hassan. That explained the balaclavas, too. They didn't want footage of themselves committing murder. It was then that Knox knew he was going to die. He kicked and struggled, but he was too tightly bound. The driver revved his engine like a young biker throwing down a challenge. Its back wheels spat sand. Then it began speeding away, rope hissing as it paid out. Knox braced himself; he screamed into his gag. The man with the camera phone moved closer to frame his climactic shot as the rope lifted, shivered and went taut.

Chapter Fifteen

I TRUST YOU HAVE GOOD NEWS FOR ME," said Hassan.

Nessim, even though talking to a phone, closed his eyes as if in prayer. "We've had a setback, sir."

"A setback?"

"Someone else got to him first."

"Someone *else*?"

"Yes, sir."

"I don't understand."

"Nor do we, sir. He went into a hotel. He came out again. He walked around to the back and down an alley. Another man followed him. We thought nothing of it until a black car pulled up and he was bundled into the back."

"You mean you just let them take him away?"

"We were across the street. There was a tram."

"A tram?" asked Hassan icily.

"Yes, sir."

"Where did they go?"

"We don't know, sir. Like I say, there was a tram. We

couldn't get past." The damned thing had just sat there as he tooted at it, the fat driver smirking at them, enjoying their frustration.

"Who was it? Who took him?"

"We don't know, sir. We're working on it now. If we're lucky, it's someone who heard what he did to you and thinks they can sell him to us at a price."

"And if we're not?"

"According to his file, he has plenty of enemies. Maybe one of them spotted him."

Silence. One beat. Two beats. Three. "I want him found," said Hassan. "I want him found as a matter of urgency. Do I make myself clear?"

Nessim swallowed. "Yes, sir. Crystal clear."

KNOX FELT INCOMPARABLY OLDER as he trudged north, following tire tracks in the sand. When the rope had paid out and stretched taut, he knew he was going to die. It was a qualitatively different thing, knowing you were going to die as opposed to fearing you might die. It did strange things to your heart. It made you think differently about time, the world, and your place in it.

Apparently the rope had been cut clean through, then fixed back together again with duct tape. The tape had ripped free as soon as the rope went taut, so that the two sections of rope had pulled apart, and Knox had flopped down on the sand, his bladder venting, his heart bucking like a terrified steer, bewildered by his reprieve. The driver had come around in a great loop over the sand to collect his comrades, who had been squatting there all the time, filming his reaction, the way he pissed himself. They had all laughed uproariously at that, as though it was the funniest thing they had ever seen. One of them had thrown an envelope out the window, and then they drove off, leaving him tied there to the stake, his trousers soaked, his throat raw with burns from the rope.

It had taken him two hours to free himself from his various bonds. He was shivering by then, full-body tremors. Desert nights were cold. He had dried his trousers as best he could by smearing them with handfuls of dusty sand, then gone over to the envelope. Plain white. No writing on it. When he had opened it, some sand fell out. Ballast to stop it blowing away. Apart from that, it contained only an Egypt Air compliments slip with four words on it: "You have been warned."

He climbed a small rise. Far ahead, the pinpricks of headlights were headed in both directions on a busy road. He walked at a slow, tired, dispirited pace. It was easy enough to be bold when you faced abstract dangers, but it was different now that they clearly knew where he was. And he had others to think of, too, particularly Augustin and Gaille. He couldn't risk putting them in danger.

It was time to get out.

NICOLAS DRAGOUMIS was an early riser by temperament, but this morning he awoke earlier than usual, eager as a child at Christmas. He went straight to his laptop to check his e-mail. There was one from Gabbar Mounim, as promised. He downloaded and decrypted the movie file attachment impatiently while he read the message, nodding approvingly as he did so. His father had always insisted that Knox wasn't to be harmed, and Mounim made it clear that his men hadn't harmed Knox, not in any real sense. A little chloroform, a tap on the skull, a jolt to his system. That couldn't count as harm. On the contrary, it would make him appreciate life all the more.

Nicolas played the movie for the first time: Knox abducted; Knox lying unconscious on the floor of the car; Knox dragged onto the desert sands; the look of terror on his face as the car accelerated away! Nicolas was exultant. To think that this wretch had once caused him and his father such grief! And now look at him! Pissing himself like an eight-year-old. He played it again, then a third time, his back soothing with every frame. A good night's work. A very good night's work indeed. Because, unless Nicolas wasn't the judge of character he knew himself to be, that would be the last he ever saw of Knox.

IT WAS GROWING LIGHT when Knox finally reached the coast road, but the traffic was still thin. He ran across, then over a bank of dunes and down the beach to the Mediterranean. He peeled off his trousers and boxer shorts, washing them in the lapping waves, wringing them out

as best he could. He draped them over his shoulder and
walked along the beach, his feet caking pleasantly with
the chill, thick sand.

The sun rose orange, laying a fiery comet on the foamy
backwash of a wave. He reached a walled compound of
holiday homes, a gate swinging on the breeze. It looked
deserted. These estates came alive only on weekends and
holidays. Many of the homes had clotheslines outside,
several draped with swimming costumes, towels, and
clothes. He went in, wandered among them until he spotted an old cream djellaba and headdress, faintly damp,
perhaps because of the early hour and the nearness of
the Mediterranean. He left his trousers in part exchange,
along with as much cash as he could afford. Then he took
them and fled before he was spotted.

It was all very well for those men to warn him to get
out. But he needed his bank cards, passport, and papers,
all of which he'd left at Augustin's. Most of all, he needed
his Jeep. It took him an hour thumbing before a three-
wheeler stopped to offer him a ride. The driver addressed
him in gruff Arabic, so Knox replied in kind without even
thinking, his mind elsewhere. They talked of soccer; the
man was a passionate Ittihad fan. It was only after Knox
had got out that he realized he'd been mistaken for an
Egyptian. His Bedouin clothes and genes, no doubt, plus
his deep tan and a day's worth of stubble.

He was almost out of money, so he took buses to Augustin's apartment block, walking the last kilometer. He
was on alert as he made his way through the parking lot,
or he wouldn't have spotted the two men in the white
Freelander, one smoking a hand-roll, the other hidden in

the shadows. He went closer. Through its rear window, he saw a familiar red overnight bag, a black laptop case, and a cardboard box packed with his own belongings from his Sinai hotel room. He spun on his heel and hurried away, but he hadn't gone far before he realized that there was no real point in fleeing. If Hassan had wanted him captive or dead, he wouldn't have let him go last night. These men were surely here to make sure he really did leave.

He turned again and walked boldly over to the front steps, his back to the Freelander, trusting his Egyptian robes to act like a cloak of invisibility. A janitor was mopping the red terra-cotta tiles. Knox stepped around the wet patch and risked a glance as he waited for the elevator. The men were still sitting in the Freelander. He took the elevator up to the seventh floor, walked down a flight, crouching below window level to let himself in. There was no sign of Augustin. He had evidently been playing away. Knox packed his belongings, then wrote a brief note thanking Augustin for his hospitality, letting him know he'd hit the road, promising to call in due course. He was just finishing up when he heard footsteps outside, then a key scraping in the lock. He watched in frozen horror as the handle turned and the door opened and Nessim came in with a translucent bag of electronic equipment in his left hand.

Chapter Sixteen

KNOX AND NESSIM stared spellbound at each other for a moment, each equally startled. Nessim recovered first, reaching inside his jacket. The glimpse of his shoulder holster jolted Knox into action. He charged Nessim, knocking him over backward. The gun went skittering away, tumbling into the stairwell, plummeting six floors before clattering at the bottom. Knox raced for the stairs. Nessim scrambled to his feet. They bounded down, leaping a flight at a time, bouncing off the walls as they turned corners, Nessim barely an outstretched arm behind. Knox reached the ground-floor lobby, tiles still slick from their mopping. He slowed just enough to keep his footing, but Nessim's feet went from under him and he crashed into the bank of elevators, turning his ankle, cursing loudly. Knox burst out the door and sprinted for his Jeep. He risked a glance behind. Nessim had emerged, too, hobbling badly. He had retrieved his gun but was holding it flat against his side—this place was too public for such things. He shouted at his colleague, who started up the Freelander and drove over to pick him up.

Knox ran to his Jeep, jumped in, turned on the ignition. The engine caught on the first try. He was away at once, up a narrow alley to a main road, which he cut into so sharply that cars behind him had to swerve and brake, getting in each other's way, honking like enraged geese. A glance in his rearview mirror told him the Freelander was struggling to bull its way through this sudden traffic jam. Knox took advantage, turning left, left again, losing himself in the maze of streets, constantly checking his mirrors, but there was no sign of them. He allowed himself to relax a little. Then he checked once more, and there they were. How the hell had they managed that? He stomped on the gas, but the faster and more maneuverable Freelander was catching him inexorably.

Up ahead, at a level crossing, a passenger train crawled into view on his side of the road. Traffic slowed to allow it past, but Knox stamped his foot down and swerved into oncoming traffic, honking furiously to move others aside. The train was still coming. There was almost no room, but he kept his foot to the floor and charged across the tracks, the train's engine flicking his rear bumper and nudging him against a wooden gatepost, but then he was through and swerving back into his own lane with nothing but clear road ahead, ignoring the fists being shaken and horns angrily honking. A glance in his mirror. The train had come to a complete halt across the road. He'd have at least a minute, probably two. He turned a corner and parked. No way had Nessim picked up his trail just like that, not in a maze like Alexandria. If Augustin's place had been under sur-

veillance, maybe they'd found his Jeep, too. He got down
on all fours to search and found the transmitter taped to his
undercarriage. He pulled it free and ran back to the street,
flagged down a taxi, and paid the driver to deliver it to the
Sheraton in Montazah Bay. Then he jogged back to his
Jeep and drove off in the opposite direction.

Nessim wasn't a fool. He'd soon realize he'd been
tricked. Knox had to make the most of this short window.
But Alexandria wasn't like other cities, with a hundred escape points. His choices were essentially to head south to
Cairo, east to Port Said, or west to El Alamein. But Nessim
would have backups, that was for sure. Hassan didn't operate on the cheap; he'd have those routes watched for an old
green Jeep. So maybe he should lie low until they dropped
their guard. But where? He was toxic; he dare not inflict
himself on any more friends. Nessim would certainly check
all of Alexandria's hotels. And he couldn't stay on the street.
Anyone could spot him. He needed to get underground.

The idea, when it came to him, was both so outrageous
and so fitting that he gave a snort of laughter and almost
rear-ended the van in front of him.

AN UNWELCOME SURPRISE awaited Nicolas Dragoumis
when he and his bodyguard, Bastiaan, drove in from Alexandria Airport to the necropolis site. He wanted to get
right to raising the plinth to find out what lay beneath,
but Ibrahim had evidently decided to make an event

of these proceedings. All the excavators were lined up in a greeting party to shake his hand, and there were tables set up, their white cloths laden with cups of tea and disgusting-looking cream cakes. Clearly, he was expected to exchange small talk with these people. It wasn't something he was skilled at, being polite to nonentities. But he was playing for high stakes, so he gritted his teeth and hid his scowl and did his best.

KNOX STOPPED AT THE FIRST ATM he saw and pillaged it for money. Hassan knew he was in Alexandria anyway; there was no point keeping a low profile. Then he went shopping for supplies: a bulky waterproof bag, food, water, an underwater flashlight, a battery lamp, spare batteries, books to read. From an automotive store he bought a green tarpaulin. Then he drove off to the forbidding residential district south of the main train station, parked, and hid his Jeep beneath it.

He packed all his other supplies into the waterproof bag and strapped it tight around his waist, placing the bulk over his stomach so that, beneath his robes, he simply looked overweight. Then he hurried to the site, flashing his SCA pass at the security guard on the stairwell, who nodded him through without a murmur. Down in the rotunda, two laborers were fixing a steel gate over the entrance to the Macedonian tomb, being supervised by Mohammed and Mansoor, who glanced up as Knox passed. Mansoor frowned in half recognition. "You!" he called out. "Come here." Knox ducked his head and hurried deeper into the necropolis. "Hey!" cried out Mansoor. "Stop!"

But Knox kept going, pushing his way past excavators bringing baskets of human remains to the rotunda. Footsteps behind only made him go faster. Several of the chambers had already been completely cleared of artifacts, the lights taken from them and redeployed where they were needed. He had intended to slip into one and hide in an empty loculus until nightfall. Now there was no chance of that.

"Hey!" cried Mansoor behind him. "Stop that man! I want to talk to him." Knox hurried on down the steps until he reached the water table and could go no farther. Since they removed the pump, the level had risen again, so that it was now as it had been, with all the air expelled. He had no time. He walked slowly into the water, so as not to disturb it too much. Bubbles escaped from his robes; the waterproof bag around his waist bellied and tried to float. The search drew closer behind him; they were checking each of the chambers in turn. He filled his lungs with air, pressed his left hand against the wall, then ducked his head beneath the black water and propelled himself along the corridor, navigating by memory. His hunger for breath built steadily. He reached the third chamber and swam to its top corner and was relieved to find that his internal compass hadn't let him down. He kicked up out of the water and hauled himself up into the chamber beneath the rotunda, the waterproof bag of supplies still around his waist. He took off his soaking robes, untied the bag, dried himself, and put on trousers and a T-shirt.

It wasn't the Ritz exactly, but it would keep him safe for a while, at least. A cubic meter of air would last him the better part of an hour if he didn't exert himself. There were about forty-eight cubic meters in this place, which meant he could stay here tonight and tomorrow. Then he would head back after the excavators had left and hide overnight in an empty loculus before leaving with the others at lunch—as long as no one figured out where he'd vanished to, of course.

He tried to get comfortable, but it wasn't easy. Alone and in darkness, surrounded by underwater tombs filled with mortal remains, half expecting someone to pop up at any moment, it wasn't surprising he felt anxious. But as time passed, he felt other emotions, too. Envy. Anger. He was the one who had realized there was something beneath the plinth. Yet here he was, a fugitive, while others got to open it. And he was so close to it! After all, the necropolis came around in a great spiral, so that the Macedonian tomb was just a few meters away from where he was now.

Yes, he frowned. Just a few meters away.

Quarrying stone was brutal work under the best of conditions. It was twice as difficult if your only access was via a narrow shaft. Electricity made it easy to forget how difficult a problem lighting had been for the ancients. Candles and fat-burning lamps had eaten up oxygen, so that rudimentary ventilation systems had been invaluable. Two access points were far better than one, allowing both laborers and air to circulate. And once the quarrying had been completed and secrecy became paramount, it would have made sense to seal up for good the larger means of access, maybe by laying stone over it and covering it with a mosaic.

He set down his lamp on the floor, then began a diligent survey of the walls, tapping them with the base of his flashlight, listening to the echo, hoping to hear a slightly higher pitch that might indicate a cavity behind. He worked from base to apex, then shuffled half a meter to his left and began again. Nothing. He checked the floors and ceilings, then the staircase. Still nothing. He bit his teeth in frustration. It had made such good sense. Yet it seemed he'd been wrong.

NICOLAS HAD HAD AS MUCH OF BEING POLITE as he could take. He grabbed Ibrahim by the arm and dragged him to one side. "Perhaps we could get started," he said tightly. "I need to get back to Thessalonike tonight."

"Of course. Yes. But there's just one more person I'd like you to meet."

"Who?" sighed Nicolas.

"Mohammed el-Dahab," said Ibrahim, pointing to a mountain of a man. "He's site manager for the construction company."

"And then we can start?"

"Yes."

"Good." They walked across. "*Salaam alekum,*" said Nicolas curtly.

"*Wa alekum es salaam,*" replied Mohammed. "And thank you. Thank you."

Nicolas frowned. "What for?"

"The sick girl I told you about," beamed Ibrahim. "She's Mohammed's daughter."

Nicolas looked back and forth in surprise between the two men. "You mean there really is a sick girl?"

"Of course," frowned Ibrahim. "What did you think?"

"Forgive me," laughed Nicolas. "I've been dealing too much with your compatriots in Cairo. I assumed baksheesh."

"No," said Mohammed emphatically. "This money makes all the difference to us. Your money gives my daughter a chance. We'll hear our results tonight. But whatever the outcome, my family is forever in your debt."

"It was nothing," said Nicolas. "Really." He turned back to Ibrahim, glanced at his watch. "Now, really, we must get started," he said.

KNOX SAT IN THE DARKNESS with his back against one of the support walls, biting the knuckle of his thumb in frustration. It just made too much sense for this place to be connected to the lower chamber. Yet he'd checked every square inch of the chamber's exterior he could get at, everything except for those areas blocked by the support walls.

He frowned. There had to be at least two feet of lime-

stone above his head, and yet there were support walls.
He pushed himself up onto his knees, placed his palms
flat against one of them, and rested his cheek against it, as
though to listen to its secrets. Why on earth would anyone
have bothered? This chamber was excavated out of solid
rock. The ceiling didn't need props. There were dozens of
chambers in this necropolis, and dozens of necropolises
in Alexandria. In none of them had Knox ever seen support walls like this. So maybe they weren't support walls
at all. Maybe they had another purpose. Maybe they were
hiding something.

He walked up and down, inspecting them closely. They
were each made up of six columns of six blocks. Each
block was a little more than a foot high and wide, and about
three feet long, stacked sideways, with the old mortar between them crumbled into dust. He went to where the support wall abutted the exterior wall, and pushed hard against
the top block. It grated but slowly gave, revealing a glimpse
of solid limestone behind. He left it for the time being
and went to the second support wall. This time, when he
pushed back the top block, he exposed the edge of a hole in
the exterior wall. He tried to push the top two blocks back
together, but they were too heavy for him, so he climbed
up between the walls like a climber in a rock chimney, then
pushed the blocks back with his feet until they were pinned
precariously between the remaining blocks beneath and the
ceiling above. He dropped down again and went to inspect
what he had revealed. A tight hole into a compact space the
size of a broom closet, another wall at its far end. He filled
his pockets with everything he might need, then squeezed

through headfirst, falling hard on his hands and landing with a grunt.

He turned on the flashlight, brushed off his palms, and went to inspect the far wall. It was built of bricks rather than blocks, small enough for one person to manage with relative ease. Knox felt his breath coming faster as he spread his palm out on it. Whatever lay on the other side had to be connected with the plinth, which Ibrahim was due to raise at any moment. He cupped an ear against it but could hear nothing. It was crazy even to consider going on. If he were found, he'd be looking at serious jail time. But he was so close. Surely one brick couldn't do any harm. Not if he was careful.

He scratched away the dead mortar, then pulled out a single brick and rested it ever so gently on the floor. He listened intently for half a minute. There was complete silence. He tried to peer through, but the hole was too small for both his eyes and his flashlight together. He reached the flashlight through the gap instead, then squinted as best he could along the line of his arm. But the flashlight was now pointed in the wrong direction, so he couldn't make out a thing. Trying to twist his hand around, his fingers involuntarily opened a fraction and the flashlight slipped agonizingly from his grasp. He tried to grab it back but it fell in spirals and landed with a splashy thump in shallow water, its beam making ghostly white ripples on the facing wall.

Chapter Seventeen

Knox had no choice but to retrieve the flashlight. Ibrahim, Mansoor, and others were about to raise the plinth, and if they found it, he was certain to be discovered. Besides, he had time. The place was still quiet. He began dismantling the wall, brick by brick, placing them precisely on the ground, the old mortar still resting on them, so that he would be able to rebuild the wall exactly as he'd found it. When he had created enough space, he poked his head through, catching a pungent whiff of ammonia. It was a low, arched corridor with a watery floor, like some Victorian sewer. Its walls were even scratched with lines to make it look as though it had been built of bricks rather than ex-cavated, perhaps to disguise the passage he had just broken through, but possibly because the ancients had simply con-sidered construction more prestigious than excavation.

He stretched down for his flashlight but couldn't quite reach it, not without leaning on the wall, which he didn't trust to hold his weight. He removed another two rows of bricks, then straddled what remained. The water felt sharp on his bare foot as he stooped to retrieve the light. He listened intently. Nothing but silence. He was here now. It would be criminal not to take a quick look.

He splashed along the corridor, brushing aside cobwebs, his imagination sensing eels and nocturnal creatures around his bare ankles. He came to a compact chamber beneath a chimney shaft, its mouth blocked by some kind of slab. The plinth, no doubt. He went back the other way and came to a marble portal with an Ancient Greek inscription cut into its architrave:

Together in life; together in death. Kelonymus.

Kelonymus. The name was familiar, as Akylos had been. But the memory wouldn't come and time was short, so he passed beneath it, reaching the foot of a broad flight of stone steps that spread out like a fan as it rose. And at the top . . .

"Jesus Christ!" muttered Knox.

"WHAT'S GOING ON?" demanded Nicolas, as a large crowd of senior excavators and other guests descended the stairwell to the rotunda.

"How do you mean?" frowned Ibrahim.

"All these people?" said Nicolas. "You can't seriously be inviting them all."

"Just to watch. From the antechamber. This is a big moment for us."

"No," said Nicolas. "You, me, your archaeologist, Elena. That's all."

"But I've already—"

"I mean it. If you want the remainder of your Dragoumis sponsorship money, you'll kick these people out now."

"It's not that simple," protested Ibrahim. "We need Mohammed to lift the plinth. We need the girl to take photographs. Moments like these don't come often, you know."

"Fine. Those two. No others."

"But I—"

"No others," said Nicolas emphatically. "This isn't a circus. This is supposed to be a serious excavation."

"Fine," sighed Ibrahim. And he turned with a sagging heart to disappoint the crowd of excited excavators.

KNOX'S MOUTH HUNG OPEN as he played his flashlight over the chamber like a searchlight over a bombarded city. He struggled to believe his eyes. To his right, a terrace had been hewn in the limestone. Sixteen golden larnaxes, or burial caskets, stood on each of two shelves, making thirty-two in all. Glass bowls had toppled and fallen both over the shelves and the floor, scattering their contents of precious and semiprecious stones. Also on the floor were countless precious artifacts: swords and spears and shields and amphorae of silver and clay. White marble had been inlaid into the far wall, a lengthy inscription carved into it, though too distant for him to make out what it said.

But it was the left-hand wall that mesmerized Knox. It was a huge mosaic, framed at the top by turquoise-painted plaster that represented the sky, and which contoured the main subject matter like a chalk mark around a corpse. Thirty-three men, clearly soldiers, though not all armed, were gathered into two overlapping clusters, one in the foreground, the other farther back. They looked remarkably relaxed and cheerful. Some talked among themselves, arms around each other's shoulders. Others wrestled on the sand or played dice. But kneeling at the center was the mosaic's focal point and the group's clear leader: a slight, handsome man with russet hair, who looked out of the wall with a purposeful gaze. Both his hands were clasped on the hilt of his sword, plunged deep into the sand. Knox blinked. No one could study Greco-Roman history without developing a knowledge of mosaic. Yet he'd never seen anything like this.

He had no camera with him except for the one in his mobile phone. He hadn't even turned it on since Sinai, worried that it would lead Hassan straight to him, but there was no chance of it transmitting a signal this deep underground. He tiptoed carefully into the chamber, photographing the mosaic, the burial caskets, the grave goods scattered on the floor, the inscription. He became so completely absorbed in this work that it was only when he heard a grinding, ripping noise from way behind him that he belatedly remembered the raising of the plinth.

Chapter Eighteen

Bastiaan and three burly Egyptian security guards kept the disgruntled excavators out of the Macedonian tomb while Mohammed and Mansoor attacked the plinth as they had on the day before, working the tips of their crowbars beneath one end and levering it up. It came more easily this time. They raised it a few inches, just enough for Ibrahim to slide in a hydraulic jack, which they pumped high enough to slide a pallet-trolley beneath. Then they repeated the process at the other end and simply wheeled the plinth back against the wall.

There was a fat black shaft in the floor, just as Ibrahim had glimpsed. They all gathered around. Mansoor directed his flashlight down. Light glinted brightly from five yards below.

"Water," said Mansoor. "I'll go first." He turned to Mohammed. "Tie a noose in a rope. You'll lower me, yes?"

"Yes," agreed Mohammed.

KNOX HAD NO TIME FOR FINESSE. He clutched his hand over the bulb of his flashlight to dim it yet allow him just enough light to see what he was doing; then he stripped off his T-shirt so that he could use it to erase his footprints in the dust as he backed out of the chamber and down the steps. But Mansoor was already being lowered on a rope, flashing his light all around him and down the passage, so that Knox had to duck back out of sight. "There's a corridor!" shouted Mansoor as he splashed into the shallow water and stepped off the stirrup. "I'll take a look."

"No!" said Ibrahim. "Wait."

"But I'll just—"

"Wait for us."

The light vanished momentarily. Knox risked another glance, saw the stirrup slithering back up. But then Mansoor shone his flashlight again down the corridor, his frustration evident, giving Knox no chance to escape. Someone else was being lowered now: Gaille, twisting this way and that on the rope. Mansoor turned to help her down. It was Knox's only chance. He ran along the corridor to his dismantled wall, trying hard not to make waves. But Gaille gave a shriek of alarm. "There's someone there!" she cried.

Knox stepped through the hole in the wall as Mansoor blazed his flashlight down the corridor. "There's no one," he laughed. "How could there be?"

"I could have sworn," said Gaille.

"Just your imagination," said Mansoor. "Places like this will do that."

Knox was only half listening, his heart still hammering, frantically rebuilding his wall from within, taking care to keep as silent as possible. He couldn't risk his flashlight, so he had to work by feel and what little light reached him from Mansoor, Gaille, and the others as they gathered one by one. But by the time they were all down, his wall was still only three-quarters rebuilt.

"Okay," said Ibrahim. "Lead on."

Knox froze. He couldn't do any more now except press himself back into the shadows and pray. Light flickered and flashed and then grew almost blinding. There was still a great, gaping hole in his wall. They had to spot it. But somehow, first one then the next walked past with heads bowed, watching the floor to make certain of their footing. Ibrahim, Mansoor, Elena, Gaille, and then, shockingly, Nicolas Dragoumis. Nicolas Dragoumis! Last night's mock execution suddenly had a completely new suspect.

They paused, as he had, to illuminate and read the inscription on the architrave. "Look!" said Elena excitedly, nudging Nicolas. "Kelonymus!" Her tone, and the presence of Nicolas Dragoumis, triggered recognition in Knox, so that he remembered at last why the names Kelonymus and Akylos were so familiar.

IBRAHIM ENTERED THE CHAMBER FIRST. He stood there in silent awe as the others arrived behind him and took their own places on the bottom step. He gazed almost drunkenly around the chamber. It was only when Nicolas made to step up into the chamber that he came back to his senses. "Stop!" he said. "No one goes in."

"But—"

"No one goes in," he repeated. He felt, suddenly, a surge of authority. He was the senior representative here of the Supreme Council for Antiquities, and this—as no one could for a moment doubt—was a find of historic importance. He beckoned for Mansoor. "We have to inform Cairo at once," he said.

"Cairo?" winced Nicolas. "Is that really necessary? Surely this isn't a matter for—"

"It's a matter for whoever I say it is."

"But—"

"You're our sponsor and we appreciate your support. This is no longer a matter for you. Is that clear?"

Nicolas had to force his smile. "Whatever you say."

"Gaille. You will take photographs, yes?"

"Of course."

"Mansoor, you stay with her."

"Yes."

"I'll instruct Mohammed and the security guards not to let anyone else down. I'll arrange for the necropolis to be cleared. When you're satisfied that Gaille has enough photographs, replace the plinth over the shaft. Then make sure the site is empty and seal off the mouth of the stairwell. I'm sure Mohammed can find a way. Sealed tight, mind. No one is to get in or out. Understood?"

"Yes, sir."

"I'll have Maha arrange around-the-clock security. You're not to leave until they arrive. Then bring Gaille to my villa. Drive her yourself. And don't let her camera out of your sight."

"Yes, sir."

"As for me, I'm going to notify the Supreme Council that we've just discovered the most important antiquity in the modern history of Alexandria."

KNOX QUIETLY FINISHED rebuilding the wall before Ibrahim and the others left. Since Gaille and Mansoor remained behind taking photographs, he didn't dare move, scared the noise would give him away. Cramps built agonizingly in his thighs and calves until Mansoor was finally satisfied, and they left.

There was no time to waste. If he didn't get out quick, he'd be sealed in with all the other corpses. He cleared the area of traces of his presence, then squeezed back into the chamber beneath the rotunda, replacing the blocks as he'd found them. He stripped naked and stuffed everything into his bag, dropped down into the water, breathed deeply, then navigated his way back to the steps, pulling the bag behind him. He was lucky, there was no one waiting. In fact, the whole necropolis was eerily dark and silent. He brushed himself dry, pulled on his trousers and T-shirt, filled his pockets with everything of value, then stuffed the rest deep into an empty loculus. Then he hurried for the rotunda. Metal screeched and banged as he reached it. He looked up to see daylight already partially eclipsed by the bottom of a blue container, with a second already being positioned next to it to complete the seal. Knox pounded up the steps, his thighs protesting, diving out just as the container was maneuvered into place. Everyone stared incredulously as he rolled up onto his feet and ran for the gates. "Stop him!" yelled Mansoor. "Someone stop him!"

At the site exit, two security guards blocked his way. He dropped a shoulder, feinted right, sidestepped left, spinning one of the guards around, bursting out into the street, across traffic, dodging a minibus, putting distance between himself and the chasing pack, shouting at people to stop him, yelling into their phones. He cut down an alley toward his Jeep, three men chasing hard. A shopkeeper jumped out to block his path, but he broke through the halfhearted tackle, glancing around to see the three getting closer. And now two soldiers appeared ahead, reaching for their guns. This was turning ugly fast, but it was too late to stop now. He ducked left, his chest aching, a stitch burning in his side, his legs on fire with lactic acid. He vaulted a wall, crawled beneath a gate, then ran to the dark alley where he'd left the Jeep. He pulled the tarpaulin back just far enough for him to sneak beneath, unlock and open his door, and climb inside, where he sprawled across the front seats, keening for breath while simultaneously struggling for silence, listening to frantic footsteps hurrying up the alley behind him, praying he hadn't been seen.

Chapter Nineteen

IBRAHIM GREETED GAILLE and Mansoor impatiently when finally they arrived at his villa. "There was a problem at the site," explained Mansoor. "An intruder."

"An intruder?"

"Don't worry. Nowhere near the Macedonian tomb."

"Did you get him?"

"They're still looking. He won't get far." He held up his cell phone. "They'll call when they have news."

"Good. And the site?"

"Sealed. The guards are in place, too. It'll be fine for the moment. How about our secretary general? Have you notified him yet?"

"He's in a meeting," said Ibrahim.

"A meeting?" frowned Mansoor. "Didn't you have him called out?"

Ibrahim's cheeks flamed. "You know what he's like. I'm sure he'll call back soon." He turned to Gaille. "May we see your pictures?"

"Of course."

She transferred her pictures to her laptop and opened them one by one. Nicolas and Elena joined them as they gathered around the kitchen table to look. "Demotic," muttered Ibrahim gloomily when she showed him the inscription. "Why did it have to be Demotic?"

"Gaille knows Demotic," volunteered Elena. "She's working on the Sorbonne dictionary project."

"Excellent," beamed Ibrahim. "So you can translate this for us?"

Gaille gave a dry laugh. Demotic was a brute, as Ibrahim had to know full well. Asking her if she could translate this was like asking someone if they spoke English, then jabbering at them in coarse Anglo-Saxon.

Ancient Egypt had had just the one main spoken language, but that language had been written down with a number of different alphabets. The first was hieroglyphics, the stylized pictographs familiar from temples, tombs, and Hollywood movies. These had first appeared around 3100 BC. Pioneering Egyptologists had assumed the language to be pictorial, each symbol representing a single concept. But after the Rosetta Stone was found, with identical text inscribed in hieroglyphics, Demotic, and ancient Greek, Thomas Young and then Jean-Francois Champollion had deduced that these pictographs had had phonetic as well as symbolic value—that they were, in short, letters that could be combined in multiple ways to form words and thus a broad vocabulary, and that this language had its own syntax and grammar, too.

Hieroglyphics, while they looked fantastic on the walls of temples and palaces and formal documents, had been far too elaborate to be practical for everyday use. Almost from the start, therefore, a simpler and quicker alphabet had developed alongside. This was known as Hieratic, and it had become the language of literature, business, and administration in ancient Egypt, which was why it was usually found on cheaper materials like wood, papyrus, and ostraka. Then, around 600 BC, a third written language, called Demotic, had evolved, reducing Hieratic to a series of strokes, dashes, and dots, like Egyptian shorthand. To make matters worse, it had neither vowels nor breaks between words, its vocabulary had been large and vernacular, its alphabet had varied significantly from region to region, and it had evolved massively over the centuries, so that it was really a family of related languages, not just one. Mastery took years of dedication and a set of dictionaries the size of a Volkswagen Beetle. Depending on how mainstream this inscription was, and what resources would be available to her, decipherment could take hours or days, or even weeks. She summed this all up with a wry glance at Ibrahim.

"Yes, I know," he said, having the grace to blush. "But still."

Gaille sighed, though in truth she felt exhilarated by the challenge. It had been too dark in the chamber to make much of the inscription earlier. But her camera had astonishing resolution and her photographs had come out crisply, despite the dust and cobwebs, making the Demotic characters clearly legible. She zoomed out again. Something about the inscription was bothering her, but she couldn't figure out what.

"Well?" asked Ibrahim.

"May I have a minute by myself?"

"Of course." And he ushered everyone out to give her some peace.

KNOX LAY ABSOLUTELY STILL across the Jeep's front seats. The chasing pack had gathered directly outside and now were discussing plans and catching their breath. Sweat was cooling all over his body, giving him chills despite the warmth of the day. The Jeep lurched as someone sat on its hood. He heard the rasp of a lighter, cigarettes being lit, people gossiping and bantering, chiding each other for being too slow, too old. The Jeep creaked as someone else leaned against it. *Christ!* How long before one of them thought to check beneath the covers? But there was nothing he could do but lie still. Nothing except make plans. Yet what plans? Hassan, Nessim, the Dragoumises, the police, and the army were all after him, and Christ knew who else. He couldn't risk turning on his cell phone to review his photographs lest Nessim trace the signal. Besides, he'd barely be able to see anything on the tiny screen, and anyway he needed them deleted as soon as possible, because if they were found, they would prove he'd been inside the lower chamber and earn him ten years in jail. Ideally, he would have liked to transfer them to his laptop, but that was in the back of Nessim's Freelander along with the rest of his stuff, and anyway it didn't have a USB port, so his only way of getting the photos to it was by e-mailing them to himself, then downloading them. But none of that was going to happen while he was lying in his Jeep with his pursuers on his hood.

He turned his thoughts elsewhere: The names Kelonymus and Akylos. The Ptolemaic archives in Mallawi that he and Richard had discovered had included letters, bills, reports, codices, poems, religious texts, and all the other kinds of documents that you would expect in a small town. There had been far too much for them to translate as they went along, so they had conserved them instead, then cataloged them and passed them to the SCA for safekeeping and later study. Their preferred method of cataloging had been to collect the fragments of a particular papyrus together and photograph them, then assign the fragments and the photograph a single file name, based on where they were found or (if too many had been found in one place) a name of a place or a person from the text. And two of the names that had cropped up most during this process, and almost always in tandem, had been Akylos and Kelonymus.

The originals had long ago been taken by Yusuf Abbas of the SCA for "safekeeping," so God only knew where they were now, but Knox had photographs of them on CDs. Unfortunately, they, too, were in the trunk of Nessim's Freelander, probably under closed-circuit television surveillance in the parking lot of some high-end Alexandrian hotel; and he wasn't exactly in a position to go hunting from hotel to hotel in hopes of a smash and grab. No, he needed another way.

The Jeep lurched as the man got off his hood. Footsteps scuffed and faded. Knox waited until there had been silence for a good couple of minutes, then climbed out

and stripped off the tarpaulin. He had no time to waste.
He had phone calls to make.

DESPITE STARING FURIOUSLY at the inscription, it
still took Gaille several minutes to work out what was
bothering her. But finally she got it. The bottom line of
text was incomplete, and it was written left to right. Yet
Demotic, like Arabic, had been written right to left.

The inscription in the Macedonian tomb had been in
Greek. The few words of text in the antechamber paintings had been in Greek. The dedication on the architrave
was in Greek. The shield bearers had been Greek. The
gods they invoked had been Greek. This looked like Demotic, but it didn't read that way, not initially at least.
And it seemed perverse to switch to Demotic just for the
inscription. So maybe it had simply been too sensitive to
be written in plain Greek. Maybe the writer had used the
Demotic alphabet instead. Codes, after all, hadn't been
unknown to the ancients. Alexander himself had used sub-
terfuge to hide sensitive messages. The Admonitions of
the Sons of Dawn, one of the Dead Sea Scrolls, had used
code for particularly sensitive words. Valerius Probus had
written an entire treatise on substitution ciphers. They had
been simple things, because people had believed them un-
breakable. But Gaille didn't.

She copied the inscription out onto a pad, checking for
patterns as she did so. If this was a simple transliteration

cipher, and the same word was encrypted more than once, then it would produce identical sequences every time. It wasn't long before she had her first strike, then a second and a third. The third looked particularly helpful: ten characters long, and appearing no fewer than four times. That surely had to be a single word—an important one, too. What could it signify? A person's name, perhaps. Mentally, she ran through all the names they had come across in the upper chamber. Akylos, too short. Likewise Kelonymus and Apelles, Bilip and Timoleum. She had a little surge of excitement when she thought to try Alexander, but that fell short, too. Her spirits sank again. She stood up and walked in brisk circuits around the small room, sensing she was missing something, scowling in an almost physical effort to impel her mind to the answer.

When finally it came, her cheeks flushed and she looked around, worried that her schoolgirl error might have been observed. For "Alexander," the name by which the world knew him, was in fact a Latin name. To Greeks, he had been known as Alexandros. She sat back down and used the letters in "Alexandros" to begin a transposition alphabet, replacing the Demotic symbols with the matching Greek letters wherever they appeared throughout the text. That gave her enough to guess the word adjacent to the first Alexandros: Macedonia. With half the alphabet now broken, the rest swiftly followed.

Ancient Greek was her thing; she made the translation on her pad, so utterly absorbed in her task that she lost track of time and her surroundings until her name was suddenly called, bringing her back to the real world.

She looked up to see Ibrahim, Nicolas, Mansoor, and

Elena standing in a semicircle, looking expectantly at her, as though someone had just asked her a question and they were waiting for her answer.

Ibrahim sighed and said, "I was explaining to Nicolas how difficult Demotic can be. We want as few people as possible to know about this, so we very much want you to work on it by yourself. How long do you think you'll need? One day? Two? A week?"

It had to be the most gratifying moment of Gaille's professional life. "Actually," she said airily, holding up her pad, "it's already done."

Chapter Twenty

NESSIM WAS IN HIS HOTEL ROOM, discussing plans with Hosni, Ratib, and Sami. There was no great zest to their conversation, however. Knox had vanished off the radar, and nothing they tried had picked him up again.

It was late afternoon when Nessim's phone rang. It was Badr, his contact from the phone company, who had been waiting for Knox to use his cell phone. "He's turned it on," he said excitedly. "He's making a call."

"Who to?"

"No one—he's sending pictures to an e-mail account."

"Where?"

"Near the railway station."

"Stay on the line," said Nessim. "Tell me if he moves." Hosni, Ratib, and Sami had already risen to their feet. He nodded at them. "We've got a trace," he said. "Let's go."

"WELL?" SAID IBRAHIM EXCITEDLY. "Don't keep us in suspense."

Gaille nodded. She cleared her throat and began to read aloud: *"I, Kelonymus, son of Hermias, brother of Akylos, builder, scribe, architect, sculptor, lover of knowledge, traveler in numerous lands, give homage to you, great gods, for allowing me to bring to this place below the earth these thirty-two shield bearers, heroes of the great victor, Alexander of Macedonia, son of Ammon. I now make good my pledge to bring together in one place the thirty-three who died carrying out the last wish of Alexander, that a tomb be built for him in sight of the place of his father. And to fulfill his wish, Akylos and these thirty-two built such a tomb and appointed it with goods fit for the son of Ammon."*

Gaille hadn't properly registered the text until now—she'd been too busy translating it. But even as she read it out, she realized how explosive it was. She glanced up and saw on everyone's faces the same astonishment that she knew must be on her own.

"Go on," said Elena hungrily.

"And to fulfill his wish, they seized his body from the White Wall to take it through the red land of great dryness to the mouth of the place prepared below the earth. And near that place, Ptolemy, who is styled Savior, trapped these men so that they took their lives rather than be subjected to his torture. And so Ptolemy crucified them in vengeance and left them crucified for the carrion to feed on. Akylos and the thirty-two gave their lives to honor the wishes of Alexander, son of Ammon, in defiance of Ptolemy, son of nothing. I, Kelonymus, man

of Macedonia, brother of Akylos, beseech you, great
gods, to welcome these heroes into your kingdom as you
welcomed Alexander."

She looked up again to indicate that she had finished.
The looks of excitement had given way to a kind of
stunned disbelief. No one spoke for a good five seconds.

It was Nicolas who finally broke the silence. "Does
that . . . ," he began hesitantly. "Does that mean what I
think it means?"

"Yes," said Ibrahim. "I believe it does."

THE MOMENT HIS PHOTOGRAPHS WERE SENT,
Knox deleted the images from his cell phone, then turned
it off altogether and roared away in his Jeep before Nessim had a chance to get to him. Just one more phone call,
and he'd be in business. He parked near Pompey's Pillar,
bought himself a ticket, and went inside. The site was a
walled enclosure of about a hectare, surrounded by high-
density housing. The pillar itself occupied pride of place
on the small hillock at its center, but in fact the whole enclosed area was historic as the onetime site of the famous
Temple of Serapis.

Knox had always felt a great fondness for Serapis,
a benign and intelligent deity who had somehow fused
Egyptian, Greek, and Asian religious myths into a single
theology. According to one thesis, he was a Babylonian
god; in fact, when Alexander had lain dying in Babylon,

a delegation of his men went to the Temple of Serapis to ask whether Alexander should be brought to the temple or left where he was. Serapis replied that it would be better for him to be left where he was. The delegation obeyed, and Alexander died shortly afterward, that being the better thing. Other scholars, however, asserted that Serapis had its roots in the Black Sea city of Sinope, while still others claimed that Serapis was Egyptian, because Apis bulls had been sacrificed for centuries and buried in huge vaults known to the Greeks as the Sarapeion, a contraction of "Osiris-Apis" or "dead Apis bull."

Knox glanced around to make sure no one was looking, then hid himself from view behind the base of Pompey's Pillar. He checked his watch, took two deep breaths, turned on his cell phone, and began pressing numbers.

"WHAT DO YOU MEAN, you've lost him?" yelled Nessim.

"He's turned off his phone."

Nessim punched his dashboard so hard, he scraped skin from a knuckle. "What was his last location?"

"I told you: near the railway station."

"Stay on the line," ordered Nessim, hurtling through the streets. "If he makes another call, I want to know at once." It was five minutes before they reached the station. Nessim drove around for a while, but there was no sign of

Knox or his Jeep. Then Badr spoke again. "He's turned it back on. He's making another call."

"Where?"

"South of you," said Badr. "He must be right next to Pompey's Pillar."

Nessim and his men ducked to look out the windows as they drove. Passing a side street, he glimpsed the marble pillar thrusting upward just a kilometer away. "We're on our way," he said. He roared down the road, cut across traffic to Sharia Yousef, then headed along a wide boulevard with a brownstone wall to his right, Pompey's Pillar on the left. He pulled a U-turn and swerved up onto the pavement, and the four of them jumped out and hurried inside to the ticket booth. "Is this the only entrance?" he asked the woman, pushing some bills through the window.

"Yes."

"Stay here," he ordered Hosni, as he and the other two men went into the site. Then he asked Badr on his phone, "Is he still on the line?"

"Yes," confirmed Badr. "You're right on top of him."

"Then we've got him!" exulted Nessim.

Chapter Twenty-one

Nicolas took Ibrahim to one side. "Do you have an upstairs bathroom?" he asked, patting his stomach. "All this excitement seems to have done strange things to my digestion."

"Of course," said Ibrahim, pointing him to the stairs. "First on your left."

"Thank you." He hurried up and locked himself in. Then he took out his cell phone to call and brief his father on the blizzard of events and relay the gist of the inscription, too.

"What did I tell you?" said the elder Dragoumis.

"You've been right at every step," acknowledged his son.

"And it was the girl who broke it? Mitchell's daughter?"

"Yes. You were right about her, too."

"I want to meet her."

"I'll arrange for it once we're done," said Nicolas.

"No. Now. Tonight."

"Tonight. You're sure?"

"She worked out that there was a lower chamber in the Macedonian tomb," said Dragoumis. "She realized the inscription was a cipher, and broke it, too. She'll be the one to find what we're looking for; I feel it in my heart. She must be on our side when that happens. You understand?"

"Yes, Father. I'll take care of it." He took further instructions, then finished the call and rang Gabbar Mounim in Cairo.

"My dear Nicolas," enthused Mounim. "I trust you were satisfied with—"

"More than satisfied," said Nicolas. "Listen. I need something done right now."

"Of course. Whatever you wish."

"I believe our friend Yusuf at the SCA is in a meeting," said Nicolas. "When he comes out, he'll have a message on his desk to call Ibrahim Beyumi in Alexandria. Mr. Beyumi is going to ask him for an urgent meeting. I want our friend to invite a third party to that meeting and to look favorably upon what she asks. Her name is Elena Koloktronis." He spelled it out. "You may let our friend know that he'll be *very* generously rewarded, as you will be, too. You know I'm a man of my word."

A chuckle rolled down the phone line. "I do, indeed. Consider it done."

"Thank you." He made another few phone calls to get things under way, then flushed the toilet, washed his hands, and went back downstairs.

"Any better?" asked Ibrahim solicitously, meeting him at the bottom.

Nicolas smiled. "Much better, thank you."

"You'll never guess what's happened. Yusuf Abbas, my

secretary general, just called from the SCA. He's invited me to Cairo for an immediate meeting."

"What's surprising about that?" frowned Nicolas. "Isn't that what you wanted?"

"Yes, but he's invited Elena, too. And none of us can work out how he even knew she was in the country."

NESSIM COULD SEE no immediate sign of Knox inside the Sarapeion—little sign of anyone, indeed, except for two Korean tourists taking pictures of each other in front of Pompey's Pillar, and a young family enjoying a modest picnic. He motioned for Ratib and Sami to spread out and comb the site. They went slowly, checking each of the various pits, cisterns, and chambers. But they reached the red-brick wall at the far end without a trace of him.

Badr was still on the line. "Are you quite sure he's here?" Nessim asked icily.

"You must have walked straight past him. I don't understand it."

Nessim looked over at Ratib and then at Sami. They shrugged and shook their heads. He pointed to the pillar, suggesting they meet at its base. He reached it first. A brown paper bag rustled in the light breeze. He gave it a wary nudge with his foot, carefully pulling it open. There was a cell phone inside. He picked it up and turned it around, frowning, wondering what it signified.

There was a crash of broken glass at the far side of

the wall. It was only when his car alarm began to wail
that Nessim realized that was where he had left the Freelander—with all Knox's belongings in the back. An old
engine roared and raced away before any of them could
react. Nessim closed his eyes and clutched his forehead.
He hated Knox. He *hated* him. But he couldn't help but
rather admire him, too.

NICOLAS DREW ELENA to one side to explain how
he had arranged her meeting with Yusuf Abbas, and what
she should try to achieve in it. Yusuf was greedy but cautious. If Elena could provide him with an excuse to let her
explore Siwa, and thus earn himself his fat commission,
then he'd do so. But it would need to look legitimate. A
low-level epigraphic survey, say—just her and the girl.

"The girl?" frowned Elena. "Can we trust her?"

"My father believes so. Well? Can you take care of
Yusuf?"

"Leave him to me."

Nicolas walked over to Gaille, who was transferring
photographs onto Ibrahim's laptop to show to Yusuf.
When she was finished, he asked her for a word, then
steered her out into Ibrahim's small garden. "My father
wants to meet you," he told her.

"Your father?" Gaille looked a little alarmed. "I don't
understand. I don't even know who he is."

"He's the founder and backer of the Macedonian Archaeological Foundation," explained Nicolas. "That makes him your boss. He was also the person who suggested Elena employ you."

"But . . . why?"

"He knew your father," said Nicolas. "He admired him greatly. And he's kept an eye on your career over the years. When Elena needed a replacement, he naturally thought of you."

"That was . . . very good of him."

"He's a very good man," nodded Nicolas seriously. "And he wants you to have dinner with him this evening."

Gaille frowned. "He's in Alexandria?"

"No. Thessalonike."

"But . . . I don't understand."

Nicolas smiled. "Have you ever flown on a private jet before?" he asked.

Chapter Twenty-two

KNOX RACED THROUGH the back streets of Alexandria, his recaptured belongings piled high on the seat beside him. It had felt good putting one over on Nessim. A man can only run for so long before his pride begins to smart. He drove east toward Abu Qir, putting distance between himself and his pursuers; then he parked to see what he had.

His laptop battery was old and had only an hour's juice. He flicked through his photograph CDs, checking file names, but he couldn't find a trace of Akylos or Kelonymus. He scowled in frustration. Nessim had either left them behind or removed them from his car. How unlucky was that? It was a minute or two before another possible explanation occurred to him.

There was a pay phone on the corner. He didn't dare telephone Rick directly. Instead, he called a mutual friend who worked next door at the water-sports center in Sharm, and asked her to fetch him. He came on the line a minute later. "Hey, mate," he said. "You forgotten my number or something?"

"It may be tapped."

"Ah. Hassan, huh?"

"Yes. Listen, you haven't borrowed some of my photographic CDs, have you?"

"Christ, mate, I'm sorry. I was just practicing my Greek."

"Not a problem. But I need them. Any way you can get them to me?"

"No sweat. There's nothing happening here. Where do you want to meet?"

"Ras el-Sudr?"

"You mean that dump south of Suez?"

"That's the one," said Knox. "There's a hotel there called the Beach Inn. When do you think you can make it?"

"Give me four hours. Maybe five."

"Perfect. Will you come in your Subaru?"

"Unless there's a reason not to."

"You might want to check it for tracking devices first. And make sure you're not followed. These guys are serious."

"So am I, mate," Rick assured him. "So am I."

MOHAMMED AND NUR clutched hands as they waited for the phone call to tell them the results of the bone marrow tests. They had used a private health care group with medical centers in Alexandria, Cairo, Assiut, and Port Said to make it easier for far-flung friends and family.

Especially family. Bone marrow compatibility was heritable, so the chances of finding a match was significantly higher among kin. They had tested another sixty-seven people, using up all the funds Ibrahim had made available. Dr. Serag-Al-Din had promised to call with the results an hour ago. Waiting for the phone to ring was about the most grueling experience of Mohammed's life. Nur winced as he squeezed her hand too tightly. He apologized and let go. But she needed the contact as badly as he did, and within moments their hands found each other again.

Layla was in bed. They had decided not to inform her of this process until it was done. But she was a sharp child, sensitive to atmosphere. Mohammed suspected that she knew all too well what was going on: the sentence of life or death that would shortly be passed on her.

The phone rang. They looked at each other. Nur made a face and started to weep. Mohammed's heart started pattering as he picked up the receiver. "Yes?" he asked. But it was only Nur's mother, anxious to learn if they had heard. He bit his lip in frustration and passed her across. Nur got rid of her with promises to call the moment they knew. Mohammed crossed his legs. His bowels felt loose and watery, but he dare not go to the toilet.

The phone rang again. Mohammed breathed deeply and picked it up. This time it was Dr. Serag-Al-Din. He said: "Mr. el-Dahab. I hope you and your wife are both well."

"We're fine, thank you. Do you have our results?"

"Of course I have your results," he said genially. "Why else do you think I'd call?"

"Well?"

"Bear with me a moment. I seem to have lost my place in your file."

Mohammed closed his eyes and clenched his fists. *Come on, you son of a dog. Say something. Anything.* "Please," he begged.

There was a rustling of paper. Dr. Serag-Al-Din cleared his throat. "Yes," he said. "Here we are."

IT WAS DUSK when Ibrahim and Elena arrived in Cairo for their meeting with Yusuf Abbas, secretary general of the Supreme Council for Antiquities. The great man was waiting for them in an ornate conference room, talking on the phone. He looked up sourly, then waved them vaguely at chairs. Ibrahim set up his laptop while he waited for Yusuf to finish discussing mathematics homework with his son. He found dealing with his boss immensely trying, not the least because he himself was a fastidious man, and Yusuf had grown grotesquely fat since orchestrating his palace coup and unseating his energetic, popular, and highly respected predecessor. Even watching Yusuf wrest himself from his chair was a mesmerizing sight, like seeing some ancient ship of war setting sail. He would prepare for the feat moments ahead of time, readying his muscles as if wind were filling the unfurling sails, and the rigging would creak and the anchor would haul and, *yes, yes, yes, movement*! Right now his forearms rested like giant slugs on the polished walnut table, but every so often he would lift a finger to his throat, as though his glands and not his incessant consumption of rich foods were to blame for his obesity. And when people addressed him from the side, he would move his eyes rather than his head to look at them, his pupils sliding to the corners— the very caricature of shadiness. Finally, he ended his call and turned to Ibrahim. "Such urgency," he said. "I trust it has a purpose."

"Yes," said Ibrahim. "It does." And he turned his laptop to show his boss Gaille's pictures of the lower chamber, while explaining how they had been found.

Yusuf's eyes lit up when he saw the burial caskets. "Are those . . . *gold*?" he asked.

"We haven't had time for analysis yet," said Ibrahim. "My priority was to seal the site and inform you."

"Quite right. Quite right. You've done well. Very well." He licked his lips. "This is a remarkable discovery. I see I will have to supervise the excavation personally."

Elena leaned forward—not much, just enough to catch his eye.

"Yes?" he asked.

"We're both aware of our exceptional good fortune that you could spare time from your other commitments for this meeting, Mr. Secretary General, for we know you are a man with extraordinary demands upon your time." Her Arabic was stilted and clumsy, noted Ibrahim, but her posture and use of flattery were impeccable. "We're glad that you, like us, consider this find to be of historic importance, and are delighted that you'll be involved in its ongoing excavation. However, sharing this exciting news with you wasn't the only reason Mr. Beyumi and I were anxious for this meeting. There's something else that needs your wisdom and urgent consideration."

"Something else?" asked Yusuf.

"The inscription," said Elena.

"Inscription? What inscription?" He glared at Ibrahim. "Why haven't you told me about this inscription?"

"I believe I did, Secretary General."

"Are you contradicting me?"

"Of course not, Secretary General. Forgive me." He re-opened his photograph of the inscription.

"Oh, *this*," said Yusuf. "Why didn't you say you were talking about this?"

"Forgive me, Secretary General. The fault is mine. You'll note that the characters are Demotic, but the inscription is actually in Greek." He nodded at Elena. "A colleague of Ms. Koloktronis's deciphered it. I can explain how it works, if you're interested. Otherwise, here is a copy of the translation."

Yusuf's mouth worked as he read the text, his eyes going wide as he assimilated the implications. It wasn't surprising, reflected Ibrahim. Memphis had been known to ancient Egyptians as White Wall. The word desert came originally from Desh Ret: the Red Land. Kelonymus referred to Alexander as the "Son of Ammon," so the place of his father, it followed, was the Oracle of Ammon in Siwa Oasis, where old sources suggested Alexander had asked to be buried. The inscription, therefore, asserted that a group of shield bearers had stolen Alexander's body from under Ptolemy's nose in Memphis and had taken it across the Western Desert to a tomb they'd prepared within sight of the oracle of Ammon in Siwa Oasis. Ptolemy, however, had pursued them, and they had killed themselves rather than fall into his hands. All except Kelonymus, Akylos's brother, who had avoided capture and who had later brought all his comrades' remains back to Alexandria for burial, in fulfillment of his vow.

When Yusuf had finished he blinked twice. "Is this . . . is this to be believed?" he asked.

"The translation is correct," answered Ibrahim carefully. "I've checked it myself. And we believe it to be sincere as well. After all, as you've seen from the photographs of the underground chamber, this man Kelonymus went to extraordinary lengths to honor these men. He wouldn't have done it for a hoax."

"But it would have been madness," frowned Yusuf. "Why would these men throw their lives away on such a venture?"

"Because they believed that Alexander's dying wish had been to be buried in Siwa," answered Elena. "Ptolemy betrayed that wish when he started to build a tomb in Alexandria. You must remember, Alexander was a god to these people. They would have risked anything to carry out his orders."

"Please, you're not asking me to believe that Alexander is buried in Siwa, Ms. Koloktronis," sighed Yusuf. Ibrahim knew what was on his boss's mind. In the early 1990s, another Greek archaeologist had announced to the world's media that she had found the tomb of Alexander in Siwa Oasis. Her claim was universally rejected, but not before Siwa and Alexander had become something of a joke in the archaeological community.

"No," acknowledged Elena. "Alexander's embalmed body was on display in Alexandria centuries after this inscription was made. No one's denying that. However, surely it's possible that they seized his body and set off towards Siwa, where they had a tomb ready and waiting."

Yusuf sat back in his chair and looked sternly at Elena. "So," he remarked, "the *true* purpose for your presence at this meeting becomes clear. You're not here out of concern for the proper excavation of this Alexandria find. Oh, no. You're here because you believe that somewhere in Siwa there is a tomb appointed with—how does this . . . Alexander cipher of yours put it, again?—yes, with 'goods fit for the Son of Ammon.' And you want my permission to look for them, no doubt."

"Alexander was the most successful conqueror in history," said Elena. "One of Egypt's greatest pharaohs. Imagine what finding this tomb of his would mean for this country. Imagine what honors would befall the secretary general whose enlightened leadership made it possible. Your name would rightly be venerated along with the great patriots of this nation."

"Go on."

"And you have nothing to lose. I know the chances of finding anything are extremely thin. I know the resources of the Supreme Council are inexcusably tight. But something should be done. Something small. A low-level epigraphic survey of antiquities, say, conducted with the permission of the SCA. Just me and one colleague. Anything more substantial will only provoke rumors. You know what it is with Siwa and rumors."

Yusuf frowned. "Every hill in the Oasis has been

searched and searched again," he observed. "If this tomb does exist and has lain hidden for twenty-three centuries, do you truly expect to find it in a matter of weeks? Do you know how *wide* the Siwa Depression is?"

"It won't be easy," admitted Elena. "But it has to be worth a try. Think of the alternative. When the contents of the Alexander cipher leak, every treasure hunter in the world will converge on Siwa. If we find the tomb first, we can preempt that, or at least announce that there's nothing to it. Either would be preferable to a gold rush."

"There'll be a gold rush only if word gets out," pointed out Yusuf.

"But it *will* get out," insisted Elena. "We all know it will. That's the nature of these things."

Yusuf nodded to himself. "Siwa is the territory of Dr. Sayed," he said sourly, as though he rather resented his colleague. "And Dr. Sayed has his own ways. You'll need his permission, too."

"Of course," nodded Elena. "Apart from anything else, I understand he has an outstanding collection of reference materials. Perhaps you might speak to him yourself— ask him to give us access. I know, of course, that it will make no difference whatever to *your* decision, which will be taken solely for the greater benefit of Egypt, but you might perhaps let *him* know that our backers have set aside very significant fees for all our SCA consultants, including yourself, naturally."

"I cannot agree to an open-ended expedition," said Yusuf. "Siwa may be a large oasis, but it is a small community. Whatever your cover story, people will eventually note what you are doing. Your presence will trigger the very result you seek to avoid."

"Six weeks," suggested Elena. "That's all we ask."

Yusuf rested his hands on his belly. He liked to have the last word on everything. "Two weeks," he declared. "Two weeks from tomorrow. Then we'll talk again, and I'll decide whether to give you another fortnight or not."

NESSIM PACED BACK AND FORTH in his hotel room, willing his phone to ring, for one of his sentinels to spot Knox before he could drop out of sight once more. There had to be a good chance. The simple fact that Knox had broken cover to get his belongings back suggested he was after something, that he had a purpose and was prepared to take risks in its pursuit. Yet, for all that, there was something about Knox that made Nessim feel inadequate, almost fatalistic.

He stopped in mid pace, daunted suddenly by the prospect of confessing another failure to Hassan. He needed to show he was doing something. He needed to demonstrate that he was *active.* He had kept the hunt largely in-house up till now, but the time for discretion had passed. He unzipped his money belt, checked his cash, and turned to Hosni, Ratib, and Sami. "Get on your phones," he told them. "A thousand dollars to whoever finds Knox's Jeep. Two if he's in it."

Ratib pulled a face. "But everyone will know it was us," he protested. "When Knox turns up dead, I mean."

"Do you have a better suggestion?" snapped Nessim. "Or perhaps you'd like to tell Hassan yourself this time why we haven't found Knox yet."

Ratib dropped his gaze. "No."

Nessim sighed. The stress was getting to him. And Ratib had a point. "Okay," he said. "Only people you trust. One in each town. And tell them not to blab, or they'll be answering to Hassan themselves."

His men nodded and reached for their cell phones.

BY THE TIME the Dragoumis Group's Lear jet touched down in Thessalonike that night, Gaille had decided that she could get used to traveling like this, despite the twinge of guilt she felt at all these carbon emissions for so whimsical a trip. White leather seats so comfortable they made her groan with pleasure, a window the size of a wide-screen TV, a butler on hand to prepare meals and drinks, the copilot coming back to talk her through her preferred arrangements for flying back in the morning. An immigration officer came out to greet her with cloying politeness ("any friend of Mr. Dragoumis, Ms. Bonnard . . ."), and a chauffeur-driven blue Bentley that whisked her away up into the hills above Thessalonike just so she could sit back and admire the night sky.

They reached a walled estate patrolled by guards. They

were waved through, down to a whitewashed palace lit up like son et lumiere. And then, to cap it all, Dragoumis himself emerged from his front door to meet her, his hands clasped behind his back, a vivid birthmark near his left eye. After all she had imagined of him on her journey, it was a surprise and relief to her to see how short and slight he was. He hadn't shaved; he looked rustic and very Greek. Just for a moment, she thought she would be able to handle him easily, that he was nothing to fear. Then she drew closer and realized she had been wrong.

Chapter Twenty-three

K NOX CUT CROSS-COUNTRY to get to Ras el-Sudr, his route taking him through Tanta, the largest town of the Delta. Something about Tanta niggled in his brain; someone had mentioned it to him recently, but he couldn't think who. Then he remembered Gaille's offhand remark about her Tanta concierge, and he pulled the Jeep to the side to think. He hadn't given much thought to Elena's Delta excavation; too much else had been going on. But maybe that had been a mistake. Especially now that Nicolas Dragoumis had appeared on the scene.

It was no secret that Elena's Macedonian Archaeological Foundation was sponsored by the Dragoumis Group. And the Dragoumises had no interest in Egypt, Knox knew—only in Macedonia. If they were financing an excavation in the Delta, therefore, they were after something Macedonian. And just maybe it was connected with that site they had just found in Alexandria. It certainly couldn't hurt to find out more.

He found a Tanta bar with a phone directory, then

rang local hotels asking for Elena. He got a hit on his fifth attempt. "She not here," the night clerk told him. "Alexandria."

"What about her team?"

"Who you want to speak to?"

Knox ended the call, jotted down the hotel's address, and hurried back to his Jeep.

PHILIP DRAGOUMIS LED GAILLE through arches and across polished mosaic floors to a drawing room with gorgeous oils and tapestries on the walls. "A drink," he said. "Then we eat. Red wine? It's from my estate."

"Thank you." She looked around as he opened a bottle and poured two glasses. An oil portrait of a fierce-looking black-bearded man with a mess of scar tissue around his left eye had pride of place above the huge fireplace. A portrait of Philip II, father of Alexander the Great. Her eyes flickered back and forth between the picture and Dragoumis, and she realized with a slight shock that the portrait was intended to draw some kind of subliminal parallel between the two, implying that the birthmark around Dragoumis's own left eye was some kind of stig-mata, as though he were Philip reborn. "You don't really believe in reincarnation, do you?" she asked.

He laughed loudly and unaffectedly, pleased by her boldness. "There is a saying: 'When a wise man does business with the Chinese, he speaks Mandarin.'"

"And when he does business with the superstitious?" suggested Gaille.

His smile broadened. He nodded at a second painting: a beautiful young dark woman in ragged peasant clothes. "My wife," he said. "I painted her myself. From memory." He gave a sharp little nod. "She's buried outside. She loved the view from this hill. We used to walk up here. That is why I bought this land and built my home here."

"I'm sorry."

"When I was a young man, I was a troublemaker. I used to go from village to village preaching the Macedonian cause, so the Athens secret police wanted to speak with me. You can imagine, it was not a desire I shared. When they couldn't find me, they visited my wife instead and demanded she tell them where I was. She refused. They poured petrol on her stomach, breasts, and arms, but she told them nothing. Then they lit it. Still she wouldn't talk. They poured petrol onto our baby son. Finally she talked. My wife was left with terrible burns, yet she could perhaps have survived with proper treatment, but I had no money for such treatment. My wife died because I had chosen to preach rather than to work, Ms. Bonnard. The day I buried her was the day I decided to stop playing at politics and become rich."

"I'm sorry," said Gaille helplessly.

Dragoumis grunted, as if to acknowledge the inadequacy of words. Then he said, "I knew your father."

"So your son told me. But I wasn't that close to him, you know."

"Yes, I do know. I have always felt bad about that."

Gaille frowned. "Why should you feel bad about it?"

Dragoumis sighed. "You were due to go to Mallawi with him, were you not?"

"Yes."

"But then he postponed?"

"He had urgent personal business."

"Yes," agreed Dragoumis. "With me."

"No," said Gaille. "With a young man called Daniel Knox."

Dragoumis made a vague gesture, as if to imply it came to the same thing. "Do you know much about Knox?" he asked.

"No."

"His parents were archaeologists themselves. Macedonian specialists. So they often visited this part of the world. A charming couple, who also had a delightful daughter. They worked closely with Elena, you know. Ten years ago they went to visit one of her excavations in the mountains. Elena's husband collected them from the airport. Unfortunately, on the drive up to the site . . ."

Gaille looked at him numbly. "All of them?" she asked.

Dragoumis nodded. "All of them."

"But . . . what's that got to do with my father?"

"It was an accident. A terrible accident. But not everyone believed this."

"You mean . . . *murder*? I don't understand. Why would anyone want to kill Knox's parents?"

"Not Knox's parents. Elena's husband. Pavlos."

"But who would want to kill him?"

Dragoumis smiled. "Me, Ms. Bonnard," he said. "Me."

KNOX ARRIVED IN RAS EL-SUDR FIRST and loi-
tered near the Beach Inn's parking lot so he could watch
out for Rick and then make sure he hadn't been tailed.
When he was satisfied, he went to meet him. "Good to see
you, mate," grinned Rick.

"You, too."

"Interesting times, eh?" He nodded at a nearby bar.
"You want a drink? You can tell me all."

"Sure." They took a table in the shadows, where Knox
filled him in on everything that had happened since he
fled Sharm.

"I don't believe it," said Rick. "That bastard Hassan
had a noose put around your neck and attached it to a car?
I'll kill him."

"Actually," said Knox, "I don't think it was Hassan.
Hassan wouldn't have had the rope cut."

"Then who?"

"Have I ever told you about what happened in
Greece?"

"You mean with your parents? You just told me there'd
been a road accident. You never said there was a story
to it."

"A winding road, an old car, a misty night in the moun-
tains. The kind of tragedy that happens all the time, right?
The only trouble was, the driver was a guy called Pavlos.
The husband of that woman Elena I was telling you about.
A journalist, very outspoken. A muckraker. He was run-

ning a campaign against a very powerful and rich family called the Dragoumises, demanding an inquiry into their businesses—that kind of thing."

"And you figured he was killed to shut him up?"

"I did at the time," nodded Knox.

"So what did you do about it?"

GAILLE LOOKED AT PHILIP DRAGOUMIS IN HORROR. "You murdered Pavlos?"

"No," he assured her. "I swear to you on my wife's grave that I had nothing to do with his death—or the deaths of Knox's family. All I meant was that certain people believed I had the motive to do it."

"Why? What motive?"

"You must understand something, Ms. Bonnard. I am a Macedonian patriot. This whole region used to be Macedonia, but then it was cut up by the Treaty of Bucharest and handed out to Serbia, Bulgaria, and Greece. I have made it my life's work to undo that gross injustice. But others, men like Pavlos, believe this region rightly belongs to Greece, and they try to stop me. Pavlos was skilled at insinuation. He wanted an inquiry into my life and businesses not because he thought me corrupt, but because he knew it would leave an indelible smear. When he died, the pressure for an inquiry died with him. So you can understand why people believed I was responsible. But I was not responsible, I assure you. I never even considered Pavlos my enemy, only my opponent, and there is a world of difference between the two. Even if I were a man of violence, which I am not, I would never have sanctioned it against Pavlos. And the truth is, I had no need." He leaned closer. "Can I trust you never to tell Elena what I am about to reveal to you?"

"Yes."

"Good. Pavlos had been indiscreet, and I had irrefutable evidence of this. The release of this information would have been . . . *problematic* for him. We had spoken together about it. I assure you, he was no longer a threat to me."

"So you say."

"Yes. So I say." There was a trace of impatience in his manner. "Tell me something, Ms. Bonnard. You have been working closely with Elena Koloktronis these past three weeks. Do you really believe that she'd work for me if she thought me guilty of murdering her husband?"

Gaille thought about it for a moment, but there was only one answer. "No."

"And you should understand, Ms. Bonnard, Pavlos was everything to Elena. Trust me: If she believed me responsible for Pavlos's death, she would make sure the whole world knew about it."

"She would have spoken out?"

"Oh, no," Dragoumis grunted. "She'd have killed me." He smiled at Gaille's startled reaction. "It's a fact," he said. "It would have been a blood matter, which is still a powerful force in this region. But when you consider how intensely she loved him . . ." He shook his head. "I was half fearing she'd do something. So much grief needs venting.

But, you see, she knew the truth of it. Her husband was a wild and reckless driver who never serviced his car. No. Elena was brokenhearted, but not a problem. It was your father's young friend, Knox, who was the problem."

"Knox? In what way?"

"He believed I'd murdered his whole family to silence Pavlos," said Dragoumis. "He didn't think I should get away with that. It isn't hard to understand his point of view. So he took up Pavlos's campaign himself. He wrote endlessly to local politicians, newspapers, TV stations. He picketed government buildings and police stations. He spray-painted 'Dragoumis Inquiry' in huge letters outside my head office. He printed it on helium balloons, threw leaflets from tall buildings, draped banners over railings at televised sporting events, rang radio shows and—"

"Knox? Knox did all this?"

"Oh, yes," nodded Dragoumis. "It was impressive, especially when you consider that he believed me quite capable of murder. And damaging, too. He cut a sympathetic figure, as you can imagine. He got people talking. I asked him to stop, but he refused. He was deliberately trying to goad me into doing something rash, as though that would prove his case. I grew worried for him; he was only doing this because he was sick with grief. And there were people, sympathetic with my cause, who wanted to silence him. It reached a point where I couldn't guarantee his safety anymore. And if anything happened to him . . . you can imagine. I needed him gone, but he refused to listen to me. So I looked to someone he would listen to."

"My father," said Gaille numbly.

"He was a close friend of the Knoxes, and I knew him,

too. I asked him to come speak with me. He was reluctant at first, since Mallawi had been about to start, as you know. But I assured him it was a matter of life and death. He flew in and we struck a deal: he'd take Knox away and keep him quiet, while I'd put out the word that Knox wasn't to be touched. Your father visited Knox's hotel, where Knox apparently gave him a speech about standing up to tyrants. Your father listened politely and slipped knockout drops into his retsina. By the time he woke, they were both captive on a slow boat to Port Said, and your father had time to talk sense into him. And that, Ms. Bonnard, is why I feel badly about your falling-out with your father. It would never have happened, you see, had I not asked him to intervene for me."

IN THE RAS EL-SUDR BAR, Rick nodded slowly as he digested Knox's account of his feud with the Dragoumises and how he'd come to Egypt with Richard Mitchell. "And here I was thinking you were just another quiet Yank," he said. "Do you have any other international gangsters on your trail, or is that the lot?"

"That's the lot—as far as I know, at least. But guess who I saw this afternoon?"

"This man Dragoumis?"

"His son. Nicolas."

"And he's as bad?"

"Worse. Much worse. I don't much like the father, but

you've got to admire what he's achieved. And he has principles, too. When he gives his word, he keeps it. The son's just a wanker with an inheritance, you know?"

"All too well. So you figure this desert 'lynching' was the son getting his own back?"

"Probably."

"And you're not going to take that lying down, are you?"

"No."

Rick grinned. "Cracking. So what's our plan?"

"*Our* plan?"

"Come on, mate, you're outnumbered. You could use some help. And Sharm's dead, like I say."

Knox nodded. "If you're serious, it would be fantastic."

"Absolutely. So what's our first move?"

"We head up to Tanta."

"Tanta?"

"Yes," said Knox, checking his watch. "And we're on a bit of a deadline, too, so how about I explain when we get there?"

DRAGOUMIS LED GAILLE through to his dining room. It was a vast space, with a long walnut table running down its middle. Two places had been set at one end, lit by candles. A servant was waiting by a trolley to serve their food, a dark and meaty stew swimming with unfamiliar spices.

"Forgive my simple tastes," said Dragoumis as he began to eat. "I have never developed a refined palate. If it's haute cuisine you enjoy, you must dine with my son."

"I'm sure it'll be delicious," said Gaille, prodding at her meal uncertainly with her fork. "Excuse me, Mr. Dragoumis, but I'm curious. Did you fly me all this way just to talk about my father?"

"No," said Dragoumis. "I flew you here to ask for your help."

"My help?" she frowned. "With what?"

Dragoumis leaned forward. Candlelight struck his eyes obliquely, making his dark-brown irises appear flecked with gold. "This so-called Alexander cipher talks of a tomb in Siwa filled with goods fit for the son of Ammon."

"But . . . how do you know about that?"

Dragoumis waved her question impatiently aside. "The cipher also says that the shield bearers killed themselves before Ptolemy had a chance to . . . *learn* from them where this tomb was."

"Yes."

"Have you ever heard of such a tomb? A tomb in Siwa filled with goods fit for a man like Alexander?"

"No."

"Then it remains to be discovered?"

"If it ever existed."

"It existed," stated Dragoumis. "It exists. Tell me, Ms. Bonnard, would it not be something to discover it? Can you imagine what goods might be considered fit for such a man, the greatest conqueror in history? The weapons he was given from the Trojan wars? His personal copy of Homer, annotated by Aristotle? Be honest: do you not *yearn* to be the one to find it? Fame. Wealth. Admiration. You'd never again need to ask yourself in the dark hours of the morning what your purpose is upon this earth."

"You misunderstand how these things work," said Gaille. "Ibrahim Beyumi is reporting all this to the secretary general of the SCA. What happens next will be up to them. And it won't include me."

"Perhaps you have not heard. Elena was at this meeting, too."

"Yes, but—"

"And she has persuaded the secretary general that she is the best person to lead this search."

"What? But . . . how?"

"Elena is skilled at negotiation, believe me. However, she is not so skilled at other aspects of archaeology. That is why I asked you here. I want you to go to Siwa with Elena. I want you to find this tomb for me."

"Me?"

"Yes. You have a gift, as your father did."

"You overestimate my—"

"You discovered the lower chamber, didn't you?"

"Actually, that was—"

"And you deciphered the inscription."

"Someone else would have deciphered—"

"Humility does not impress me, Ms. Bonnard," he said. "Success impresses me. Elena has many virtues, but she lacks imagination and empathy. These are your gifts. They are gifts our cause needs."

"Your cause?"

"You think it old-fashioned to have a cause?"

"I think 'cause' is a politician's word for bloodshed,"

said Gaille. "I don't think archaeology should be about causes. I think it should be about the truth."

"Very well," nodded Dragoumis. "How about this truth? My grandfathers were both born in Greater Macedonia. By the time they were men, one was Serbian, the other Greek. To people like you, people without causes, it may seem an excellent thing that families like mine can be cut up and parceled out like slaves. But one group of people feels strongly that this is not acceptable. Can you guess, perhaps, who these people are?"

"I imagine you mean those people who call themselves Macedonian," answered Gaille weakly.

"I do not seek to change your mind, Ms. Bonnard," said Dragoumis. "I simply ask you this question: who, in truth, should decide who a person is—they themselves or someone else?" He paused, perhaps to give her a chance to respond, but she found she had nothing to say. "I believe that there's a legitimate nation of Greater Macedonia," he continued. "I believe that this nation has been illegally divided between Bulgaria, Serbia, and Greece. I believe that the Macedonian people have been unfairly oppressed for centuries, that they've suffered decades of ethnic cleansing, that they are persecuted still because they have no voice, no power. Hundreds of thousands in this region agree with me, as do millions more across the world. They share culture, history, religion, and language with each other, not the states to whom they've been allocated. They call themselves Macedonian, whatever world opinion tells them they're called. I believe these people deserve the same rights to liberty, religion, self-determination, and justice that you take for granted.

These people are my cause. They are why I ask your help." His gaze seemed to grow in intensity as he looked at her; there was something almost triumphal about it, about his self-certainty. She tried not to meet his eyes, but she couldn't help herself. "And you will give it," he said.

Chapter Twenty-four

KNOX WAS KEEN to stash his Jeep somewhere Nessim wouldn't easily find it. He turned down a narrow country lane just south of Tanta, Rick following in his Subaru. Then they drove in convoy for fifteen minutes or so, until he saw in the moonlight a line of derelict farm buildings in an overgrown field used as a makeshift dump site. Perfect. He lurched his way down a rutted earth track to a yard of broken concrete. A row of barns stood along the opposite side, open to the elements, their floors muddy, their corners filled with windblown litter, their mouths blocked by a line of drinking troughs partially filled with rainwater. To his left was a low, ugly concrete-block outbuilding with a wide steel door that screeched on the concrete when they swung it open on its hinges. The building was empty inside except for the pungent smell of spilled diesel and urine, and white splashes of bat and bird droppings on the floor. Knox parked inside, took everything he might need to the Subaru, then covered the Jeep with his tarpaulin.

"You ready to explain now?" prompted Rick as they started for Tanta.

"Sure," said Knox. "Did I ever tell you about my Mallawi excavation?"

Rick snorted. "Did you ever stop?"

"Then you'll remember the basics," said Knox, opening his laptop and checking the CDs Rick had brought. "Richard Mitchell and I found an archive of Ptolemaic papyri. We passed them for safekeeping to Yusuf Abbas, now secretary general of the SCA. He liked what he saw so much, he took over the whole excavation."

"And then you spotted some of the papyri on the black market."

"Exactly. Now, there isn't a wide market for Ptolemaic papyri, even with good provenance. But *stolen* papyri? I mean, most of the usual buyers are academic institutions, and they won't touch anything hot. But Philip Dragoumis is interested in anything Macedonian, particularly if it's got a connection with Alexander."

"And you think these papyri do?"

"I think there's a good chance. The names Kelonymos and Akylos cropped up in a lot of the Mallawi papyri. Look." He turned the laptop around so that Rick could see the list of file names, dominated by "Akylos" and "Kelonymus." "And we found these same two names in a necropolis in Alexandria, and there's no doubt that *they're* related to Alexander. Akylos was one of Alexander's shield bearers, and Kelonymus was his brother. And Nicolas and Elena recognized the name Kelonymus yesterday. I'll swear to that."

"Okay. So there's a link between the Mallawi papyri and

this Alexandrian tomb of yours. But that doesn't explain what we're doing in Tanta."

"The Dragoumis Group is funding an excavation near here. They're not people to sponsor just any dig, not in a foreign country. They're looking for something specific." They reached the hotel that had acknowledged Elena as a guest, then parked across the street to monitor its front door. "I think it's all part of why Nicolas came personally to see the tomb in Alexandria, which means it has to be important. I want to know what it is. But I can't exactly just ring up and ask. All the excavation crew have signed confidentiality agreements, so no one's going to talk, particularly not to me."

"Ah," said Rick, nodding at the hotel. "But they're staying there, are they?"

"Exactly. And in an hour or two, they'll set off for their day's work, so we're going to follow."

ELENA WOKE EARLY, sunlight streaming in the open window of Augustin's apartment, noises reaching them from below: cars starting, doors slamming, families bickering. She had had every intention of breaking it off with Augustin when she returned to Alexandria late last night, before their fling could grow serious. But then he had appeared at her hotel room to take her out to dinner, and he smiled that smile at her, and she suffered an exquisite cramp in her stomach, and she knew that she'd been fooling herself.

She lay there, staring fondly at him. It was strange—and utterly unfair—how men could look beautiful even when a complete mess. His hair was a medusa of lank snakes all over his face, and a thin trail of saliva leaked from the corner of his mouth to darken the pillow. Yet still she desired him. For the first time in a decade, she found herself helpless with lust. And to think, she and Gaille were off to Siwa later this morning! She needed to make the most of their remaining time together.

She drew back the cotton sheet, the better to look at him. She reached down and began to tickle softly the inside of his thigh from just above his knee rising all the way up to his scrotum. He swelled, unpeeled, and flopped upward onto his belly. A wicked grin spread across his face, though his eyes were still closed, and not a word was said. She kissed him on his brow, his nose, his cheek, his mouth. His breath tasted sour but not at all unpleasant. Gradually their embraces grew more intimate, both too eager to wait. He turned onto his side and fumbled in his bedside table for a condom, which he tore open with his teeth and unrolled deftly with one hand. He grimaced as he forced himself inside her, resting his weight on both hands, holding himself up high. He half withdrew, jiggled and teased, so that she ached for him and pulled him back in. She craned up her neck so that she could look down at the point of junction between them, the long, hard, dark shadow of him drawing out of her, pushing slowly back in. She'd forgotten what a mesmerizing sight fucking could be—so ruthlessly animal, so distinct from all the effete ritual of romance that surrounded it. He pushed her back down and they stared hard into each other's eyes until it was too much for her, and she twisted and cried out as she came, and they spilled together onto the floor. They lay there for half a minute or so, wrapped together, grinning, gathering breath. He jumped up easily to his feet. "Coffee?" he asked.

"Chocolate."

He padded naked to his kitchen, discarding his condom into an overflowing wastebasket. A pearly strand depended from his penis, so he wiped it dry with a paper towel, then checked his fridge. *"Merde!"* He scowled. "No milk."

"Come back to bed," she complained. "I have to go collect Gaille from the airport soon."

"I need coffee," he protested. "I need croissants." He pulled on yesterday's trousers and shirt. "One minute only, I promise."

She watched him walk out the front door. Something like happiness swelled in her chest. All these years of sating her desires with milksops and fops. Christ, but it felt good to have a real man in her life again.

IT WAS HARD WORK STAYING AWAKE, so Knox bought two cups of sludge coffee for Rick and himself from the first café to lift its shutters. Four men and three women in work clothes came down the hotel steps, where they joined a number of Egyptians who had been loitering outside. They all climbed aboard two flatbed trucks, squeezing up front or stretching out in the back. One of the men did a quick head count; then they lumbered away along the road toward the town of Zagazig.

Rick gave them twenty seconds' head start, then followed. Tailing people was easy in Egypt. There were so few roads, you could afford to hang well back. The trucks turned toward Zifta, then down a farm road. Rick waited until they were nothing but a cloud of dust, then headed after them. They drove for another two or three kilometers before they saw one of the trucks parked, and no one in sight.

"Let's get out of here before we're spotted," suggested Knox.

Rick wheeled around and they headed off. "Where now?"

"I don't know about you," yawned Knox, "but I haven't slept in two days. I vote we find ourselves a hotel."

THE DAY HAD PASSED with wretched slowness for Mohammed el-Dahab, but now it was late afternoon, and time was almost up. He paced back and forth outside the cancer ward of Alexandria's Medical Research Institute. At times he sucked great heaves of air into his lungs; at others his breathing became so short and shallow he thought he would faint. Waiting for the phone call with the test results had been grueling enough, but nothing like this. He walked to the window, stared blindly out over the night-lit city, the harbor. So many millions of people, none of whom he cared one jot for. Let Allah take them all but leave him Layla.

Dr. Serag-Al-Din had given them good news. He had found an HLA match: Basheer, a third cousin of Nur's mother, who herself had come close to death when her Cairo apartment block collapsed years ago. Mohammed had thought nothing of it at the time, had been completely indifferent to her life or death. But if she had died . . . He closed his eyes and brought a fist up to his mouth. It didn't bear thinking about.

But the HLA match meant nothing in itself. It mattered only if Professor Rafai now granted Layla a berth for a bone marrow transplant. Mohammed was here to learn of his decision.

"*Insha' Allah, insha' Allah,*" muttered Mohammed again and again. The mantra did him little good. If only Nur were here—someone who understood. But Nur hadn't been able to face it. She was at home nursing Layla, more terrified even than he. "*Insha' Allah,*" he muttered. "*Insha' Allah.*"

The door of the oncology ward swung open. A plump young nurse with huge brown eyes came out. Mohammed tried to read her expression, but it was beyond him. "Will you come with me, please," she said.

Chapter Twenty-five

KAREEM BARAK'S FEET WERE RAW AND ACH-ING. Too much tramping these wretched roads in tight boots with leaky soles. He cursed himself for having answered Abdullah's summons and for agreeing to his terms. One hundred dollars to whoever found this one wretched Jeep! It had seemed too good to be true. But when Abdullah had assigned districts to search, he received this godforsaken stretch of farmland. How the others had sniggered! As if anyone would park out here! He ought just to give up, but those dollars had him by the throat. For Abdullah to offer a one-hundred-dollar reward, he had to be looking to make five or ten times that himself, which meant opportunities for a smart young man like Kareem to exploit. But first he needed some luck.

It was dusk when he saw the farm track and the ramshackle buildings some two hundred meters along it. The way his feet burned, it might as well have been two hundred kilometers. He had a sudden craving for a huge bowl of his aunt's *kushari* with extra fried onions, mopped up with

great chunks of *aysh baladi,* then the welcoming embrace of
his mattress. No way was the Jeep down there. Enough! He
scowled and turned, hobbling painfully back the way he had
come. But he'd barely gone twenty steps when a minibus
of schoolgirls rattled past. One of them caught his eye and
smiled shyly. She had good skin and huge brown eyes and
luscious red lips. Staring after her, he forgot all about *kushari*
and bed and aching feet. That was what he truly wanted: a
beautiful, coy young woman to call his own. And for all his
romantic dreams, he was a realist enough to know he would
never have one until he earned some serious money.

He turned yet again and made the painful trudge up the
track to the farm buildings.

MOHAMMED FOUND IT DIFFICULT even to walk as
he followed the nurse. He had to remind himself how it
was done: one foot and then the other. She led him to a
large office, where Professor Rafai was flicking through
the dividers of a white filing cabinet. Mohammed had
seen him often on his rounds but had never before been
granted a private audience. Mohammed didn't know how
to read this. Some men delighted in granting good news;
others felt it their duty to break bad. Rafai turned to Mohammed with a bland, professional smile that gave nothing away. "Sit, sit," he said, gesturing to his small round
corner table. He pulled out a brown folder and came to
join him. "I hope you've not been waiting long."

Mohammed swallowed. Did Rafai truly not understand? Then, suddenly, all Mohammed wanted was to go back outside and wait some more. When hope was all a man had, he fought hard to hold on to it. Rafai opened the brown folder and peered through his half-moon glasses at a sheet inside. He frowned as though he had just read something of which he had previously been unaware. "You understand what a bone marrow transplant would have involved?" he asked without looking up. "You understand what you were asking me to put your daughter through?"

It was a numb feeling, catastrophe. Mohammed felt cold and sick, yet at the same time immensely calm. He wondered bleakly how he would break this to Nur, if Layla would understand what it meant.

Rafai proceeded remorselessly: "We call this procedure bone marrow transplantation, but that is misleading. In ordinary chemotherapy we target only cancerous fast-dividing cells, but in this procedure we deliberately poison a person's entire system in order to destroy *all* their fast-dividing cells, cancerous or otherwise. That includes the bone marrow. The transplant is not the treatment. The transplant is necessary because after we annihilate all these fast-dividers, the patient will die without new marrow. It is a traumatic and extremely painful experience, without guarantee of success. Rejections occur despite perfect matches. And even if the new marrow takes, convalescence is extensive. Tests, tests, always tests. This is not the treatment of a few days. Scars stay for life. And then there's infertility, cataract blindness,

secondary cancers, complications in the liver, kidneys,
lungs, heart . . ."

Mohammed understood something then. Rafai wasn't
here because the task was difficult; he was here because
he relished exercising power. Mohammed reached forward to push down Rafai's folder. "Say what you have to
say," he demanded. "Say it straight. Look me in the eye."

Rafai sighed. "You must understand that we cannot
give a bone marrow transplant to every patient who needs
it. We allocate our resources on the basis of clinical evidence, on who will be most likely to benefit. I am afraid
the lymphoma has advanced so far in your daughter—"

"Because you would not do the tests in time!" cried
Mohammed. "Because you would not do the tests!"

"You must understand that everyone here loves
your—"

Mohammed rose to his feet. "When did you decide
this? Did you decide *before* we did the tests? You did,
didn't you? Why didn't you tell us? Why did you let us
go through that?"

"You're wrong," said Rafai. "We didn't make the
final—"

"Is there anything I can do?" pleaded Mohammed.
"Anything at all? I beg you. Please. You can't do this."

"I'm sorry." He smiled blandly. The interview was
over.

Mohammed had never previously understood failed
suicides; the ones commonly described as cries for help.
But in a moment of insight he realized that some conversations were simply too difficult to broach without some
kind of act to demonstrate the overwhelming strength of

feeling involved. He couldn't face Nur and Layla with this news. It was beyond him. So he picked Rafai up by the lapels of his jacket instead and slammed him against his office wall.

IT WAS A GOOD SEVEN-HOUR DRIVE from Alexandria to Siwa Oasis, where Elena and Gaille were due to begin a survey of antiquities as cover for their search for Alexander's tomb. It was an uninspiring journey, too, first heading west along the scrubby, overbuilt Mediterranean coast, then south through flat and empty desert, with nothing to see for mile after mile but the occasional service station or herd of wild camels, until they topped a rise and the relentless emptiness was suddenly broken by glittering white salt lakes and orchards of silver-green.

They pulled into Siwa's market square as a muezzin called the faithful to prayer, and the sun vanished behind the dark rose ruins of the old Shali Fortress. The streets here were wide, spacious, and dusty. There were few cars or trucks. People walked, cycled, or took donkey carts. After the bustle of Alexandria, Siwa seemed gloriously leisurely and content. Gaille rolled down her window and inhaled deeply. Her spirits lifted. Siwa was truly the end of the road. There was nothing beyond it but the great Sea of Sand. The oasis had no purpose but itself.

They found available places in a hotel located in a date

palm orchard. Their rooms were newly painted, clean, and polished, with sparkling windows and gleaming bathrooms. Gaille took a shower and put on some fresh clothes; then Elena knocked on her door, and they set off to visit Dr. Aly Sayed, Siwa's representative of the Supreme Council for Antiquities.

KNOX AND RICK ducked down in the front seats of the Subaru as one of the flatbed trucks left for the night, its headlights flickering over the grove of trees where they had hidden. A good day's sleep had recharged Knox's batteries, and his laptop's, too. He reopened it once the flatbed had driven off, resuming his study of the Mallawi papyri, fragments of ancient letters, and other documents.

"I reckon the other one must have already left," said Rick. "I mean, they can't excavate in the dark."

"Let's give it ten minutes, just to be safe."

Rick pulled a face but let it go. "How you getting on?" he asked.

"Not too bad." His laptop screen was old and fuzzy. The photographs had been taken for cataloging purposes, not for decipherment. The lighting was variable, to put it kindly. Most of the papyri were completely unreadable. Yet he could still make out occasional words and even phrases, many of them in a recognizable hand, so written by a single person. Often they were vague, almost deliberately so, such as "and then the thing happened that brought me to Mallawi." Elsewhere, the author referred again and again to "the enlightened," "the truth bearer," "the knowledgeable," "the holder of the secret." And in other places they were downright treasonous. "I don't know who wrote this," he told Rick, "but he wasn't very respectful."

"How do you mean?"

"Ptolemaic pharaohs were all called Ptolemy, so they distinguished themselves by their cult titles instead. For example, the first Ptolemy was known as Soter, the Greek word for 'savior.' But here he's referred to as Sotades."

"Sotades?"

"A scurrilous Alexandrian Greek poet and playwright. Wrote a lot of homoerotic verse, invented the palindrome, then got himself into trouble for mocking Ptolemy Two Philadelphos for marrying his sister. Speaking of which, Philadelphos actually means 'sister lover,' but he's referred to here as 'sin-lover.' Ptolemy Euergetes, 'the benefactor,' is 'the malefactor.' Philopator, 'the father loving,' is 'the lie-building.' Epiphanes, 'the manifest god,' is 'the manifest fraud.' You get the idea?"

"Not exactly the world's greatest satirist, was he?"

"No. But even *referring* to the Ptolemies like this . . ."

Rick leaned forward in his seat, squinting through his windshield into the moonlit night, impatient to get moving. "They must have left by now," he muttered, turning on his ignition. "Let's go in."

"Five more minutes."

"Okay," grumbled Rick, turning the engine off again.

He leaned across to look at the laptop. "What else are you finding?"

"Lots of place names. Tanis, Buto, Busiris, Mendes. All important Delta towns. But the place that comes up by far the most is Lycopolis."

"Lycopolis. City of the Wolves, yeah?"

"It was the Greek name for ancient Asyut," nodded Knox. Asyut was some fifty miles south of Mallawi, where the papyri had been found, so it made some sense. But all the other place names were in the Nile Delta, well over a hundred miles north of Asyut. Besides, something was knocking at his memory, and it wasn't Asyut.

Another pair of headlights came down the farm track. They both ducked again. "Looks like you were right," grinned Rick, his teeth glowing white. The second flatbed came to a complete stop as it reached the road, waiting for a car to pass. They could hear its turn signal clicking, and the tired banter of laborers in the back, glad that a long day was over. Then it pulled out onto the Tanta road and was gone. "Right," said Rick, turning the ignition on once more. "Let's do it, yeah?"

"Yes."

The moon was bright enough for them to drive with only their sidelights on, not wanting to advertise their presence yet not wanting to look unduly stealthy, either. They reached the line of trees where the flatbed had parked earlier. A stake hammered into the ground declared in Arabic and English that this was a restricted area, reserved by the Supreme Council for Antiquities in partnership with the Macedonian Archaeological Foundation. They retreated a little way, concealed the Subaru in a small copse, then went searching. Rick had been out shopping while Knox had slept, and now he handed Knox a flashlight, though it was light enough not to need it. A cool breeze rustled and whispered in the branches. A bird hooted. They could see the static umber glow of a distant settlement, and yellow headlights crisscrossing on a road. Their boots balled up with soil as they crossed a field. In its far corner they found a site in midexcavation, a honeycomb of roped-off four-by-four-meter pits divided by balk walls, then a series of emptied graves, each a meter deep, their contents removed, their bases hidden in shadow from the slanting moonlight, freshly dug earth by their sides. It took them barely fifteen minutes to check it all out. "Not exactly the Valley of the Kings, is it?" muttered Rick.

"You can't expect them to—"

"Shhhh!" went Rick suddenly, crouching down, a finger to his lips. Knox turned to look at what had caught Rick's eye. Several seconds later, he saw it: a small orange glow moving between the trees. "Two people," whispered Rick. "Sharing a smoke." He motioned at an empty grave, its foot in darkness. Knox nodded. They climbed down inside, watching over the rim as two men in dark uniforms and caps advanced. Private security contractors, rather than army or police, but with black holsters on their belts. One of them was holding the leash of a huge German shepherd, growling and baring its fangs as if it had caught a scent but wasn't yet quite sure of what. His companion was curious enough to turn on his flashlight, which he shone around as they drew closer, discussing some TV movie they both had watched earlier. Rick smeared earth on his hands and the back of his neck and gestured for Knox to do likewise; then they lay motionless and facedown in the grave as the two guards walked right up to them, the German shepherd getting thoroughly excited but being hauled back and cursed at. A flare of light bloomed in the bottom of the grave, then was gone. A still lit cigarette butt landed by Knox's cheek. One of the men, while talking to his companion, unzipped his trousers and took a leak on the earth above, the splash-off spattering around Knox and Rick, while his companion made lewd comments about some actress he fancied. Then the two men turned and trudged away, dragging the agitated dog with them.

Rick was first to stir. "Fuck me, that was close," he muttered.

"We should get out of here," said Knox.

"Ballocks," said Rick. "Two men and a German shepherd guarding an empty field—I want to see what they're *really* protecting."

"They had guns, mate," said Knox.

"Exactly," grinned Rick. "This is getting interesting."

"I don't want you getting hurt," said Knox. "Not on my account."

"Fuck that; I haven't had this much fun in years." And he set off before Knox could argue further, keeping low to the ground, using his experience to find the stealthiest path. Knox followed, grateful to have such a friend. The moon made ghostly shadows through the trees as they mounted a gentle but lengthy rise. He glimpsed gray ahead and pointed it out. Rick nodded and motioned for

Knox to stay where he was. He vanished for a minute before reappearing out of the shadows. "Two buildings," he whispered. "One large, one small. Made of concrete block. No windows. Steel doors. Padlocks. But both guards are outside the small one. That's the one we need to get inside."

"I thought you said it was a concrete-block building with no windows. How the fuck are we going to get inside?"

Rick grinned. "You'll see."

GAILLE AND ELENA found Dr. Aly Sayed easily enough. He lived in an impressive two-story house at the end of a narrow tree-lined lane. A dark man with snowy hair, eyebrows, and trimmed beard sat outside, a tumbler in one hand, a bulbous fountain pen in the other, his tabletop spread with papers. "Hola!" he cried cheerfully. "You must be my secretary general's friends." He rested his tumbler on his papers to stop them from being blown away, then bounded across. Siwa had been on the ancient slave route, and he clearly had Negro as well as Arab blood, which he seemed to emphasize deliberately with his open sandals, khaki shorts, and short-sleeved gold and scarlet shirt.

"You must be Ms. Koloktronis," he said to Elena, shaking her hand. "And Gaille Bonnard," he said, turning to her. "Yes! Your father's eyes."

Gaille was shocked. "I beg your pardon?"

"You are not Richard Mitchell's daughter?"

"Yes, but—"

"Good! When Yusuf tell me to expect Elena Kolok-tronis and Gaille Bonnard, I think to myself, ah, yes, I recognize this name! When your father dies in his terrible fall, I post to you I think a great package of papers and belongings. You received it, I trust?"

"That was you? Yes. Thank you."

Aly nodded. "Your father was my very good friend. He stay with me often. You are welcome for your own sake, of course. But the daughter of such a good man is a thousand times welcome."

"Thank you."

"Though I must say I am surprised that Yusuf Abbas commended you so warmly to me." He raised an eyebrow. "It couldn't be that he is unaware of who your father is, could it?"

"I don't know," blushed Gaille, who always felt slightly awkward when her father was discussed in Egypt.

"Perhaps I should tell him myself next time we speak," he mused. But then he saw her expression, and touched her elbow. "Of course you know I'm joking. I would never do such a thing. You have my word. Now, come inside. You'll honor and adorn my humble home. Inside! Inside!"

Gaille and Elena exchanged a glance as they followed. They hadn't expected such an exuberant welcome. He slapped his hand against the rough yellow exterior wall. "Kharshif," he announced. "Mud and salt. Strong like rock but with one weakness. She turn back into mud again when she rain!" He put his hands on his sides and laughed uproariously. "Fortunately, she not rain like this often in Siwa. Not since 1985! Now Siwa is all one concrete block." He thumped his chest. "Me, I like the old ways." His front door opened onto a long hallway. Framed photographs jostled for space. More were stacked on the floor. Discolored patches from previous hangings showed that he often changed them around. He wasn't camera shy, that was for sure. He appeared in picture after picture: Discussing excavation matters on-site; out hunting with an army officer, holding up a white gazelle with a gunshot wound in its head; in mountaineering kit halfway up some cliff; sightseeing in Paris, St. Louis, Granada, and other cities she couldn't place; shaking hands with dignitaries, celebrities, and Egypt experts. Not an ego wall so much as an ego house.

They reached his kitchen, its broad fireplace open to the night sky. A huge old yellowing refrigerator clicked on as they entered, and began to rattle loudly. He kicked it, and the rattling became more subdued. "A drink?" he suggested. "You may not know, but Siwa is dry of alcohol. Our young men enjoy too much the labgi, the alcohol we make from dates, and labgi makes them enjoy too much each other, so no more alcohol! In this sense, however, *my* house is the oasis!" Gaille found his boisterous good humor disconcerting, as though he was laughing up his sleeve at them. He opened the refrigerator door to reveal a jungle of fresh fruit and vegetables inside, stacks of beer and white wine. He wagged a finger at Gaille. "Your father teach me wicked habits. A terrible thing, the love of alcohol. Each time I run low

I must invent SCA business in Cairo, and I *hate* Cairo. It means I have to pay respects to my secretary general, and, believe me, that is a privilege made all the greater by its rarity."

He poured them drinks, led them back to the hallway, where he unlocked a blue door, pushed it open, flipped on a light, and stood aside. A wave of delicious cool air wafted out. The room was large and lushly carpeted. A single heavy air-conditioning unit stood hissing beneath the closed, bolted, and shuttered windows. A computer, a flatbed scanner, and a color printer rested on two archival tables next to three gray steel filing cabinets and white-painted shelving stacked with books above locked glass-fronted cabinets. She noted the straight lines on the walls. There was no risk of this room, at least, turning back into mud. "I understand you're here to research our old sites, yes?" He waved his hand. "My collection is at your service. If it is published about Siwa and the Western Desert, it is here. And if not published, also."

"You're extremely kind," said Elena.

He waved her thanks away. "We're all archaeologists here. Why would we keep secrets from one another?"

"Do you have photographs?"

"Of course." He opened the top drawer of a filing cabinet, withdrew a large map, and spread it out. Grid lines ran north to south and east to west, giving each square a unique reference number that corresponded to an indexed folder in the cabinets, which contained grainy black-and-white aerial photographs as well as occasional color, ground-level site prints. While he explained his system to Elena, Gaille wandered along the shelves, fingering sheaves of press cuttings on the golden mummies of Baharriya; histories of Kharga, Dakhla, and Farafra and of the geology of desert. Two entire ranges had been given over to Siwa, the shelves packed so tight that she had to pull hard to pluck out a first edition copy of Qibell's *A Visit to Siwa.* She turned the crumbling yellow pages with great tenderness. She loved the whimsy in the accounts of pioneer travelers like this.

"You know these?" murmured Aly, suddenly at her side.

"Not all of them," she admitted. "In fact . . ."

He laughed warmly, then stooped to unlatch and open a low cabinet. Inside, wire racks bulged with gray and tan folders of loose papers. Notebooks and journals were stacked in separate piles. He found and removed a thick green folder and handed it to her. "You know the Siwan Manuscript? The history of our Oasis kept by the Mosalims since . . ." he waved his hand to indicate forever. "These notes in red pen are mine. You'll find them valuable, I think." He set the folder down and returned to his books. "Ah, yes! Ahmed Fakhry. A great man. My mentor and my very good friend. You have read his works?"

"Yes." It was the only research she'd managed so far.

"Excellent. Ah! And this! W. G. Browne's *Travels in Africa, Egypt and Syria from the year 1792 to 1798.* The first European for centuries to visit Siwa—or to write of it, at least. He thought us nasty, dirty people, while we hurled stones at him because he pretended to be a man of faith. How far the world has come! Here's Belzoni, ev-

eryone's favorite circus strongman. And Frederick Horne-
mann—German, of course, but he wrote in English. His
journey was sponsored by the London African Society in,
let me see, yes, 1798."

"Is there nothing more up-to-date?"

"Of course, of course. Many books. Copies of
every excavation log. But, believe me, when these old
people visit, our monuments and tombs were in much
better condition. Now many are nothing but dust and
sand. *'My name is Ozymandias, King of Kings.'* " He
sighed, shook his head sadly. "So much lost. You read
German, yes?"

"Yes."

"Good. One never knows these days. Even reputa-
ble universities seem to hand out doctorates to people
who can barely speak their own language. Here is J. C.
Ewald Falls's *Siwa: Die Oase des Sonnengottes in der
Libyschen Wüste.* Cailliaud's *Voyage à Meroe;* you must
read that. And that criminal Drovetti! I had to travel to
Turin to see the Canon of Kings. *Turin!* Worse even than
Cairo! They tried to kill me with their trams!"

"When can we start?" asked Elena.

"When you would like?"

"Tonight."

"Tonight!" laughed Aly. "Do you never relax?"

"We only have two weeks."

"Not tonight, I'm afraid," said Aly. "I have plans. But
I'm an early riser. You're welcome here at any time from
seven."

"Thank you."

RICK AND KNOX CIRCLED DOWNWIND so that the German shepherd wouldn't catch their scent. It was another ninety minutes before the guards set off on their rounds once more. The moment they were gone, Rick hurried into the clearing and over to the smaller building. He examined its two hefty padlocks, produced a hooked length of thick steel wire from his pocket, then proceeded swiftly to unlock them both.

"Where in hell did you learn that?" murmured Knox.

"Australian Special Forces, mate," grinned Rick, pocketing the padlocks and ushering him inside. "They don't teach knitting." There was a deep hole in the floor, a wooden ladder tied to one wall. "It's sixteen minutes to the other site," said Rick. "I timed it. Sixteen more back makes thirty-two. We need to be out of here in twenty-five tops. Okay?"

"We'd better hurry," agreed Knox, adrenaline pumping as he led the way down. The ladder creaked but held, and he was soon crunching on stone chips. Rick joined him a moment later. They walked side by side down the narrow corridor, Rick picking out a wall painting with his flashlight. "Jesus!" he muttered. "I thought Wolf-man was out of the Marvel comics."

"Not Wolf-man," corrected Knox. "Wolf *god*. Wepwawet."

Rick was looking at him strangely. "What's the matter?" he asked. "You seen a ghost?"

"Not exactly."

"Then what? Have you worked out where we are or something?"

"I think so. Yes."

"Come on, then, mate. Spill."

Knox frowned. "What do you know about the Rosetta Stone?" he asked.

Chapter Twenty-six

Boss! Boss!"

Nessim glowered at Ratib. Since they offered their reward, their phones had been ringing constantly. Knox's Jeep had been spotted everywhere from Marsa Matruh down to Aswan, as had Knox himself. Nessim was longing for a result, if only so they could call off this damned search and get some peace. But the more time that went by, the lower his hopes fell. "Yes?" he asked.

"It's Abdullah, boss," said Ratib. "You know, from Tanta. Says one of his crew has found the Jeep."

"Where?"

Ratib shook his head. "Kid won't say until he's got his money. And he wants more. Kid's demanding a thousand dollars just for himself. And Abdullah wants the same."

Nessim scowled. The money itself didn't bother him; it was Hassan's, after all. But being held to ransom did. *Yet, if this was for real . . .* He checked his money belt to see how much he had on him. "Tell him we want proof," he said. "Tell him to send photographs. If it is, they can each have seven fifty."

Ratib shook his head. "The kid refuses to go back," he said. "Reckons Abdullah will have him followed, and then he won't get anything."

Nessim barked out a laugh. He had met Abdullah twice himself, and both times he instinctively checked his pockets afterward to make sure he still had his wallet. "Ask him to describe exactly what he saw."

Ratib nodded and complied. "He says it was covered with a green tarpaulin," he reported back. "He says he took a peek inside. He says he saw a box of CDs and books."

Nessim grabbed the phone from Ratib. "What books?" he demanded.

"I don't know," answered the kid. He sounded terrified, way out of his depth. "They were in foreigner writing."

A flashback of Knox's hotel room and the archaeology books he had taken away. "Did they have pictures?"

"Yes."

"What kind?"

"Ruins," said the kid. "You know. And those people who dig in the desert."

Nessim clenched his fist. "You stay exactly where you are," he told him. "We're on our way."

"THE ROSETTA STONE?" frowned Rick, snapping a couple of shots of the painting with his digital camera before moving on. "I know what you'd expect me to know. Why?"

"And that is?"

Rick shrugged. "It's a large chunk of a monumental stela. Black basalt, something like that."

"Quartz-bearing rock," corrected Knox. "It should actually be sparkling gray with a pink vein. The black comes from too much wax and London dirt."

"It's inscribed in three languages," said Rick. "Hieroglyphics, Demotic, and Greek. And it was found in Rosetta by Napoleon's men. Seventeen ninety-nine, wasn't it?"

"Yes."

They reached a second painting, similar to the first. Rick took two shots; the flash was blinding in the darkness. "They realized it might hold the key to deciphering hieroglyphics, so they hunted for other fragments. Worth their weight in diamonds, as someone put it." He squinted at Knox. "Is that what we're after? The lost pieces of the Rosetta Stone?"

"No."

"They didn't find anything; but then the stone wasn't from Rosetta originally; it was only transported there as building material." As they walked, the walls turned black with char; great scars scored the baked clay. "One hell of a fire," muttered Rick as he photographed.

"You were telling me about the Rosetta Stone."

"Yes. Copies were made, and there was a race to decipher it. Jean-Francois Champollion made the final breakthrough. He announced his results sometime in the 1820s."

"Eighteen twenty-two. Friday, September 27, to be exact. Considered by many to be the birth date of modern Egyptology."

Rick shrugged. "That's pretty much it."

"Not bad," said Knox. "But you know what you haven't mentioned yet?"

"What?"

"The inscription itself. What it says."

Rick laughed ruefully. "You're right. How about that?"

"You're not alone. This great monument, this iconic image, and hardly anyone knows what it says."

"So what does it say?"

Knox shone his flashlight ahead. The white marble of a portal glowed pale, and on either side lay ghostly wolves. "It's known as the Memphis Decree," he said as they pressed forward. "Written to commemorate Ptolemy Five's accession in one nine six BC. The Golden Age of the Ptolemies had been well and truly over by then, of course, thanks to Ptolemy Four."

"The party animal," nodded Rick, crouching to photograph the wolves.

"Exactly. The Seleucid king Antiochus Three thought he was soft and ripe for plucking. He seized Tyre, Ptolemais, and much of the Egyptian fleet."

"Spare me the detail," said Rick. "We're on the clock, remember."

"Okay," said Knox as they moved on. "There was a

great battle at Raphia. The Egyptians won, and peace was restored to the land. It should have been good news."

"But?"

"Taxes were already punitive, but Ptolemy had to raise them even higher to finance his war and then the victory celebrations. People left their farms and homes because they couldn't afford to pay. Discord spread. There were massive uprisings across Egypt. Ptolemy Four was assassinated, and his successor, Ptolemy Five Epiphanes, was still only a child. When a group of rebels attacked military posts and temples in the Nile Delta, Epiphanes' men went after them. The rebels took refuge in a citadel."

"That's right," said Rick, snapping his fingers. "They thought they'd be safe. They were wrong."

"They were very wrong," agreed Knox as they walked down two steps to a second doorway. "According to the Rosetta Stone, Epiphanes' men stormed it and put them all to the sword."

"Charming."

"You know where it all happened? A place called Lycopolis, in the Busirite administrative district."

"The Busirite administrative district? Wasn't that pretty much where we are now?"

"Exactly," nodded Knox as they reached the portal. "Welcome to the citadel of ancient Lycopolis."

Rick went through first, his flashlight held out ahead. "Oh, Jesus!" he muttered when he saw what was inside. And he turned and looked away, as though about to be sick.

"COME," SMILED ALY SAYED. "This is no evening to waste in a library."

Gaille and Elena followed him to his outside table. A breeze had turned the evening cool. Birds twittered in the distance. Gaille listened as Elena and Aly chatted amiably, exploring connections, mutual friends, and obscure sites they both had visited. After a while, he turned to Gaille. "Your poor father," he said. "I think about him often. My esteemed secretary general did not greatly respect him, as you may know. For myself, I work only with people I respect. No man loved this country more."

"Thank you."

He smiled and turned back to Elena. "Now, tell me what it is you do in Siwa. Yusuf hinted mysteriously that you'd found something interesting in Alexandria."

"You could say that."

"And it has implications for Siwa?"

"Yes." Elena took a set of Gaille's photographs from her bag. "Forgive me, but Yusuf insisted I make you promise not to say a word."

"Of course," nodded Aly. "My lips are sealed."

"Thank you." She passed them to him, explained how they had been found and what they meant, then read out a translation of the Alexander Cipher.

"A tomb fit for Alexander," murmured Aly as he leafed through the pictures. "And you hope to find it in two weeks?"

"We hope to make progress in two weeks," said Elena. "Enough to be granted another two."

"How?"

"The text gives several clues." She ticked them off on her fingers. "It states that the tomb was in sight of the oracle of Ammon, that it was within a hill, that its mouth was beneath the sand, that it was excavated in secret. Tomorrow morning, with your permission, we'll compile a list of all hills in sight of the oracle. Then we'll visit them."

He raised his eyebrows. "Do you know how many sites that will be?"

"We can eliminate a few. This place was built in secret; that cuts out anything near ancient settlements or trading routes. And quarrying is thirsty work. They'd have needed fresh water."

"This is the oasis of a thousand springs."

"Yes. But many are salt, and most of the freshwater ones are settled."

"They could have dug their own well."

"And we'll search for it," agreed Elena. "We've a list of features to look for. For example, as you well know, you can tell quarried rock from the grooves left by the tools. Any significant quantities of such rock will be interesting. Digging in the desert is brutal. The sand's so fine and dry, it runs like liquid. Macedonian soldiers were experienced engineers, so maybe they used a cofferdam. Your aerial photos might help us find its outlines. I'm also having some remote sensing equipment shipped in: a caesium magnetometer, a remote-controlled aircraft for more aerial photographs."

Aly was still flipping through the photographs. Gaille was watching him idly when his expression froze. He caught himself almost immediately, glanced around with attempted nonchalance, then hurried through the other photographs before passing them back. "Well," he said. "I wish you luck."

Bright lights flickered between the trunks of date palms. A canvas-covered truck roared up the drive and stopped in a squeal of brakes. Aly rose to his feet. "Yusuf suggested you would need guides," he said. "I took the liberty of contacting Mustafa and Zayn for you. They are the best in all Siwa. They know everything."

"Thank you," said Elena. "That's most helpful."

"No trouble. We must work together, must we not?" The truck doors opened, and two men jumped down. Aly turned to Gaille and said, "I thought of them the moment Yusuf told me your name."

Gaille frowned. "Why?"

"Because they were the guides with your father on that terrible day, of course." And, just for a moment, all warmth left his expression. He squinted at her with an almost clinical detachment, curious of her reaction. But then he caught himself; his smile was back, and he was the perfect host again, crackling with benevolent energy, making everybody welcome.

KNOX SWUNG HIS FLASHLIGHT AROUND to see what had made Rick flinch. There were skeletons lying every-where on the floor, some of them tiny, many still wearing ragged fragments of clothing, along with jewelry and amulets. "Oh, man," grimaced Rick. "What the hell happened?"

"The siege, remember?" said Knox, more calmly than he felt. "The men would have fought. The women, children, and elderly would have taken refuge. An underground temple would have seemed perfect. Until they got shut in and someone lit a fire between them and their only escape."

"Christ! What a way to go."

Knox nodded absently as he was forcibly reminded of an incident from Alexander the Great's conquests. Samaria had risen in revolt, killing its Macedonian governor. In punishment, Alexander destroyed the city, executing every rebel he could lay his hands on, then hunting two hundred others to a desert cave. Instead of going in after them, he had built a fire in the mouth and asphyxiated them all. Their remains had recently been discovered, along with seals and legal documents that were considered the oldest cache of Dead Sea Scrolls ever found. Knox had never paid much attention to the incident, an almost inconsequential sidebar to Alexander's campaigns, but suddenly he felt an empathetic sadness for all those people who had gotten in the way of Alexander's glory juggernaut.

Rick tapped his arm. "No time for daydreaming, mate. We're down to ten minutes."

Knox tore his gaze from the huddled corpses to look around the rest of the space. It was effectively a subterranean Greek temple, with Ionic columns embedded in the exterior walls and in front of the pronaos. A wooden walkway had been set up on concrete blocks to enable excavators to move around quickly and without causing damage. Knox went into the pronaos, its walls carved with pastoral scenes, ivy, fruit, and animals, then into the naos, dominated by a white marble statue of Alexander on a rearing horse. "Look!" said Rick, pointing to the far corner. "Steps."

They led down into a crypt, a sarcophagus against the far wall, with Greek writing on its side. "Kelonymus," read Knox. "Holder of the secret, founder of the faith."

"Kelonymus?" frowned Rick. "That's your friend from the papyri, right?"

"And from Alexandria," agreed Knox. There were stone vats around the walls, filled with limestone and earthenware ostraca. Knox picked one out and squinted at the faded writing. "A petition to the gods," he said.

"So this is a temple? A temple to Kelonymus?"

Knox shook his head. "To Alexander. That's his cult statue upstairs. But Kelonymus must have been the founder or chief priest or something." He crouched down. "So what have we got?" he asked rhetorically. "An old man in Mallawi writes about his childhood in Lycopolis. He reveres Alexander, Akylos, and Kelonymus and despises the Ptolemies, dismissing them as liars and frauds. And why were Epiphanes' men so ruthless when they stormed the citadel? Everyone was slaughtered or taken for execution." He glanced at Rick. "Doesn't that smack of more than an ordinary uprising? I mean, the southern rebels were granted amnesties. So why did these people all have to be killed?"

"They knew something," suggested Rick. "They needed to be shut up."

"The holder of the secret," nodded Knox. "Must have been one hell of a secret."

"Any ideas?"

Knox frowned at the glimmer of a possible answer. "The Ptolemies were never really taken into Egyptian hearts," he said. "They were only tolerated because of their direct succession from Alexander. That's why they tried so hard to associate themselves with him. They spread rumors that Ptolemy One had been Alexander's brother, you know, and they built his great mausoleum in Alexandria partly so they themselves could lie next to him. Imagine what would have happened if the legitimacy of that succession came into question."

"I'll imagine it later, if you don't mind," said Rick, tapping his watch. "We need to scoot."

Knox nodded. They hurried up the steps, then back along the walkways and the corridor to the wooden ladder. Rick climbed it first, going for haste rather than quiet, Knox struggling to keep up. "Okay," murmured Rick, when they reached the top. "Let's do it." He opened the steel door, ushered Knox out, and padlocked it behind them. Away to their left was a flutter of lamplight and the growl of a dog. "Perfect timing," grinned Rick. But then the second guard stepped out from behind a tree directly in front of them, zipping up his pants. They all looked at each other in shock.

"Run!" cried Rick. "Run!"

Chapter Twenty-seven

Knox and Rick fled headlong into the trees, forearms up to protect their faces from slapping branches. "Stop!" cried the guard. "Stop or I shoot." A shot cracked out. "Stop!" he shouted again. But they kept running, bulling their way through the woods until they reached a tilled field, then running across it in the direction of the Subaru, their feet plunging deep into the moist soil, their boots growing heavy with accreted mud. Behind them, the German shepherd was barking crazily with excitement. A stitch began in Knox's side. He wasn't as fit as Rick, and began to fall behind. He glanced back. They'd gained good distance on the pursuers, but that damned German shepherd had their scent. "Keep going," called out Rick from ahead, sensing that Knox was flagging. "The car's not far."

They ran on for another minute before he looked around again. The night had grown overcast, but he could just make out the guards silhouetted upon a low ridge. One of them stopped to aim at Knox, snapping off a couple of rounds that cracked past, making him stumble on the heavy soil, his thighs protesting as he pushed himself back up, finding the running really hard labor now, fighting for every breath, the stitch stabbing brutally in his side, Rick getting farther and farther ahead of him.

The guards must have realized they wouldn't catch him themselves, so they unleashed the German shepherd instead, then stood and urged it on. It came bounding over the soft earth, panting as it raced up behind him, snarling and snapping at his leg. Knox twisted to kick it away, but he tripped and fell, and immediately the dog sprang on top of him, going for his throat, saliva drooling, sharp teeth snapping an inch from his face. The two guards were closing, wheezing heavily after their long chase. Knox thought he was done for, but then he heard the roar of an engine, headlights flashed on, and the Subaru raced up beside him. Rick jumped out and charged screaming at the bewildered dog, which leaped off Knox and cowered away just long enough for both men to scramble back into the car. The dog regained its nerve quickly, however, jumping up at Knox's door, barking furiously. The guards were almost on them. Rick thrust the Subaru into reverse and stomped on the gas. They zipped backward, turning in a crescent out onto the field; then Rick threw it into first and accelerated up through the gears. Gunfire cracked. Knox's side-window shattered, and the windshield turned opaque. Rick punched out a viewing hole as he raced toward the track, then toward the Tanta road. Knox looked around, but their pursuers were finally lost in the darkness. Private security guards firing off guns would scarcely be keen to contact the authorities, but maybe they had colleagues who would come out looking for the Subaru. "We'd better go for the Jeep," panted Knox.

"You think that's wise? Shouldn't we just lie low for a bit?"

Knox shook his head. "Kelonymus was constantly referred to as the holder of the secret. I want to know what that secret is. Five will get you fifty that the answer's in that damned inscription from the lower chamber in Alexandria. The one in Demotic."

"But I thought you didn't know Demotic."

"I don't," admitted Knox. "Which is why we need to go see a friend."

"Ah! And where's he, then?"

"Ever been to Farafra?"

"Farafra!" protested Rick. "But that's halfway across Egypt!"

"Then we've no time to lose, have we?"

KAREEM'S EYES BULGED when Nessim unzipped his money belt and drew out a brick of fifty-dollar bills. He had never seen so much cash. He had never even imagined it possible. He watched, entranced, as Nessim counted out fifteen notes for Abdullah, then another fifteen, which he held tantalizingly out to Kareem. "Take us to the Jeep," he said.

Kareem climbed in the back of the Freelander, whose smashed rear window was patched with plastic sheeting.

It had started raining, making it harder for Kareem to give coherent directions in the unfamiliar landscape. He had never felt so scared in his life, or so excited. He was terrified that he had somehow made a gigantic mistake or that the Jeep's owner might have returned for it in the past hour. And it wasn't just the reward that Kareem stood to lose, he knew. One look was all it took to know that Nessim and his men would want someone to vent their frustrations on.

They reached the track and drove up it to the yard. They parked and trudged through the mud to the outbuilding's steel door, then swung it open on its hinges. For a moment, Kareem saw nothing inside, and his heart bolted crazily, but then the tarp-covered Jeep came into view, and he swallowed convulsively with relief.

One of the men lifted up the tarpaulin to check the license plate. "It's his, all right," he announced.

"Good." Nessim unzipped his belt again and counted out Kareem's cash. "Now, get out of here," he admonished him. "And don't come back."

Kareem nodded vigorously. He clutched the banknotes tight as he splashed off back down the track, the devil on his heels. He glanced around once to see Nessim passing out flashlights and handguns, then again to see him deploying the Freelander and his men for an ambush. Someone was clearly in mortal danger, but Kareem didn't care. He felt exultant, his life finally about to begin.

IT HAD STARTED TO RAIN. Flurries swept through the broken windows and punctured windshield as Knox and Rick approached Tanta. "You want to wait it out?" asked Knox.

"Nah," replied Rick, squinting ahead. "Shouldn't last long." He evidently knew his weather, for the squall passed quickly. They turned the heaters on full blast, deliciously warm against their sodden trousers. They cut south of Tanta and turned off the main road. "Where the hell is this place?" muttered Rick as they searched for the derelict farm.

"Just ahead," said Knox, with more confidence than he felt. Their headlights lit up a young man tramping along the road toward them, a strange look on his face as he stared at Rick and Knox through the windshield. The visibility was so poor that they drove past the mouth of the track and had to reverse a little way to turn up it. Rainwater had filled the potholes; they kept lurching violently into them, their suspension creaking, headlights dancing on the trees and barns. Rick hunched forward over the wheel, peering intently ahead, crawling along.

Knox glanced at his friend. "What is it, mate?" he asked.

"That kid we passed," muttered Rick. "He gave me a bad feeling."

"Want to turn back?"

He shook his head. "We won't get ten miles with the windshield like this; not once we get on the main roads."

"Take it slow, then."

"The fuck do you think I'm doing?"

Nerves taut, eyes skinned, they lumbered on down

the track to the yard. Rainwater had gathered in shallow puddles on the concrete, reflecting their beams brightly. There was a muddy patch ahead. They both saw the fresh footprints in it together. "Shit!" swore Rick. He stamped on the accelerator and roared into a violent U-turn, tires screeching, flinging Knox hard against his door.

Nessim's white Freelander surged out from the trees, headlights springing on high beam, dazzling them both. Rick tried to swerve around it, but he lost traction in the wet and slithered head-on into it instead, hoods crumpling, glass shattering, airbags deploying, pinning them in their seats. It took Knox a moment to gather himself—a moment he didn't have. His door was hauled open, and something cracked him on the temple, leaving him stunned. He was hauled out by his collar and dragged roughly along the concrete, too dazed to resist, his ears ringing like a bell tower, until he was inside the outbuilding—and Rick, too—the steel door closing like a trap behind them both. Nessim kicked him onto his back, and stood astride him, aiming down at his chest. "Who's your friend?" he asked, pointing his flashlight at Rick, who was groaning and rubbing his forehead, mussing a trickle of blood into his hair. He tried to push himself up onto his knees but promptly collapsed again, vomiting hard, making the Egyptians laugh.

"Not friend," mumbled Knox, still hopelessly disoriented. "Driver. Knows nothing about this. Let him go."

"Sure," snorted Nessim.

"I swear," said Knox. "He knows nothing."

"Then it's his unlucky day, isn't it?"

Knox pushed himself up onto an elbow, his scattered

senses beginning to return. "Good money, is it?" he asked. "Working for a gangster like al-Assyuti?"

Spots of red flared momentarily on Nessim's cheeks. "You know nothing about my life," he said.

"And you know enough about mine to end it, do you?"

"You brought this on yourself," spat Nessim. "You must have known what would happen."

Rick pushed himself up, successfully this time. "What's going on?" he slurred. "Who are these people?"

"Don't worry about it," said Knox.

"They've got guns," said Rick, sounding fearful and bewildered. "Why have they got guns?"

Knox frowned at his friend. Somehow his tone didn't ring quite true. Maybe it was simply a concussion, but maybe he was trying to lull Nessim and these others into taking him lightly. They'd have no idea of his background, after all. If that was so, then it was down to Knox to buy him some time to go to work. Time and perhaps darkness. The only light in this place was from the various flashlights, after all, and if he could get them all pointed at him . . .

He glared up at Nessim. "I overheard you tell that girl in Sharm you used to be a paratrooper," he said. "You fucking liar."

"It wasn't a lie."

"Paratroops have honor," sneered Knox. "Men of honor don't sell themselves to rapists and murderers."

Nessim slapped Knox hard across the cheek with the barrel of his gun, sending him sprawling. "Men of honor don't refuse duties just because they dislike them," he said tightly.

"Honor!" snorted Knox, pushing himself back up onto his knees. "You don't know what the word means. You're just a whore, selling yourself for—"

Nessim slapped Knox even harder this time, so that he collapsed, dazed, to the floor, his cheek scraping like stubble on the rough concrete. And it was lying there, in a daze, that he watched Rick blur into action. A single punch sent the first man sprawling. An elbow doubled up the second, Rick wresting his gun from him as he went down, shooting the third through his thigh before turning the gun on Nessim, who was still standing frozen over Knox.

"Drop it!" yelled Rick. "Fucking drop it!" Nessim's gun and flashlight both clattered to the concrete. "On your knees!" he shouted. "All of you. On your fucking knees. Now!" The Egyptians complied, even the wounded man, whimpering piteously with shock, his cream trousers staining red. "Hands behind your fucking heads!" roared Rick, enraged partly by their treatment of Knox, but more by having been made to fear that he was going to die. The Egyptians must have read their fate in his expression, because the color drained from their faces. Nessim alone showed defiance, bracing himself as Rick aimed down at the bridge of his nose. Knox remembered the shame on his cheeks earlier, how he had bridled at the accusation of lacking honor. "No," he said, grabbing Rick's arm just before he could pull the trigger. "We're not like that."

"You may not fucking be," retorted Rick, trying to shake him off, "but I am."

"Please, mate," said Knox.

"And what the fuck do you suggest we do?" yelled Rick. "Let them go, they'll come straight after us. This is self-fucking-defense, mate. Nothing more."

Knox looked again at Nessim. His expression gave nothing away, yet Knox was certain Rick was wrong. Let Nessim go, and his personal code wouldn't allow him to come after them. But as for the others . . . He stooped to pick up Nessim's handgun, then looked around for inspiration. The outbuilding was small and windowless and built of concrete blocks. Its door was solid steel with strong hinges. He grabbed the tarpaulin from the Jeep, threw it on the floor in front of Nessim, then aimed down at his chest. "Off with your clothes," he ordered. "All of you."

"No," scowled Nessim.

"Do it," said Knox. "If not for yourself, then for your men."

Nessim's jaw tightened, but he looked around at his men and seemed to deflate a little. He began reluctantly to undress, as did his men, throwing their discarded clothes into the tarpaulin. When they were down to their underpants, Knox made a bundle of the tarpaulin and tossed it in the back of the Jeep.

"Can you handle them on your own?" he asked.

Rick snorted. "Weren't you watching?"

Knox drove the Jeep over to the Subaru and Freelander. The Subaru was dead, but the Freelander started up on the third try, its engine clattering with terminal damage. He wrestled it into reverse and bunny-hopped over to the outbuilding. Rick came out backward, swinging the steel door closed with his foot, allowing Knox to drive tight up alongside it and put on the hand brake. Not perfect, maybe, but it should hold them for a few hours, by which time they'd be halfway across Egypt.

They hurried to the Jeep. Rick took the wheel, roaring off unnecessarily fast as if to burn off his residual anger, not once looking Knox's way. As for Knox, he stared out the windshield, badly shaken by the revelation that his friend had been prepared to execute those men. The silence between them grew distinctly uncomfortable, so that Knox began to fear that things between them might never be quite the same.

It was Rick who finally spoke. "I thought you said those guys were serious," he muttered.

"What can I tell you, mate," grinned Knox. "I thought they were."

Chapter Twenty-eight

GAILLE AND ELENA took Aly at his word, arriving at his house at seven sharp to find him already at work outside, his papers pinned down with a pot of Siwan tea and some glasses, as though he'd been expecting them. He greeted them warmly, poured them each a glass, then showed them into his library and left them to it.

Elena started with the aerial photographs; Gaille, with the books. When she pulled down her first volume, it came more easily than the night before, as though the bookshelf was less tightly packed. She looked more closely. Yes. She distinctly remembered a red-leather-bound volume that had left stains on her fingers. She pulled out a modern academic text and checked the bibliography against his shelves. Two of the best-known books on Siwa were missing. Yet this was supposed to be a definitive collection. Then she remembered that strange look on his face the night before, when he was looking through her photographs. "Elena," she murmured hesitantly.

Elena looked up crossly. "Yes?"

"Nothing," said Gaille. "Sorry." Knowing Elena, she would go straight out to confront Aly, and bang would go their cooperation. Instead she made a note of the missing titles. She would call Ibrahim at her first opportunity and ask him to send copies directly to her hotel.

KNOX WAS FAST ASLEEP in the passenger seat of the Jeep when Rick shook him awake. "What?" he asked blearily.

"Checkpoint," muttered Rick.

"Damn it," said Knox. Checkpoints were so rare in Alexandria and the Delta that he had stopped worrying about them, but in Middle and Southern Egypt, and in the desert regions, they became commonplace. The Jeep drifted to a halt. Two weary-looking soldiers wearing thick uniforms against the morning chill trudged across. One of them rapped the driver's-side window. "Passports," he said in English when Rick lowered it, evidently figuring them both for foreigners. Knox still had Augustin's papers for Omar Malik, but to use them now would only raise suspicions. He fetched out his American passport and handed it across. The soldier yawned as he took it and Rick's to his cabin to check.

The second soldier, meanwhile, remained standing beside the Jeep. He lit a cigarette, stamped his feet, then glanced in the rear window. Too late, Knox remembered the tarpaulin bundle containing the clothes and other belongings of Nessim and his men, including their handguns.

The soldier opened the back door and leaned inside. "What's this?" he asked, putting his hand on the bundle.

"Just some clothes," said Knox, trying his best to sound relaxed.

The soldier pulled back the flaps to rummage inside. He pulled out a jacket and held it up against himself to check his reflection in the glass before throwing it back and taking a couple of shirts instead, then a pair of trousers, checking the pockets, pulling out an expensive cell phone, and grinning ingratiatingly at Knox, as if to suggest that a gift wouldn't go astray. Knox's mouth was dry. If this prick found any of the guns, they'd have one hell of a lot of explaining to do. He said: "Excuse me, but those are our belongings."

The soldier grunted irritably and threw the trousers and the phone back into the tarpaulin, then slammed the door unnecessarily hard. His comrade inside the cabin had finished his call and was coming back out. Knox's heart was banging violently in apprehension, but the soldier handed back their passports without a flicker, then waved them through. They kept the smiles off their faces until they were well away. "What do you know," said Rick. "Maybe Hassan's given up on you."

"I doubt it, mate," said Knox. "I reckon he just doesn't want the authorities knowing he's on the hunt."

"That's something, at least."

"Yeah," agreed Knox. "It is." He glanced around at the

bundle in the back. "But I reckon we should dump this shit before it gets us into grief. What do you say?"

"I reckon you're right," nodded Rick.

NICOLAS ARRIVED AT IBRAHIM'S OFFICE with delicate business to discuss. His father had charged him with acquiring certain artifacts from the Macedonian tomb for his private collection: at least one golden burial casket, plus a selection of weapons. Now that Yusuf had taken personal control, it was just a matter of creating convincing replicas and arranging a switch. But Ibrahim was still involved in the excavation and would need to be dealt with, not least because Yusuf insisted on having a plausible scapegoat in place should their switch be discovered. "I'm not disturbing you, am I?" Nicolas asked.

"Nothing that can't wait," smiled Ibrahim. "Just sending some books on Siwa to Gaille. Though I can't believe Dr. Sayed doesn't have copies."

Nicolas settled himself at the corner table. "I'm sure you must be aware how pleased we are at the Dragoumis Group at the outcome of our partnership," he began.

"We're pleased, too."

Nicolas nodded and drew a thick envelope from his jacket pocket. "My family makes it a policy to reward success." He set the envelope down on the table midway between them and smiled at Ibrahim to indicate that he should take it.

Ibrahim frowned at the wad of banknotes inside. "For me?" he asked.

"As a token of our appreciation and gratitude."

Ibrahim squinted suspiciously. "And what do you want for this money?"

"Nothing. Just a continuation of our partnership." Nicolas was, in fact, wearing a miniature camera on his chest, its lens disguised as his second button. Everyone in the SCA accepted bribes, but that didn't make it legal. If Ibrahim took this baksheesh like a good little boy, the film would be used to coerce him, step-by-step, until he was completely compromised. If he didn't, Nicolas had many other avenues to explore and exploit.

Ibrahim hesitated, then pushed the envelope back across the table. "If you wish to contribute further to our partnership," he said, "we have a bank account set up for the purpose, as I'm sure you already know."

Nicolas smiled tightly and took back the money. "Whatever you think best."

"Is there anything else? Or may I return to—"

There was noise outside. The door burst open, and Mohammed rushed in. "I'm sorry, sir," said Maha, hanging gamely on to his arm. "I couldn't stop him."

"It's all right, Maha," said Ibrahim. He frowned at Mohammed. "What do you mean by this?"

"It's Layla," said Mohammed, tears streaming down his face. "They've said no. They've said no. They won't give her the treatment."

"My dear friend," winced Ibrahim, standing awkwardly, "I'm so sorry."

"She doesn't need sympathy; she needs *help*."

"I'm sorry. I don't see what more I can do."

"Please. I've asked everyone else. You're her last hope."

Nicolas stood and backed away. Talk of disease was always uncomfortable to him. The books Ibrahim had collected for Gaille were perched on the corner of his desk. He picked one up and flipped idly through the pages.

"I suppose I can ask around," Ibrahim was saying. "But I don't know anyone at the hospital."

"I beg you. You must do something."

The book was filled with black-and-white sketches. Nicolas turned to one of a hill and a lake called Bir al-Hammam. There was something strangely familiar about it. He put the book down and picked up another. It, too, had a picture of Bir al-Hammam, a photograph this time. He stared and stared at it, and finally he realized why the images were familiar, and a great orgasmic shudder ran through him.

"Nicolas? Nicolas?" asked Ibrahim anxiously. "Are you all right?"

Nicolas shook himself back to his senses. Ibrahim was looking strangely at him. He smiled and said, "Forgive me. Miles away, that's all." He looked around to see that Mohammed had gone. "Where's your friend?" he asked.

"He had to leave," said Ibrahim. "His wife's in a dreadful state, apparently. I promised to do what I could. But what *can* I do? That poor girl!"

Nicolas frowned thoughtfully. "If I could help her, you'd be grateful, yes?"

"Of course," said Ibrahim. "But I really—"

"Good," said Nicolas, tucking Gaille's books under his arm. "Then come with me. Let's see what we can arrange."

Chapter Twenty-nine

THE ORACLE OF AMMON proved to be a hump of rock some four kilometers out of Siwa Town. Despite its onetime fame, there was no parking lot, no concession stand, and no entry charge. When Gaille, Elena, and their guides arrived early the next morning, they were alone except for a wizened old man sitting against a wall opposite the entrance, holding out a trembling hand in hope of alms. Gaille reached for her purse. "You'll only encourage them," warned Elena. Gaille hesitated, then gave him a banknote anyway. He smiled gratefully.

Two young girls with plaited waist-length black hair came forward, hoping to sell them some of the homemade bracelets around their wrists. Zayn scowled at them and they ran away giggling.

Gaille had been a little uncertain at first of Mustafa and Zayn, but she quickly warmed to them. Their knowledge of Siwa was impressive. And there was something touching about their friendship: an ancient tradition of homosexual marriage was dying hard in Siwa; local song and poetry still celebrated such close relationships, and she couldn't help but wonder.

Mustafa was big, with bark-rough skin darkened by sun as much as genetics, to judge from the paler bands around his neck and beneath his watchband. He was absurdly fit and nimble despite smoking incessantly. He had a special relationship with his ancient and temperamental truck. No gauges or dials worked anymore, and every frill was long gone, from the ball of the gearshift to the rubber of the pedals and the carpet beneath, but he could still make it run.

Zayn was a whip of a man, no more than forty, though his hair and beard were streaked with silver. While Mustafa drove, Zayn obsessively oiled and polished a thin-bladed ivory-handled knife that he kept folded beneath his robes. Each time he put it away, the slick and spotless blade would scrape against the sheath, so that instantly it needed cleaning again, and he'd draw it back out and examine it and mutter Siwan obscenities.

A short but steep flight of steps led up beneath a lintel into the main body of the oracle, a skeleton of walls like a wooden ship that had rotted in estuary mud and later dried out. Gaille felt a moment's quiet awe as she stood there. There weren't many places in the world where you could be certain that Alexander himself had once occupied that exact space, but this was one of them. The oracle had been esteemed throughout the Mediterranean during Alexander's time—a rival to Delphi, perhaps even its superior. Legend had it that Heracles had visited, and Alexander had claimed Heracles as his direct ancestor. Perseus was reputed to have made the trek, too, and Perseus had been associated with the Persian Empire, which Alexander intended to make his own. Cimon, an Athenian general, had famously sent a deputation to Siwa to ask whether his siege of Cyprus would succeed. The oracle had refused to answer, except to say that the person who asked the question was already with him. And when his emissaries had returned to the fleet, they learned that Cimon had died on that exact day. Pindar had written a hymn of praise to the oracle and, upon asking it for the greatest luck available to humans, had promptly died. But perhaps the incident that had the greatest impact was the invasion of Egypt by the Persian king Cambyses. He sent out three armies: one to Ethiopia, the second to Carthage, and the third across the desert to Siwa. This third army had vanished without a trace, and the oracle had gained a certain awed respect as a result. "How did the oracle work?" asked Gaille.

"The priests carried the physical manifestation of Zeus-Ammon in a golden boat decorated with precious stones, while young virgins chanted," said Elena. "The chief priest read out the questions of supplicants, and Ammon answered them by dancing forward or backward. Unfortunately, Alexander was granted a private audience, so we don't know for sure what he asked or was told."

"I thought he asked about his father's murderers."

"That's one tradition," acknowledged Elena. "The story goes that he asked whether all his father's murderers had been dealt with, and that the Oracle replied that the question was meaningless because his father was divine and therefore couldn't be murdered; but all the murderers of Philip II had been appropriately dealt with, if that was what he meant. Probably apocryphal, of course. All we know for sure is that Zeus-Ammon became Alexander's favorite God, that he sent emissaries here when Hephaiston died, and that he asked to be buried here, too." She picked up a pinch of soil, examined it momentarily, and threw it away.

"It must have been a terrible blow to the oracle's priests," said Gaille. "Thinking they were going to get Alexander's body, then learning it was going to Alexandria."

Elena nodded. "Ptolemy soothed their pain. According to Pausanias, he sent them a stele of apology and handsome gifts."

Gaille climbed as high as she could safely go, then gazed all around. The landscape here wasn't like Europe, where the hills and mountains had been thrust upward by geological pressure and time. This entire region had once been a sandstone plain high above, but most of it had collapsed. The hills that remained were simply the last men standing. She oriented herself north, Al-Dakrur to her right, the great salt lake and Siwa Town to her left. Ahead, the air was so clear, she could see dark ridge lines through her field glasses, many kilometers away. The sand in between was punctured by thrusts of nicotine-brown rock, some no bigger than small cars, others like tower blocks. "Where the hell will we even start?" she asked.

"All great tasks are just a large number of small tasks," observed Elena primly. She spread a chart out on flat ground and rested a stone on each corner. Then she set up a tripod, screwed in a camera and telephoto lens, and began a rigorous study, taking a line from the Siwan Hill of the Dead, sweeping her camera to the horizon, then back again before adjusting it a hairsbreadth to her right. Each time she found a new rock or hill, she photographed it, then invited Mustafa and Zayn to study it through the lens. They squabbled for a while before making a mark on the chart. Each mark would mean a visit and a survey.

Gaille sat on a hump of rock and stared out over the desert, the breeze buffeting her back, whipping strands of hair forward into her eyes. It was unexpected, coming to an alien land yet feeling so at home. And she realized, almost to her surprise, that she was happy.

NICOLAS NEEDED SOMEWHERE PRIVATE to make the kind of phone calls that would secure Layla her medical treatment, so he asked Ibrahim if he wouldn't mind his borrowing Ibrahim's villa for the afternoon. Ibrahim was so eager to help that he drove him there himself. "You couldn't excuse me for a few minutes?" asked Nicolas when they arrived.

"Of course."

As ever, he first rang his father.

"Well?" asked Philip Dragoumis.

"I've found it."

"You're sure?"

"I'm sure I've found the place. Whether there's anything inside . . ." He explained what had happened, how he had seen the pictures in the books Gaille had asked Ibrahim to send down to her, and their significance.

"I told you she'd be the one," said Dragoumis.

"Yes, Father, you did."

"Well? What's our plan?"

Nicolas told his father how far he had gotten. They discussed and refined his ideas, decided on the team, the equipment they would need, the weapons and logistical supplies. "I'll take operational charge, of course," said Nicolas.

"No," said Dragoumis. "I will."

"Are you sure?" asked Nicolas anxiously. "You know we can't guarantee your safety away from—"

"You think I'd miss this?" asked Dragoumis. "I've spent my whole life striving for this."

"As you wish."

"And good work, Nicolas. This is well done. This is very well done."

"Thank you." Nicolas had to wipe his eyes. It wasn't often that his father congratulated him, but that only made it all the more special when he did. He ended the call and sat there in a glow. Then he shook his head sternly to refocus himself; this was no time to wallow. Nothing had been achieved yet, and it wouldn't be unless he got busy. He rang his Cairo fixer, Gabbar Mounim, first.

"Yes?" asked Mounim. "I trust everything is to your satisfaction."

"As always," agreed Nicolas. "But there's something else I'd like you to do for me. Two things, actually."

"A pleasure."

"Our mutual friend. I'd like him to summon his colleague Dr. Aly Sayed of Siwa Oasis to an emergency meeting." If Sayed had deliberately hidden these books from Gaille, as Nicolas suspected, he must have made the connection, too, which meant they needed him out of Siwa while they went to work.

"How much of an emergency, exactly?"

"Tomorrow, if possible."

Mounim sucked in a breath. "It won't be easy, but I'll see what I can do. And the other?"

"I don't suppose you have influence at Alexandria's Medical Center, do you?"

ELENA WAS DRIVING back into town when Nicolas called on her cell phone. "We need to meet," he said. "How soon can you get to Alexandria?"

"For crying out loud, Nicolas, I've only just arrived here."

"This can't wait, Elena. Something's happened. My father wants to discuss it with you."

"Your father? He's coming to Alexandria?"

"Yes."

Elena breathed deep. Philip Dragoumis didn't leave Northern Greece on a whim. If he was coming here, it had to mean something truly significant. "Fine," she said. "Where?"

"Ibrahim's villa."

"When?"

"Tomorrow morning. Nine o'clock."

"I'll be there." She snapped her phone shut, already making plans. Leave now and she could be there in time for a night with Augustin. "I'm needed back in Alexandria," she told Gaille.

"Alexandria?" frowned Gaille. "Will you . . . be gone long?"

"How am I supposed to know that?"

"You want me and the guys to start looking?"

Elena frowned. Gaille had a distressing habit of finding things without her help. "No," she said. "Do nothing until I come back."

"As you wish."

"YOU MEAN TO TELL ME that Knox escaped you again?" asked Hassan incredulously when Nessim had completed his telephone report.

"He had a friend with him," said Nessim.

"A friend?"

"We'll find them," said Nessim, striving to sound more bullish than he felt. His confidence had been shot by what happened. Having the tables turned so completely would do that to a man, as would a night spent struggling to escape from an outbuilding, or wandering half-naked across farmland with a wounded comrade. But, to Nessim's surprise, the thing that had struck him deepest about the entire fiasco were Knox's words about his lack of honor. Nessim was old enough and wise enough to know that insults didn't hurt unless they rang true, and so now he couldn't stop asking painful questions of himself: How had it come to this? What was he doing working for a man like Hassan? Was money really that important to him? "We'll watch all his friends and associates," he said. "We'll put out another reward. It's just a matter of time before we find him again."

"So you keep telling me," said Hassan.

"I'm sorry," said Nessim. "He's better at this than we imagined possible. But now we know. Now we're prepared. Next time we'll have him."

"Next time? How can I be sure there'll be a next time?"

"Another week. That's all I ask."

"Can you give me one good reason why I shouldn't fire you and hire him instead?"

"You'd have to find him first," muttered Nessim beneath his breath.

"What did you say?"

"Nothing."

There was a stony silence. Then, "I think it's time we discussed this face-to-face, don't you?"

"Face-to-face?" asked Nessim bleakly.

"Yes," said Hassan. "Face-to-face."

MOHAMMED WAS ASTONISHED to see Professor Rafai step out of the taxi and slam its door behind him. He had not expected to see Layla's oncologist again, certainly not on his building site. "There is somewhere private?" demanded Rafai, trembling with anger.

"Private?"

"To talk."

Mohammed frowned in bewilderment. "Now?"

"Of course now! You think I'm here to book an appointment?"

Mohammed shrugged and led Rafai to his cabin office.

"I don't know how you do this!" shouted Rafai as the door closed. He removed his half-moon glasses and jabbed them like a scalpel at Mohammed's face. "Who do you think you are? I base my decisions on clinical evidence. *Clinical evidence!* You think you can bully me into changing my mind?"

"I'm sorry for my behavior in your office," frowned Mohammed. "But I've already apologized. I was under immense strain. I don't know what else—"

"You think this is about that?" cried Rafai. "This isn't about that."

"Then what?"

"Only your daughter!" yelled Rafai. "Only ever your daughter! You think she's the only one sick. A young boy called Saad Gama waits for bone marrow. A true scholar of Islam. You want to explain to him that we must postpone his treatment because you have more influential friends? You want to tell his parents he must die so that your daughter might live? You think they don't care for him?"

"Professor Rafai, in the name of Allah, what are you talking about?"

"Don't deny it! Don't insult me by denying it! I know you've done this, though how you have the power . . . Well, let me tell you, Saad's blood is on your hands! Your hands, not mine."

Mohammed went cold. He asked dizzily, "What are you saying? Are you saying you'll give Layla her transplant?"

Rafai glared furiously. "I'm saying I won't risk my department over this."

"But her transplant?" insisted Mohammed. "Layla will receive her transplant?"

"Tell your friends in Cairo to stay away from me and my staff. If the procedure goes wrong, we'll not be held accountable, you hear? Tell your people that. Tell your people!" He stormed out of the office. Mohammed's hands were shaking as if from palsy, so that he couldn't even hold his phone steady when he tried to dial Nur.

NICOLAS WAS ON THE PHONE with his bodyguard, Bastiaan, when Ibrahim knocked and entered, bringing with him a cup of coffee and a plate of cakes, which he set down on the corner of his desk. Nicolas didn't bother to stop talking, but he slipped into euphemism and turned his back. "You've arranged for the purchases?"

"Vasileios is flying in with your father. He's been briefed on what we need."

"And when will you be at the villa?"

"I'm on my way now. Shouldn't be more than fifteen minutes."

"Good. And make sure . . ."

Behind him, Ibrahim gave a little gasp. Nicolas turned to see him holding open one of Gaille's books, staring in shock at a picture of Bir al-Hammam. Nicolas closed his eyes in irritation with himself. "Make it ten minutes," he told Bastiaan in his coarsest Greek. "We've got a problem." He killed the call and plucked the book from Ibrahim's hand. "There's something I need to tell you," he said.

"What? But have you seen this picture of—"

"Quickly," said Nicolas, grabbing Ibrahim's arm and hustling him through to the kitchen.

"What is it?" asked Ibrahim, bemused. "What's going on?" Nicolas opened and shut all the drawers until he found a kitchen knife, and he held it up so that its blade glinted. Ibrahim paled. "What . . . what are you doing with that?"

Nicolas held the knife out wide in his left hand, so that Ibrahim's eyes followed its glittery menace. Then he punched the archaeologist with his right, sending him flailing onto his back. He knelt down and pressed the sharp steel against Ibrahim's throat before he could recover. "My colleague Bastiaan is on his way," he said. "You're going to be nice and quiet until he arrives, aren't you?"

"Yes," agreed Ibrahim.

KNOX HAD TAKEN OVER THE WHEEL while Rick caught up on his sleep. It was midafternoon when he reached Farafra, where his friend and Demotic expert Ishaq lived. He nudged Rick awake. "We're here, mate."

"Always the way," grunted Rick irritably. "Loveliest bloody dream."

Knox hadn't been to Ishaq's home in several years, but Farafra was small, and the house wasn't hard to find. He was looking forward to seeing his old friend. They went back a long way, to Knox's first season at Mallawi. A small and ridiculously intelligent man, Ishaq had spent most of his leisure time in his hammock, staring lazily up at the sky. But give him some Demotic to translate, and there was no one better in Egypt.

Unfortunately, when they parked outside his home, everything was shuttered. They banged on his front door, but there was no response. They went a couple of doors down the road to the information center, which doubled as his office, but there was no one there, either. "He must be out on excavation," said Knox, checking the time. "He'll be back soon."

"Let's have a look at the bloody photos of this inscription of yours, then," muttered Rick.

"I don't have them with me."

"You *what*?"

Knox gave him a look. "You don't really think I'm stupid enough to travel halfway across Egypt with enough incriminating evidence on my laptop to get me ten years?"

"So how the hell's your mate going to translate them?"

"I e-mailed them to myself. Ishaq's wired."

They sat in the shade of a date palm to wait. Torpor set in. When flies settled on them, they lacked even the energy to swat them away. A young boy in robes pushing an old bicycle much too big for him approached tentatively. "You look for Ishaq?" he asked.

"Yes. Why? Do you know where he is?"

"He leave for Cairo. A meeting. A big meeting. All the desert archaeologists are to be there."

"Did he say when he'd be back?"

"Tomorrow," shrugged the boy. "The day after."

"Ballocks," muttered Rick. "What now?"

"I don't know," said Knox. "Let me think."

"I don't believe this Kelonymus bastard. Everything else was in Greek. Why the hell did he have to switch to Demotic for this bloody inscription?"

Knox's jaw dropped; he turned to look at his friend.

"What?" asked Rick. "What did I say?"

"I think you've just gone and cracked it," said Knox.

Chapter Thirty

MOHAMMED WAS STILL IN A DAZE from his good fortune when his phone rang. "Yes?" he asked.

"This is Nicolas Dragoumis. You remember, I helped finance the tests for—"

"Of course I remember, Mr. Dragoumis. What can I do for you?"

"I believe you should have heard some good news."

"That was you? You are my friend in Cairo?"

"Yes."

"Thank you! Thank you! I am in your debt, Mr. Dragoumis. I am forever in your debt. I swear, anything you ever want . . ."

"Anything?" asked Nicolas dryly. "Do you really mean that?"

"On my life."

"I hope it won't come to that," said Nicolas. "But tell me: do you have a mechanical digger on your site?"

THERE HAD BEEN LITTLE for Gaille to do that afternoon. Although they had recruited Mustafa and Zayn for
the next fortnight, she gave them the day off, then went
to Aly's house, hoping to do some more research, only
to find it locked, and a note on his door saying he'd been
summoned to Cairo. She went back to her hotel and lazed
away the afternoon in a hammock before reviving herself
beneath a cold shower and hiring a rickety bicycle that
she was now pedaling down to a local freshwater spring.
Coasting along one short stretch, she passed a donkey
cart carrying three Siwan wives enshrouded in their dark
blue embroidered cotton *tarfottet.* One lifted her cowl
and gave Gaille a shy yet radiant smile. She couldn't have
been more than fourteen.

Her bicycle tires were soft, and pedaling was hard work
on the road, whose surface was sticky from the sun. She
was relieved when she saw the spring ahead, a small, deep
pool bounded by stone, the water clear down to grayish
rocks, with floating clumps of lurid green algae. Several
zaggalah sat around, their work on the date palms finished for the day, eyeing her with obvious interest. She'd
been looking forward to a swim, but she couldn't face
their stares, so she went instead into the orchard to share
a cup of bitter Siwan tea with the young custodian.

The sun sank behind the great salt lake and the hills
beyond, the horizon blazed orange and purple before the
colors faded, and another day was gone. She thought of

the young Siwan girl on the donkey cart, married at the onset of puberty to spend the rest of her life hidden from the world, her vision reduced to the narrowest of eye slits, and Gaille had an epiphany—a vivid understanding of the change wrought in herself by the past few weeks. She knew in that moment that she could never again take refuge from life in the physical and intellectual comfort of the Sorbonne, compiling arcane dictionaries of dead languages. Such work was immensely valuable, but it was a step removed from reality, shadows on the wall. She wasn't an academic. She was an archaeologist, her father's daughter.

It was time to make her peace.

RICK AND KNOX FOUND A HOTEL with a modem jack so they could download the photographs of the lower chamber and the inscription. But deciphering wasn't Knox's strength, and progress was slow. Meanwhile, Rick looked through the other photographs of the lower chamber. When he came to the mosaic, he frowned and said, "Haven't we seen this before?"

"How do you mean?"

He fetched out his own digital camera and scrolled through to the painting of Wepwawet holding the banner of Alexander. Knox saw it at once. The skyline in the mosaic and in the painting were identical. In the mosaic, it silhouetted the two groups of soldiers. In the painting, it contoured Wepwawet and his banner. And it was see-ing Alexander's face on the banner that gave Knox the inspiration he needed to find a keyword and so crack the cipher. When he was done, he scrawled out the text, then translated it for Rick.

"A tomb filled with goods fit for Alexander," murmured Rick. "Jesus!"

"No wonder the Dragoumises are after it," said Knox. "And they've got a head start, too. We need to move."

"Where?"

"The place of Ammon, Alexander's father. Siwa."

They consulted a guidebook. Siwa wasn't that far away, not as the crow flies, but reaching it on proper roads meant driving all the way up to Alexandria, then along the coast to Marsa Matruh and south again. Three sides of a square, perhaps fourteen hundred kilometers in all. Alternatively, they could take the old caravan route, which would save them the best part of a thousand kilometers, but it meant crossing a fierce and unforgiving desert. "What do you reckon?" asked Rick.

"The desert," said Knox unhesitatingly. "At least Nessim and his men won't be able to find us."

Rick grinned. "I was hoping you'd say that."

First task was getting permission. There were army posts dotted across the desert with nothing to do but has-sle the few hardy tourists who ventured through. Setting off without proper authorization was asking for grief. But now that Knox's passport had been cleared at the check-point, that was only a matter of baksheesh and time.

The local army commander begged a couple of hours to arrange the paperwork. Knox and Rick used it to buy supplies: crates of water and baskets of food, an extra spare tire, cans of oil and petrol. Then they set off, making the most of the cool of the night while it lasted.

AUGUSTIN ANSWERED HIS FRONT DOOR with a stained white sheet wrapped like a sarong around his waist. The way his face fell, Elena knew at once. She felt an exquisite calm as she pushed past him into his bedroom. The girl had spiked blond hair, and a brass ring through her lower lip. She had flat breasts with big nipples, and a shaved pubic mound. "You his wife, then?" she asked, reaching down for a soft pack of Marlboro Lights and a plastic lighter.

Elena turned. Augustin was about to say something, but when he saw her expression he seemed to think better of it. She exited, hurried down the stairs, and walked briskly to her car. She felt no regret at not warning him of her visit; between ignorance and knowledge, she'd choose knowledge every time. But she grew angrier with every step. At a traffic light, her cell phone started to ring. She recognized Augustin's number. She rolled down her window, hurled it out, and watched it spark and skitter on the road. Traffic was thick. She clenched the steering wheel and yelled, drawing concerned looks from pedestrians. She cut in front a truck and roared out of the city on the Cairo road. She had no destination in mind. She just wanted to push the car until it fell apart.

This was not about Augustin. Augustin was nothing, she realized now, merely a screen onto which she had projected memories of Pavlos. Pavlos was her man, the only man she had ever truly loved. For ten years, she had craved to be with him. For ten years, her life had been shit.

A semi approached fast on the other side of the highway. Her hands twitched almost unconsciously on the steering wheel; she veered toward it, almost able to taste the sweet release of oblivion. The truck driver blared his horn in warning, startling her from her reverie, and at the very last moment she wrenched the wheel and swung back safely onto her side of the highway.

Not now. Not yet.

She had lost more than a husband when she lost Pavlos. She had lost honor. Dragoumis was flying in. He would be away from home soil. He'd be vulnerable. They said you could buy anything in the back streets of Cairo, and Cairo was just two hours' drive south. It was time to put that old maxim to the test.

Elena had a blood debt to settle.

Chapter Thirty-one

IT HAD RAINED during the night, leaving the roads slick and black. Thin traffic threw up spray that glinted like diamonds in Mohammed's headlights. Before he even reached the outskirts of Alexandria, stress was twisting his spine like a tourniquet. He drove hunched over the steering wheel, consulting his watch and the speedometer. He dared not take the flatbed truck and its load over seventy kilometers per hour, yet he dare not be late, either. Nicolas had been adamant that he reach Siwa by sunset tonight.

It had been years since he handled a rig this size and weight, but he got the hang of it quickly enough, especially once he was out on the Marsa Matruh Highway, where the road became wide, straight, and easy. He took Layla's picture from his wallet and laid it on the dash to remind himself why he was doing this. A police car loomed in his wing mirror. It slowed as it came alongside. He kept his eyes on the road ahead, and at last it sped on. His heart settled.

He touched Layla's photo. If all went well, her intense chemotherapy and radiotherapy conditioning treatment would get under way tomorrow. Her condition was so severe, there was no time to waste. Doctor Rafai and her medical team would deliberately and systematically fill her system with poisons. In a fortnight or so, if Allah willed it, they would harvest marrow from Besheer's pelvis, remove fragments of blood and bone, and inject them into Layla. If that worked, Layla would begin months of tests, treatment, rehabilitation. It would be a year at least before they knew for sure. Until then, he had no choice but to do what Nicolas wanted, because Nicolas had made it quite clear to him that what had been given could just as easily be taken away.

Mohammed had had a mechanical digger on site. It had been finding the heavy-duty flatbed transporter truck that proved difficult. All his usual suppliers had been out, but he had kept on the phone, calling friends and friends of friends until finally he found one. Then it had been a matter of filling in paperwork, collecting the truck and bringing it to his site, and loading and securing the mechanical digger all by himself, because Nicolas had been adamant that he let no one else know what he was up to.

And all the while, Mohammed had brooded on why Nicolas would want such equipment in Siwa. None of the possible answers made him feel any better. The rising sun threw his truck's shadow far ahead of him on the black highway. Mohammed drove into it as into a dreadful premonition.

KNOX STARED THROUGH the Jeep's windshield at the sands stretching out before him. The desert was at its most beautiful in the early morning and late afternoon, when the angle of the sun created chiaroscuro shadows in the golden dunes, and the heat was less intense. But when the sun was high, the landscape turned monochrome and flat, except for those areas covered by a layer of salt crystals from some long-vanished sea, where it was so dazzling he had to squint to protect his eyes.

The track he was driving had been in use since ancient times—an old caravan trail from the Nile to Siwa. On either side lay the bones of camels, empty petrol cans, burst tires, discarded water bottles. They had been here perhaps a week, perhaps decades. The Western Desert didn't recycle like other places; instead, it froze like a time capsule. On one of his trips with Richard, retracing the tracks of the Zerzura Club explorers who had mapped the Western Desert and the Gilf Kabir, Knox had encountered the remains of a man in Bedouin dress sitting by the ashes of a fire in a dune valley, who had apparently died abruptly of a heart attack, and his hobbled camel nearby, which, unable to move, had perished with him.

His lips were badly cracked with dehydration; his tongue kept gluing itself to the roof of his mouth. He took another swig from the water bottle he kept clamped between his legs, swilling it around before swallowing. Within seconds, however, his mouth was as dry as before.

He glanced over his shoulder to reassure himself that he and Rick had gotten sufficient supplies.

"What's that?" frowned Rick, pointing ahead.

The Jeep's windshield had smeared so badly that Knox had to lean his head out the window to make it out clearly. There was a low darkness on the horizon, like rain, except that there were no clouds in the sky, and rain was the least of one's worries out here in the Western Desert. "Trouble," muttered Knox.

ELENA WAS IN A FIERY MOOD when she reached Ibrahim's villa, fresh from her trip to Cairo.

"You're late," said Nicolas angrily, leading her into the kitchen, where Philip Dragoumis was at the table discussing plans with Costis, his longtime head of security, and several of his team, battle-hardened veterans of the various Balkan conflicts. "I told you to be here at nine."

Just the sight of Dragoumis made Elena's bag weigh heavier on her shoulder, but this wasn't the moment. "I had something to do," she said. "What's the rush, anyway?"

"We need to be in Siwa by nightfall."

"Siwa!" she protested. "You made me drive all the way up here just to drive straight back down again."

"It's for your own good," said Nicolas, nodding at the security monitor. "You've been recorded arriving. Tomorrow evening you'll be recorded leaving. And Ibrahim will swear you've stayed here all the time in between."

"Then how—"

"There's a back gate," said Nicolas. "We've rigged the camera on it to show nothing." He glanced at his watch. "But we need to get moving. Can I have your cell phone, please?"

"Why?"

"Because if you use it while we're traveling, you can be traced," he said with exaggerated patience. "There's not much point in having an alibi if you're going to blow it with a phone call."

"Then how will we communicate?"

"We have phones in the cars," said Nicolas. "Now, please just give it to me."

"I don't have it," admitted Elena, a little sheepishly. "I threw it away."

He frowned. "You threw it away? Why?"

"Does it matter? Now, what's this about? It had better be good."

"I think you'll find it good," growled Dragoumis. She frowned at him. He beckoned for her to join him at the table. He opened the two books of Siwa for her to see and laid them alongside a photograph of the mosaic from the Alexandrian tomb.

"Christ!" murmured Elena.

"Yes. We've found it at last. Now all we have to do is bring it home."

She looked at him in horror. For all that she sympathized wholeheartedly with the Macedonian cause, she was an archaeologist, too. Sites and artifacts were sacred to her. "Bring it home?"

"Of course. What else do you think we've been working for?"

"But . . . this is crazy. You'll never get away with it."

"Why not?"

"For one thing, it may not be there."

"If it isn't, it isn't," shrugged Dragoumis. "But it is." He put his hand over his heart. "I know it in here."

"But an excavation like this can take months. Years."

"We have one night," grinned Nicolas. "Tonight. A mechanical digger will meet us there. Eneas and Vasileios are bringing other equipment and a container truck. One of our ships is headed to Alexandria. It'll be docked by morning, in plenty of time to load whatever we find. Believe me, our captains are skilled at playing the three-card trick with sealed containers. Within days it will be back in Thessalonike, and then we can make the announcement."

"Announcement? But you can't! Everyone will know we stole it."

"So? They won't be able to prove it. Especially when you say that the Macedonian Archaeological Foundation made this discovery in the mountains of Macedonia. As a respected archaeologist, people will accept your word."

"I don't believe this!" protested Elena. "I'll be an international joke."

"I don't see why," said Nicolas. "If it's possible Alexander had a tomb prepared for him in Siwa, why not in Macedonia?"

"We have an explanation for Siwa: the Alexander Cipher."

"Yes," said Dragoumis. "And what does it say, exactly? That the shield bearers prepared a tomb for Alexander in the place of his father and that they crossed the desert to take him there. That applies to Siwa, certainly. Ammon was Alexander's divine father, and Siwa lay across the Western Desert. But it applies to Macedonia, too. Philip was Alexander's mortal father. And the shield bearers would have had to cross the Sinai desert to reach it."

Elena's mouth fell open. She couldn't refute the logic, yet still she felt appalled. "But people would still know," she said weakly.

"We certainly hope so," grinned Nicolas.

"How do you mean?"

"What do you imagine the reaction will be when Athens tries to wrest it off us, as international pressure will force them to do? Can you imagine the outcry? Macedonia will never stand for it."

"There'll be war," said Elena numbly.

"Yes," agreed Nicolas.

Elena turned to Dragoumis. "I thought you were a man of peace," she said.

"And so I am," he agreed. "But every nation has the right to defend itself. And we are no different."

THE PLACE WHERE GAILLE'S FATHER had fallen to his death was at the eastern edge of the Siwa Depression, some three hours' drive from Siwa Town. When Gaille asked Mustafa and Zayn to take her out there, they looked deeply uncomfortable. But she pointed out to them that she was his daughter, that she had never had a proper chance to say good-bye to him, and finally they agreed.

They drove east along the Bahariyya track for the best part of a hundred kilometers, then turned north. It was a beautiful though slightly eerie setting. High cliffs jutted from the great Sea of Sand. There was no greenery out here. A white snake slithered down a steep dune. Apart from that, Gaille saw no life at all, not even a bird.

It was a five-minute scramble from where they parked to the foot of a high, sheer cliff. A cairn of stones marked the exact spot. His full name, Richard Josiah Mitchell, had been scratched crudely into the top one. He had always hated being called Josiah. His closest friends, knowing this, had teased him mercilessly with it. She picked it up and asked her guides if either of them was responsible. They shook their heads, then suggested it must have been Knox. She set it back as she had found it, uncertain what to think.

As she stood there, Mustafa explained how they and Knox had hurried down here to find her father already cold, his blood everywhere, how they had offered to help Knox take his body back to the truck, how he had snarled at them.

She looked around at where they had parked. "You mean *that* truck?" she asked.

"Yes."

She felt a little weak. "My father's body was in your truck?"

Mustafa looked a little sheepish. He told her how much he and Zayn had respected her father, what a tragedy it had been, how unnecessary. Gaille stared upward while he talked. The rock face rose sheer and high above them. It made her toes tingle. She felt light-headed, a little nauseated. She had never been good with heights. She took a step back, stumbled, and might have fallen had Zayn not grabbed her by the arm and restored her to balance.

Her sense of vertigo stayed with her as she and Mustafa climbed the rock face. Zayn elected to stay behind with the truck, in case of robbers. Gaille had snorted softly when she heard that. Robbers! There was no one for fifty miles. But she couldn't blame him. The growing heat and the gradient made the climb far more difficult than she had anticipated. There was no path, just a series of steep shelves of rock too sandy to provide secure footing. Mustafa led the way, dancing up in his ragged flip-flops, careless of his thick white robes and heavy pack, five times bulkier than her own. Each time he got far enough ahead, he would squat like a frog on an outcrop to smoke one of his foul cigarettes and watch amiably as she labored to catch up. She grew increasingly indignant. Didn't he know that men his age shouldn't be able to ingest tar so relentlessly and still be fit? Didn't he realize he should be a physical wreck? She scowled up at him. He waved cheerily back. Her feet ached despite her leather boots; her calves and thighs were trembling with exertion; her mouth was tacky with thirst. She reached him at last, slumped down, fetched out her water bottle, swilled and swallowed a mouthful, and asked plaintively, "Are we nearly there yet?"

"Ten minute."

She squinted suspiciously at him. He had said that every time.

THE SANDSTORM HIT LIGHTLY AT FIRST. Rick sat back in his seat with a relieved smile. "This isn't so bad," he said.

"If it doesn't get any worse."

It was still light enough outside that he could see the track, despite the sand being blasted against his door and window. Sandstorms tended to fall into two broad categories. One was effectively a dust storm, hundreds of feet high, that blocked out the sun and was disorienting without being particularly brutal. The other—like this one—was a true sandstorm: a fierce wind picking up sand from the dunes and firing them like shotgun pellets.

It wasn't long before Rick was regretting his complacency. The wind buffeted them so hard, they were creaking back and forth on their suspension; the paint and windows were being assailed by a nonstop barrage, loud and frantic, that seemed certain to break through the fragile old glass. Visibility deteriorated so badly that Knox could barely see the track anymore. He kept skewing into soft sand that cloyed beneath their wheels, or over stray sharp rocks that threatened their tires, so that he had to go down into first gear and slow almost to a crawl.

"Shouldn't we stop?" asked Rick.

Knox shook his head. Stop for even a minute, and the wind would blow away the sand beneath their tires, making them sink into the pits it created, until they were stuck. Then it would pile up a drift against their side until they were completely buried and their doors pinned, making them dependent on being rescued. And there wasn't much chance of that out here.

The winds grew indescribably fierce, causing the Jeep to rock precariously back and forth. The left wheels dropped suddenly just as a gust blew viciously hard, so that for a moment it felt as if they were about to be blown onto their side.

"Christ!" muttered Rick, clutching his door handle as they slammed back down onto four wheels. "Have you been through one like this before?"

"Once," said Knox.

"How long did it last?"

"Seven days."

"You're fucking with me."

Knox allowed himself a small smile. It wasn't often he had seen Rick rattled. "You're right," he admitted. "It was more like seven and a half."

A WAFT OF TOBACCO SMOKE tickled Gaille's throat and made her cough. Mustafa held up a hand in apology, then screwed the butt into the dust with his flip-flop. Gaille dribbled water onto her palm, ran it over her brow, and rose reluctantly to her feet. "How much further?" she asked.

Mustafa nodded keenly. "Ten minute," he said. She clenched her teeth together. Damned if she would give him

the satisfaction of begging for more recovery time. She followed him wearily up a gully in the hillside. After a little
while, it suddenly sheared away, so that she could see for
tens of kilometers over the golden desert. It looked endless.
"You see," said Mustafa with an impresario's whirl of the
hand. "Ten minute."

By God, they were high up. Gaille inched closer to the
edge. It fell away beneath her directly to the rocks below,
fawn cliffs riven by black shadows. A ledge ran above
the precipice before reaching again the safe embrace of a
gully, but it was ridiculously narrow, more like stepping
stones than a path. "You crossed *that*?" she asked.

Mustafa shrugged. He kicked off his flip-flops and
walked quickly across, left hand against the cliff wall,
soles of his feet molding themselves to the meager holds.
He dislodged a small stone, and she put a hand against the
cliff wall and leaned out to watch it fall. It hit a knob of
rock and bounced away from the cliff. Still it fell . . . and
still. She could barely see the cairn on the rocks far
below.

Mustafa reached the far side. "See?" he grinned. "Is
nothing."

She shook her head. There was no way she could do it.
Her balance was poor; her ankles were tired. It would be
difficult enough at ground level, but up here . . . Mustafa
shrugged and came back across. Chills cramped Gaille's
toes just watching him. He placed his hand on her back to
give her courage. She reached her left foot tentatively onto
the first small outcrop and brought her right foot to join
it. She spent an age looking at the place where she had to
set her foot next. She made that step jerkily, then another.

The world warped and grew indistinct around her, shearing away from her at the same time that it rushed up at her face. She wanted to go back, but she couldn't move. She closed her eyes, pressed her back against the cliff wall, stretched out her arms for balance. Her fingers and toes felt bloodless and weak; her knees threatened to buckle. It was then that she understood at last what had happened to her father, and Knox's part in it. Tears sprang from her eyes as she realized how wrong she had been about him, about everything. "I can't do this," she said. "I can't—"

Mustafa grabbed her hand and pulled her to safety. "You see," he grinned. "That was all Knox must do."

She shook her head at him and collapsed, dry-heaving, into a bowl of rocks from which she couldn't possibly fall. She turned onto her back, covering her eyes with her hand while wiping away the tickle of tears from her cheeks. Her father's life insurance policy had included a handsome bonus for accidental death, enough for Gaille to buy herself an apartment. *An apartment!* She felt wretched. She struggled to her feet and, with weak, rubbery legs, followed Mustafa on the long, silent walk down to the truck.

Chapter Thirty-two

Knox and Rick drove through the sandstorm for what seemed like hour after hour. The whine and screech and roar got to them both, like furious harpies clawing at the Jeep's metalwork, trying to get at them. The engine was increasingly strained, too, with unsettling glugs and belches coming from the radiator. But finally the storm began to abate; and then, in what seemed little more than a moment, the wind died away altogether and they were through, with nothing but open desert around them.

They had driven off the track some time before, and there was no sign of it, either, or any landmarks to give them guidance. They had neither GPS nor a decent map against which to plot it.

"You know where we are?" asked Rick.

"No."

"Then what the fuck do we do now?"

"Don't worry," said Knox. He climbed up onto the Jeep's hood and scoured the horizon through binoculars.

People thought of the desert as a single flat landscape, bereft of personality and recognizable features, but it wasn't like that at all, not once you had been out here a few times. Every region had its own personality and look. Some parts were like those Utah salt flats where the land speed records were set. Others were like raging high seas frozen into dunes, and though the sands shifted, the underlying shapes themselves were immortal and unchanging. And there were numerous cliffs and ridges, too, many of which Knox had climbed.

The air was still hazy, but away to the north he spotted a familiar escarpment. Half an hour's drive, and they'd be back in business. "We should eat," he told Rick. "Give the engine a rest."

They sat in the shade of the Jeep and washed cold rice and vegetables down with water, the engine creaking and groaning as it cooled. When they were done, they topped up the water in the radiator and set off again, reaching the track right where Knox had thought they would, then drove on through the seemingly endless desert. Yet it wasn't endless. In fact, it was only a little after dusk that they reached a sealed track, and then progress was even swifter. Within another hour, they pulled into Siwa's main square.

"I could kill a cold drink," muttered Rick.

"Not if I see it first," answered Knox.

MOHAMMED REFUELED FIFTY KILOMETERS north of Siwa, then drove for half an hour with his phone on the seat next to him, waiting for it to pick up a signal. When finally it did, he pulled off the road to call Nur. It did him good just to hear her voice. His premonitions of his own doom had been growing stronger with every passing minute, but then Nur mentioned Layla's name and Mohammed blurted out suddenly how much he loved them both, that if something went wrong and she shouldn't see him again—

"Don't talk like that!" The distress in Nur's voice shocked him.

He breathed in to calm himself and assured her that he was fine; he'd see her tomorrow evening. He hung up, switched off the cell phone before she could call back, and checked his watch. He had made excellent time. He jumped down and walked back along the side of the road, crouched. He scooped up a handful of sand, let it trickle away, and watched the peaks that remained on his fingers, the valleys between them. The sand was so hot from a day of baking in the sun that it left his skin reddened. He scooped up another handful, as though he believed that by punishing himself now, he might avoid more grievous punishment later.

A Bedouin in a dusty white truck honked his horn and leaned out of his window to ask cheerfully if he needed help. Mohammed thanked him but waved him on. He was so tired, time seemed to move at half its usual speed. The sun lowered to the horizon and finally set, and it quickly grew dark. He kept glancing up and along the road to the coast, which was so straight and flat, it would have made a Roman weep for joy. When he saw two four-by-fours and a container truck approaching, he stood, brushed the sand from his trousers, and climbed back into his cab. The vehicles slowed as they drew alongside. An interior light came on in the four-by-four, and Nicolas leaned out its window and motioned for Mohammed to fall in behind them. Mohammed gave him the thumbs-up and pulled out behind them. He followed the convoy a few more kilometers along the road to Siwa, then across the sands and deep into the desert.

GAILLE WAS OUT WALKING when she saw Knox and another man glugging bottles of ice-cold water under the awning of a café. It was a profound shock to see him, not least because she had been thinking of him all day, about his role in her father's death and the letter he had sent her afterward. She hesitated but then walked over. He looked up, startled to see her. "Gaille," he said awkwardly.

"Daniel." She nodded.

"This is Rick," said Knox, nodding at his companion.

"Nice to meet you."

"Likewise."

She turned back to Knox. "Can we talk? In private?"

"Sure." He gestured at the road. "Want to take a walk?" When she nodded, he turned to Rick. "You don't mind, do you, mate?"

"Take your time. I'll get something to eat."

Knox and Gaille walked off side by side. "Well?" he asked.

"I went out there today."

"Out where?"

"To where my father died. Mustafa and Zayn took me."

"Ah."

She turned to face him. "I want to know what happened, Daniel. I want the truth."

"I'm sure they told you the truth."

"I think they told me what they saw," replied Gaille, walking on again. "But that's not quite the same, is it?"

He gave her a sideways glance. "What's that supposed to mean?"

"You stuck with my father when no one else did. You wouldn't have done that unless you cared about him. So why did you let him fall?"

"I didn't."

"Yes, you did. And you must have had a reason. And I think I know what it was. He was already dying, wasn't he?"

"I don't know what you're talking about."

"What was it? AIDS?"

"It was an accident," said Knox.

She shook her head. "Mustafa and Zayn told me you snarled at them when they offered to help you with his body. All that blood. That's why I'm thinking AIDS."

"It was an accident."

"And then, of course, you had him cremated so quickly."

"I told you, it was an accident."

"You'd have to say that, wouldn't you, or you'd be

complicit in insurance fraud." Knox opened his mouth to speak, but nothing came out. In the darkness of the back street, it was tough to read his expression, but she persevered anyway. "He made you promise to write to me, didn't he? To tell me he'd been thinking of me? Please. I just need to know."

Knox was silent for a while. "Yes."

She nodded several times. Although she had known it in her heart, it still took some effort to assimilate. "Tell me," she said. "Tell me everything."

"It wasn't just AIDS," sighed Knox. "His whole body was in meltdown. He had cancer; his organs were failing. It was just a matter of time. Time and pain. He was never the kind of man to eke things out in a hospital or be a burden. You should know that. He wanted to go on his own terms, in a place he loved. And he wanted to do something for you, to make up for being a bad father."

"A bad father?" asked Gaille bleakly. "Is that what he said?"

"Yes."

"And you just let him . . . go ahead with it?"

"He didn't give me a choice. At least, my choice was to be there or not to be there. He was my friend. I chose to be there." Then he added mulishly: "I'm sorry if you think that was wrong."

"I don't," she said. "I just wish I could have been there, too."

"You had your chance. He tried often enough to mend fences with you."

"Yes," she agreed. "You don't need to tell me I've behaved badly. I know that. And I'm sorry."

They had looped around in a circle. Rick saw them and waved, so they went to join him. "Cracking chicken and fries," he said. "So you're this famous Gaille, then?"

"Gaille, yes," she acknowledged. "I don't know about famous."

"You are to me. Your man Knox here talks about you nonstop."

"Shut it, Rick," said Knox.

Rick laughed. "So how you getting on with your search?"

"What search?"

"Come on, love. Goods fit for the son of Ammon. "

She looked back and forth between them. "How do you guys know about that?"

Knox shrugged and smiled. "You're not the only one who's been behaving badly."

"How do you mean?"

"Remember when you got lowered beneath the plinth?" He pulled a face and mimicked her voice outrageously: "There's someone there!" he cried.

Her eyes went wide. "That was you!" she laughed. "Daniel, that's *awful*!"

"I know," he grinned. "So have you had any luck?"

"I can't talk about it. I gave my word."

"Who to?" scoffed Knox. "Elena? Nicolas Dragoumis?"

"No. Yusuf Abbas."

Knox laughed out loud. "That crook? The man's corrupt, Gaille."

"He's the head of the SCA."

"He destroyed your father."

"I don't know," sighed Gaille, putting her hands on her head. "I don't know who to trust anymore."

"You can trust me," said Knox. "Your father did. Or if you want to talk to someone in authority, try Dr. Sayed. You can trust him with your life."

"Are you sure?"

"How do you mean?"

She hesitated, then said, "He saw something in my photographs of the lower chamber. I'll swear he did. And then some books went missing from his shelves."

Knox frowned. "And you think he took them to stop you making some kind of connection?"

"Maybe."

"Believe me, Gaille, if that's the case, it wouldn't have been to stop you. It would have been to stop Yusuf. Let's go see him."

She shook her head. "He's not here. He's been called to Cairo. And his house is locked."

"Then it's just as well we've got Rick," grinned Knox. "He's got a talent we can use."

Chapter Thirty-three

IBRAHIM'S NERVE, never particularly strong, had completely failed him since Nicolas pressed that sharp blade against his throat. Courage was easier in daydreams. He had let himself be bullied into calling in sick, then writing out and signing multiple authorizations on SCA paper for an excavation in the Western Desert, even though the Western Desert was completely outside his jurisdiction. Since then, he had been forced to stay by his phone in case Nicolas was challenged and he was called to verify his signature.

He hadn't been left alone. Manolis and Sofronio, Nicolas's pilot and copilot, were with him. They had locked all the exterior doors and windows, pocketed the keys, and confiscated his cell phone. Now they followed him everywhere: to his bedroom, even to the bathroom. And Sofronio spoke enough Arabic to listen in on his conversations whenever the telephone rang, his finger poised to disconnect should Ibrahim try anything.

Nicolas and his men were clearly intent on looting a

priceless historical treasure from Siwa. Ibrahim had dedicated his life to Egypt's heritage, yet now he was helping
these gangsters pillage it. He turned abruptly and walked
toward his office. Manolis followed. "I'm only fetch-
ing my work," he sighed. Manolis came with him all the
same. Ibrahim pulled some papers from his top drawer
and glanced at the lock as he left. The key was on the
inside, as he had thought. He walked back out with Manolis, then tutted at himself. "My pen," he said.

Manolis waited while Ibrahim returned into his office,
picked up a bulbous red fountain pen from his desk, and
held it up for Manolis to see. His heart began pounding
unhealthily fast, and his mouth went dry. He regretted his
sedentary life, which had rendered him hopelessly unfit
for heroics. Still, he put his hand on his office door and
told himself this was the moment. His mind urged his
hand to slam the door and twist the key, buy himself some
time, allow him to redeem himself . . . but his hand didn't
obey. Then he lost his nerve and walked on out. His heart
rate slowed. The adrenaline ebbed, and he felt an urgent
need to urinate. He bowed his head in shame at the truth
of himself: a coward, a failure, a nothing. A man's life
was the gift of Allah; what a waste he had made of his.

BIR AL-HAMMAM PROVED to be twin peaks of rock
connected by a low ridge, with steep slopes of sand
that fell away like a pyramid on every side. There was

a freshwater lake at its southern foot, bounded by reeds
and vegetation, and the moonlight shimmered off its waters, rippled by the skipping of insects and the fish that
hunted them. Fruit bats shrieked as they left their caves
in the worn limestone to gorge themselves on the nearby
orchards.

In order to hide their activity, Nicolas arranged all the
vehicles in a semicircle around the precise spot at the base
of the hill where he intended to dig, where Kelonymus
had marked the spot all those millennia ago. Not that anyone was likely to be passing. They were ten kilometers
north of Siwa, after all, and three from the nearest road
or settlement. He supervised the unloading of equipment,
distributing shovels, picks, flashlights, and weapons. He
ordered Leonidas to take one of the AK-47s and climb
onto the container to keep lookout.

Moonlight gave Mohammed enough light to work by.
He munched great scoops out of the desert with his mechanical digger and dumped them behind him, his vehicle
gradually tipping forward so that he had to reverse out
and then dig himself an approach trench. The hill was an
iceberg, most of its mass hidden beneath the sand. After
three hours, his entire digger had been swallowed by the
pit he had created, but still he found nothing. Nicolas and
his men had watched eagerly at first, but their interest
ebbed as the hours passed without success. Still, every so
often Nicolas asked him to pause while he inspected the
newly uncovered rock. During these intervals, Mohammed took the chance to look around. The dunes were so
cold and white, one would think them snowdrifts. Leonidas came down from his sentry duty on top of the con-

tainer, moaning about how bitterly cold it was, and no one went up to replace him. They stood together with their shoulders hunched, and cupped cigarettes.

Mohammed filled another scoop, dumping it behind him. The sand cascaded hard down the slopes; it sounded like rain. His mind fizzed and blurred with fatigue. He was by now so deep in his own pit that he couldn't help but imagine that he was digging his way down to hell. Nicolas held up a hand to ask him to idle his engine once more, then went forward with his father to inspect the sandstone. He shook his head in frustration and kicked the rock angrily. Mohammed tried not to show gladness. His best hope was to obey orders and pray he found nothing. Nicolas trudged out of the pit and came over to him. Mohammed lowered his window.

"Enough," said Nicolas. "There's nothing. We must leave."

Mohammed nodded at the vast trench he had created. "Do we fill it in?"

Nicolas shook his head. "The first wind will take care of it for us."

"As you wish." Mohammed looked over his shoulder to back out of the trench. He was so tired, he forgot to change gear and jumped forward instead, clattering against the rock of the hill with his scoop. A sheet of solidified sand cracked and fell away. He shook his head in annoyance, but as he shifted gears and reversed there was a shout of excitement, then a chorus. The Greeks all clustered around the rock, shining flashlights. Mohammed stood up in his cab. He could just make out a smooth piece of pink marble the size of an outspread hand. His heart sank. Whatever it was these men were looking for, he had just found it for them.

IT WAS DARK AND QUIET at Aly's house. The windows were shuttered and the front door locked. Rick produced his steel wire, and soon they were inside.

"I don't like this," said Gaille nervously.

"Trust me. Aly's a friend. He'll understand. Let's just find these books."

It was Rick who did so, beneath Aly's mattress. There were five volumes, all told. They took one each and flipped through the pages. It was Gaille who spotted the line drawing of Bir al-Hammam. "Look!" she said, setting it on the bed. "The silhouette of the hills. It's exactly the same as the mosaic."

"And the Wepwawet painting from Lycopolis," said Knox.

Gaille stared at him in surprise. "You've been there, too?"

"We've been everywhere, sweetheart," grinned Rick.

"The holder of the secret," muttered Knox. "So now we know what it was: the location of the tomb the shield bearers built for Alexander, with all the grave goods still inside."

"The *exact* location," added Rick, pointing out the two outcrops of rock that mapped exactly onto Akylos's splayed knees and Wepwawet's outspread feet, and between which both sword and standard were planted.

Gaille sucked in a breath anxiously. Knox squinted at her. "What?" he asked.

"It's just, I asked Ibrahim to send me copies of these books. And then Elena was summoned to Alexandria. And Aly to Cairo. You don't think someone's . . . *trying* something, do you?"

"I don't know," said Knox grimly. "But I think we should make sure."

Chapter Thirty-four

IT WAS THE WEE HOURS OF THE NIGHT, so Knox took it easy on his Jeep until they were out of town; then he opened it up over the rutted desert track, the old suspension groaning and squeaking as they bounced and jarred. Icy air blew through the cracks in the doors and the empty ventilator slots. Rick was in the back, leaning forward between the front seats, while Gaille clamped her hands beneath her armpits. "We must be mad!" she said, shivering. "Why don't we come back in the morning?"

"We can't risk it."

"Risk what?" she grumbled. "Even if people know about the tomb, they can't exactly just loot it."

"Trust me, the Dragoumises will do exactly that if the prize is big enough."

"But is it big enough? I mean, they're certain to be found out. Would they really risk international condemnation and life in prison just for some goods fit for Alexander?"

"Maybe that's not what they're after. Maybe there's more."

"Like what?" asked Rick.

"There's only one thing they'd risk everything for."

"Come on, mate. Spill."

"Dragoumis wants an independent Macedonia. That's only going to happen through an all-out war. He knows that. But nations don't go to war for nothing. They need a cause, something greater than themselves that they can all believe in. The Jews followed the Ark of the Covenant into battle. Christians followed the true cross. If you were Macedonian, what would you follow?"

"The body of Alexander," said Gaille numbly.

"The immortal, invincible lord of the world," agreed Knox.

"But that's not possible," protested Rick. "Alexander was on display in Alexandria hundreds of years after the shield bearers all died."

"Was he?"

"Of course," said Gaille. "Julius Caesar visited him. Octavian. Caracalla."

Knox waved impatiently. "Think about it from a different perspective for a moment. Imagine you're Ptolemy, just settling into Egypt. News comes that these bastard shield bearers have made off with Alexander's body. You *need* that body. It's the only thing that gives your reign legitimacy, so you set off after them, but by the time you catch them, there's no sign of Alexander, and the shield bearers have all killed themselves. What the hell do you do now?"

"A double?" frowned Rick. "You're suggesting he used a double?"

"It has to be possible, doesn't it? I mean, Ptolemy had already used a decoy once to send Perdiccas off in the wrong direction. Surely the idea would at least have *occurred* to him."

"But Alexander had the most famous face in antiquity," protested Gaille. "Ptolemy couldn't just embalm a substitute and hope no one noticed."

"Why not? There was no TV, remember. No photography. There was memory and there was art, but all of it was idealized. Listen, Ptolemy kept Alexander's body in Memphis for thirty or forty years before he moved him to Alexandria; archaeologists have been arguing about the reason for that for decades. Do you really believe it took that long to build an appropriate tomb? Or that Ptolemy held the transfer back deliberately so he'd have a grand state event for his son's succession? Bullshit. Maybe *this* is why. Maybe Ptolemy couldn't risk bringing the body to a Greek city because it wasn't Alexander at all, and he had to wait until everyone who'd known Alexander well was either dead or too gaga to remember what he looked like."

"You're dreaming."

"Am I? You showed me the painting yourself."

"What painting?"

"In the antechamber of the Macedonian tomb, of Akylos with Apelles of Cos. Tell me this: why would Alexander's personal portrait painter waste time on a humble shield bearer? Could it be because Akylos was sitting in as Alexander's model? I mean, we never found his body in Alexandria, did we? And you saw the mosaic. Akylos was short and slight with reddish hair. Now, describe Alexander."

"No," said Gaille weakly. "It can't be."

Knox read it on her face. "What?" he asked. "Tell me."

"It's just," she said, "it seemed odd that Kelonymus buried the shield bearers in the Royal Quarter. I mean, that was the absolute heart of Ptolemy's power. Taking them there would have been suicidal."

"Unless?"

"Kelonymus wrote in the Alexander Cipher that he'd pledged to reunite the thirty-three in death as in life. If you're right—I mean, if it really was Akylos buried as Alexander in Alexandria—then the necropolis would have been as close as Kelonymus could possibly have got the other shield bearers to him. This was his effort to reunite them."

Knox stomped on the gas pedal. They roared across the sand.

ELENA WATCHED RAPTLY as Mohammed cleared the marble slab of sand and set the teeth of his scoop between the top of the marble and the limestone lintel, then toppled it forward. She flinched as it fell, professionally appalled by such cavalier vandalism, but the sand was soft and it didn't shatter. She was still as determined as ever on her vendetta, but she also had to see what lay inside. In every way possible, this was the climax of her career.

They each took flashlights, shining them down into the black mouth. A flight of steps almost entirely submerged beneath a slant of sand led down to a rough-hewn corridor just tall and wide enough for two men to stand shoulder to shoulder. Elena followed Nicolas and his father fifty paces into the hill before the corridor opened out into a cavernous chamber. But as they shone their flashlights eagerly around, they soon realized it was empty except of dust and detritus: a broken drinking vessel, an earthenware amphora, the hilt of a dagger, the bones and feathers of a bird, presumably trapped here centuries before. Only the walls repaid in any way the efforts they had made to find this place, for the raw sandstone was handsomely sculpted like the stations of the cross, with scenes from Alexander's life in deep relief, furnished with real artifacts.

In the first, to their left, Alexander was a gurgling infant in his cot, strangling snakes like Hercules—and evidently there had once been real snakes there, though time had disintegrated them, leaving only wafer-thin translucent skins. In the second, he was leading his famed horse Bucephalus away from his own shadow, the better to tame him. The third showed him with other young men around the feet of an elderly man, perhaps Aristotle himself, reading from what would once have been a parchment scroll but which had long since crumbled into fragments that lay at his feet. The fourth showed Alexander on horseback, exhorting his men to battle. The fifth had him plunging a wooden-shafted javelin through the chest of a Persian soldier with a bronze ax. Then came the celebrated Gordian knot. Legend had promised sovereignty over all Asia to the person who could untie it, even though untying it was impossible—a conundrum that Alexander resolved with his customary directness by cutting straight through the rope, represented here by a carved trunk of wood, one end looped around the metal yoke of a chariot, the other anchored inside a slot in the rock wall. The next scene showed him consulting the oracle of Siwa itself, the chief priest assuring him of his divinity. And so it went on, his victories, his setbacks, and his deathbed, all beautifully recorded. The final scene showed his spirit ascending a mountain to join the other gods, being welcomed as an equal.

Their flashlights played among these mesmerizing sculptures, creating shadows that stretched and danced and ducked and darted with life after twenty-three hundred years of utter stillness. No one dared speak. For though this was a remarkable find, Elena knew that it wasn't what Philip and Nicolas Dragoumis had come for, it wasn't what they needed for their mission. Either the shield bearers had never made it this far with Alexander's body or someone had been here before them.

"I don't believe this," muttered Nicolas, balling his fist. "I don't fucking believe this. All our work! All our work!" He gave an inarticulate cry of frustration and kicked the rock wall.

Elena ignored his tantrum and crouched down instead by the foothills of the mountain up which Alexander's spirit was ascending. "There's an inscription," she told Dragoumis.

"What does it say?"

She wiped away the dust and held her flashlight at an

angle to accentuate the shadows and make it easier to see. " *'Go up into the secret skies, Alexander,'* " she translated aloud, " *'while your people here mourn.'* "

"There's another one there," said Costis, pointing his flashlight at the base of the relief of the infant Alexander strangling the snakes.

Dragoumis translated this one himself: *"You do not know your strength, Alexander. You do not know what or who you are."* He glanced doubtfully at Elena. "Does it mean anything to you?"

"It's from the *Iliad,* isn't it?"

Dragoumis nodded. "They both are. But what are they for?"

Elena went down on her haunches by a third scene, a depiction of fierce fighting. " *'Shield clashed against shield, and spear with spear. The clamor was mighty as the earth turned red with blood.'* "

Dragoumis was by the Gordion Knot, he and Costis working their flashlights in tandem, the better to see. " *'Whichever man undoes the knot that fixes this yoke will find himself the Lord of all Asia.'* "

" *'Talk not of running, nor of fear,'* " said Elena, " *'for I know of neither.'* "

They went on around the walls, deciphering the inscriptions. When they were done, Elena looked at Dragoumis. "What do you think?"

"I think we need more—"

A heavy thump reverberated from up the passage at that moment. The floor shook; dust shivered from the walls. Nicolas looked around, then closed his eyes in anger as he realized what it was. "Mohammed," he muttered.

OPPORTUNITY HAD TAKEN MOHAMMED BY SUR-
PRISE. The Greeks, every last one of them, had gone inside the hill. Curiosity had gotten the better of them. He
had waited a minute or two, half expecting one or another
of them to realize their mistake and come back out. When
they didn't, his courage began to mount. If he could block
them in, he could go into Siwa and bring back the police.
They would all go to jail for years, unable to affect Layla
or exact revenge.

His first idea was to ram the mouth of the passage with
one of the vehicles, but they were all the wrong shape. He
decided instead to reseal the passage with the marble
slab, then swamp it beneath sand. He slid the teeth of his
hydraulic scoop beneath it and tried to lift it, but it was
so heavy, his rear wheels left the ground, his hydraulic
mechanism screeched and stalled, and the slab slipped
sideways and clapped loudly on the sand. He cursed himself. They were bound to have heard that. Shouts of alarm
came from within, so it was too late to back down now.
He reversed a little way, then accelerated forward, using
momentum to pick up the marble slab. A Greek arrived at
the mouth just as it tipped back neatly into its slot. Mohammed felt jubilant as he scooped sand and more sand
onto it. He exulted as the pink marble quickly disappeared,
imprisoning them all inside. He could hardly believe how
simple it had been. Nur was right: she always said that if
you faced your demons, you could conquer any—

A muffled burst of gunfire. A second burst.

Mohammed watched numbly as a cone was sucked out of the sand in front of him, as it widened and deepened. A small black hole appeared. A man clambered through. Mohammed swung the scoop at him, but he ducked it easily and aimed his AK-47 at Mohammed's face. Mohammed took his hands off the controls and raised them numbly. A second man crawled out, and a third. He thought of Layla, what would happen to her now, and felt despair. More Greeks scrambled out, like so many rats. Costis opened the cab door, switched off the ignition, and took away the keys. Nicolas appeared, brushing down his sleeves and trousers. He said, "If any of my people knew how to work this machine, you would be dead now. Do you understand?"

"Yes."

"You have a daughter," he said. "Her life depends upon our goodwill. Do you understand?"

"Yes."

"You will cooperate?"

"Yes."

He nodded at Costis, who had returned with a pair of handcuffs. He closed one cuff around the steering wheel and the other around Mohammed's left wrist, allowing him enough movement to work the controls but not enough to escape. He added the key to a key ring on his belt. Then he frowned and looked over his shoulder, out over the dunes. It was a moment before Mohammed heard what had distracted him: the faint growl of an engine coming from the direction of Siwa. Costis glanced at Nicolas, who held up his hand for silence. The noise died away momentarily, then returned even louder. Nicolas grimaced with foreboding. It was the early hours of the morning. No one should be out driving in the desert, not unless they had a very specific purpose.

"You want us to check it out?" asked Costis.

"Yes," said Nicolas.

Costis signaled to Leonidas, Bastiaan, Vasileios, and Dimitris to go with him. They grabbed weapons and sprinted for their four-by-fours.

Chapter Thirty-five

THERE WERE OLD RUTS and tire tracks in the sand. Knox used them as a water-skier uses wake, jolting all three of them, so that they bounced in their seats. It was a point of pride for Gaille that she wouldn't remark on it, even though the passenger-side seat belt had broken years ago and Knox had to fling out his arm every so often to hold her in her seat. The Jeep's antique suspension squeaked, squealed, and banged. Knox downshifted, turned, and roared up a dune, straining the old engine the last few yards. As they crested the dune, she could see the now-familiar silhouette of Bir al-Hammam ahead. Then they were on the downslope, taking it at such an oblique angle that the right wheels left the ground for a moment, hanging in space. Knox pinned Gaille in her seat until they bounced back onto all four. She threw him a grin, but then he glanced in the mirror and frowned in obvious concern. Gaille turned to see a four-by-four coming up fast behind them, headlights off, evidently not wanting to give itself away.

"What the hell?" muttered Rick.

"It's those bloody Greeks," said Knox. He raced down a dune, gaining speed to climb its far bank. They flew over the top and bounded down the other side, roaring away along the compact valley sand.

"There's a second one," said Rick, as another four-by-four appeared over the dune to their left, plunging down the bank, forcing Knox into an evasive skid, his wheels throwing up sprays of sand and bringing them almost to a stop. He shifted up through the gears, turning back the way he had come, but the Jeep was no match for the four-by-fours. They gained inexorably, pulling up alongside on either flank, motioning for him to stop. Knox spun hard and cut left, forcing the driver to slam on his brakes. He roared up another dune, but the gradient was steep and the sand soft, and the balding tires lost traction and began to churn.

Knox stopped fighting, let gravity roll them back down, then swung the Jeep around. A four-by-four nosed into his right side so that both his right wheels left the sand. It nudged them again, harder this time, tipping them up onto their side, so that they plowed a short furrow in the sand before crashing onto their roof. Gaille shrieked and threw up her hands to protect her head as Knox tried to hold her in her seat, but the momentum was too much for him, and she smacked the windshield hard.

They came to a stop. Gaille felt dizzy and sick. The passenger door opened and a man stood above her aiming an AK-47 at her face. She looked numbly up at him. He motioned for her to get out. She tried to obey, but her limbs wouldn't function, so he grabbed her by a hank

of hair and hauled her viciously out, ignoring her shriek
of pain. Knox crawled out after her, bracing himself to
spring at the man, but another of the Greeks was waiting
in ambush and clubbed Knox on the back of the head
with the butt of his gun, so that he collapsed face-first
on the sand.

Rick came out next, hands over his head, looking
cowed. But it was only an act. His first punch knocked
the first Greek onto his backside. He wrenched the AK-47
from him and twisted it around at the second man, his
finger already pulling the trigger. But he didn't quite
make it. A yellow burst of flame spat from the second
man's muzzle, accompanied by the percussive noise of
automatic gunfire, and Rick's chest exploded red. He was
thrown backward onto the sand, the AK-47 falling from
his grasp.

"Rick!" cried Knox, crawling over to his friend. "Oh,
Christ! Rick!"

"Jesus, mate," slurred Rick, trying to raise his head.
"What the fuck . . . ?"

"Don't talk," pleaded Knox. "Just hold on." But it was
already too late. The tension went from his neck, and
his head slumped lifelessly. Knox turned around, hatred
in his heart, purpose in his eye, but the Greek gunman
was watching him with perfect self-assurance. He spat
nonchalantly onto the sand, as if to indicate that was all
Rick's death meant to him, then pointed his weapon at
Knox's chest. "Hands behind your head," he said. "Or it's
the same for you and the girl."

Knox glared at him, but there was nothing he could
do. Vowing silently that he wouldn't leave Rick un-

avenged, he clasped his hands behind his head, while another of the Greeks bound him hand and foot.

IBRAHIM COULDN'T SLEEP. He had lain awake brooding for hours. Every time he managed to soothe himself to relative peace, he would suffer another spasm of shame. He had dedicated his whole life to the study of ancient Egypt. To be complicit in the rape of a tomb—and such a tomb!—would blacken the Beyumi name forever. He couldn't allow this further stain on his honor. He couldn't. Yet each time he sat up, resolved to do something, his nerve wilted. He wasn't that kind of man. He was no kind of man at all. And what could he achieve anyway? They had taken his cell phone, his bedside phone, and his modem jack. They had locked his doors and windows and taken the keys. He rose once more, went to his bedroom door, and stood there with his hand on the handle. He returned for his dressing gown, then took three deep breaths for courage before opening his door. Manolis was asleep on a mattress in the corridor outside. Ibrahim stood still, waited for his heart to calm. He reached his left leg over Manolis. A floorboard creaked beneath the carpet. Ibrahim froze.

Manolis's eyes opened; Ibrahim could see the luminous white rings of his corneas. "What are you doing?" he grunted.

"My stomach," said Ibrahim. "I need tablets."

"Wait. I come with you."

"It's okay. I—"

"I come with you."

THE TWO FOUR-BY-FOURS pulled up in front of Nicolas with a screech of brakes and a spray of sand. Bastiaan threw open the back door of the first and hauled two figures out. First was some lifeless stranger half wrapped in a rug, his chest a mess of blood and pulp. Then the girl, Gaille, dizzy and pale, her wrists and ankles tied with rope. She looked around, evidently terrified, and her eyes locked on someone standing behind him. "Elena!" she cried plaintively. "How *could* you?"

"Because she's a patriot," retorted Nicolas coldly when Elena didn't speak.

Costis was hauling another man from the back of the second four-by-four. He glared up from the sand. *Knox!* Nicolas felt a little nauseated suddenly, as though he had eaten something that disagreed with him. There was something about the man that made him feel just that little bit helpless. Knox's gaze slid past Nicolas to where his father was standing. "So!" he said contemptuously. "A common tomb robber."

"Scarcely a *common* tomb robber," replied Dragoumis, unruffled, "as I suspect you know full well."

"Have you found him, then?" Knox asked despite himself.

"Not yet," admitted Dragoumis.

"Not yet?" frowned Nicolas. "What do you mean, not yet? There's nothing there."

Dragoumis looked sourly at his son. "Have you learned nothing about this man Kelonymus?" he asked impatiently. "Do you really believe he's the kind to surrender his greatest secret at the first breach?" He pointed at Gaille, then said to his men, "She understands his mind better than anyone. Bring her inside."

"Don't do it, Gaille," said Knox tersely. "Don't give them anything."

Dragoumis turned to him. "You know I am a man of my word. So let me make you an offer. If you two help me find what we're looking for, I vow I'll let you both go free."

"Sure!" scoffed Knox. "After everything we've seen!"

"Believe me, Daniel, if we find what we're looking for, the more you two talk, the better it will be for us."

"And if we refuse?"

Dragoumis gave a small, sorrowful shrug. "Do you really want to put that to the test?"

Nicolas kept his eyes on Knox while he debated his response. It was clear that he was still burning with rage for what they had just done to his friend, that he was only waiting for an opportunity to exact revenge. He turned to warn his father, but his father silenced him with a look, as though he was already five moves ahead, so he shrugged and turned back to Knox. The man was still struggling with himself, with his conscience, but then he glanced at Gaille, her face ashen with fear and streaked by tears, silently pleading with him not to do anything crazy.

He blinked and sighed. "Okay," he said. "We'll do what we can."

"Good," said Dragoumis. He turned to Costis. "Untie their ankles, but not their wrists. And keep a close eye on this one," he added, gesturing at Knox. "He's more dangerous than he looks."

Costis nodded seriously. "I know," he said.

IBRAHIM AND MANOLIS walked downstairs together. The carpet was lush, but the soles of Ibrahim's feet felt icy. He glanced down, almost expecting them to be glistening blue-white, like diamonds. Sofronio was snoring on the couch. When Manolis turned on the lights, he sat up, disoriented with sleep, then cursed Manolis in Greek and covered an expansive yawn.

Ibrahim made a show of looking through his kitchen cabinets, slamming drawers, muttering. He heard the two Greeks conferring. Their Greek was so guttural, he couldn't understand a word, but the way they looked suspiciously at him . . . "They're not here," he said brightly. "They must be in my desk." He walked briskly toward his office. Sofronio and Manolis were still muttering. It was now or never. Ibrahim leaned his weight forward and broke into a run.

"MOVE, DAMN YOU," said Costis, jabbing Knox in the small of the back with the muzzle of his Kalashnikov.

Knox glowered over his shoulder. "You're going to pay for what you did to Rick," he promised.

But Costis only snorted and jabbed him harder. And in truth, Knox was in no position to make threats. Walking along this dark passage into the belly of the hill, the bloom and flare of flashlights all around, having to duck every so often to avoid scraping his scalp on the low ceiling, he felt sure that it wasn't just Alexander's tomb he was walking into, but his own and Gaille's, too, unless he could somehow turn this situation around.

The passage opened out abruptly. Evidently, the Greeks had been here before, for they expressed no surprise at the marvelous sculptures around the walls. But to Knox they were so remarkable that for a moment he almost forgot about his predicament. His wrists were still bound, but his hands were in front of him. He took a flashlight from one of the Greeks, then went over to a sculpture of Alexander leading a charge. Gaille came with him, and then Elena and Dragoumis, too, creating the surreal impression of four academics at a conference discussing some obscure artifact.

Gaille stooped to translate the inscription. " *'Then Pallas Minerva gave him courage that he might outdo all others. Fire blazed like the summer sun from his shield and helmet.'* " She turned to Elena. "Is that what you made of it?" she asked.

"Pretty much," agreed Elena. Then she added, a touch uncertainly, "It's from the *Iliad*, isn't it?"

"Yes," agreed Gaille. "Adapted a little, but yes."

Elena nodded more confidently. "He certainly likes his Homer," she said. "All of the inscriptions are from the *Iliad*."

"Not all," corrected Dragoumis. He nodded at the far wall. "The Gordian knot wasn't in the *Iliad*."

"No," agreed Knox. He walked over to it and stooped to read the inscription. *"He who unties the knot on this yoke will find himself the Lord of all Asia."* He snorted and glanced around at Dragoumis. "You gave us your word, yes?" he asked.

"Yes," said Dragoumis.

"Good," said Knox. He walked over to the tableau of Alexander spearing the Persian and grabbed the bronze ax in both hands. It was cool to the touch and surprisingly heavy.

"Stop him!" cried Nicolas.

"Be quiet," said Philip Dragoumis irritably.

Knox took the ax to the Gordian knot, bringing the blade down hard, slicing splinters out of the wood. He struck again, then a third time, the blows sending shivers up his fingers and palms. But the dull blade still did its work, and the old wood shattered and tore apart. One end lay still; the other slithered like a fugitive snake into the rock wall—apparently attached to some kind of weight. There was a low scratching sound, then silence. They waited expectantly, but seconds ticked by and nothing more happened.

"Is that it?" sneered Nicolas. "I hope you don't think that—"

And then it started: a low rumbling in the rock above their heads, growing louder and louder, shaking dust from the ceiling and making tiny vibrations in the floor. Everyone looked up and then, apprehensively, at one another. The noise stopped, and there was silence again. Everyone shrugged and began to relax and—

The wall to Knox's right suddenly exploded, sending shards of stone flying everywhere. He had virtually no time to react. He dropped the ax and threw himself to the ground, taking Gaille down with him, hugging her face against his chest as fragments of rock thudded and crashed into his legs and back, glancing off his scalp, bruising and stinging, drawing blood.

It was over almost before they realized it was happening at all. The shrapnel settled; the thunderous noise died, leaving their ears ringing. People began muttering and coughing and choking on the dust and powdered sandstone, gingerly checking themselves for injuries. One of the Greeks was cursing, but not too seriously, as though he had sprained a wrist or turned an ankle. Other than that and a few cuts and bruises, it seemed they had been lucky. It took Knox a moment to recognize the opportunity for him and Gaille to make a break for it. But when he glanced around, the first thing he saw was Costis, grinning knowingly at him and pointing his gun.

He picked himself up and helped Gaille up, too. Someone retrieved a flashlight and shined it at where the wall had been—a great, gaping hole was now torn in its heart. There was blackness beyond, indicative of an even greater space, and the glint of metallic objects on the floor. They edged closer, treading tentatively on pulverized sandstone littered with fragments of a tougher stone, like marble, that crackled beneath their feet.

Knox looked up at the circular shaft that rose almost vertically above him into the hill before vanishing into darkness. Cutting the Gordian knot must have triggered a rockfall. But then he was through to the other side, and other matters took his attention. The hewn passage zig-zagged left and right, shielding it from the blast of the falling rock. Then it began to funnel open. Niches were cut in the walls, and in them were life-size painted alabaster statues of nymphs and satyrs, a rearing horse, Dionysus on a couch, his head thrown back, drinking from a goblet, surrounded by tendrils of ivy and fat bunches of purple grapes. They passed other objects, too: Attic vases of brown, red, and black painted with scenes from Alexander's life. Too crude to be the work of Kelonymus, perhaps they were the personal tributes of the shield bearers themselves. A wooden model of a chariot. Some crude pottery figurines. A silver wine jug and matching drinking vessels. A bronze cauldron. A golden bowl containing fistfuls of uncut precious and semiprecious stones: rubies, turquoise, lapis lazuli, amethyst, diamonds, sapphires. A golden cup inscribed with a sixteen-pointed star, and next to it a golden handbell that reminded Knox poignantly of Rick. And then, set in the right-hand wall, a painting of Alexander in his chariot, carrying a golden scepter, just like the frieze described by Diodorus Siculus as part of the funeral catafalque, enabling Knox to answer at last the question of how Kelonymus and the shield bearers had financed all their endeavors. They had had the cata-falque. Perhaps these shield bearers were the very unit that Ptolemy had tasked with bringing it back to Egypt, only for them to change their plans once they realized that he meant to betray Alexander's last wish.

Costis nudged him in the back again. They moved on, passing what could only be described as an ancient library: scrolls bound with ivory holders and stacked in loculi cut in the sandstone walls, and books in open silver and golden caskets, the handwriting still faintly visible on their yellow parchment and papyrus, as well as drawings of herbs, flowers, and animals.

"My god!" muttered Gaille, looking at Knox with wild eyes, all too aware of the intrinsic and historic value of this find.

They kept walking and the passage opened up again into a great domed chamber twice the size of the previous one, its floor glittering like shattered quartz with metallic arti-facts, its walls and ceiling decorated with gold leaf, so that their flashlights reflected dazzlingly from all sides. And there were grave goods here, too, set on twelve altars: rings and necklaces and amphorae and coins and caskets. Weap-ons, too: a shield, a sword, a helmet, a breastplate, a crested helmet. And in the center of the chamber, at the heart of all the altars, at the focal point of their flashlights, stood a high pyramid, rising in steps on every side to a peak on which rested a magnificent golden anthropoid coffin.

And no one could be in any doubt now about what they had found.

Chapter Thirty-six

IBRAHIM SLAMMED HIS OFFICE DOOR and turned the key in the lock just as Sofronio charged the door with his shoulder. Ibrahim jumped back and cried out as the panels bulged and the frame shook, but the door held. Sofronio charged again; still it held. Ibrahim gained confidence. He strode to his desk, picked up his phone, and dialed the police emergency number. It rang twice before it was answered. He gave his name and address and had begun to explain his situation when the line suddenly went dead. His eyes tracked the white cable to the point where it pierced the wall and ran out to the rest of the house. He stared at it dumbly. A different kind of pounding started on the door, sharp and loud: a boot, not a shoulder, two men taking it in turns. The frame by the jamb at last began to give. Ibrahim dropped the telephone handset and backed away, watching sickly as the wood began to splinter. There was nowhere to hide. The door to the main room was the only way out except for the windows, but they were locked and Manolis had the keys. A letter opener and a paperweight lay on his desk. The knife was sharp and steely, but he knew in his heart that he lacked the nerve to wield it in anger, so he hurled the paperweight through the window instead, then jumped up onto his desk. The door finally gave, the jamb a streak of yellow wood beneath its coat of gloss. The two men charged in. Ibrahim dived for the hole in the shattered window, but Sofronio grabbed his ankle, stopping him dead, so that he plunged down onto a long, jagged shard of glass. It was a strangely dull sensation, more a blow than a cut. All strength ebbed from his limbs. He was dragged back into the room, his chin thumping onto his desk and carpet. He felt his abdominal wall flap open as he was turned onto his back, and saw with a certain perverse pride the deep shock on Manolis's face as he pressed his hands on either side of Ibrahim's belly in a futile effort to stem the evisceration. Sofronio simply closed his eyes.

Ibrahim lay there as the two men discussed what to do. Manolis tipped books from the shelves while Sofronio left the room and returned with a large, translucent bottle of white spirits, which he splashed over the papers, carpet, and wooden desk. He stooped to set fire to it with a yellow plastic lighter; then both men hurried away. A teaching of the Prophet came irreverently to Ibrahim's mind: that a Muslim should keep inviolate his blood, property, and honor. He almost managed an abstract chuckle at this, to have lost all three in such spectacular fashion. His fingers and toes began to tingle like a swallow of good tonic water. He had long had a queasy fascination with the mechanics of death, wondering whether oblivion would follow instantly from his heart stopping or whether his mind would fade out like an antique radio. Fire filled the room with choking thunderclouds, causing his eyes to burn. He heard sirens, a screech and clash of metal, gunshots, and then men in masks and uniforms rushing in, kneeling beside him. But too late, far too late. To his surprise, he felt a mild but growing euphoria. He had brought indelible dishonor on his name, his family, and his city; but at least people would say he had given everything he could to put it right.

IN THE CHAMBER WITHIN THE HILL, Knox, Gaille, and all the Greeks climbed the pyramid together to the summit. There was a moment's awed silence as they stood around the coffin, raised to waist level on a white marble plinth, its lid lushly carved with scenes of hunting and war. With the side of his hand, Knox brushed away the skin of sand and dust that had settled there over the millennia. One could tell gold from bronze because bronze tarnished over the centuries, and this was definitely gold.

Like a high priest, Dragoumis rested his palms on it. "Open it," he ordered.

The lid was so heavy, it took all of them heaving together to raise it and shift it sideways and then lay it on the floor beside the coffin. They all stared hungrily down inside, pressing and craning past each other, the better to see. A man's body lay snugly within, deep in dust and the traces of petals and spices, a giant ruby diadem on his brow, his arms folded across his chest, a sword on one side, a golden scepter on the other. He had evidently once been covered in gold leaf, but it had peeled away in places, exposing blackened, parchmentlike skin and limbs shrunken down to the bones beneath. Black and gold, like so many of the world's most dangerous creatures.

In the dappled, moving light, Knox looked for the signature scars on the body. Yes. Even after all these centuries, it was possible to discern faint traces of the throat slash of Cyropolis, the shoulder puncture from a Gaza catapult, the nipple pierced by a Multan arrow, and the thigh gashed at Issus. Knox's skin prickled. He felt weak. There could be no question. "It's him," he murmured. "It's Alexander."

Dragoumis's eyes were wet when he looked around. "Then it's time to bring him home," he said.

IT WAS EASY ENOUGH taking the coffin lid out to the container truck. That was just a function of exertion and time. The coffin itself, however, was another matter altogether. It was far too heavy for them to lift, so they slung ropes around it to lower it carefully down the pyramid, using sand as a lubricant on the steps and the passage floor, dragging it behind them, all pulling together, even Knox and the girl, though they got only a foot or so with every heave. They brought it finally to the passage mouth, already turned into a ramp by the sand Mohammed had dumped. They tied a thick rope to the tow bar of a four-by-four and tried to tow it out, but the vehicle's wheels spun uselessly. They brought in the second four-by-four, and all heaved together and finally managed to haul it to the truck.

Getting it up into the container was even more problematic. Mohammed tried to lift it with the hydraulic arm of his digger but only tipped himself forward. In the end it was Philip Dragoumis who suggested the solution: Mohammed dug a trench in the sand in front of the coffin; then the truck reversed into it, so that the mouth of the container was below the coffin. They plugged the intervening gap with sand, then dragged the coffin in until it was over the front axle, as stable as they could make it.

Nicolas wiped his brow, well pleased, then looked over to his father for approval. But his father only gestured toward the east, where the sun was already beginning to show on the horizon. Nicolas nodded. Perhaps one day they might come back for all the other treasures inside the hill. For the moment, though, they had what they needed, and it wouldn't pay to be greedy.

No one noticed when Elena slipped away from the container and walked across to the four-by-fours to collect her bag. She had bought her gun last night by the simple expedient of flagging down the first taxi she saw in Cairo and thrusting cash at its driver until he realized she was serious. The cabbie had begun a relay of telephone calls, and two hours later, a dealer had shown her his collection. She knew the one she wanted before he even picked it up. It was black and chunky, and just looking at it gave her confidence. When she pointed it out to him, he nodded keenly. A shrewd choice, he had enthused: the Walther P99, a semiautomatic with two clips. After explaining how it was put together, he had taken her out into the alleys of the City of the Dead and shown her how the safety catch worked, and she pumped four bullets into a wall. It had given her a warm glow in her belly, the same warm glow she got now as she took it in her hand.

Three lives to take. Then her blood debt would finally be settled.

She turned around to see Mohammed reburying the mouth of the tomb beneath sand. Knox and Gaille were being herded by Nicolas, Leonidas, and Bastiaan to the four-by-fours, while the other Greeks were sitting on the back of the container, smoking well-earned cigarettes. Costis and Dragoumis were standing together, watching benignly. Costis had an AK-47 slung over his shoulder, but he looked relaxed, not expecting trouble.

Elena couldn't have asked for a better opportunity. She walked toward them, the Walther hidden behind her back. The men turned when they saw her coming. Dragoumis frowned, as though puzzled by her expression. "Yes?" he asked.

She took Costis first, pulling the trigger even as she was raising the gun. The round punctured his rib cage. The recoil kicked up her hand, so that the second round tore through his upper chest beneath his throat, flinging him onto his back. Her sense of time and space distended. To her left, men yelled in panic and scrambled for their weapons. She paid them no heed. She felt strangely invulnerable, protected by destiny. Costis was making strange high, keening sounds. He raised his head to look down at his punctured front, then tried to hold his hands over himself. She stepped astride him, aimed at his nose, and fired once more. The bullet tore through the ridge above his eye, and his head slumped lifelessly to the sand.

She turned to Dragoumis. His face was white. He seemed frozen. She walked up to him and pressed the muzzle against his heart. "Tell your men to be still," she said. Dragoumis said nothing, so she raised and pressed the gun against his forehead. When she saw him tremble, she felt a great gladness inside. Then she realized he was trembling not with fear but with anger. "I didn't kill Pavlos," he said flatly.

"Yes, you did."

He shook his head. "You have my word: that crash was an accident."

"It was no accident," she assured him. "Believe me. I know everything. I know you hired a whore to seduce Pavlos. I know you had them filmed together, that you showed him the footage. I know you threatened to send me a copy unless he stopped calling for an inquiry."

"Then you also know that I had no need to kill him."

Elena could feel tears prickling on her cheeks. "Did you really believe you could control Pavlos? Not a chance. Not you. Not me. Not anyone. He came to me. He confessed everything. That's how I know you were responsible."

A muscle flickered on Dragoumis's temple. "I give you my word," he said. "I swear on Macedonia. On the body of Alexander. On the death of my wife. I never ordered for Pavlos to be killed."

"No," said Elena. "But *I* did. I had him killed because of your fucking film." She smiled as Dragoumis assimilated this, worked out the import, looked at her for the first time in the certain knowledge of his own death; and seeing that, savoring it, she shot him once through the forehead, scattering bits of brain and bone like seed corn over the sands. Then, thinking of Pavlos, longing for him, she stuffed the hot muzzle against the roof of her mouth, closed her eyes, uttered his name, and pulled the trigger one final time.

Chapter Thirty-seven

NICOLAS DRAGOUMIS FLINCHED and closed his eyes a millisecond before Elena killed his father and then herself. When he opened them again, his father was lying on his side, one arm splayed out, the other tucked awkwardly beneath him, legs folded like half a swastika. He found himself staring and staring, unable to take in what he saw. It was impossible that such a man could be so quickly and utterly extinguished. He stepped unsteadily across Elena's prostrate corpse to stand beside his father, waiting for him to move—to rise, brush himself down, give orders.

He jumped as someone touched his elbow. He turned to see Leonidas talking to him. He could see his lips move but could make no sense of the words. He looked down again, and slowly his brain began to recover. All men died, but their missions lived on. His father's mission lived on. It was up to him to complete it. The thought strengthened Nicolas. He looked around again. The sun had already cleared the horizon. The mouth of the tomb had already vanished beneath sand. His men were gazing expectantly at him.

"Dig a pit," he said. "We bury Costis and Elena here." The calmness and authority of his voice surprised him. But then, why should it? His father had been Philip II reincarnate, the father of Alexander the Great. And what did that make him? Yes, what did that make *him*?

"And your father?" frowned Leonidas.

"You think I'd leave him here?" snapped Nicolas. "We bring him with us. He is to be buried with full honors."

"What about those two?" asked Leonidas, nodding at Gaille and Knox, being herded by Bastiaan into the back of one of the four-by-fours.

Nicolas felt a resurgence of his anger, and an opportunity to vent it. His jaw tightened. He stooped to take the Walther from Elena's loose grip. He checked the clip: five gone, four left. He walked over to the four-by-four. "Get Knox out," he ordered.

Bastiaan dragged Knox out by the arm and threw him on the sand. Nicolas aimed down at his chest. The girl cried out, pleading for mercy, but Bastiaan punched her in the temple, so that she fell sprawling unconscious across the rear seats. Nicolas stared down at Knox. "No one can say we didn't give you fair warning," he said.

"Your father gave us his word he'd let us go if we helped you find Alexander."

"My father is dead," said Nicolas.

"Yes, but he—"

He got no further, because Bastiaan slammed the butt of his gun into the back of his skull, and he collapsed facedown on the sand.

"Thank you," said Nicolas. He smiled as he aimed at the back of Knox's head and tightened his finger on the trigger.

MOHAMMED RUBBED HIS LEFT WRIST where the hard steel handcuff chafed. He didn't recognize the man Nicolas was about to shoot, but he recognized Gaille, who had always been nice to him during the necropolis excavation, enquiring after Layla and wishing them all well. And he recognized murder, too, and that he was colluding in it.

He had thought Layla's life worth any price. Now he realized he had been wrong.

The cuff was too tight to slip his hand free. And though he was a strong man, he wasn't strong enough to rip the steering wheel from its mount. But the handcuff key was on a chain on Costis's belt. That, at least, gave him a fighting chance. He started up the digger, thrust it into gear, and accelerated forward. The suddenness of his charge caught the Greeks by surprise. Nicolas turned and fired twice, but Mohammed used the scoop as a shield, and the bullets pinged and whined away, and then he was upon Nicolas, so that he had to dive aside, rolling over and over. Bullets sprayed; Mohammed ducked as he worked his controls to scoop Costis up from the sand. Then he turned down the slope, the gradient helping him speed away, glancing over his shoulder to see the Greeks streaming down after him on foot and in the vehicles. The digger bucked and jolted, and Costis danced in the scoop but didn't fall. Mohammed reached flatter terrain and dumped Costis to the sand, then pulled up alongside him, placing the bulk of the digger between himself and the Greeks. He threw open the cab door and stretched down, but he couldn't quite reach Costis. He twisted the steering wheel as far as it would go, and tried again. Still no good—he could only brush him with his fingertips, however hard he strained. The Greeks were yelling as they hurtled down toward him, loosing wild shots, roaring their vehicles. He hooked his right boot beneath Costis's head, lifting him high enough to snatch a hank of hair. He grabbed his chin, collar, finally his belt, the chain, the key ring. Four keys. Two bore BMW insignia; the others were small, unmarked. He had to lift Costis bodily from the sand to get the first key up to the cuff. No good. He was trying the second when something exploded behind his ear, and his world went black.

NICOLAS ARRIVED AT THE FOOT OF THE SLOPE to find Mohammed unconscious, blood leaking from a cut in his scalp. "New plan," he said tightly. "Put the bodies in the flatbed. Dump it and the digger in the lake."

Vasileios pulled up in the second SUV and nodded at the backseat. "And the girl?"

Nicolas peered in. Gaille was sprawled unconscious across the backseats. It made him realize suddenly that he'd forgotten about Knox in the chaos, and he suffered

a sudden lurch of premonition. He looked around. All his
men were down here with him—every last one of them.
Without Costis or his father to lead them, they had degen-
erated into an undisciplined rabble. "Where's Knox?" he
demanded, even though in his heart he already knew the
answer. "Who the fuck was looking after Knox?" No one
spoke. Their eyes wouldn't meet his when he glared their
way. He clenched his fists as he gazed up to where Knox
had been. There was no sign of him except for the ropes
that had bound him, now lying discarded on the sand. He
closed his eyes for a moment to let the swell of fury pass.
Sometimes it almost seemed as though God wasn't on
their side. He jumped in the four-by-four with Vasileios
and Bastiaan and drove back up. The place was a mess
of footprints, impossible to track. Knox could have vanished anywhere. He could have hidden beneath the sand
or climbed the hill or gone round the other side of it by
now. The sun was getting higher all the time, and daylight wasn't safe. You could see forever in the desert on
a clear day; their vehicles would stand out like beacons.
The tourists and the bird-watchers would already be leaving their hotels. Reveille would have sounded in the army
barracks. They had to leave now.

Nicolas half pulled Gaille out of the backseat and
pressed the muzzle of the Walther against her temple.
"Hear this!" he shouted. "The girl dies if you give us
trouble. You hear? Any trouble at all, your old friend's
daughter dies."

His voice echoed off the hill, then faded to silence.

Chapter Thirty-eight

Kₙₒₓ ᴡᴀᴛᴄʜᴇᴅ ꜰʀᴏᴍ ʜɪꜱ ʟᴇᴅɢᴇ as Nicolas and several of his men drove off north in the container truck and one of the four-by-fours, leaving others behind to load Rick, Elena, and Costis into the flatbed, which they then drove out into the lake. It plowed up a great white wash as it floated before tipping onto its side, belching out air, and sinking. Knox felt sickened watching the body of his old friend Rick consigned so unceremoniously to the deep—and guilty, too, because Rick had only come here to help him. But now wasn't the time for regret or mourning or vengeance. Those would come later. Right now he had work to do.

The Greek driver of the flatbed swam in a leisurely breaststroke back to the bank. He shook himself down, walked over to the mechanical digger, started it up, and repeated the trick. The driver hauled himself out the window as the cab vanished beneath the surface. He was halfway back to the bank when the lake erupted behind him and the big Egyptian spluttered up, coughing and choking. His revival lasted only a few moments until the digger dragged him back down beneath the surface, still handcuffed to the wheel. One of the Greeks cracked a joke. They all laughed as they climbed into the second four-by-four and set off after their comrades.

Knox waited until they were out of view, then scrambled down the cliff face and bounded down the sand dunes to the lake, stripping as he went.

CHOKING HAD SHOCKED MOHAMMED back to consciousness, but it seemed only so that he could experience terror as the digger pulled him remorselessly down. He managed a last despairing breath before it tugged him beneath the murky water. The engine stalled, the door was hanging open, and the whole vehicle was tilted at a precarious angle as though it might tip over on the soft lake bed. He pulled himself inside, where a little air had been trapped against the cab's curved roof. He breathed in, felt for and switched on the domelight. It cast rings of reflected yellow light on the disturbed water, revealing how small his air supply was. He ducked back down, strained to pull his hand free of its cuff, but his thumb prevented him. He tried to wrench the wheel from its mount. Useless. The exertion was only burning through his meager supply of oxygen. The key was in the ignition, so he turned it, but the engine didn't respond. He went up for another breath, and the digger lurched and tilted further, sending precious bubbles streaming away. He remembered reading about some mountaineer who had sawed off his arm with a pen-knife to free himself from rockfall. Yes. He could do this for Layla. He took a breath, ducked down, and fumbled on the floor for shards shattered by gunfire, but he found only pebbles of safety glass. He went back up.

A flurry of water, a tug on his sleeve. He almost died of fright when a man's head bobbed up beside him. The man Nicolas had wanted to kill. "Where's the key?" he asked curtly.

"The dead Greek," gasped Mohammed. "On his belt."

The man nodded, ducked, and vanished.

There was so little air, it was already beginning to go bad. He pressed his cheek against the exposed metal roof and tried to keep calm. An eternity seemed to pass. The air grew fetid, and his mind fuzzed. A headache pounded between his eyes. He prayed for Layla, that somehow she would get through this, that her life would be good once this dreadful disease was behind her. What could stop her then? All fathers were proud of their daughters, but who among them had such cause?

The cab lurched again. A small shriek escaped him as more air bubbled away. That was the trouble with hope: it came at the cost of intense fear. He had to pull his cuffed wrist almost taut to reach the remaining air. It was rank, poisoning him, and he had to breathe harder and faster to harvest any oxygen from it at all.

The cab lurched and tipped remorselessly sideways, spilling up the last of the air. He clamped his mouth with his hand as long as he could, but then he couldn't fight the need in his lungs anymore; he had to open it. Water flooded in. He choked once but then sucked in again, and the liquid poured down his throat. A swirl of random yet comforting colors, patterns, sensations, aromas, all bathed in the warm love of Nur and Layla . . . and then a burst of bright, white light.

NICOLAS CALLED IBRAHIM'S VILLA as he led his small convoy north on the Marsa Matruh road. There was no reply. He called Manolis and then Sofronio on their cell phones. Neither answered. Something was wrong. Anxiety gnawed at his stomach. He glanced at Vasileios.

"What is it?" asked Vasileios.

"I don't know."

He looked around at the second SUV, and then the container truck immediately behind it. Burdened by its precious cargo, it was struggling to reach and maintain 70kph. At such a rate, it would take them at least ten hours to reach Alexandria. Ten hours. Christ! Who knew what might happen in that time, especially with Knox on the loose? And he had thought everything would go so smoothly! He picked up his phone to try Ibrahim and the guys again, only to see his signal fade and die altogether. If their journey down was any way to judge, his phone wouldn't pick up again until they neared Marsa Matruh and the coast.

There was nothing for it but to press on.

STREAMS OF RELEASED AIR and lake bed gasses simmered the surface of the lake, and slicks of oil, algae, and detritus made overlapping circles, marking the places where the vehicles lay on the bottom. Knox swam from the center of one to the other, then kicked down. The flatbed truck had made it farther into the lake than the digger, but the water, usually so clear, was badly roiled; Knox had to work by feel. His lungs were about done when he touched something metallic. He surfaced for more air, then dived once more, pulling himself through an open window into the flatbed's cab. He searched with his hands. The first corpse he found was Rick. He felt that sickness in his gut again but squashed it down. The second body had long hair. A woman—Elena. He pushed her aside and grabbed a foot instead, following it up a trouser leg to a belt. He fumbled along it, found a key chain, then unbuckled the belt and slipped the key chain off. Clutching it tight, he pulled himself out of the cab, kicked for the surface, and heaved in a breath, then swam back until he judged himself to be above the digger. Filling his lungs with air, he kicked down. His eyes were raw and burning as he searched for the excavator, which had tipped completely onto its side. He pulled himself in the broken window to find all the air escaped, and Mohammed slumped and lifeless. In his haste, Knox dropped the keys. By the time he found them and picked them up again, the pressure was building relentlessly in his own lungs, his brain

screeching for air. He took Mohammed's wrist. The first
key didn't fit; the second, either. In panicked disbelief, he
tried the keys again. Still nothing. He wanted to scream.
He needed air. The other cuff was locked around the steering wheel. He tried the first key on that, then the second.
This time it went in. He turned it, and the cuff released.
Grabbing the big man's collar, he dragged him to the window, out and up to the surface, then sidestroked to the
shallows, hauling Mohammed behind him with one arm
across his chest, pulling him up onto the bank.

He put one hand on the unmoving chest, his other on
the throat. The big man's heart had stopped. Of course
it had fucking stopped—he'd been breathing nothing but
water for the past three minutes. Knox thought back to
the drowning and near-drowning course he had attended
as a diving instructor. When water entered the airway,
people automatically experienced larygnospasm, which
was to say that their throat constricted to divert the inhaled water to their stomachs. But after cardiac arrest,
the airways often relaxed again, allowing water to enter
the lungs. Kurt, a beanpole Austrian with a beard down
to his nipples, had taught no-drainage cardiopulmonary
resuscitation straight from the book; but in an acerbic
aside had remarked that if *his* life depended upon it, he'd
want the Heimlich first, whatever the current thinking
was, because if your airways were blocked, your brain
was fucked anyway. Knox stretched both arms around
the big man's waist, made a fist of his right hand, thumb
just below the solar plexus, then squeezed his abdomen
with a sharp upward thrust. Frothy dark water flooded
from his mouth and nose. He pumped until nothing more

came out, then tilted back his head to open the airway, pinched the nose, and ventilated him twice. He checked for a pulse, found nothing. He kept pumping and ventilating, pumping and ventilating, until the big man suddenly convulsed, choked, gasped, expelled a dribble more water from his throat and mouth, and began again to breathe. Knox slumped onto the muddy sand beside him, naked and drained and trembling.

Then he remembered with weary horror that Nicolas had Gaille. *Let her be alive. Please God, let her be alive.*

He pushed himself to his feet and gathered his clothes. His legs were weak and rubbery, but he forced himself to run across the dunes to see if he could salvage the Jeep.

Chapter Thirty-nine

NICOLAS LEANED OUT HIS WINDOW to wave the container truck to the side of the road. He needed to refuel and make phone calls, but he couldn't exactly pull into a service station with Gaille lying across his backseats. His men opened the back doors of the container. The sun was still low enough that it hadn't heated up inside yet.

They waited until the road was clear in both directions, then dragged Gaille inside, gagged her, and tied her to the steel handrail at the front end. Then he ordered Eneas to stay inside with her to make sure she didn't try anything.

Back in the four-by-four, they raced on ahead. The road was straight and true and untroubled by uniforms. Vasileios turned on the radio and searched for music; Nicolas turned it off again. They finally reached a service station, where a couple of trucks were parked outside, on their way to or from Siwa. Vasileios refueled while Nicolas made calls. There was still no answer from Ibrahim, Sofronio, or Manolis. What the hell was going on? He called his office in Thessalonike and ordered Katerina to look into it. But his apprehension was growing worse all the time as he climbed back into the SUV.

KNOX'S JEEP WAS LYING AT AN ANGLE on its roof, a third of the way up a dune. He pushed and pushed, achieving a little back-and-forth resonance, but not quite enough to take it to its tipping point. He dug sand from beneath the roof with his bare hands to increase the angle of tilt, then tried again. Finally, with a great crash, it fell onto its side and then almost onto its wheels, teetering there for a moment before threatening to fall back. Knox hurled himself against it, and though his feet were slipping and slithering in the soft sand, he refused to give way, and finally the Jeep clattered upright, throwing up clouds of sand and dust.

The key was still in the ignition. He turned it with trepidation, but it caught the first time. Tears of gratitude moistened his eyes. What a beautiful, wonderful fucking car. He raced back to the lake, where Mohammed was breathing shallowly but regularly, though he hadn't regained consciousness. Even with Gaille to worry about, Knox couldn't just leave him. The man weighed at least 250, and it was all Knox could do to heave him into the back. Then he set off back to Siwa and its general hospital, devising plans as he went.

IT WAS LATE MORNING when Nicolas drew close enough to
the coast to pick up a cell signal. He called Ibrahim's home
number at once, then Manolis and Sofronio. Still nothing.
He called Thessalonike, but now Katerina wasn't answering, either. Fear was a pool of acid in his gut. Manolis and
Sofronio were his pilot and copilot, so without them he'd
be stuck in this shit-hole of a country. Alexandria was still
a six hours' drive away, but he had to know what was going
on, so that he could make contingency plans. He glanced
around at the other SUV directly behind him, and then the
container truck, weighted by all that gold, slowing them
all down.

He called the second SUV on the cell phone; Bastiaan
answered. Nicolas ordered him to drive on ahead, to find
out what had happened in Alexandria. Bastiaan gave him
the thumbs-up; they pulled out to pass, then speeded on
ahead and soon had vanished out of sight.

KNOX PULLED UP OUTSIDE SIWA GENERAL HOS-
PITAL, tooting his horn frantically. A nurse came out,
shielding his eyes from the morning sun, and Knox flung
open the rear door to show him Mohammed, who still had
a handcuff locked around his wrist.

"What happened?" asked the nurse, moving already into diagnosis.

"His heart stopped," replied Knox. "He almost drowned."

The nurse ran back inside, reappearing a few moments later with a doctor and a gurney. "The police will want to talk to you," said the doctor.

"Of course."

They loaded Mohammed gently and wheeled him inside. "Come with us," said the doctor. "You'd better wait inside."

"In a moment," said Knox. "I need something from my Jeep." He went back out. Police be damned. It wasn't just Nicolas's warning about what he would do to Gaille if he encountered trouble; it was that the Egyptians were notoriously trigger-happy in hostage situations, and there was no way he would entrust Gaille to their care. Anywhere else in the world, he wouldn't have had a hope of catching Nicolas after the head start he had. But this wasn't anywhere else. This was Siwa, and Siwa was unique. There was no way the container truck could cross the desert, which meant it had only one possible route out: north to the coast, then east to Alexandria. Once they were in Alexandria, all Egypt would open up, but that was still many hours away.

He put his hand on the dashboard. "Just one more trip," he pleaded. "Just one more." Then he roared away.

THE HOURS PASSED with grinding slowness for Nicolas as his four-by-four and the container truck crawled east along the Mediterranean coast. He kept thinking that Bastiaan and his crew must have reached Alexandria by now, but it wasn't until they neared El Alamein that his phone finally rang. "Yes?"

"Bastiaan here. We're at the villa."

"And?"

"It's burned out. No sign of the guys. But there are uniforms everywhere—fire, police, medical."

Nicolas fell silent as he realized the extent of this disaster. The alibis that had been meant to protect them were now going to hang them. They had all been filmed entering the villa on the security cameras. Even if the fire had by some miracle destroyed the tape, the rental cars outside would still lead the police inexorably to the airport, to their immigration details, to their plane. Going for it now would be like salmon leaping for the net. He ordered Bastiaan to head back and meet them outside Alexandria. Then he called Katerina in Thessalonike again. She answered this time, but he had barely said a word when she cut in and told him primly that she wasn't at liberty to discuss company policy on that matter, but she could get someone to—

"There are people with you?"

"Yes."

"Police?"

"Yes."

"They're listening in?"

"No."

"Recording calls?"

"Not yet."

"You can get somewhere and call back?"

"Not immediately."

"As soon as you can."

Nicolas chewed his knuckles while he waited. Twenty minutes passed before she rang back. "I'm sorry, sir," she said breathlessly. "There are police everywhere. They have warrants. Apparently, the Egyptians asked them to—"

"You've heard from Manolis and Sofronio?"

"Not directly, sir, but I overheard a policeman. I think there's been a fight with the Egyptian police, and I think Manolis is hurt. He had to go to the hospital. Sir, they're saying he killed a man. What's going on? They're accusing us all of terrible things. Everything's going crazy. People are terrified. They're searching our files. They're freezing our accounts. I heard two of them talking about ordering our ships back to port."

"They can't do that," protested Nicolas. "Put Mando on it."

"I already have. He says it's going to take him a couple of days to—"

"I don't have two days!" yelled Nicolas. "Sort it out now."

"Yes, sir."

"And call me the moment you learn anything."

"Yes, sir."

"And I need Gabbar Mounim's phone number again. Quick as you can."

"Yes, sir."

THE DREAD WAS BUILDING IN KNOX. He had been pounding the poor Jeep for seven hours and still hadn't caught up with the truck, and Alexandria was now only thirty kilometers ahead. Was it possible he had miscalculated? Was it possible Nicolas had got here already, or found another route out? A plane from Marsa Matruh? Across the border into Libya? No. Both of those would be madness, let alone impossible to organize on such short notice. This *had* to be their route. He just had to keep on going.

Five kilometers shy of the first main road junction, he glimpsed a container truck ahead. He speeded up. Yes. And one of the SUVs in front of it. He took his foot off the gas at once, dropped back to a discreet distance, and followed.

Chapter Forty

THE MOMENT BASTIAAN and his crew rejoined the convoy after their Alexandria sortie, Nicolas ordered everyone off the road. They took a sandy track to the edge of a lake: mist rising from the water, shabby fishermen poling their weather-beaten punts along narrow channels between reed-covered islets. He had intended to explain the situation to them all, canvass their ideas, discuss plans, but their nerves were so strained by fear as they realized the extent of their predicament that they quickly began shouting, jostling, and blaming one another. It was just as well that Katerina called at that moment, giving everyone a chance to calm down.

She had Gabbar Mounim's number for him, so he called it at once. A woman answered, and Nicolas asked for Mounim, giving his own name. Without even checking, she told him politely that Mr. Mounim couldn't come to the phone right now. He asked her more forcefully, but she just repeated her message. When he screamed at her, she repeated it once more, completely unperturbed. Nicolas breathed deep, then asked as politely as he could when Mr. Mounim might be able to call him back. Mr. Mounim was very busy all this week, apparently. Perhaps next week or the week after. Nicolas ended the call, suddenly fearful that they might run a trace. News of leprosy traveled so fast in his world, it defied Einstein. He slammed the heel of his hand against the side of the container, which rang dully. Their plane was tainted, their ship. Their names, descriptions, passport numbers, and license plates would already be spreading like disease along the wires. He closed his eyes. Dismay curdled to anger.

Knox. It could only be Knox. Knox had blabbed.

He went to the rear of the container. It wasn't his fault now; he had made the penalty for interference clear. If you wanted people to take you seriously in this world, you had to be prepared to execute your threats. The container door was open, and it was still hot and stifling inside. The girl was lying gagged on the floor, her wrists bound around the interior handrail, her lips dry and chapped. Nicolas untied her and dragged her by one ankle to the mouth of the container. She struggled limply, weak with dehydration. He dumped her onto the sandy earth. Surplus baggage. Dangerous baggage—baggage with a mouth. He had left the Walther in the four-by-four. He held out his hand to Leonidas. "The AK, please."

Leonidas blinked. "She's just a girl."

"Are you stupid?" shouted Nicolas. "She's seen everything. You want to spend your life in a Gippo fucking jail?"

The girl spat out her gag so that it hung like a noose around her neck. "Please," she sobbed. "Please." Her face was ugly with tears and mucus. Nicolas couldn't bear to look at her. "Don't kill me," she wailed, shuffling toward him on her knees. "Oh, God, I won't talk. I swear. Don't kill me. Please don't kill me. I don't want to die. I don't want to die."

"Your father rejected violence," said Leonidas. "Your father—"

"My father is dead," snapped Nicolas, his hand trembling. Weaken now, and he'd be a joke. "Give me your fucking gun." He snatched it from Leonidas's grip. Looking nauseated, Leonidas turned his back. It was just as well to know who had the stomach for the hard tasks.

The girl was still mewling, clawing at his trousers. He clubbed her with the butt, took a step back, and raised the rifle to his shoulder. He had never killed anyone before. He'd given orders, sure, and they had brought a few corpses from the morgues up into the mountains for training purposes. Puncturing human flesh helped harden you, even if it was lifeless. He had come almost to enjoy the sensation of plunging a bayonet into a belly. You had to attack it with commitment, or the blade would push back rather than penetrate the skin. But this was different. He had thought it would feel clean and sharp and fine to kill; in truth, it felt squalid and deformed.

She was kneeling, hugging and kissing his feet. It was better now that he couldn't see her face. He filled his sights with the dark hair on the top of her skull, but then her face bobbed up. Again he balked. The thought of shooting her through the eyes or forehead made him feel distinctly uncomfortable. Why couldn't she just keep her face down? Didn't she have any consideration? He

menaced her again with the gun. She fell onto her back,
wailing, her face gray and contorted with terror. He gestured for her to roll onto her front, but she wouldn't. She
lay there, squirming perversely, as though she knew the
turmoil she was putting him through. He gritted his teeth.
This was the price of leadership. This was the price of
Macedonian liberation. He steeled himself by imagining
all the accolades and glory that would be his due. Then he
pressed the butt to his shoulder and filled his sights with
her face once more.

KNOX HAD FOLLOWED THE CONVOY off the road at
a safe distance, concealing the Jeep behind a rocky bank,
then watching the Greeks argue and panic. Though he
was too far away to hear their exact words, it was clear
from their confrontation that their plans had gone seriously awry and they were scared.

Nicolas vanished purposefully into the container. A
minute later, he dragged Gaille out, then demanded the
AK-47 from one of his men. Knox watched miserably,
but there was nothing he could do. He had no cell phone
to summon the police or army, and he was unarmed and
alone. Trying to save her now would be suicide. His only
sane option was to go and fetch help. He had done his
best, after all, and now it was someone else's turn. No one
would blame him.

He crouched over to the Jeep and started it up, the highway traffic close enough to muffle the sound. Then he just sat there a moment, because he knew in his heart that to go for help was to condemn Gaille to death. He couldn't accept that; he just couldn't. It wasn't simply the debt he owed her father, though that was part of it. It was Gaille herself. It was the way he had come to feel about her.

His skin prickled with fear as he realized what he was going to do. *Don't be a fool,* he told himself. It did no good. He took a deep breath and closed his eyes, almost in prayer. Then he stamped his foot to the floor, like some knight of old spurring on his faithful steed, and charged.

AN ENGINE ROARED BEHIND NICOLAS. He whirled around to see an old Jeep hurtling directly at him. *Knox!* He was standing there in numb disbelief when Leonidas snatched back his AK-47 and sprayed a burst at the Jeep's hood, which sprang up open. The engine spouted geysers of steam, and flames licked up from below. He could hear Knox revving futilely, but the Jeep rolled slowly to a stop in front of them, and the hood clanged back down. Knox opened the door and fled, but a round scorched his leg, and he cried out with pain and fell headlong, only to have Bastiaan and Eneas on him a moment later.

Nicolas wrested back the gun from Leonidas. Killing the girl was one thing, killing Knox another. He walked over, lifted the gun to his shoulder, and aimed down. "Wait!" cried Knox desperately, turning onto his back, holding up his arms as if that could protect him. "Listen! I can get you out. I can get you out of Egypt."

"Of course you can," mocked Nicolas, his finger on the trigger. "You can sprout wings and fly us, no doubt."

But Leonidas pushed down the muzzle of Nicolas's gun. "How?" he asked.

"I'll ask the questions," snapped Nicolas. He turned back to Knox, raising the gun once more. He felt ridiculous suddenly. "How?" he asked.

"I know people," said Knox.

"Oh, you *know* people?" sneered Nicolas. "We all know people."

"I know Hassan al-Assyuti," said Knox.

Nicolas frowned. "The shipping agent?"

"I saved his life," nodded Knox. "A diving accident. I gave him mouth-to-mouth. He said if I ever needed a favor—"

Nicolas squinted at him. "You're lying."

"Take me to see him. He's in Suez. Ask him yourself. He'll tell you."

"*Take* you to see him?" snorted Nicolas. "He's your best fucking friend and you don't even know his phone number?"

"I never had to call in the favor before."

Nicolas hesitated. Knox was up to something, he was sure of it. But if there was any truth whatever to his claim . . . He opened his cell phone again, called Katerina, and asked her to find a number for Hassan al-Assyuti. He walked in circles as he waited for her to call back, stamping his feet. When she finally did, he dialed it himself. He didn't trust Knox one bit. He asked for Hassan al-Assyuti and was put on hold. He kept his eyes on Knox all the time, waiting for him to blink, to back down and admit that this was bullshit. A woman picked up and tried to fob him off with the practiced spiel about Hassan being in a meeting, and could she please take a message that she would make sure he received at the very first—

"I need to speak to him now," said Nicolas. "Tell him it's Daniel Knox."

"Daniel Knox?" She was clearly taken aback. "Oh. Yes. Right. I . . . I'll put you straight through."

Nicolas couldn't hide his astonishment. He held the phone in such a way that Knox could talk, but so that he could listen in as well. Hassan came on. "Knox?" he demanded. "Is that really you?"

"That's right," said Knox quickly. "Listen, I want to come see you."

There was a pause. Then Hassan asked incredulously: "You want to come to see *me*?"

"That's right. I need something shipped out of Egypt. If I come to see you, will you take care of it for me?"

There was silence. "You'll come yourself? In person?"

"If you agree to help me get this shipment out."

"What kind of shipment? Where headed?"

"I'll tell you when I see you."

"Very well. Can you get to Suez?"

"Sure. Give me six hours."

"Six hours, then. At my container terminal." He snapped off directions, which Nicolas jotted down. The line went dead. Nicolas closed his phone.

"Well?" asked Leonidas.

"He agreed to help," admitted Nicolas reluctantly. Something stank, though he wasn't sure what. Still, it was a lifeline, and he had no option but to grab it. "You'll stay in the container until Suez," he told Knox. "One sound and you're dead. Understand?"

"Yes."

"Get us out of Egypt and you and the girl can go. You have my word." He looked directly into Knox's eyes. Nicolas couldn't afford to have him realize there was no way on earth he would let two witnesses to all this mayhem simply walk away.

Chapter Forty-one

KNOX AND GAILLE were gagged and tied to the hand-rail at the cab end of the container. One of the Greeks, a burly man they called Eneas, was handed a flashlight and ordered to watch over them. Knox's thigh throbbed from the gunshot wound, but from the quick examination he had been allowed, it looked worse than it was, plowing a furrow along his skin, but missing the muscle and bone.

The container was stiflingly hot once the rear doors were closed, and stuffy, too, particularly when Eneas lit a cigarette. After he finished and stubbed it out, he drank great gulps from a water bottle, then splashed it prodigally over his hair and forehead. Just the sound of it was torment. Knox closed his eyes and dreamed of waterfalls and crushed ice.

The coffin and lid were so heavy that the container truck's brakes shrieked when they slowed to refuel. Eneas stood above Knox, menacing him with the butt of the rifle until they rumbled off again, so that he rocked back ever so slightly on his heels. Gears crunched, and the engine whined as they struggled to pick up speed. Just as well that Egypt was so flat.

Gaille began sobbing behind her gag. She had had two or three such bouts already, interspersed with long periods of calm. Terror was too intense to sustain. Knox, too, had had two periods of icy shudders when his shirt became saturated with sweat, worsening his dehydration. In between, however, his mind felt clear as he sought a way to get himself and Gaille out of their dire predicament. So far, nothing came to mind.

He stopped trying to force it. Experience had taught him that answers often appeared when he focused on something else. Their guard lit another cigarette, the flame of his lighter glowing orange off all the gold, and Knox found himself staring at Alexander's coffin. What an end for such a man, a pawn in the never-ending game of politics and personal advancement. But there was a certain appropriateness, too. Alexander's life itself had ended in anticlimax in Babylon, triggered perhaps by the horrors of the Gedrosian Desert, into which he had led forty thousand men, and out of which he had brought just fifteen thousand. Death had been in the air for months. An elderly Indian philosopher called Calanus had joined Alexander on his campaigns but had fallen sick. Unwilling to rot away, he burned himself alive instead, assuring Alexander that they would meet again soon. In a drinking contest to celebrate Calanus's life, forty-one Macedonians had died, including the winner. Then Alexander's closest friend, Hephaiston, had died, too—perhaps the greatest blow of all. But there was also a lesser-known incident, when Alexander visited the tomb of Cyrus the

Great at Pasargadae. Cyrus had been the greatest conqueror and emperor before Alexander, a semidivine figure worshipped throughout Persia. Yet Alexander discovered his bones lying scattered on the floor by bandits who had tried unsuccessfully to steal his golden sarcophagus. The inscription on Cyrus's tomb read, "*O man, whoever you are and from wherever you may come—for I know that you will come—I am Cyrus, who won the Persians their empire. Therefore, do not begrudge me this little earth which covers my body.*" But his plea had gone unheard.

They said that when Alexander was lying on his deathbed in Babylon, aware his end was upon him, he tried to drag his failing body down to the river that ran by the palace, so that he would be swept away by the waters, and the world might believe him taken up to his rightful place among the gods. But maybe he had also sought to deny his successors the chance to treat his mortal remains with the disrespect they had shown Cyrus's. So maybe that was the fate Alexander had wanted for his body: not Siwa, not Alexandria, not Macedonia, but the oblivion of water.

The oblivion of water. *Yes.* And finally, the germ of an idea came to Knox.

It seemed forever before the truck stopped next. The back of the container shrieked as it was opened. Knox leaned his head back against the steel wall, fear tickling his chest like the beads of a rosary. Stars lay low on the horizon. The day was gone. Perhaps his last. Nicolas climbed up inside, one side of his hair spiky, as though he had napped against the window. He pointed the Walther at Knox. "We're in Suez," he said as Eneas untied Knox's bonds and pulled the gag from his mouth. Knox clenched and unclenched his hands to get the circulation back, then stood gingerly, grimacing at the pain in his thigh.

Nicolas gestured for Knox to go to the mouth of the container, but Knox ignored him. He picked up the guard's water bottle and found a few mouthfuls left. He removed Gaille's gag, held the bottle to her lips, tipped it up for her until it was empty, then kissed her on her crown. "I'll do my best," he promised her.

"I know you will."

"Move," said Nicolas, jabbing him with the Walther's muzzle.

Knox hobbled to the end of the container, making more of his injury than it really warranted, hoping to convince Nicolas that he was badly hurt. He helped himself gingerly down onto tarmac, giving a little cry of pain as he landed, then hopping a couple of times on his good leg. They were in the corner of a huge empty parking lot that stank of stale fumes and scorched rubber. Arabic music drifted from a distant petrol station. Over a wall of trees, the sky glowed orange.

"This is how it's going to work," said Nicolas. "You and Leonidas will go to see al-Assyuti. You'll negotiate our safe passage back to Greece. When Leonidas is satisfied, he'll call me and—"

"Fuck that," said Knox. "I do nothing until Gaille is safe."

Nicolas gave a tight smile. "When Leonidas is satisfied, he'll call me, and both you and the girl can go free."

"Forget it. Let Gaille go now, and I'll do my best for you. You have my word."

Nicolas sighed. "The girl's our leverage. You can't expect us to release her."

"And Hassan's my leverage," replied Knox. "I'm not going to deal with him for you until the girl's safe."

A siren wailed out on the main road. Flashing blue and red lights. They all turned as casually as they could, competing to show the least alarm. It was only an ambulance. They waited until it was out of sight.

"We keep the girl," said Nicolas. "That's not up for discussion."

Knox shrugged. "Then how about this," he suggested. "I go see Hassan, like you want. And I take your man with me. But Gaille comes, too."

Nicolas snorted. "What kind of fool do you take me for?"

"You want to get out of Egypt, don't you? All I want is this over and done with. We'll all go in together, if you don't trust me."

"Sure!" mocked Nicolas. "Straight into your trap."

"What trap? How on earth could I have arranged a trap? Besides, you're going to have to entrust yourself to al-Assyuti at some point."

Nicolas glared at him for a few moments, trying to read what he was up to. But then he shook his head and beckoned for Leonidas and Bastiaan to come with him. The three of them walked off a few paces, conferring urgently but quietly. When they were done, Nicolas came back. "We'll all go in together," he said, as though it had been his idea. "But the girl will stay in the container with Eneas." He held up his cell phone. "Try anything, and if I even *sniff* a trap, it'll be the end of her. Understand?"

Knox looked into his eyes. The devil and the deep blue sea, rocks and hard places, Scylla and Charybdis. Hurling nitro at glycerine in hopes of crawling out of the resulting crater wasn't much of a strategy, but he had no alternative. "Yes," he said.

Nicolas gestured at the nearer SUV. "Good. Then, come with me."

"If Gaille's in the truck, I'm in the truck."

"Very well," scowled Nicolas. "We'll ride up front with Bastiaan."

ONCOMING HEADLIGHTS spiked into Knox's eyes as he sat between the two Greeks in the container truck's high cab. Adrenaline added luster to the ink-blue night sky, and his mind felt almost unnaturally sharp. Bastiaan drove anxiously, grinding the gears, muttering and cursing, uncomfortable, perhaps, with such a heavy load and—no doubt—with the situation he found himself in. Nicolas kept the muzzle of his Walther pressed unnecessarily hard into Knox's ribs while giving Bastiaan directions at the same time.

They turned off the main road into an industrial park of low warehouses and cracked concrete. There was no other traffic. All the offices were closed. Every twenty meters or so, streetlights made yellow pools in the sea of black. A line of tall cranes marked the waterfront. A series of PRIVATE: KEEP OUT signs bearing the logo of Al-As-

syuti Trading ran along a high chain-link fence. Bastiaan
checked his side mirrors and slowed as they neared the entrance. The brakes began to sing, so he released them. He
turned to make the approach, then pulled up at a wooden
barrier and lowered his window to attract the attention of
the elderly security guard playing checkers against himself in a glass-walled booth, watched by a Doberman on a
leash. The old man sighed, hobbled across, squinted up at
Bastiaan, and asked in Arabic what he wanted. Bastiaan
shrugged and looked at Knox and Nicolas for assistance.

"I'm Daniel Knox," said Knox. "Mr. al-Assyuti is expecting me."

"All of you?" asked the man.

"Yes."

A ship's horn sounded in the distance. The guard
shrugged and shook his head, then returned to his booth
and made a call. With the window open, cool night air
flooded in, bringing the smells of diesel, salt, and rotting
fish. A security camera whirred and focused; then the barrier lifted. Bastiaan drove on through, struggling to pick
up speed. The office buildings were at the far end of the
terminal. Stacks of colored containers were everywhere,
like a gigantic set of child's building blocks. There was no
one in sight, no laborers, no forklift drivers, no truckers,
no crane operators. Emptiness and silence. The four-by-
fours fanned out like wingmen on either side of the truck.
A huge ship lumbered along the canal, the lights of its
bridge and deck doubling in the water, and Knox had a
disembodied yet overpowering sensation that the past decade of his life was now reaching its climax. The deaths
of his parents and his sister, his conflict with the Drag-

oumises, his years with Richard, the quest for Alexander. And Gaille, too—Gaille most of all.

As if reading his mind, Nicolas punched a number into his cell phone. A moment later, Knox heard it ringing in the container behind them. When Eneas answered, Nicolas held it up for Knox to see. "I'll do it," he warned. "I'll have her killed if you try anything. I swear I will."

Something about his choice of words made Knox frown. A memory of Elena came unexpectedly to his mind—of her standing before Dragoumis in the moment before she shot him, and the words she had used to explain herself. "Elena didn't *kill* Pavlos," he muttered. "She *had* him killed. That's what she told your father."

Nicolas scowled. "So?"

"Elena was an archaeologist, not a mafia wife. How would she have someone killed?"

"How the fuck should I know?" But there was an edge of anxiety in Nicolas's voice.

"How long has Costis worked for you?" demanded Knox, certain he was onto something.

"Shut up!"

"I bet he was working for you back then, wasn't he? Did Elena know him?"

"Where do you get this bullshit?" protested Nicolas shrilly.

"Elena went to Costis," asserted Knox. "She hired him to kill Pavlos."

"Stop this!"

"And that's why Elena shot him. Not because he was standing next to your father, but because he was the one who actually arranged the crash."

"I said stop it!"

"And Costis was on your payroll."

"I'm telling you, this is your last warning."

"He would never have accepted a job like that without clearing it with you first."

Nicolas smacked Knox on the head with the barrel of the Walther. "I warned you!" he yelled.

"Did you know my family would be in that car?" demanded Knox.

"For fuck's sake! Shut up, will you!"

"Did you know my sister would be in it?"

"Just fucking shut up!"

"She was sixteen years old," said Knox. "She was sixteen fucking years old."

"This is war!" shrieked Nicolas. "Don't you understand? War! Sacrifices have to be made."

There was a moment of shocked silence, as though neither man could quite believe the confession. Nicolas pointed the Walther at Knox's brow, his hand trembling with shame and fear, his finger on the trigger, ready to murder him merely to avoid his reproach. But then the truck's brakes began to sing again as Bastiaan pulled up outside the office building, and a man pushed through the darkened double doors ahead, letting them swing shut behind him.

"Who's that?" muttered Nicolas. "Is that Hassan?"

Knox shook his head. "Nessim."

"Nessim?"

"Hassan's head of security."

"Security?" Nicolas's voice went flat, deadened by presentiment.

Nessim waited until all the vehicles had come to a
halt. Then he gave a signal, and all around them, on the
roofs of containers, men armed with automatic weapons
stood up, aiming down, poised to fire. Sash windows were
raised in all the offices, and more gun barrels slithered
out. "You're completely surrounded," shouted Nessim,
hands cupped around his mouth. "Turn off your engines.
Put away your weapons. Place your hands on your heads.
Open your doors slowly. Then come out one by one. No
one needs to die."

Nicolas glared at Knox with utter loathing. He raised
his cell phone. "It's a trap," he snarled. "Kill the—"

Knox smashed the phone from Nicolas's hand before
he could finish his command, but Nicolas still had the
Walther, and he turned it on Knox as he pulled the trigger.
Knox flung back his head so that the bullet only scorched
his cheek before shattering the driver's-side window. It
was like a starter's pistol, setting everyone off. Bursts of
gunfire flashed orange from the SUV to their left. Nessim flung himself down. A countering firestorm erupted
from on top of the containers and the office windows,
turning the vehicle instantly into a sieve, bullets clanging
and whistling and shrieking through the metal and off the
asphalt. Knox grabbed Nicolas's wrist and twisted it until
he dropped the Walther, while Bastiaan crunched the truck
into reverse, gunning the engine in a desperate effort to
pick up speed. There was yelling all around, cries of pain,
people running, constant gunfire, but somehow the truck
remained unscathed. The second four-by-four turned in a
circle, automatic weapons blazing from its window. The
firestorm turned its wrath onto the four-by-four, glass and

metal puncturing and shattering. A back door opened, and a man jumped out. He ran five paces, firing blindly behind him before being cut down by a barrage of bullets.

The truck was finally picking up speed. Nicolas and Knox fought for the Walther as it slid around the floor beneath the cab's seats. A single bullet put a cobweb in the windshield, and Bastiaan grunted and was thrown back, a small hole in the front of his forehead. Then he slumped forward, revealing a great red crater in the back of his skull. They began at once to lose speed. Nicolas seized the Walther and turned it on Knox, but Knox butted him on the bridge of the nose, then grabbed his wrist and slammed it repeatedly against the dashboard until he dropped the gun. Knox pushed Bastiaan's body aside and reached his foot across to hit the gas, causing them to accelerate once more. He wrenched the steering wheel around, reversing them toward the canal. Nicolas picked up the Walther again and aimed it at Knox just as the rear wheels dropped off the jetty's edge, and the undercarriage scraped and screeched on the canal wall. The weight of gold in the container used the jetty's edge as a fulcrum to hurl the cab into the air. Nicolas shrieked as they were flung upright, then plunged down into the water. The truck shuddered as it hit, then again as gravity threw Alexander's golden coffin and lid like twin battering rams into the rear doors, tearing them off their hinges, then spilling out into the canal, plunging down through the water.

The truck bobbed twice, then flopped onto its belly. Without the golden coffin weighing it down, there was enough trapped air to keep it afloat for now. Nicolas tried

to wrest open the passenger door to get out, but the weight
of water wouldn't allow it. He rolled down the window
instead, letting the canal gush in, frothing silver. He tried
to climb out, but Knox grabbed his ankle and rolled the
window back up, pinning his waist. The cab tipped onto
its side, trapping Nicolas underwater. He kicked and
kicked in an effort to break free, but Knox, his own head
still above water, hardened his heart by reminding himself of his sister, his parents, and Rick. It seemed an age
before Nicolas finally went still, then Knox climbed out
the other window, keeping the container between himself
and the gunmen now lining the jetty. His eyes were soon
on fire from the polluted water, so that he had to feel his
way around, but when he opened them in a blurry squint,
he was sure for a moment that he could see the twin eye
sockets of a skull staring back at him before it fell on its
side, releasing bubbles like a dying breath, and swirling
away down into the deeps.

He shook his head to clear it. Let the dead bury the
dead. He had Gaille to save. The container's rear doors
had been ripped off, so he was able to pull himself inside. The heavy steel box was already two-thirds underwater and filling fast. Everything had tipped out during
the plunge—everything but Gaille, saved by her rope
cuffs around the handrail, as he had prayed she would
be. But the water was already up to her throat, and she
had her head tilted back, straining upward for air. Knox
ducked underwater to find and then untie her bonds, but
the wet knots had pulled tight, and the water level was
rising all the time, over her chin now, her mouth, her nostrils. He kept on at the rope until he felt at last a little give

in it, enough to work in a nail and then a fingertip, and suddenly the knots were loose. Gaille slipped her wrists free, and they both turned and swam for the mouth of the container, emerging from it together, gasping for breath, turning around to watch it vanish underwater with a final belch of released air.

A line of men stood along the waterfront, rifles raised and aimed. Nessim, standing out front, pointed them to a flight of steps that led up out of the water. The fight that had kept Knox going finally deserted him. He knew that it was all up for himself, and all he could hope for now was to give Gaille a chance. He swam tiredly across, then helped her out by her elbow. She took his hand. He tried to pull free, to put distance between them, but she realized what he was up to, and refused to let go. They climbed the steps silently together, still holding hands, giving each other courage.

"Follow me," ordered Nessim.

Knox's leg had started bleeding again. It pulsed with pain, so that his limp was no longer an act. Hassan's men were pulling bodies out of the SUVs. A rear door fell open, and Vasileios's head flopped out, his Kalashnikov rattling onto the concourse. Weapons immediately turned toward the noise, safety catches off. Then they realized there was no danger, and someone cracked a joke and everybody laughed—relief from the nervous tension of combat. Knox's sodden clothes grew increasingly chilled. He put his arm around Gaille, squeezed her shoulder, kissed her temple. She smiled bravely at him. The polluted water burned tears from his eyes, which ran freely down his cheeks. Wiping them away, he kept thinking about the moment Nicolas had shuddered and died, the door between life and death, where they themselves were now standing. Despite his fear, he had no urge to run. It was out of his hands; the jury had retired. Nessim showed them into a drab office with a huge stuffed fish in a glass case, and tattered charts of freshwater and marine species on the wall. He left for a moment, returned with two dirty hand towels, and tossed them one each. They wiped dry their faces and arms. Knox sat down and clamped his towel over his leg. "What happens now?" he asked.

"We wait," said Nessim.

"For what?"

"Mr. al-Assyuti was in Sharm when you called. He'll be here any minute."

"This has nothing to do with the girl," said Knox. "Let her go."

"We wait for Mr. al-Assyuti," said Nessim.

"Please," begged Knox. "I let you and your men go in Tanta. You owe me. Let her go."

But Nessim only shook his head. Knox closed his eyes, weary, frightened and dismayed. It galled him that al-Assyuti, of all men, would be the one to benefit. He would have no trouble hauling up the sarcophagus and lid from the mud and murk of the canal bed, and once he did, he would pry out the gemstones and melt down the gold, destroying forever one of the great finds of modern archaeology. And who could say that he wouldn't get his hands on the rest of the Siwa treasure, too—him or Yusuf Abbas or the two of them together? The thought of such corrupt men turning so glorious a find to their own benefit made him feel physically ill. His whole life,

Knox had searched for such objects—not for their intrinsic value but for the knowledge they brought with them. And yet, first by cutting the Gordian Knot, then by reversing the container truck into the canal, he had willfully played a part, just to give himself and Gaille a chance of life where there had seemed no chance at all. And it hadn't even worked. Then he looked sideways at her sitting beside him, and he felt a certain peace, because he knew absolutely that if he had it to do over again, even knowing what he knew now, he wouldn't hesitate. He took her hand again, interlaced fingers, and gave her a little squeeze of reassurance. She smiled and reciprocated, caressing his skin with her thumb.

Fifteen minutes passed before headlights sprang through the window. Knox's heart accelerated. He glanced again at Gaille, who was looking as frightened as he felt. Footsteps grew loud; then Nessim opened the door, and Hassan al-Assyuti walked through, hands clasped behind his back. He looked bigger than Knox remembered. His eye and jaw were both puffy, and he grimaced as he moved, as though still feeling the beating he had taken.

"Let the girl go," said Knox at once. "She knows nothing about this."

Hassan smiled wolfishly, showing a flash of gold where previously there had only been white. "You're a hard man to find, Mr. Knox. My men have been scouring all Egypt."

"We had a deal," said Knox. "I said I'd come to see you. You said you'd get a shipment out for me. I'm here. She's the shipment. Keep your word. Get her out."

"You don't think you've breached the terms of that

particular contract? You don't think three vehicles filled with armed and hostile men allows me to—"

"Please," said Knox. "I'm begging you. Do what you want with me, but let the girl go."

"What? So she can walk straight out of here and sell her story to the press?"

"She won't do that. Tell him, Gaille. Give him your word."

"Fuck him," said Gaille through chattering teeth. "I'm staying with you."

Hassan barked out a laugh of mixed amusement and admiration. "You prefer looks to intelligence in your women, I see."

"You won't get away with this."

"Get away with what?" shrugged Hassan. "All I've done so far is rescue you from a situation of extreme jeopardy. You should be thanking me. As for what I'm going to do next . . ."

"Yes?" asked Knox.

"You humiliated me in Sharm, Mr. Knox," said Hassan, the tendons taut in his neck. "People have been *laughing* at me. At me, Mr. Knox. At *me*. I'm sure you appreciate that I can't allow such things to go . . . *unremedied*." He came a step closer, leaning down so that the tip of his nose was almost touching Knox's, his breath sour in Knox's nostrils. "It's a simple matter of respect."

"Respect!" snorted Knox. "You were raping a girl."

Hassan's eyes narrowed. He stood up once more, his fists clenched. Knox braced himself for a punch, but Hassan restrained himself and even managed a tight smile. "I'd almost given up hope of finding you," he said. "But then, this afternoon, you called out of the blue. I thought it was a joke at first. I thought you were *taunting* me. You had to be aware, after all, of what I'd do to you. But then an extraordinary news story began to break. A man recovering in Siwa Hospital began babbling about discovering the tomb of Alexander the Great, and golden coffins and a conspiracy of Greeks and how a young man called Knox had come to his rescue. And suddenly your telephone call began to make some sense. What else could your shipment be but these renegade Greeks, this plundered treasure?"

"How happy you must have been," said Knox bitterly, "having me deliver it straight to your door! Don't you have enough gold?"

"A man can never have enough gold, Mr. Knox," retorted Hassan. "And yet, you're right, in a way. Money has never been a problem for me. There are other things, however, that I've found more difficult to acquire. Do you see where I'm going, Mr. Knox?"

"My guess would be to prison for life."

Hassan laughed. "You couldn't be more wrong. This isn't some crude heist; it's an official operation. Semiofficial, at least. Those men out there are paratroops—Egypt's finest, old comrades of Nessim's. After all, you don't really imagine I have thirty armed marksmen to call on at such short notice, do you? And why do you think your convoy wasn't challenged on your approach to Suez? And why do you think no one shot at your container, except when your driver tried to get away?"

"I don't understand," protested Gaille. "What's he talking about?"

"I'm talking about a way for you two to walk out of

here alive," he told her. "I'm talking about a way for everybody to win."

"Go on," said Knox.

"The ambitions of youth aren't the same as the ambitions of maturity, Mr. Knox, as you've probably realized for yourself. When I was a young man, I craved only money, because money is like air—if you don't have it, nothing else matters. But once you have it . . ." he made a dismissive gesture.

"So what *do* you want?"

"Legitimacy. Respectability. A place in the hearts of my people. An opportunity to serve."

"An opportunity to serve!" snorted Knox. "I don't believe this! You're going into *politics*?"

Hassan allowed himself a smile. "Our nation is led by an aging generation," he said. "A generation out of touch with its people. Egypt is crying out for new leadership, for people with fresh ideas and energy, for people who understand the new ways. I intend to be one of those people. Yet politics in Egypt is not an easy world to penetrate, particularly for a man with my . . . background. Egypt is riddled with nepotism, as you know. Too many sons are already waiting in line, and I'm sure you realize that patience isn't my strongest point."

"So that's it," muttered Knox. "You're going to make yourself the hero of the hour. The savior of Egypt's heritage."

"And you're going to help me, Mr. Knox," nodded Hassan. "You're going to tell the world that the reason you contacted me earlier today was because when you realized that these great Egyptian treasures were in danger, you knew I was the person to go to, because I always put my country and my people ahead of anything else; and you've been proved right by events, because I've done exactly that."

"And if I don't?"

Hassan reached out to stroke Gaille's cheek. "It's already a bloodbath outside, Mr. Knox. Do you really believe that two more corpses would make any difference?"

"You're bluffing."

"Is that a challenge, Mr. Knox?"

Knox stared at him, trying to read behind his eyes, but the man was made of stone; he gave nothing away. He glanced instead at Gaille, who was bracing herself for the worst, yet prepared to suffer it on his account; and he knew then that he had no choice. "Fine," he said. "You have a deal."

"Good," said Hassan. He nodded at Nessim, still standing stolidly by the door. "You have my head of security to thank, you know. This was his idea. I was *angry* with you, Mr. Knox—you have no idea how angry. After your call came, I wanted you shot. But Nessim persuaded me this was the wiser course." He leaned in close once more, as if to confide a secret. "I'm a bad enemy to make, Mr. Knox. You'd do well to remember that."

"I will," Knox assured him. "Believe me."

Hassan looked back at him, amused by his defiance, and the two men locked gazes long enough for both to realize that it wasn't over between them just yet, that unfinished business remained. But it could wait. It *would* wait. They each had too much to lose.

Knox stood, helped Gaille to her feet, and put his arm

around her. They walked together to the door, held open
for them by Nessim. Knox nodded slightly at him as they
passed, and Nessim nodded back—an acknowledgment
of debts settled, perhaps even of mutual respect. Then
he and Gaille passed through the door and into a whole
new life.

Epilogue

SO THIS IS WHAT FAME FEELS LIKE, thought Knox, roasting beneath the arc lights as he gazed out over the bank of microphones to the squatted rows of photographers and the TV crews and the press journalists perching forward on their chairs, taking notes with one hand while straining to be noticed with the other, eager to pose their questions, if only to show their bosses they were doing their jobs, because they must realize by now that they wouldn't get any answers worth a damn.

"I'm sorry," declared Yusuf Abbas for the umpteenth time. "It's far too early to know exactly what we've found. Archaeology doesn't work that way. We need time to secure and examine the sites. We need time to retrieve and study what we find. In a year or two, perhaps, we'll know a little more. Now, just three more questions, I think. Who wants to—"

"Daniel!" shouted out a young redheaded woman. "Daniel! Over here!" Knox turned toward her and was momentarily dazzled by the flash of a camera bulb. "How can you be sure it was Alexander?" she yelled.

"Is it true there's more gold?" called out a Japanese journalist.

"Gaille! Gaille!" cried a gray-haired man. "Did you think you were going to die?"

"Please," begged Yusuf, holding up both hands, loving every moment. "One at a time."

Knox scratched his cheek, itching with fatigue and several days' stubble. How bizarre this all was. To think that at this very moment, people around the world were watching him on TV. A few would almost certainly be old acquaintances. They'd squint at the screen in disbelief, maybe mutter an obscenity beneath their breath, or hoot with laughter and pick up the phone to alert mutual friends. *Have you seen the TV? Remember that guy Knox? I swear to God, it's him!*

He glanced across at Gaille. She smiled and raised an eyebrow back at him, as though she understood exactly what was going through his mind. The past twenty-four hours had been bewildering. Their police debriefing in Suez had initially been conducted in a jubilant, self-congratulatory mood: jokes cracked, hands shaken, him and Gaille treated as heroes. Mohammed's story seemed to have captured the popular imagination. And to make things even sweeter, they had watched Yusuf Abbas on live TV struggling haplessly to explain his relationship with the Dragoumises, and why he had given the MAF permission to excavate in the Delta and conduct a survey in Siwa, and why Elena Koloktronis had visited him in Cairo.

But then, suddenly, the tone had changed. A new investigator, called Umar, had arrived at the police station. His first act had been to have Knox and Gaille locked up in separate cells; then he proceeded to interrogate them unrelentingly. He had scimitar sideburns and sharp eyes, and he seemed absurdly suspicious of their story. He had tried to trick Knox into contradicting himself, and to twist his words against him, and he had shown no interest at all in Nicolas Dragoumis and his men, as though robbery and multiple murder were unimportant to him. He had focused on Knox's own movements, pressing him particularly on the SCA sites in Alexandria and the Delta, trying to force him to admit that he had broken into them.

"I don't know what you're talking about," Knox had insisted. "I know nothing about those sites."

"Really," Umar had said, frowning theatrically. "Then perhaps you can explain how photographs of them were found on a laptop and a digital camera in your Jeep." Knox's heart had plummeted. He had forgotten completely about those. To clam up now or ask for a lawyer would be tantamount to admitting he had something to hide. To lie to a man like this would be madness, but so would coming clean. And he had Rick's reputation to worry about, too. In no way could he allow his friend's good name to be tarnished as a tomb robber, not after the sacrifice he had made. Umar had smiled with infuriating smugness. "I'm waiting," he said.

"I've done nothing wrong," Knox had protested.

"That may be your opinion. In my country, we consider breaking into historic sites a very serious crime—especially for a man already known to have sold antiquities on the black market."

"That's bullshit!" Knox had protested furiously. "You know that's bullshit."

"Explain the photographs, Mr. Knox."

Knox had scowled and sat back in his chair, arms folded across his chest. "What photographs?"

Umar had snorted. "Do you know the penalties for antiquities theft? Even for *attempted* theft, you could serve ten years."

"This is ridiculous. I've just helped save a great treasure for Egypt."

"Nevertheless," said Umar, "a wise man would be aware of the seriousness of his position. Are you a wise man, Mr. Knox?"

Knox had narrowed his eyes, sensing subtext in Umar's words. "What do you mean?"

"I mean that there is *one* explanation for your presence in these sites that I would gladly accept."

"And that is?"

"That you were there with the authority of the SCA— specifically, with the knowledge and blessing of the secretary general, Yusuf Abbas."

Knox had closed his eyes as he finally caught on. "So that's it," he laughed. "I say I was working undercover for Yusuf, and suddenly he wasn't best friends with the Dragoumises anymore; he was *investigating* them. Tell me: what do you get out of it?"

"I've no idea what you're talking about," Umar had replied primly. "But perhaps we should go through your statement one more time. The media are clamoring for the full story, as I'm sure you appreciate. Only this time, why don't you start by describing the phone call you made to Yusuf Abbas to alert him to your suspicions about the Dragoumises, and the authority he granted you to act covertly on his behalf."

"Or?"

"Or everyone loses: Yusuf, you, the girl."

Knox had felt sick. "The girl?"

"Egypt needs someone to punish, Mr. Knox, and the Greeks are all dead. But your friend Gaille was working for them. She was flown to Thessalonike on a private jet just days ago to meet Philip Dragoumis, and she was with Elena Koloktronis in Siwa. Trust me, I can make her look guilty as the devil with far less material than this. Such a sweet young thing, too! Can you imagine what even a month in an Egyptian prison would do to her?"

"I don't believe this."

Umar had leaned forward. "And think of this, too. If you agree, you'll be a hero. I've been authorized to tell you that the SCA will welcome you back into the fold with open arms and look favorably upon any future excavation applications you might choose to make."

For a moment, Knox had felt the urge to hurl the offer back in Umar's face. Five years ago, younger and more headstrong, he would have done so. But the wilderness was a good teacher. "If I agree," he said, "it'll be on one condition."

"And that is?"

"A new SCA award. The Richard Mitchell Award, presented annually to a promising young archaeologist by the secretary general himself. The first to go posthumously to my friend Rick Hannah."

Umar had allowed himself a small smile. "You will excuse me one minute?"

Knox had stretched out his leg as he'd waited for Umar to return; the bullet wound felt pleasantly tight and sore. Nothing but flesh, he had been assured. In a week, it would be only a scar and a memory. Umar had come back in. "Not the Richard Mitchell Award," he had said. "Just the Mitchell Award. A recognition of the contribution the whole family has made, including your friend Gaille. My contact assures me that any more would be impossible. I believe him."

Knox had agreed. Frankly, he'd been surprised that Yusuf buckled even that far. It was effectively an acknowledgment that Richard had been innocent of selling antiquities on the black market; and if he was innocent, then who but Yusuf could be guilty? Yusuf had to be really feeling the heat. For a moment, for precisely that reason, Knox had considered rejecting the deal, but it hadn't been just his own skin at stake. "Fine," he had said. "But you'll need the girl's agreement, too."

"I already have it," Umar had told him, patting his pocket. "It seems she didn't want you in jail any more than you wanted her there."

"May I see her?"

"Not yet. Once we've rewritten your statement, we'll hold a press conference. You, the girl, and Yusuf will tell the world how you worked together with Hassan to foil those dastardly Greeks. After that, you and she can do as you please."

"Once we're irretrievably compromised, you mean."

Umar had only smiled.

And so here they all were, Yusuf Abbas wrapping up the press conference, thanking the journalists for coming, and insisting they contact him directly, not Knox or Gaille, with any further questions. Then he rested his palms flat on the table, clenched his jaw, braced his hams, and launched himself up out of his chair onto his feet before beaming around the room as if expecting applause. When it didn't come, he beckoned Gaille and Knox to stand beside him for a few final group photographs, an arm around the shoulders of each, as though they were the best and oldest of friends. The cameras clicked their fill; then the arc lights started going out. Journalists called friends and offices on their cell phones as they filed out in a muted hubbub. The world's attention moved on, leaving Knox feeling oddly deflated. He had never sought the spotlight, yet there was something undeniably intoxicating about it.

Yusuf kept his arms around their shoulders as he steered them through the rear doors of the conference hall, inquiring solicitously about their plans. The moment the doors shut behind them, however, he scowled and stepped back and rubbed his hands with distaste, as though he suspected Knox and Gaille of carrying diseases. "Don't even think about talking to the press without my permission," he warned them.

"We gave our word."

Yusuf nodded sourly, as though he knew how much the word of such people was worth. Then he turned his back emphatically on them and lumbered away.

Knox gave a little shudder as he turned to Gaille. "Want to get out of here? I arranged for a taxi."

"What are we waiting for?"

They made their way along a maze of corridors. "I can't believe Yusuf's going to get away with it," muttered Knox.

"We had no choice," Gaille reassured him. "There's no evidence against him, but there is against us. And it's not our fault Egypt appointed him secretary general."

"Your father would never have agreed."

"Yes, he would. He made a deal with Dragoumis, didn't he?" She smiled and took his arm. "Anyway, it's done now. Please let's talk about something else."

"Such as?"

"Such as, what are you going to do now?"

He thought bleakly of Rick. "I've got a funeral to attend."

"Oh, Christ. Of course." She bowed her head a moment, then asked, "And afterwards?"

"I haven't thought about it," said Knox, though this was a lie. The prospect of excavating again had been in his nostrils ever since Umar made the offer. "And you?"

"I'm off to Paris, first flight I can get."

"Oh." He stopped dead. "Really?"

"I've decided to leave the Sorbonne," she said. "I owe it to them to tell them in person, don't you think? They've been very good to me."

Knox couldn't prevent a smile from spreading across his face. "And then?"

"I'm planning to come back here. Find myself some excavating work and learn the ropes, you know. I understand that Augustin is always looking for new assistants. Maybe I could—"

"Augustin!" protested Knox appalled. "That old goat! You can't be serious!"

"I thought he was your friend."

"He *is* my friend. That's precisely why I don't want you working for him."

"I need a job," insisted Gaille. "Do you have a better suggestion?"

They reached the back doors, pushed through them, and went down the steps to the waiting taxi. Knox opened the back door for Gaille, then climbed in beside her, giving directions to the driver. He rolled down his window as they pulled away, allowing in the scents of Egypt: the spices, the fumes, and the sweat. This was more like it—away from the politics, the ambition, the bargaining, the corruption, the deceit. In pursuit of the raw truth once more. He turned to Gaille. "I'll be needing a partner myself, as soon as all this has blown over," he told her.

"Really?"

"Yes. Someone who'll work for a pittance, just for the love of it. Someone with the right skills to complement my own. A languages expert, ideally. Preferably one who can take a half-decent photograph, too. Two employees for the price of one, you know. I'm cheap like that."

Gaille laughed, her eyes sparkling. "And may I ask what the two of you will be going in search of?"

He grinned at her. "Don't you mean, what will the two of us be going in search of?"

"Yes," she said happily. "That's exactly what I mean."

WILL ADAMS, a full-time writer, previously worked for a communications agency in London and for a firm of business history consultants based in Washington, D.C. He lives in Essex, England.

Enjoy a special peek at
the next exciting thriller
featuring famed adventurer
Daniel Knox.

Please turn this page
for a preview of

The Exodus Quest

Available in hardcover

Prologue

The southern shore of Lake Mariut, AD 415

THE PLASTER HAD DRIED AT LAST. Marcus scooped up handfuls of dirt and sand from the floor, then smeared them across the fresh white surface until it was dulled and dark and virtually indistinguishable from the rest of the wall. He held his oil lamp close to examine it, adding more dirt where needed until satisfied, though in truth it needed the eyes of a younger man. A last walk through the old, familiar passages and chambers, bidding farewell to his comrades and ancestors in the catacombs, to a life-time of memories, then up the steps and out.

Late afternoon already. No time to waste.

He closed the wooden hatch, shoveled sand and stone down on it. The crash and scatter as it landed, the swish of robes, the crunch of his iron-shod spade. He began to hear in these noises the distant chanting of a mob. It grew so strong, so convincing, he paused to listen. But now there was only silence, save for his heavy breathing, the hammer of his heart, the trickle of settling sand.

Nothing but the fears of a solitary old man.

The sun was low in the west, tinting orange. They usually came by night, as evildoers will, though they were growing bolder all the time. He'd seen strange faces along the harbor that morning. Onetime friends muttering among themselves. People whose diseases he'd treated without thought for his own safety looking at him like contagion.

He began to shovel again, faster and faster, to quell the panic before it could overwhelm him.

He'd thought they'd be able to ride it out. Their community had survived many previous pogroms and wars, after all. He'd imagined, foolishly, that their ideas would prevail in the end because they were so much stronger and more rational than the pious cruel nonsense of the so-called right-thinking. But he'd been wrong. It was human nature, when fears were stirred, that reason lost all power.

Poor Hypatia! That beautiful, wise, and gentle woman. They said her lynching had been ordered by Pope Cyril himself. Epiphanes had witnessed the whole thing. A mere boy; too young for such a sight. The mob led by that sanctimonious monster Peter the Reader. No surprise there. They'd torn her from her chariot, stripped her naked, dragged her to their church, cut her flesh from her bones with oyster shells, then burned her remains.

Men of God they called themselves. How was it possible they couldn't see what they truly were?

The sun had set and the night began to cool. His pace

slowed. He was far from the prime of youth. But he didn't stop altogether. The quicker he finished, the quicker he could set off, catch up his family and fellows in their quest for sanctuary near Hermopolis or perhaps even Chenoboskion, depending on how far this madness had spread. He'd sent them on ahead with all the scrolls and other treasured possessions they'd been able to carry, the accumulated wisdom of centuries. But he himself had stayed behind. They'd grown lax these past few years. It was no secret they had an underground complex here, he knew; not least because absurd rumors about their wealth and hidden treasures had found their way back to him. If the villains looked hard and long enough, they had every chance of finding these steps, however well he buried them. That was why he'd plastered up the entrance to the baptism chamber: so that some small fraction of their knowledge might survive even if the underground complex itself was discovered. And maybe one day sanity would return, and they could, too. If not himself, then his children or grandchildren. And if not them, then perhaps the people of a future age. A more rational, enlightened age. Maybe they'd appreciate the wisdom on these walls, not hate and vilify it.

He finished filling in the shaft, trod it down until it was hard to see. Time to go. The prospect dismayed him. He was too old for such adventures, too old to start again. All he'd ever sought in life was the peace in which to study his texts, learn the nature of the world. But that was now denied him by these swaggering cruel bullies who'd made it a sin even to think. You could see it in their eyes, the pleasure they took in the wanton exercise of their power. They wallowed in their villainy. They raised their hands up high as though the blood on them shone like virtue.

He was traveling light, just his robes, a small sack of provisions, a few coins in his purse. But he hadn't walked ten minutes before he saw a glow over the ridge ahead. It meant nothing to him at first, lost as he was in private thoughts. But then he realized. Torches. Approaching from the harbor. The direction of the breeze changed, and he heard them. Men and women shouting, singing, jubilant in the anticipation of another lynching.

He hurried back the way he'd come, his heart pounding. Their settlement was on a gentle hill overlooking the lake. He reached the crown and saw the glow on every side, like a pyre just lit, flames licking up the tinder. A cry to his right. A rooftop began to blaze. A second and then a third.

Their homes! Their lives! The clamor grew louder, closer. That hateful baying! How these people loved their work. He turned this way and that, seeking a path, but everywhere he went torches forced him back, penning him into an ever-smaller space.

The cry went up at last. He'd been seen. He turned and fled, but his old legs weren't up to it, even though he knew what would happen to him if he was caught. And then they were all around him, their faces enflamed with bloodlust, and there was nothing more he could do save go with dignity and courage, try to shame them into compassion. Failing that, perhaps when they woke in the morning they'd look back on their work this night with such horror and revulsion that others might be spared.

That would be something.

He fell to his knees on the rocky ground, his body trembling uncontrollably. Tears streamed down his cheeks. He began to pray.

Chapter One

DANIEL KNOX WAS WALKING NORTH ALONG Sharia Bab Sedra when he saw the earthenware bowl on the street trader's flapped-out tablecloth. Filled with matchbooks and packets of white napkins, it was propping up one end of a line of battered Arabic schoolbooks. His heart gave a little flutter; he suffered a moment's déjà vu. He'd seen one like it before, he was sure of it. Somewhere interesting, too. For a few seconds he almost had the answer, but then it eluded him. The feeling slowly faded, leaving him merely uneasy, unsure whether his mind was playing tricks.

He paused, crouched, picked up a garish plastic vase with wilting artificial yellow flowers, then a ragged geography textbook with all its pages falling out, so that out-of-date maps of Egypt's topography and demographics fanned out over the tablecloth like a deck of cards swept by a magician's hand.

"Salaam alekum," nodded the trader. He couldn't have been more than fifteen years old, made to look even younger by hand-me-down clothes at least two sizes too big.

"Wa alekum es salaam," replied Knox.

"You like this book, mister? You want to buy?"

Knox shrugged and put it back, then glanced around as though uninterested in anything he saw. But the young hawker only gave a crooked-toothed smile. He wasn't a fool. Knox grinned self-deprecatingly and touched the earthenware bowl with his finger. "What's this?" he asked.

"Sir has a fine eye," he said. "A wonderful antique from Alexandria's rich history. The fruit bowl of Alexander the Great himself! Yes! Alexander the Great! No word of a lie."

"Alexander the Great?" said Knox. "Surely not."

"No word of a lie," insisted the young man. "They find his body, you know. They find this in his tomb! Yes! The man who find Alexander, he is a man called Daniel Knox, he is my very good friend, he give this to me himself!"

Knox laughed. Since that particular adventure, he'd been everyone's very good friend. "And you're selling it out here on the street?" he teased. "Surely if it belonged to Alexander, it's worthy of the Cairo Museum itself!" He picked it up, again felt that reprise of déjà vu, a curious tingling in his chest, a dryness at the back of his mouth, a slight pressure at the base of his cranium.

He turned the bowl around in his hands, enjoying the

sensation of touch. He was no expert on ceramics, but all field archaeologists had a certain knowledge, not least because about nine out of every ten artifacts on any given site were some kind of pottery—a fragment from a plate, cup, or jar, a shard from an oil lamp or perfume flask, perhaps even an ostracon, if it was your lucky day.

But this wasn't broken. It was some seven inches in diameter and three inches deep, with a flat base and curved sides and no rim to speak of, so that you could hold it in both hands and drink directly from it. From the smooth texture, the clay had evidently been well sieved for grit and pebbles before it had been hard-fired. It was pinkish gray, though coated with a paler wash that gave it a swirling texture, like cream just stirred into coffee. Maybe local provenance; maybe not. He'd need an expert to determine that. He had little more success with the dating. Fine ware like oil lamps and expensive crockery had changed constantly with prevailing fashions, if only to show off the wealth of the owners, but coarse ware like this had tended to keep its form, sometimes for centuries. Circa AD 50 at a guess, plus or minus a couple of hundred years. Or a couple of thousand. He put it back down, intending to walk away, but it just wouldn't let him go. He squatted there, staring at it, rubbing his jaw, trying to read its message, work out how it had put its hook in him.

Knox knew how rare it was to find valuable artifacts in a street market. The hawkers were too shrewd to sell high-quality pieces that way, the antiquities police too observant. And there were artisans in the back streets of Alexandria and Cairo who could knock out convincing replicas in a heartbeat if they thought they could fool a gullible tourist into parting with his cash. But this particular bowl seemed too dowdy to be worth the effort. "How much?" he asked finally.

"One thousand US," replied the young man without blinking.

Knox laughed again. Egyptians priced the buyer, not the piece, and clearly he was looking unusually wealthy today. Wealthy and stupid. Again he made to walk away; again something stopped him. He touched it with his fingertip, reluctant to be drawn into a haggle. Once you started, it was rude not to finish, and Knox wasn't at all sure he wanted this piece, even if he could get it cheap. If it was a genuine antiquity, after all, then buying it was illegal. If it was fake, then he'd feel annoyed with himself for days at being taken in, especially if his friends and colleagues ever got to hear about it. He shook his head decisively, and this time he did stand up.

"Five hundred," said the young hawker hurriedly, sensing his fat fish slipping through his fingers. "I see you before. You a good man. I make you special price. Very special price."

Knox shook his head. "Where did you get it?" he asked.

"It is from the tomb of Alexander the Great, I assure you! My friend give it to me because he is a very good—"

"The truth," said Knox. "Or I walk away now."

The boy's eyes narrowed shrewdly. "Why I tell you this?" he asked. "So you call the police?"

Knox fished in his back pocket for some cash, letting

him see the banknotes. "How can I be confident it's genuine unless you tell me where you got it?" he asked.

The trader pulled a face, looked around to make sure he couldn't be overheard. "A friend of my cousin works on an excavation," he murmured.

"Which excavation?" frowned Knox. "Who runs it?"

"Foreigners."

"What kind of foreigners?"

He shrugged indifferently. "Foreigners."

"Where?"

"South," he waved vaguely. "South of Mariut."

Knox nodded. It made sense. Lake Mariut had been hemmed around by farms and settlements in ancient times, before the inflows from the Nile had silted up and the lake had started to shrink. He counted his money slowly. If this bowl had indeed come from an archaeological site, he had a duty to return it, or at least to let someone there know that they had a security problem. Thirty-five Egyptian pounds. He folded them between his thumb and forefinger. "South of the lake, you say?" he said with a frown. "Where, exactly? I'll need to know precisely if I'm going to buy."

The young man's eyes refocused reluctantly from the money to Knox. A bitter expression soured his face, as though he realized he'd said too much already. He muttered an obscenity, gathered the four corners of his tablecloth, hoisted it up so that all his wares clattered together, and hurried away. Knox made to follow, but a colossus of a man appeared from nowhere and stepped across his path. Knox tried to go around, but the man simply moved sideways to block him, arms folded across his chest, a dry smile on his lips, inviting Knox to try something. And then it was too late anyway, the youngster swallowed up by crowds, taking his earthenware bowl with him.

Knox shrugged and let it go. It was almost certainly nothing.

Yes. Almost certainly.

VISIT US ONLINE

@ WWW.HACHETTEBOOKGROUP.COM

AT THE HACHETTE BOOK GROUP WEB SITE YOU'LL FIND:

CHAPTER EXCERPTS FROM SELECTED NEW RELEASES

•

ORIGINAL AUTHOR AND EDITOR ARTICLES

•

AUDIO EXCERPTS

•

BESTSELLER NEWS

•

ELECTRONIC NEWSLETTERS

•

AUTHOR TOUR INFORMATION

•

CONTESTS, QUIZZES, AND POLLS

•

FUN, QUIRKY RECOMMENDATION CENTER

•

PLUS MUCH MORE!

Bookmark Hachette Book Group
@ www.HachetteBookGroup.com.